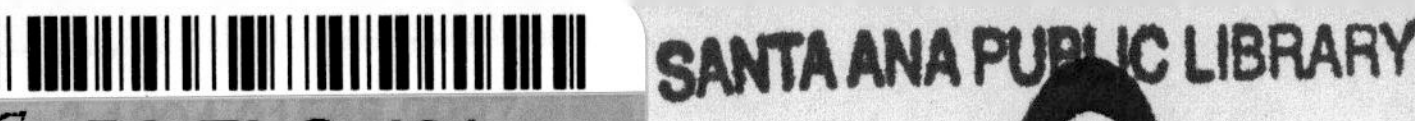

Praise for *Blind Sight*

"This has all of O'Connell's trademarks: a twisty puzzle, page-turning suspense, and a dark and complex city of corruption. Above all is the cool, scary Mallory, who sees through the smokescreen of civility to the violence within. As one character says, 'Vengeance, thy name is Mallory.'"
—*Library Journal*

"Through twelve novels featuring NYPD Special Crimes Unit detective Kathleen Mallory, readers have been taken on a wild ride with the brilliant, unpredictable sociopath and onetime street urchin."
—*Sacramento Bee*

"Mallory is scary-smart . . . An entertaining, slightly over-the-top protagonist with brains and attitude. Colorful and appealing (or appalling) characters make this one a winner for crime-fic fans."
—*Kirkus Reviews* (starred review)

"Marry the intuition and problem-solving skills of Lincoln Rhyme with the street smarts and stunts of Jack Reacher, and you'll come up with someone very close to Kathy Mallory. As long as Carol O'Connell keeps pumping out crime fiction like this, she will have a faithful reader in me."
—*BookPage*

"Keeps the reader on edge. Mallory has a lot of real brain power and a whole lot of attitude. She is one member of the law who can live, no matter what happens, on the very dangerous streets of the big city."
—*Suspense Magazine*

"*Blind Sight* has an almost Dickensian feel. For those readers looking to escape the usual police procedurals, she's the ticket."
—*Chicago Tribune*

"Mallory remains one of the most original and intriguing cops on the planet. A classy, classic, riveting read."
—*Open Letters Monthly*

Praise for Carol O'Connell

"M is for Mallory—Kathy Mallory, bestseller O'Connell's powerful and powerfully flawed New York Special Crimes Unit detective. M is also for morbid, macabre, and mordant—adjectives that can be applied to the plot, the prose, and the humor of this dazzling eleventh novel in the series. Mallory's bravura performance wreaks justice both inside and outside the legal system." —*Publishers Weekly*

"Enthralling . . . Mallory continues to be an enigmatic and fascinating character. Despite an impeccable fashion sense and movie-star good looks, Mallory is as much a feral being as she was when she was first rescued from the streets as a child. Her closest counterpoint in mystery fiction is Lisbeth Salander." —*Mystery Scene Magazine*

"NYPD Special Crimes detective Kathy Mallory is one of the most intriguing characters in crime fiction today."
—*New York Daily News*

"Like all the Mallory novels, this one is a solid police procedural with a twisty plot, and Mallory is a fascinating, rich character. Fans won't want to miss this." —*Library Journal*

"Carol O'Connell is one of my favorite writers."
—Karin Slaughter

"Before Salander took the world by storm, there was Mallory, the most gloriously original heroine to grace crime fiction's meanest and darkest streets."
—Sarah Weinman, editor of
Troubled Daughters, Twisted Wives

"Mallory is one of the great characters ever in detective fiction." —*San Jose Mercury News*

"Carol O'Connell has raised the standard for psychological thrillers." —*Chicago Tribune*

TITLES BY CAROL O'CONNELL

Blind Sight
It Happens in the Dark
The Chalk Girl
Bone by Bone
Find Me
Winter House
Dead Famous
Crime School
Shell Game
Judas Child
Stone Angel
Killing Critics
The Man Who Cast Two Shadows
Mallory's Oracle

BLIND SIGHT

CAROL O'CONNELL

G. P. Putnam's Sons
New York

PUTNAM

G. P. PUTNAM'S SONS
Publishers Since 1838
An imprint of Penguin Random House LLC
375 Hudson Street
New York, New York 10014

The Library of Congress has catalogued the G. P. Putnam's Sons hardcover edition as follows:

Names: O'Connell, Carol, [date] author.
Title: Blind sight / Carol O'Connell.
Description: New York : G.P. Putnam's Sons, [2016] | Series: A Mallory novel
Identifiers: LCCN 2016008417| ISBN 9780399184239 (hardcover) | ISBN 9780399184253 (ePub)
Subjects: LCSH: Mallory, Kathleen (Fictitious character)—Fiction. | Police—New York (State)—New York—Fiction. | Policewomen—Fiction. | Murder—Investigation—Fiction. | Missing persons—Investigation—Fiction. | BISAC: FICTION / Crime. | FICTION / Thrillers. | FICTION / Mystery & Detective / General. | GSAFD: Mystery fiction. | Suspense fiction.
Classification: LCC PS3565.C497 B58 2016 | DDC 813/.54—dc23
LC record available at https://protect-us.mimecast .com/s/6ROwBVHV0gmvsb?domain=lccn.loc.gov

First G. P. Putnam's Sons hardcover edition / September 2016
First G. P. Putnam's Sons premium edition / September 2017
G. P. Putnam's Sons premium edition ISBN: 9780399184246

Printed in the United States of America
1 3 5 7 9 10 8 6 4 2

Support your local bookstore . . . please.

The reborn samizdat of the Internet is not enough to keep ideas alive and burning bright, not in a future with only one store on a scorched landscape that used to be a marketplace.

—*Carol O'Connell*

ACKNOWLEDGMENTS

Marc Maurer, president of the National Federation of the Blind, was very kind in his advice to me, which included terminology: He calls the blind "the blind" (more sensible than the terms that seek to avoid that word for reasons known only to the politically correct). My friend Richard Hughes read the first draft of this novel, and I thank him for his peerless insults and sarcasm. More thanks to Dianne Burke, another old friend and a world-class researcher. A special thank you to Ken Gates, who *knows things about roses.* And I owe a debt to the late Dr. Kenneth Jernigan, posthumously my guide for what to leave out of the novel. This man, blind from birth, railed against writers' clichés in his essay, *Blindness: Is Literature Against Us?* I read it. I aimed for grace.

PROLOGUE

The unusual was common here, yet the heads of local people did turn to stare as she walked by. Others, the sightseers, only looked at landmarks for the way life used to be. They had little interest in life ongoing all around them, and so the woman robed in black moved past them. In plain sight. Unseen.

Shops and cafés opened under a blue sky over St. Marks Place, and the first wave of tourists, a dozen or so, gathered round their guide as he spoke of a bygone era when this neighborhood was edgy, dangerous, drugged up—and *fun,* when the nights had reeked of marijuana for three city blocks. "No need to score reefer in those days," he said. "You'd just breathe deep and get stoned. It was a party that went on for years."

"Decades," said a portly, white-haired New Yorker, who had lived all his long life in an apartment above the family bodega. He turned his back on the tourists to work a squeaky crank on the wall. With a few swift turns, he lowered a striped awning to give his flower stall some shade. The stall was shallow, sized to fit a narrow sidewalk that was choked with sneakers and sandals as the walking tour walked on.

Cars were forced to share the roadbed with two aging rock 'n' rollers on foot. The bodega's proprietor had a good eye for such people. Pilgrims, he called them. They stopped to snap pictures of their shrine, a brownstone that had appeared on an album cover dating back to music on vinyl and songs that were old when those two were young.

Stepping out from the shade of his awning, the elderly man looked up at the sky. Cloudless. How he loved these early summer days when shoplifting children were still jailed in their classrooms. By a movement caught in the corner of one eye, he knew something dark was coming his way, and this, the first shock of the morning, brought out his widest smile.

"Angie!" How many years had gone by? Too many. "So grown up!" Such a liar he was. Angela Quill had not aged a day. She was in her twenties now, but those big gray eyes were the eyes of a child who had yet to grow into them.

When he released the girl from a bear hug, he stepped back to stare at what she wore, what she had become. The veil—even that was no longer common in her trade. But what of the rest? A white wimple framed her face. The wide black robe had enough material to clothe three of her. And there was length enough to hide her feet—so out of place in this age of raised hemlines for holy women.

He plucked out his hearing aid to fiddle the volume and cure a squeal in the works. "What? Say again?" Oh, she was a *cloistered* nun? He never would have chosen that path for her. Such women were shut away from the world, sealed up behind walls until they died.

Yet here she was—out and about in the city. How could that be? What—

She wanted to buy flowers, but the ones in his stall were all wrapped by the dozen in bouquets. Would he sell her only *two* roses? She had money for two.

"For you? *Here.*" He loaded her arms with two *dozen* red blooms—so happy was he to see her again. "And I won't take your money." They talked awhile, and his every sentence began with "I remember when—" When she was only ten years old, Angie had been his flower girl, his inspiration for the stall. After an early killing frost, the little girl had taken dead rosebushes from his upstairs window box. Come spring, she had given the fruit of their seedpods to him as tender potted plants. Nowadays, all his plants and cut flowers arrived on a truck. It was not the same—not so charming as a canny child who could bring roses back to him from the dead.

Did he know the time?

"You have to go? So soon?" His attention was called away by a customer—only for a moment. When he turned back to speak with Angie, she was not beside him anymore and nowhere to be seen. How could she leave him with no goodbye? And she had not taken her roses with her. Not all of them. Only two. And a few dollar bills had been left behind. His eyes searched the street. Her long black robe should have made her a standout in this season of bare-legged people.

But no. *Poof.* Gone. And so fast. How had she—

A woman screamed.

Angie? *Oh, God, no!*

Coming his way was a gaggle of teenage girls with high-pitched shrieks of laughter. *So* loud. He turned down the volume of his hearing aid. And the scream was blamed upon them. *Damn kids.* They could stop a man's heart.

* * *

"HEADS UP, EVERYBODY." The walking tour came to a halt in front of a vacant store, and the guide pointed to the apartment house on the other side of the street.

The resident of the second floor, an elderly shut-in, thought this man might be pointing up at her, but no, he sang out the name of a long-dead poet who had once lived here.

She wished the tourists would go away. They impeded her view.

The woman in the wheelchair was a creature of the clock, and precisely fifty minutes remained of her customary hour at the window, time enough for a bit of breakfast and her crossword puzzle. Also, she secretly kept company with the old man down on the sidewalk across the street. Though she had not spoken to him in years, she was that rare old-timer of St. Marks Place who knew him by name and could recall a day when Albert Costello was a lively, talkative man. Now he was a hermit. However, he did have ritual outings, and so she knew right where to find him every morning at nine o'clock, when she would wheel her chair to the window, and there—

Oh! Where was that skinny old fool?

She had looked away from the window to fill in a few blank squares of her puzzle. In only those few seconds, her companion had disappeared, abandoning his post down there by the streetlamp—and *long* before their shared hour had ended.

Where could he have wandered off to? Albert was as old as she was. He could not move that fast, not even if he had traveled only as far as the door to his apartment building. She scanned the river of tourists on the sidewalk below, but his dear balding head was not there in the swim with them.

Well, that was different. She liked her puzzles, but this one was disturbing.

A woman's scream from the street was less interesting.

THE TOUR GUIDE faced a clothing store. "That used to be a jazz club. Charlie Parker played there. Greatest sax man who ever lived." His group paused to snap photographs of the famous nightspot that was not there anymore.

And now they had the attention of a young man in blue jeans, who stood on the sidewalk, tying an apron around his waist. The local trade never amounted to much before noon, but he was in need of a smoke before all those freaking tourists descended on the café. Aw, they were turning his way. Too late? Well, still time for a puff, maybe two. A cigarette dangled from the waiter's mouth as he leaned against the brick wall and struck a match. He watched a child come round a corner, a blind boy tapping a white cane on the pavement—and ditching school. *Good for you, kid.* Then, with a flick of the wrist, the boy's cane collapsed to a short wand in a conjuror's sleight of hand.

Neat trick. Was the kid even blind? So sure-footed was this little boy that he was either a faker or very much at home on St. Marks Place.

A woman screamed. But no heads in the approaching tour group were turning to point the way to any trouble. No, these people were focused. *Hungry.* And screaming that could not be backed up with blood was written off to street noise. Nothing more.

The tour group no longer blocked his view of the—

The blind boy had disappeared. One second he was there—then gone. He must have ducked into a doorway. But the illusion of a vanishing act remained with the waiter as yet another neat trick.

INCREDIBLY, the troop of sightseers had witnessed *nothing*, every pair of eyes turned elsewhere as they spilled into the narrow street and crossed over.

The lady from Bora Bora watched them file into the café. Though she was hungry, breakfast could wait until her son arrived. She looked to the west, the direction of his university. No sign of him. Where *was* her student prince? She spoke Tahitian, French and a smattering of Japanese, but she had no words that Americans might understand. And so, for the past week, her eldest child had been her guide through this part of the world. He was late to join her for a last meal and a kiss goodbye before she must leave for the airport.

She did not mind the wait. Her homeland in the South Pacific was a place of great beauty and deep peace, but this other island, Manhattan, was an intoxicating display of action—theater of the street. Without her son to translate, some acts would always be inexplicable. And the most recent one had been over in a snatch of seconds when two people had disappeared.

At the end of her long journey home, she would speak of the drama that had unfolded on the sidewalk. She would retell it as a fabulous fable for her youngest child, a little boy who loved nothing better than a scary story. "Flying down the street," she would say to him, "a running woman's long black robe became dark wings spread upon the wind."

In a fury, the Bird Woman of St. Marks Place had attacked a muscular man and ridden his back—and *that* part was true. "Claws dug in. Her black wings flapping. His arms flailing." The tense battle of man and giant bird had just begun when they vanished—in seconds—disappearing behind a brief curtain drawn in the form of sightseers passing by, and so it seemed that Bird Woman had flown up and away with her prey clutched in talons.

Though, in truth, at the sound of the great bird's victory scream, the lady from Bora Bora had never turned her eyes to the sky. The scream had not come from up there. But, for the sake of the story, she would only rely on the magical logic of the moment.

1

If they knew why he had come here, all these men would turn him away.

The odyssey had begun in the morning on St. Marks Place, not half a mile from this SoHo police station, and now it was night. A bank of tall, grimy windows worked poorly as mirrors, reflecting his white hair and face, but not his black cassock, and so Father Brenner's head appeared to float across the squad room—slowly—though his mission here was urgent.

Long fluorescent tubes of light spanned the high ceiling, some of them twitchy, blinking off and on with a nervous sputter, and telephones glowed with red lights, the tiny alarms of those left hanging on the line. Half the desks were occupied by tired detectives drinking coffee, tapping keyboards and talking among themselves.

All conversation stopped.

Heads lifted here and there to note his passage, and one man winced when it was apparent that the elderly priest was heading for Kathy Mallory's desk.

Understood.

Father Brenner reminded himself to address her as *Detective* Mallory, having lost the right to any familiarity when she was a child in his parish school, enrolled there by her foster mother, Helen Markowitz. That good woman had suspected that Kathy was born a Catholic, but suspicion was all that Helen and her husband ever had to work with. The little girl had told them nothing useful, not even her right age. So she *might* have been ten years old at that first meeting in his office, but certainly not eleven, the age on her application.

The child had been presented to him in the guise of a small Botticelli angel. Backlit by sunlight that day, her blond curls had gleamed like a dammed halo.

Here, he paused in his recollection and his steps.

Yes, *damned* was a fitting word for that early impression. A second look at her had pretty much killed his angel analogy. The long slants of her eyes held a shade of green not found in nature, not God's work. Even then, long before she would grow up to carry a gun, he had intuited that she was dangerous. Another early indicator was a teaching nun, who had been left with a rather bad limp to mark the close of Kathy's final semester.

The priest still carried guilt for his blindness to Sister Ursula's *eccentricity*. No, call it cruelty. Crazy old woman.

Upon his first visit to this police station, he had brought Inspector Markowitz's foster child along to explain the plaster cast on her wrist—and the nun in the hospital. The meeting had not gone well. Guided by a schoolgirl code of *Thou shalt not rat*, Kathy had refused to confirm Sister Ursula's assault on her. Honoring the child's resolve, the inspector had called it a breakeven day, "My kid's broken wrist for the nun's mangled leg." But outside of Kathy's hearing, Louis Markowitz had offered the priest the angry choice of "Put that nun in a bughouse, or put her down like a dog. Pick *one!*"

Father Brenner had selected the bughouse option.

Tonight, his eyeglasses sweated down the bridge of his nose. It was taking him such a long time to cross this room and meet with the grown-up Kathy Mallory; he was *that* anxious to see her again. He had spoken with her commanding officer in passing at the downstairs door, and Lieutenant Coffey had waived the protocol of a visitor's badge and pointed the way up the staircase to the Special Crimes Unit. And so the priest might believe that he was coming upon this young woman unannounced—catching her unawares.

Foolish idea? Oh, yes.

As a child, she had given him the eerie sense that her vision extended to the back of her head—and spookier still—to the inside of *his* head. He kept this illusion saved away with others in his mythology of her, a book of many pages.

Not a *holy* book.

So far, the young detective in blue jeans appeared normal enough, though rather well dressed for a civil servant. As a boy, he had worked in his father's tailor shop, and he well knew the quality of the wonderful linen blazer draped on the back of her chair. So good was his sartorial eye, he could even attest to her T-shirt's fine grade of silk.

Kathy Mallory's eyes were focused on the glowing screen of a computer, and the light of a desk lamp gave her another halo, but the priest was long past *that* deception. As he approached, she did not turn to him in any natural fashion. The golden head swiveled—machinelike—and she did not look up to meet his eyes. No recognition at all. He might well be a piece of furniture with a clerical collar. This was an old, cold quirk of hers, one that used to unhinge him with the thought that she was not quite like the other children, not human, no heart, no pulse.

In a more worldly sense, she was not much changed in her mid-twenties. The high cheekbones were more pronounced, but she was otherwise a taller replica of the child with the cream-white skin and cupid's bow lips. He often wondered if that lovely face had been the chief complaint of Sister Ursula, the ugly antithesis of Kathy. Yes, that would have set the old woman off. The nun would have regarded the infliction of pain as tempering temptations of the flesh, punishing a little girl for the crime of—

"Sit down, Father Brenner." Kathy Mallory's half-smile welcomed him to hell. It was a given that if she seemed at all happy to see him, it was only because she liked the diversion of toying with his soul—as if she had that power over him.

Well . . . did she not? Obediently, he settled into the wooden chair beside her desk.

"What brings you out tonight?" Her silken voice gave him no clue of inflection. Her red fingernails were more telling, drumming the desktop, prompting him to get on with his reason for bothering her.

He might begin with the news that her old nemesis, Sister Ursula, had died, but before he could open his mouth, she read his mind to say, "I'm sorry for your loss." Her condolences on the dead nun were delivered with an expression of pure pleasure, the way a cat might smile with a mouse in her teeth—at the moment before she bit down hard to break the creature's back. No mercy, no forgiveness.

No surprise there.

"I've come about another nun," he said. "A young

one, close to your age. I'm afraid for her." No sympathy was expected on this account. He could only hope to intrigue. "Sister Michael disappeared yesterday. She's already been reported to Missing Persons. They said they'd look into it. . . . I know what that means." *Goodbye, Sister, and best of luck to you.* "But I believe she was kidnapped."

"So there's a ransom demand." Hardly intrigued, the detective turned back to the screen of her laptop, a sign of dismissal even before she said, "Go talk to Major Case. They handle that. We do homicides here."

And it would take more than one homicide to interest her. Over the years spent following her career with the NYPD, he had learned that the Special Crimes Unit was best known for cases with a high body count, the bloodiest carnage in New York City.

"Ransom?" He scratched his head in a calculated show of vagueness. "Well, I don't know about that."

"No note? No phone call?" She faced him again, eyes narrowed. "Then why would you think it's a kidnapping?" Clearly, she did not believe him.

Good. That should hold her attention. Oh, just the chance to catch him in a lie, to make him twist and squirm—how she would *love* that. "This is all I know," he said. "Sister Michael was on the way to visit her mother on St. Marks Place. She started out in the morning, but never got there. That was yesterday. And we both know that Missing Persons is *not* out looking for her."

"They're swamped with runaways." Her eyes closed in the slow blink of a contented cat, and he knew he had her now, for she was playing harmless when she tossed off the afterthought that "People are always walking away from their old lives."

"If she wanted to leave her order, she would've worn

street clothes, not this." He set a snapshot on the desk. It was a bit damp from his hand. He had carried it all through this day into night. It pictured a young woman in the long robe and veil of a cloistered nun. "And I know she bought two red roses in her mother's neighborhood. I talked to the man who sold—" Oh, no, he was boring her. Well, on to the bit he had saved for last. "I can promise you that Sister Michael's mother does *not* have the mayor's ear . . . but that man knew about the disappearance *before* the Missing Persons report was filed."

He thought she might like that part, but it was hard to tell. She was tensing, as if wound by a spring and set to—

She leaned far forward. And, whiplash fast, he sat well back.

"What *else* did you hold out on Missing Persons? They're not idiots over there. If you'd told them—"

"I wasn't the one who made that report. . . . I don't even know Sister Michael."

Her eyes flickered. A eureka moment?

"So the church is *cop-shopping,*" she said. "Reaching out for a detective who'll play nice with the ugly parts. . . . That's why they picked you? Because they think we had a warm, cozy relationship when I was a kid?"

A good guess in some respects.

"I *did* go to Major Case," he said. "Their detective sent me away after five minutes. I had no proof of kidnapping. That's what he told—"

"You think there *is* proof. You think I can get it for you. So there *was* a ransom demand." Her tone accused him of lying. Fair warning. It was confession time at the police station. "Where'd you get your information, Father? I know Mayor Polk won't play golf with any priest lower than a bishop. Who told you he already knew about—"

"I can't give you a name."

"You *can!"* Her fist hit the desk as punctuation. "Nobody sent you here under the Seal of the Confessional." Her sudden expression of anger fell away in the flip of a switch to one of resignation, which must be an equally false mask. "All right, just tell me what church politician talks to the city politicians. Does that make it less like ratting out another priest?"

Yes, that would do. "Father DuPont is on the cardinal's staff. He'd be the one to—"

"And what's the nun's name?" She turned away from him to face her computer.

"I told you. Sister—"

"Her *real* name."

Not the saint's name taken with her final vows. The archangel had been a fierce choice for a nun—a name that was the battle cry of the good angels in the War of Heaven. "In her former life, she was known as Angela Quill."

The detective tapped her keyboard. "So this woman disappears, and you jump to the conclusion of . . . what? A satanic nun collector?" She tilted her head to one side, her face a parody of innocence when she asked, "Why is that?"

"Hey, Mallory." A man with hooded eyes slouched up to the desk. His dark hair was silvered with enough gray to make him at least twice her age. Raising one hand, he warded off her response. "I know. Half a day shot. I went home for lunch and walked in on a stickup. Took me forever to get through the booking." He turned an affable smile on the priest. "I live over a bar. The owner's my landlord. If I'd let the perp walk outta there with the cash, my rent would've gone up." The man sloughed off his wrinkled suit jacket and sat down at the desk that faced and adjoined Kathy Mallory's. The garment slid from his lap to the floor, and he left it there.

Not a *tidy* man.

Though the cheap suit did have an odor of spot remover, those shoes had not been polished in recent decades. This wardrobe-challenged detective introduced himself as Riker. "I'm her partner. What can we do for you, Padre?"

Not a Catholic.

Father Brenner pulled a folded sheet of paper from his cassock pocket. The bold type above the nun's grainy portrait asked, HAVE YOU SEEN HER? This was his mission statement at a glance, and he handed it to the man. "That's my last one. I've been taping them up in store windows." Sister Michael's photograph was, more accurately, a picture of what she wore. Her face was the smallest element in the frame, and not what he had counted upon to stand out in the memory of the public. But her long robe and veil would be a rare sight on city streets.

"A *dress-code* nun," said Riker. "Wearing that getup of hers must be hell in this heat. Is she from the Brooklyn convent?"

"No, she's from the Monastery of Saint Bernardine. It's about sixty miles upstate. The nuns have a website and a tractor, but otherwise, their traditions are centuries old. We have no pictures of Sister Michael in other clothes, and no family members to help with—"

"But her mother's *alive.*" Kathy Mallory smiled to say that she had caught him in another lie, though he had yet to make even one false statement. "You told me the nun was on the way to visit her—"

"The mother only had the same photo I used for my poster. I called on the woman this morning."

Detective Riker held the nun's poster at arm's length, the distance for a man who ought to wear bifocals. Brows knit together, eyes squinting, he asked, "Is that face—" The man looked to his partner, as if she might have an answer to that half a question.

And she did. As her laptop was angled toward Riker, Father Brenner saw the full-screen display of Sister Michael clad in a torn red camisole that hung from one bruised shoulder by a flimsy string. The makeup was garish. The dark hair was spiked and streaked with purple dye.

It was an old police mug shot.

Kathy Mallory raised her eyebrows, as if only mildly curious. "One of your more interesting nuns?"

Detective Riker stared at the screen image that gave up the name in bold capital letters. *"Quill!"* He looked down at the poster and tapped the date of the nun's disappearance. "*Two* Quills go missing on the same day?"

ALMOST THERE.

Detective Riker had cadged a ride out of SoHo in the backseat of a patrol car, and now he rolled north past the skyscrapers of Midtown, heading for the Upper East Side, the heart of the search for a kidnapped schoolboy.

How long had his partner intended to toy with Father Brenner before mentioning Jonah, the *other* missing Quill? Riker wasted no pity on the priest. That old man had known what he was dealing with before he walked in the door of Special Crimes.

Kathy Mallory was also—*special.*

As the car rounded a corner, he saw a familiar face on the street and leaned toward the patrolmen in the front seat. "Guys? I'm gettin' out here."

The driver pulled to the curb half a block from this precinct's station house, and Riker stepped out on the sidewalk to shake hands with an old friend, a sergeant like himself, but not in the Detective Bureau. Murray was still in uniform and now in charge of the officers canvassing Jonah Quill's neighborhood.

After their exchange of *Good to see your ugly face* and *What's up,* Riker was told why the kidnap story had not been fed to reporters. "The kid's uncle is loaded with money," said Murray. So, on good odds of a ransom demand, the crime had not gone public. And there were no worries about leaks to the press corps. The police commissioner had menaced news outlets all over town with naked threats to people's private parts, a time-honored practice officially known as *media cooperation.*

Riker slung his suit jacket over one arm as he walked down East Sixty-seventh Street alongside Sergeant Murray. They passed by a woman with a Great Dane on a leash, and the detective had to wonder how large the lady's apartment might be to accommodate a dog the size of a pony. How many acres of floor space? Downtown, south of Houston Street, Riker was considered a social climber because his bathtub was not in the kitchen.

He gave the nun's poster to Murray as they entered the local police station, a landmark building from the late 1800s. Though Riker's own station house was also more than a century old, it was less grand. This one, disguised as an oversized town house, had been built to blend in to a patch of the 19th Precinct that was filthy with millionaires. But the neighborhood had no flavor, no music. There might be some history to it; the detective did not know or care. No rockers had ever sung songs about this part of town, and that said it all for Riker.

Sergeant Murray, not so vain as the SoHo detective, put on his bifocals, the better to study the small face on the poster. "I'll be damned. Nobody told us about any nun. . . . She looks just like Jonah." He led Riker up the stairs to the second floor, saying over one shoulder, "Tell you what we got. Cops downtown reported sightings of a blind kid tapping his way up a street with a white cane. They can place him in the East Village that morning. But we got other sightings in the Bronx and Queens."

"The East Village fits with Sister Michael," said Riker. "We know she bought flowers on St. Marks Place around nine that morning."

"Well, this'll get us some leads." Sergeant Murray held up the poster for a second look. "What's up with those dicks at Missing Persons? We should've had a copy of this. The nun's even got the kid's smile."

"Shit happens."

The sergeant nodded to say, *Amen, brother*, and then he stopped by a closed door at the top of the stairs. "We keep him in here."

The door opened by a few inches to give Riker a covert look at a civilian half his age, who sat at the far end of a conference table that was littered with paper cups and take-out cartons, pens and yellow pads. The young man's head was bowed, and his hands were clenched together in a white-knuckle prayer.

Murray kept his voice low, saying, "That's the kid's uncle, Harold Quill. He won't go home. Don't expect much, okay? The guy's punchy. No sleep since his nephew disappeared."

The lean, dark-haired Quill sported a stubble of beard, and the wrinkles in his expensive suit were also a few days in the making. When the detective and the sergeant entered the room, the man looked up with the eyes of the boy and the nun, large and gray and ringed with black lashes, but his had a vacant look of no one home. His skin was bloodless. And a puff of air might push him over, not that he would notice.

Riker had seen this before—what was left of a man when a child went missing.

After Sergeant Murray made the introductions, the detective sat down beside the distraught uncle. "So . . . you got a family connection to Angela Quill. Is that right?"

No response? Was this guy debating whether or not he should answer that simple question without legal advice? Rich people—could they even answer a damn phone without a lawyer?

"Angie's my sister," said Harold Quill. "She's a—"

"A nun, yeah. Was she meeting up with your nephew yesterday morning?"

"No! Why would you—" Quill covered his face with both hands, as if that could make a cop disappear, and he shook his head. "I drove Jonah to school. . . . He should've been in class."

"The nun's gone missing, too. My partner's downtown talkin' to your mother. Do you—"

"No!" Harold Quill grabbed Riker's arm, and the detective pretended not to notice that this man's fingernails were digging into him. "Promise me," said Quill, "*promise* you won't tell my mother where I live!"

* * *

DETECTIVE MALLORY was Mrs. Quill's only visitor from the NYPD. Evidently, her son had failed to tell police that his kidnapped nephew had a grandmother on the Lower East Side. Less surprising, no one had even telephoned for a statement on the disappearance of her daughter, the nun. *Most* surprising? This woman had taken the dwindling of her family members quite well—as if one or two of them might vanish on a typical day.

"I called the prioress to tell her what I thought of my daughter for standing me up." In a lower voice, the mother muttered, "That *bitch*. That *whore*."

And would the nice detective like some tea?

Statuettes of saints cluttered every surface in this stuffy parlor that stank of scented, votive candles, the odor of cinnamon warring with rosemary and lavender. All the walls were lined with portraits of Jesus: a laughing Christ and a weeping one, but predominantly bloody, suffering Christs nailed up by hand and foot, and *these* images had set the tone of the interview with Mrs. Quill, whose mouth was forever frozen in the downturned arc of the righteous, whose eyes were way too wide and laser bright with the light of the Lord.

Mallory sat on the sofa, flipping through the family photograph album. *Useless.* Most of the faces pictured here had been scratched out, though not all of these erasures were done with the same tool. Some cuts were sharper than others. Beside her sat the scrawny matriarch of the family, dressed in a prim white nightgown. The loudmouthed crone guided the detective, page by page. And so Mallory discovered that images of the husband had been the first mutilations.

"May he rot in hell! He left me with *three* damn kids."

Next in the order of abandonment came the scratched-out face of a blond daughter.

"Gabriel. Gabby, we called her. She was fifteen when that picture was taken. That's when she ran away from me. A year later, she *died* giving birth to a bastard." Mrs. Quill said this with great satisfaction, as if that death might have been payback for a child born out of wedlock. The woman lowered her voice and leaned closer to share another happy confidence. "Gabby's son was born *blind.*"

Even a more seasoned detective would have flinched. Mallory only looked down at one more photo of a faceless girl, and this one had dark hair.

"Oh, that's my Angie, the other goddamn whore." Mrs. Quill reached out one bony hand to turn to the next page, and there was the only unscarred picture of this daughter, a recent addition that had yet to be pasted in with album corners. Sister Michael was posed in the robes of a nun. "She redeemed herself . . . with the *church.*" Sarcasm suggested that the nun had yet to be redeemed here at home.

Every picture of Mrs. Quill's son, Harold, had the face scratched out in the year he had sued her for custody of his nephew, Gabby's blind child. "Poor little Jonah. They stole him from me—Harry and that bitch social worker. By now, the boy's drowning in sin." A photograph of this child as a toddler, who had yet to commit any *known* sin against his grandmother, had survived the knife cuts of omission from the family.

Given more than a nodding acquaintance with Crazy, Mallory had to ask how this woman fancied chances for the survival of Sister Michael and Jonah. "Are they dead or alive?"

"Dead!" This firm vote revealed no guilt, but perhaps

the opinion that a nun and a little boy could deserve to lose their lives. Then Mrs. Quill added, "Dead and gone to God," a slightly better outcome, though offered up with less enthusiasm.

THE WALLS WERE BRICK. The door was metal. The grown-ups were dead.

Jonah had stepped on their flung-out arms and legs while mapping this chilly room that was fifteen steps square. A queasy horror. And now the stink of them was dulled by clogs of snot brought on by the boy's crying. He had found his aunt among the corpses.

By touch, he had recognized a long robe and veil, but he knew it was Aunt Angie by the smallest finger of her right hand, broken in her childhood and crooked out at the knuckle. Jonah had held this hand so many times. He could never mistake it for any other.

She had gone away when he was seven years old. For five years, he had waited for her in the fantasy of She Comes Back—and here she was.

He kissed her crooked finger.

High on the wall and beyond his reach, the loud motor started up again with the death rattle of an old machine, its parts clacking, broken or breaking down, but still churning out more blasts of cold air. Shivering, Jonah laid his body down beside his aunt. She gave him comfort—and warmth. Her wide robe was generous enough to cover him, too. "Thank you."

Pieces of a day were missing. Or was it two days? His internal clock was broken. There was a rumble in his stomach, but the thought of food made him want to puke. Was his brain busted, too? Dumbed down? Only now he thought to wonder what had happened to him—to her.

How could she be dead?

Aunt Angie *knew* how to fight. On her way out of his life, she had taught him that fingernails could draw blood, thumbs could gouge out eyes, and a kick to the balls could put a man in a world of hurt. And then she had walked out the door to catch a bus to God's house.

Had she known then what was coming—*who* was coming?

Her killer would never suspect him until it was too late. He could walk right up to that sick bastard and play helpless—just a kid, right?—and then *nail* him. *Kill* him? *Yes!* Beneath the blanket of the shared robe, Jonah's fists made one-two punches. *No* fear. Aunt Angie was with him, keeping him warm, teaching him how to draw blood and bring on pain. His aunt's side of this conversation was made up from saved-away memories of her, the sound of her, but all the words had the ring of true things. He knew what she would say to every—

The air conditioner shut down. Now a new sound. Metal on metal. A squeak to a door hinge. And the dead woman's voice inside his head screamed, *That's him!*

The boy shook off the robe and sat up.

Footsteps. *Heavy* ones. Aunt Angie sang out, *Get ready!*

Jonah was shaking and shot through with freaking cold, heart-a-banging panic.

The footsteps stopped a few paces into the room. Jonah rocked his body like a toddler with a wooden horse between his legs. The hard-soled shoes were crossing the floor, coming for him. *They were here!* Now the smell of cigarette breath. So close. Puffs of stinky air on his face.

Close enough! yelled Aunt Angie.

A man's deeper voice, a *real* one, said, "You can't *see*."

Jonah, get him!

Sorry, so sorry, but he could not do that. He was *crazy* scared. A small bottle of sloshing liquid was pressed into his hands—a reward for getting the rules right in a world where twelve-year-old boys were always outmatched by grown men. *Sorry.*

The bottled water tasted odd. No matter. *So* thirsty. Jonah drank it, gulped it down. All gone now. His rocking slowed—and stopped. His fear ebbed away, dulling down to nothing. Sleep was creeping up on him.

Behind him was the man's hard-sole step. Stepping over the other bodies? Light plops. Dull scrapes. A quick shuffle of shoes. The door opened and closed, shoes leaving and coming back again—and again. More steps and shuffles, rustles and—what?

No! Jonah shook his head, shaking off a mind-muddling fog.

He reached for Aunt Angie's hand. *No, no, no*—she was sliding away, *leaving* him. Her body was dragged across the floor faster than he could crawl after her. Not *fair!* He rose up on his knees, as much of a stand as he could manage, and his hands balled into fists. "Give her *back!*"

The door went *BANG!*

And the boy fell, toppling to one side. Sleep came on so fast. He never felt the pain of hard ground rushing up to meet him with a knock to the head that said, *Good night!*

2

The trees of Carl Schurz Park gave cover to Gracie Mansion, the official residence of the mayor. In the small hours of the morning, an alarm had sounded, and now this eighteenth-century landmark and its adjoining wing were surrounded by sheets of plastic tied off on ten-foot poles. Above this curtain, only the upper half of the extension building could be seen by civilians on East End Avenue. They saw nothing of the more secluded yellow mansion that overlooked the channel waters of Hell Gate—and the corpses stacked up on the lawn.

Members of the hazmat team were visible through the cloudy plastic as they moved about in helmets and bulky white suits that were sealed to protect them against deadly gasses and flesh-eating viruses or come what may.

On the broad sidewalk across the street, their audience was sporting Sunday-best T-shirts, shorts and summer dresses. The atmosphere turned festive as the crowd applauded the first sighting of bright-colored umbrellas attached to rolling carts. Food vendors had turned out to cater this new threat to public health and safety. Men in aprons hawked their wares along the roadbed, first servicing the front lines. Then hungry buyers at the rear sent their money forward, hand-to-hand, and bags of bagels and coffee were handed back to them.

Men and women in dark suits held up the IDs of Homeland Security, and they yelled at the civilians, ordering them to move on. Predictably, these federal agents were ignored. The menace implied by moon suits had scared off out-of-towners, but not blasé natives who always formed a crowd for the prospect of sudden death in New York City. And, *damn it,* it was time for brunch.

Behind the backs of the shouting agents, a cadre of uniformed police officers stood in a line down the center of the avenue, and they all wore smirks of *We told you so, you stupid bastards.* The NYPD *knew* how to do crowd control. And, clearly, the federal government did not.

Some civilians with curbside views sat on canvas camp stools sold from a cart with merchandise that included paper fans and sun visors. Most of the crowd remained standing, growing restless as they watched the slow, blurry movements of the hazmat team. New York attitude was in the air, and it demanded, *Hey, let's get on with the show!*

TWO DETECTIVES STOOD behind the gawkers. One wore an out-of-date suit that spoke well of him as a civil servant who lived within his means, though, truth be told, Riker hated shopping and had let it slide for years.

He gave his partner a gallant wave that said, *Ladies first,* so he could use tall Mallory as a wedge to move through this tightly packed mob. People tended to get out of her way, and not because they respected the badge or her tailored threads—or the running shoes that cost more than Riker's entire closet, shoes thrown in. The whole package said that she was *somebody*, but the Mallory effect on crowds was more than that. When she wanted to jangle a civilian—like right now—she dropped every pretense of being human and walked toward the poor bastard, as if she meant to walk right through him, and this was all that was needed to inspire that man's wary backwards dance.

Just a hint of crazy got a world of respect in this town, though there were detectives in the Special Crimes Unit who suspected that Kathy Mallory was not hinting. She *might* be the real deal. Riker believed she knew this and encouraged it in the same way that the clothes on her back flaunted the idea of a cop who *might* be dirty.

She liked her games. She played them well.

When they reached the street, Riker ignored the government suits—so as not to lose face with the cops on the line. He spoke to the uniform with the sergeant's stripe, "What's up, Murray? You got a body count?"

"Yeah, I seen four of 'em in there." The sergeant glanced at officers to his left and right, indicating that this was not a good time to thank him for a tip on a dead nun. "The security cameras are useless—blacked out with paintballs. But I know the perp was wearing NYPD blue last night. On the other side of the park, we found a cop knocked out cold and stripped down to his skivvies."

Mallory was distracted by an argument half a block away. It looked to be one-sided, no fists in play yet, but getting there. Riker also watched this scene as a government agent, red in the face, rose off the balls of his feet, trying so hard to be taller. The fed was outsized by the man who set a Gladstone bag down on the sidewalk at his booted feet. Chief Medical Examiner Edward Slope ripped off his protective helmet and gloves. The doctor's anger was more dignified—and more effective. The flat of one raised hand silenced the younger, shorter man from Homeland Security. Now it was Dr. Slope's turn to vent, and the federal agent came down from his tiptoes.

"A scam." Without hearing one clear word, Mallory had the gist of the ME's complaint. "Those moon suits are just for show, right?"

"That's *my* guess," said Sergeant Murray. "What we got in there is weird, but it's got shit to do with germs or poison gas. I figure the mayor wanted to keep people outta the park . . . on a *Sunday*. Well, forget that." With a nod toward the plastic curtain, he said, "So one of those clowns in there called out the hazmat team. Figured that'd scare 'em off." He turned back to the bagel-noshing sidewalk crowd. "Do they look scared to you?"

Since diplomacy was not his partner's forte, Riker walked down the street to join the kiddie agent in charge of false alarms and circuses. The detective offered this youngster the carrot of being addressed as a grown-up. "Look, pal, I know you got jerked around today, but don't go off on anybody else, okay? We need some leverage here. Just pack up the moon suits and go."

"Somebody's gotta pay for dragging out the whole damn—"

"Me and my partner, we can make that happen. We can make the pack of 'em wish they'd never screwed with you." In the hierarchy of New York City, this was a fairy tale, but the young agent seemed to like the story.

EDWARD SLOPE's shed hazmat suit was carried off by Homeland Security agents, and now the chief medical examiner wore only the uniform of a Sunday backyard barbecuer. Never mind loud—his Hawaiian shirt *shrieked* color. Even so, he was the most distinguished man on the scene. Silver-haired and tall, he had the posture and bark of a general as he issued orders to his minions, who had been waiting on the sidelines all this time. The ME had entered the red zone alone; he thought most of his people were idiots, but they were his idiots, and he would never put them in harm's way. At the top of the short driveway, two of them pulled aside the plastic curtain, and a gurney stacked with body bags wheeled past them.

Dr. Slope lowered his voice to speak with Riker and Mallory. "A very egalitarian killer. The victims are different genders, races, ages. I'd call it *pointedly* random."

The doctor marched into the tented area, and the detectives followed him past the gatehouse, beyond the extension building and along one side of the yellow mansion. At the turn of this corner, the plastic curtain was torn down to give them a view of the river beyond a wide circle of manicured grass.

Three corpses lay facedown in a careless pile at the foot of the stairs to the veranda and the mayor's front door. An old woman's stark white face was pressed to the brown hand of a young man's body, and his head was pillowed on feet that stuck out from beneath him. Most notable among the dead was the fourth corpse, Sister Michael, also known as Angela Quill. This body had been rolled over and set apart from the rest.

Riker pulled out his notebook and pen. "Likely weapon?"

"A knife," said Dr. Slope. "But when this was called in, I was told that a doctor on the scene had identified symptoms of sarin gas. *In a pig's eye*. And that doctor turned out to be a press secretary. I want her charged with falsifying—"

"Okay," said Riker. "We'll talk to her."

"Too late. I did the honors. You'll find that little moron locked in a bathroom. She was crying—but still alive when I was done with her."

"Yeah?" Riker suppressed a grin. *Liar.* A gentleman to the core, Dr. Slope would *never* make a woman cry. Though Mallory might make the doctor's lie come true soon enough.

Most of the grassy land was enclosed by a tall fence of iron bars with pointed spikes, all but a section of redbrick wall that separated the mansion's lawn from the public area of the park. This was the lowest and likeliest access. The detective reached out to snag the arm of a man he knew, a passing crime-scene investigator. "Hey, Rizzo. I know our perp didn't toss the bodies over the wall. No crushed bushes, no drag marks on the grass. So what's the deal here?"

"You gotta see this, or you'll think I'm lying." Rizzo led him around the south corner of the mansion and pointed to a jog in the brick wall, where another CSI was photographing a narrow iron gate that joined the two sections. "It was secured with—"

"A damn padlock?" It lay on the ground at Riker's feet—broken. Flimsy piece of crap.

"Yeah. Breaking in here—that's three second's work with the right tool. One of the guys on park patrol tells me this is the hooker entrance. The uniforms don't go near it after dark. Mayor Polk thinks they might scare off his call girls." CSI Rizzo pointed to the concrete stairwell leading down to the basement of the mansion's wing, and no words were needed. This entry point could be seen by any visitor on the park side of the gate's iron bars. It was an open invitation to any lunatic passing by.

"I see it—and I still don't believe it," said Riker. "Did the perp get inside last night?"

"Nope, no sign of entry anywhere but this gate. Your guy just dumped the bodies and left." On their way back to the front lawn, the man from Crime Scene Unit said, "Here's the real weak spot—no adults in charge of mansion security. The mayor's protection detail answers to the commissioner, and—"

"And he answers to the mayor," said Riker. "Got it."

When the dead bodies were in sight, Rizzo stopped, and he *had* to ask, "What's your partner doing?" As if it were not plain enough.

"She's smelling corpses," said Riker.

Mallory had finished with the nun, and now, as the ME's team rolled the other bodies, she leaned down to sniff each one in turn. Done with that, she said, "So . . . not a spree killing."

"No," said the chief medical examiner. "All different stages of decomp. There's signs of dehydration, too—except for the last kill. She's the most disturbing one." Dr. Slope looked down at the corpse in nun's regalia. The young woman's large gray eyes were open, and she wore a faint, sly smile. "I'm going to see that in my sleep for a *long* time."

MALLORY AND HER PARTNER stood on the veranda of Gracie Mansion in a face-off with a lanky young man who wore a bow tie and a sneer.

The mayor's aide, Samuel Tucker, was puffed up with all the importance of an entitled frat boy from some college of fastidious twits. He inspected their gold shields, squinting as if that might help him spot fakes—or germs. The aide then informed the detectives that they were not on the approved list for the meeting inside. He glanced at Riker's suit with a moue of distaste. Clearly, *that* detective would not even make the cut for those allowed to enter by the front door on any occasion. He shrugged as if to say, *Perhaps the back door? But not today.*

Riker and Mallory walked around him to enter the mansion's foyer, a generous space with a couch and chairs and a grand staircase.

Now that Tucker understood his true place in the world—not rising to the kneecap of a cockroach—he scrambled over the patterned floor, racing past the detectives to give the appearance of *leading* them into the library, a smaller room that might be misnamed, as it contained only a handful of books. It was a museum scheme of turquoise walls, white trim and period furnishings from the gaslight era. A dozen people milled around in a mix of suits and weekend wear. The aide walked through the low babble of conversations to approach one of the paired blue love seats in front of the fireplace, where he leaned down to whisper in the mayor's ear.

His Honor Andrew Polk was nearly fifty, but his brown hair had not one strand of gray, and Mallory pronounced it an excellent dye job. He was reported to be five-feet-four, but that might be too generous a measure for this little man with the tiny shiny eyes of a rodent. He wore the casual clothes of a Sunday sailor, and his canvas shoes tapped out the beat of nerves on the fray—or maybe this was just a sign of irritation with the man bending over him. Hands clasped together, Polk nodded at something his aide had just said.

Seated beside the city's top politician was a fair-haired man, a decade younger and miles better looking. He sported a suntan to match the mayor's, though no one would peg him as a fellow yachtsman, not dressed in *that* suit, a very nice one—and expensive for a man of the cloth. This could only be the cardinal's man, Father DuPont, *another* politician. And Mallory could put that suntan down to rounds of whacking balls on a golf green, the favored political venue of churchmen currying and bestowing favor. The priest's expression was somber to fit the occasion of finding a dead nun on the doorstep.

The police commissioner should have been the lone figure on the facing love seat, but there sat Chief of Detectives Joseph Goddard, a broad-shouldered man in a silk suit. Even before she saw his face, Mallory recognized the bullet-shaped head and the crew cut. He was an interesting choice of police confidant for Mayor Polk. All around them were civilian staff and NYPD bodyguards, most of them standing, others seated on chairs and a striped couch. In the next moment, all of them, except for the mayor's aide, filed through the door, leaving in obedience to the wave of the chief's hand and the word, "Out!"

The seat of power was now made clear.

So a deal had been struck, and the chief of detectives had a brand-new victim for his dossier collection. It was said that the use of power revealed a man's true face, but Joe Goddard's was on display all the time—a thug's face. At least, they had been spared his trademark entrance, a walk on leaden feet to make the floor quake. The chief liked to advertise that he was coming—and that he was dangerous to cops and felons alike. His political currency was information, and he was a master at acquiring dirty secrets.

Did that frighten the mayor?

It should.

"I didn't send for you." Chief Goddard addressed Riker, showing displeasure with this gatecrasher and—*the other one*. Mallory easily read the man's expression when he finally looked her way, all condescension and irritation, a warning to the puppy cop: She should *not* piss on the rug. He turned away from her, and she became invisible—dead to him. He *wished* she were dead. They had a history in a little dance of Crush Me If You Can.

"We ID'd one of the victims," said Riker. "Sister Michael. She ties in to another case." This was their passport. None could challenge it. Both cases would merge at the top of the NYPD priorities—now that the deadly virus scam had fizzled out.

When Chief Goddard grudgingly introduced the detectives, Mallory's name did not register with Father DuPont. Was he that good an actor? Her second thought was that this priest had instructed Father Brenner not to name the selection for pet cop. Maybe the phrase, *plausible deniability*, was also terminology of the church.

"So . . . four bodies." Mallory turned to Mayor Polk. "Four ransom notes?" Oh, the poor man was startled—as if she had smacked him. Well, *damn*.

It was Samuel Tucker who stepped forward to say, "We're not aware of any ransom demands."

Riker ignored the aide to speak with the mayor. "Well, sir, you can see why we'd ask. . . . That dead nun outside? You knew she'd gone missing before the cops did."

Good shot.

Polk's left hand wrapped around his right fist. Again, his aide was the one who first opened his mouth for the predictable denial, and Riker said to this younger man, "That's not a question, kid. It's a *fact.*" The detective's subtext was clear: *Don't let me catch you in a lie.* And that closed Tucker's mouth. Riker turned back to Mayor Polk. "About the nun. We have to wonder why you didn't call the police."

In a little masterstroke of deflection, Andrew Polk turned to Chief Goddard and leaned forward, as if to ask this man the same question.

Without a glance at the detectives, the chief said, "He *did* call it in. *I* knew the nun was missing. I had a detective looking into it . . . *quietly.*"

"A cop picked out by the *church?*" Mallory said this with a heavy lean on incredulity. "That's a roundabout way of assigning a case."

Joe Goddard looked up at her, quizzical at first, and then his expression changed to one reserved for stepping on a dog turd.

"That's right," she said. "I was the one who got tapped to look into it. *I'm* the church-friendly cop you were all praying for."

Surprise!

Father DuPont only widened his blue eyes, confirming her theory that he had opted not to be told which cop had won the honor of church toady. And she could see that the chief of detectives had been left out of this backroom arrangement of priests. No way had Goddard known any details about Sister Michael. But he did have the makings for conspiracy.

"Chief, I'm guessing you never got a look at the dead nun's face." Mallory thumbed keys on her cell phone to raise a crime-scene photograph of a smiling corpse.

"Maybe the ME rolled her body after you got here. This is Sister Michael." She held up the small-screen image of the dead woman—who bore a twin's resemblance to the kidnap victim, Jonah Quill. And that schoolboy's likeness had been seen by every cop in the NYPD, including the chief, who had assigned record numbers of detectives to find him. "You had a detective—*one* cop—looking into *this* missing Quill . . . quietly?"

The chief's cover-up for the mayor, exposed as a lie, hung in the air, the great stinking fart in the room. Goddard glared at Polk, his eyes yelling, *You screwup!*

THE AIR CONDITIONER clanked and whirred above him, and liquid splashed on the floor all around him. *Gasoline*—it burned Jonah's nostrils.

He was a ball of a boy, curled up and shaking, teeth clicking, his toes and fingers numbed by cold. But—odd thing—upon waking, his fear had not kicked in again. He only wondered how she could be dead, and "Is it my turn?"

Still groggy, Jonah was lifted to his feet by rough hands, *big* hands. His mouth was dry, his head ached, and there was a wobble to his knees as he was dragged across the raised threshold of a door to a warmer place. The air beyond the room was muggy. Gone was the stink of putrid meat—except for what traveled with him, trapped in his clothes. Hands, too. The smell of corpses and—

Smoke?

Behind him was the crackle of fire, a sound that terrified him—but not today. He was so calm. Crazy calm.

Weak and woozy, the boy stumble-walked as he was

pulled along. Below the sleeve of his T-shirt, the flesh of one arm brushed the sandpaper texture of a wall. The man walked alongside him, gripping the other arm to yank him through another doorway. They were outside now and climbing stairs to city sounds of horns and cars. This noise was still high above him when Jonah ran out of steps. An overpass? That would kill the sunlight, the clue of radiant heat beating down on his raised face to tell him it was daytime. There was no pedestrian noise at ground level and no word of warning to be quiet. So there was no one close by who might see him or—

Careful, Jonah. The vestige of Aunt Angie still survived in him, his homemade ghost of her, assembled from a kit of remembered things. Her soft voice whispered, *No one will hear if you scream. So don't make this maniac angry.*

A catch of metal undone for another door. Jonah was pushed through it to sprawl on a padded seat. The smell of leather. His feet were lifted and jammed in behind him and—*Slam!* The air in here was oven-toasty. The driver's door opened. Slammed shut. The engine came to life. And—*click.* A cigarette lighter? Yes, a smell of expelled smoke. They were rolling forward, and the driver had yet to say one word.

Throat parched, voice raspy, Jonah asked, "Is it my turn?"

MALLORY'S PARTNER pretended to take down notes while the mayor pretended to tell him the truth. Again, Riker asked how His Honor knew the nun was missing, and Andrew Polk offered up Father DuPont as his source.

The priest turned his back on them to look out a window. Hiding a guilty face?

Mallory lost only seconds to speculation on Father DuPont. Polk was more interesting. He had not yet blamed Missing Persons for the fumble on the nun. A timely report *had* been filed with police, and Polk knew it.

So why invite Chief Goddard to spin that lie?

"Yeah, still here." She had been left on hold with a cell phone to her ear, and now an officer in a neighboring state had returned to end their conversation with the transmission of a police report and a photograph. Mallory lowered her cell phone to study the new image on its screen. She looked up and raised her voice to say, "Jonah Quill was spotted at a tollbooth in New Jersey."

As every head turned her way, she saw no reason to add that there was no eyewitness, only a security camera, and all she had was a bad-to-useless picture of the passenger's bowed head. The driver's face was hidden by the brim of a baseball cap pulled low. She only said, "They got the car."

An SUV, stolen from a senior citizen, had been recovered from a shopping mall's parking lot. No kidnapped boy was found inside it, no evidence at all, but when Mallory said, "The boy's alive," *perhaps* they all inferred that Jonah Quill was safe in police custody.

And maybe she should clear up that mistaken impression—or not.

Father DuPont seemed happy with this news. But the mayor's face went slack. A prelude to losing his breakfast on the carpet? Mallory gave this politician a tender smile from her repertoire of rarely used expressions, and so he was unprepared when she said, "Whatever the nun knew, the boy knows it, too. Is there anything you'd like to tell us . . . *before* we talk to him?"

Mayor Polk mouthed an easy-to-read obscenity as he gave Chief Goddard a look that asked, *What now?*

The chief held up one spread hand in a tempering gesture used by mothers to quiet excited children, and this said that he had the situation *and* the young detective under control. In response to that sign language, Mallory said to him, "Yeah, *right*."

Riker gave her a shake of the head, a warning that she was overstepping.

The chief turned to face her, wary and hostile, but he said nothing about her insubordination. There could be no better test. She was bulletproof.

Goddard would not be reassigning this case to more manageable detectives. He *could* not. That chance had been missed when he was caught in a lie for the mayor—as good as a confession of collusion. Though Mallory believed the chief's involvement only extended to the hour before her arrival. It was a matter of style. In the past, this man had been careful not to step in the dirt he collected for his dossiers.

But now he had forfeited his opportunity for a power grab.

Wrong.

The bastard was confidently staring her down, silently telling her that he planned to stay in the game—and Mallory should watch her back, so certain was he that she would never see the kill strike coming to end her days as a cop.

She nodded to acknowledge that glove thrown down, and now Goddard had a startled look in his eyes, and he mouthed the word, *shit!* He was staring at something behind her.

Mallory turned to catch Andrew Polk in an unguarded moment when all eyes but Joe Goddard's were turned away. He was showing the chief his true face.

What a big toothy smile you have, Mr. Mayor. And so creepy. Were his little rat's eyes shinier now? *Yes!* He was having a *good* time.

What sick game was this?

3

On the New Jersey side of the George Washington Bridge, the unmarked police car was launched like a highway rocket at a hundred miles an hour. No siren—more fun that way for Mallory, but not for the man in the passenger seat. Though Riker climbed into a car with her every day on the job, he could still be startled by a near-death experience.

His partner loved nothing better than a long stretch of dry road with no traffic lights and no rules but hers. Mallory's only obstacles were civilians. She called them speed bumps—and fair game. So far, her fellow motorists were only fighting back with obscene hand gestures, and some of them rolled down their windows to shout colorful remarks about her driving as she sped by within inches of scraping their paint.

Riker averted his eyes from the road, putting his faith in the gods of seat belts and airbags and—

Prayers answered, the car slowed down to make the turnoff for the Jersey hospital where the detectives would find Ellen Cathery, the owner of a stolen car that *might* have transported a kidnapped child and a serial killer.

* * *

ON THE MANHATTAN SIDE of the bridge, an elderly mugging victim signed his discharge papers in another hospital. Days ago, Albert Costello had been found unconscious inside a vacant store. After suffering a fall that had left a bloodstain on the floor beneath his fractured skull, he had been unable to help police with the how or the why of it. Today, though he had not completed his stay for observation, he cast aside the flimsy hospital gown and pulled his own clothes from the closet, preparing to leave against medical advice.

"I'll be fine," he said, showing his naked rump to the young man with the stethoscope. "All I need's a decent night's sleep." Albert glowered at the patient in the next bed, whose snoring had driven him insane for two nights. One more hour in this place and he might tear out all the white hair he had left.

Also, he missed his beer and smokes.

Lost weight might be another grievance against the hospital. While tying his shoelaces, Albert wondered if his arms were bonier now. The boy doctor hovered over him, wanting to know if there was someone at home to look after him. "Naw, I outlived everybody who gave a shit." And this summed up the ten years since his wife's funeral. That long ago, he had lost the hang of making new friends to replace those who had moved away or passed away. His life had been all about people, and all the people were gone.

Albert decided to walk home, a mile or more. Occasionally he brushed up against other pedestrians, touching life before it sped up and left him behind on the sidewalk. Bouts of dizziness forced him to rest along the way. Now and then, people would stop to ask if he needed help. He pegged them for out-of-towners, easy marks, and he snagged them into conversation until they tired of the mugging story and his complaints about hospital food and the snoring man in the next bed.

He arrived at St. Marks Place in the afternoon. Had anyone been willing to listen to him as he walked along the street, he could have married up some history with these addresses, the former digs of anarchists and artsy-fartsy types. He never read poetry, but he knew that W. H. Auden had lived twenty years at number seventy-seven. And up ahead was the site of the first Mafia hit in Manhattan. He had so many stories to tell about this neighborhood—and no one to hear them. Not anymore.

After unlocking the street door, he entered his apartment house; he called it his tomb. During the day, when other tenants were at work, this old five-story brownstone always had a dead feel to it. He rarely met people on the narrow stairs, not that he would recognize them, damn transients. Albert only knew a few by habits that invaded the halls on the weekends. The ground-floor tenant was the one with the strong cooking smells. On the second floor, he passed by the apartment where the loud radio lived, but the cook and the radio player had no faces. As to the floors above his apartment—well, that was another country, and he had no reason to go there.

Albert stood before his third-floor door, pulled out his keys—and discovered that the apartment was not locked. This should have alarmed him. The town prided itself on three deadbolts to every front door. In a situation like this one, all New Yorkers were geographically obliged to be paranoid. Fearful. At least suspicious.

Yet he did not back away.

His recent mugging had left him with a taste for adventure.

NEW JERSEY RESIDENT Mrs. Ellen Cathery raised her head from the pillow of the hospital bed, her wrinkled neck attenuating as she strained to sniff the air for a fragrance that was neither antiseptic nor medicinal. The New York detective's floral perfume was faint, a single dab at most, and alien. Mrs. Cathery—"just call me Elly"—could not identify the flower by its scent, and the young blonde's accent was equally untraceable. On the other side of the bed, the man's intonations were rooted in Brooklyn as he said, "Sorry to put you through this, ma'am, but anything you can tell us will help."

On the other side of the room, Mazie Wade, a stout woman with henna-red hair, was pacing and muttering over and over, "Goddamn it."

Elly had reassured her dearest friend six times that she was fine, just *fine*—except for her memory of the event. That was gone. She could only recall that she had borrowed Mazie's SUV because her own vehicle was in the shop. They both favored the large gas hogs that fit so well with their antiquing expeditions, augments to Elly's pension. Her friend Mazie was still a kid, only fifty-two, and gainfully employed by the town's police force.

One of Elly's blue-veined hands covered the needle that fed her fluids for dehydration. She fussed with the tape that anchored it to her arm while the nice man from Brooklyn read out a list of four names. "No, sorry, I don't know any of them." Oh, she had disappointed the other one, the tall blonde, who walked away from the bed. "I'm sorry," she said to the remaining detective. "I can't remember much. But we have Mazie's car back. That's the main thing. I *do* remember waking up in her car."

The paramedics had helped her out of the front seat, where she had apparently fallen asleep behind the wheel—such a deep sleep that she had gone weak in the knees and in need of assistance to the ambulance. But her location, that strange parking lot, had been a mystery to her. Then a greater mystery had unfolded when the medics noticed a light imprint on the thin skin of her face. It had suggested to them that her mouth had been taped shut.

Detective Mallory stood beside Mazie Wade, asking, "Was Mrs. Cathery a regular at that mall?"

"No," said Mazie. "The mall's twenty miles from here. Elly's very civic-minded. She makes a point of doing all her shopping here in town."

The New York detective consulted a small notebook. "So your guys found a slick of oil on her dress and a bruise on one hip."

"Yeah," said Mazie, the hometown detective. "I figure she took a fall on a garage floor, and there's acres of parking under her apartment complex. That's where those kids must've snatched the car."

"Kids." The young blonde said this in the tone of a challenge.

"Happened once before," said Mazie Wade. "It was an old man that time."

"Ma'am?" The New York policeman called Elly's attention back to him, leaning in close to say, "So yesterday, you borrowed Detective Wade's car. Try to remember where you—"

"Don't *badger* her!" Dr. Kray stood in the open doorway, his lower lip all pouted out, playing king of the hospital, though he was only her personal physician with a rather small practice in town. *Damn bastard.* So he had finally decided to grace her with a visit. With only a curt nod from on high, he marched to the foot of her bed and picked up the clipboard that dangled there. After flipping through a few pages, he gave the three detectives a withering glance, definitely overdoing it. "She's still under the effect of the drugs. Now I want you people out of here."

"What drugs?" Detective Riker appeared not to see the doctor in the room. He addressed his question to the local detective. "Something the hospital gave her?"

"No," said Mazie. "Paramedics found an injection site on the back of Elly's neck. There were drugs in her system when they brought her in." She handed a sheet of paper to the tall blonde. "That's bloodwork from the hospital lab. I had them load her tox screen with a few extras. They only found trace amounts, but it matches up with last year's case. The first drug would've dropped her on the spot. That's a mail-order item. I'm checking retailers for veterinary supplies. The next one's Rohypnol, and way too many kids got access to that one."

"A date-rape drug," said Detective Mallory. "No wonder her memory's shot."

"There was no *sexual assault!*" The irate Dr. Kray turned to Elly, saying, "Calm *down,*" though she had yet to show a sign of being anything *but* calm. And now, turning on the trio of detectives, the doctor yelled, "Are you *deaf!* I told you to get *out!*"

They ignored the old blowhard. This won Elly's heart.

The three detectives went on to discuss which areas of the mall's parking lot had been covered by security cameras. But there were too many blind spots and no pictures to be had.

"So the car wasn't stolen," said Mazie. "You might say

it was borrowed. No parts stripped, nothing missing. Just a damn joyride, and whoever did this couldn't even hot-wire a car. They needed the keys. Now, who has to drug an old lady to steal her keys? I'll *tell* you! Goddamn rotten *kids!*"

RECENT MUGGING VICTIM and hospital escapee Albert Costello opened the mysteriously unlocked door to his apartment, a place of stingy, dirty windows, deep shadows and dust. A stranger was sitting on the couch. This man might be in his late thirties, a tough guy by the looks of his muscled arms and the way he filled out his T-shirt and jeans—and those eyes were definitely on the scary side.

Fear should have been Albert's first response, but he took his cue from this uninvited guest, who removed his blue baseball cap to reveal the dark stubble of a shaved head *and* good manners. He rose from the couch to greet his host with a smile.

And Albert smiled.

The stranger was smoking a cigarette. No problem with that. Albert also had the habit. There were many ashtrays about the room, most of them full, all of them dirty.

Aw, the place was a mess. If only he had known that company was coming.

DETECTIVE RIKER could remember a time when a drive in New Jersey smelled worse. Now this road was just like any highway in America, that other nation outside of New York City. "I liked the old days better," he said to

his partner, "when car thieves just swapped out the damn license plates." True, if there was no police report of a stolen car, there would be no search for a driver. But *this* car thief had gone to unusual lengths to avoid the scrutiny of highway patrolmen, cameras and high-tech plate scanners. "Drugging an old lady to steal her car—that's just over the top."

Their own car was approaching a scanner for their dashboard E-ZPass, and Mallory slowed down to avoid setting off the speeder alarm at the tollbooth. Once they were beyond the radar, Rocketgirl was back in form, flooring the accelerator.

Many a stout-hearted cop had turned down the opportunity to ride with her. On days like this one, Riker considered renewing his driver's license, though driving would seriously interfere with his drinking, and he believed it was only the hankering for booze that reinforced his will to live.

The bridge back to the city was still miles down the highway, and he wondered how long it would be before they attracted the attention of a road-rage nut. The detective rolled down his passenger window to slap the portable siren on the roof of the car. The effect was immediate. The Jersey drivers became more complacent about his partner riding up behind them, too close to kissing their taillights, and they glided out of the lane—*Mallory's* lane.

Riker studied prints of tollbooth photos that showed Elly Cathery's car driving into Manhattan with only a man behind the wheel and then leaving with company in the front seat. The pictures were next to worthless, only revealing the brim of the driver's baseball cap. The passenger was slumped over, face hidden, though the hair

was dark, and this rider wore a red T-shirt to fit the bulletin line of Last Seen Wearing—

"That's our perp and the kid," said Mallory.

"*If* the ME can match the old lady's drug combo to the bodies. That date-rape drug leaves the system real fast."

"We might get lucky with the nun's tox screen. She was the last one to die."

Even if Dr. Slope had not volunteered that much at the scene, Riker would have deferred to his partner's smell test for the freshest corpse. He tossed the photographs on the dashboard. "Worst case—we wasted some time."

"No," she said, just a bit testy. "That's our perp. I say he lives in New Jersey." She took one hand off the wheel to reach a back pocket, and now she laid a twenty-dollar bill on the console. "And I say he's a pro."

"No way." He figured she had only pitched this bet to make him a little crazy. "So he's a Jersey boy. Okay, maybe I'll buy that part." The perpetrator would most likely go shopping for a car to steal on his own side of the bridge. "But a *hit man?*" He snatched up one of the photographs. "It's a bad shot, but pros never get this careless. If that's Jonah Quill, he should've been out of sight in the back."

Mallory shook her head. "Not today. Thanks to the mayor's scam, there were cops parked on both sides of every bridge all morning. Homeland Security had them spot-checking cars for imaginary terrorists with chemical weapons. So the perp figures—better a doped-up kid in the front seat than a tied-up kid in the back. Dead or alive, a schoolboy would've kept the car outside the federal profile."

Riker nodded. Now he knew why they had a photo for a car with no speeding violation to trigger a camera. And putting the boy in the front seat might suggest a cool head and good planning, but there was no proof of a hired killer. And so, in the vein of fishing for more, he said, "The old lady ties him to a stolen car. That's way too sloppy for a hit man."

"That was *smart.* Elly Cathery has no job. She lives alone. No one would've noticed she was missing if she hadn't borrowed a cop's personal car."

"Not buyin' it," said Riker. "For a pro, our perp's a real screwup. If the local cops are onto the—"

"The locals are nowhere," said Mallory. "Mazie Wade thinks it's happened *once* before. It could've happened a dozen times. I wonder how often a senior citizen wakes up behind the wheel of her own car . . . in a strange place. Is that *ever* a police matter?"

No. The victim might tell a doctor. More than likely, the average senior would be too embarrassed to tell anyone. And then there was the added fear of losing a driver's license, a loss that would shrink the world to places that the elderly could walk to—until they could no longer walk.

So *maybe* one point for his partner. If the killer had driven his own car or a rental today, cops would be breaking down his door right now. But Riker could never go along with the theory of a hit man. And yet he would not take Mallory's wager—such easy money, too easy. She favored sure things, the bets that she could not lose. Riker called them setups for pratfalls.

ALBERT COSTELLO would not ask if a woman had made those scratches on the stranger's face, and this was not a matter of manners. Of *course* a woman's claws had done that, but Albert never asked stupid questions. Also, there was the matter of the guy's eyes—scary-wide white saucers with little black holes dead center. Kind of intense. They said to him, *Don't move,* without saying a word out loud. *I got you in my sights,* they said. But the old man did not take this personally. Naw, this was just luck of the draw—like a birth defect.

And so he continued to entertain the stranger with his best story, the mugging that had landed him in the hospital. Parting the grimy curtains of a window that overlooked St. Marks Place, he called the man's attention to the sidewalk below. "That's the spot." That was where he had been standing before the assault. He had no memory of entering the empty store where he had been found unconscious. "See that lamppost? I kill an hour there every day."

He turned to face his mystery guest. The man had not yet offered up a name, but that long upper lip reminded Albert of a mug from the old Irish clans. And this guy had a way of talking that would have said *homeboy* back in the day. He asked more questions than cops did, but he was no cop. He had more the look of a mob enforcer, a bone breaker.

Was that worrisome?

Naw, the Irish gangs were history, and the Italian mob was dying off, the old dons gone to jail. These days, Gangland was Russian, Chinese and Dominican. Yeah, the good old days had gone to the dogs. And he said to the stranger, "So . . . you grew up around here. Am I right?"

Ma-a-a-n, what a cold one you are. And the guy got that way all of a sudden, losing his smile, going all stiff and strange-like.

Albert shuffled off to the kitchen. "I'm gonna getcha a cold beer." This promised to be a most interesting day. Life was looking up.

DETECTIVE RIKER'S PARTNER pulled up in front of an innocuous building two blocks from the train station in the town of Jamaica, the borough of Queens. This was the address of the Crime Scene Unit. He had just put both feet on the sidewalk, and—*ZAP*—the street was clear, the car was gone, like maybe Mallory had taught it how to fly.

The captain in command of the CSU was standing in the open doorway, caught in the act of coming or going. Heller's other name was The Bear, for he clearly did not belong in that suit and tie, nor did he walk about like other men, but lumbered everywhere, taking his own time. His slow-rolling brown eyes took in every detail, noting Riker's loosened tie and the swipe of wet palms on the suit jacket.

This captain was not the first man or the tenth one to ask, "Why do you let Mallory drive?"

Riker shrugged and waved off the question without tipping his hand to a long flirtation with suicide.

When they had climbed the stairs to Heller's private office, the commander sat down at his desk and laid out the evidence gathered by his team. "Nothin' to do with black-market organs, and that comes straight from the ME's Office. Dr. Slope says the stabs run deep. So your perp damn sure nicked the hearts before he removed 'em."

"He took their *hearts?*" Riker slumped low in his chair. "Hell of a trophy collection." And this lunatic act killed Mallory's theory of a professional hit man. *Good.* He rooted for the psycho option. Pros were hell-to-impossible to catch, and, in this case, hired killings had never made sense.

Heller picked up a roll of silver duct tape. "No tape was found on the vics, but this brand matches adhesive residue on their skin. It's sold in every hardware store in America. No shot at tracing it."

"Any ideas about where the bodies were kept? We figure they died at different—"

"No freezer burns, but I know it was air-conditioned storage. Dr. Slope says the nun's rigor won't square with a likely time of death." Heller moved on to the small evidence bags and sheets of text from the Police Lab. "We got debris from the clothing. To me, it all says warehouse. Mice droppings, pieces of roaches, fibers from cardboard cartons. . . . One pinfeather. The lab tech says it comes off a gull. That might steer us to a crime scene by the water." He held up two fingers for "*Two* rivers—*miles* of waterfront property." Or, more briefly put, *Kiss that lead goodbye.*

"Got anything that might give up the transport vehicle?"

"You mean fibers? No, nothing that links to floor mats or trunks. But he dumped four bodies. I'd bet on a van."

So far, not one leg of his partner's impossible theory was panning out. What was she up to? Had she known about the trophy hearts, maybe talked to the ME? Yeah, he would bet the rent money on it. And now he had the hang of Mallory's setup: Could she get him to ask Heller the granddaddy of stupid questions? He *did* have to ask, but he couched it in disbelief when he said, "Well, could've been worse. At least we're not lookin' at murder for hire."

The CSU commander relied on the science of physical

evidence and a history of violence dating back to a time when New York City was the country's murder capital—before that title was lost to Chicago. This man could be trusted to know a lunatic from a pro by the tracks and traces left behind. And so Riker had not anticipated Heller's look of serious consideration for the insane theory of a hit man.

"Your perp has an untraceable murder kit." The captain picked up a long blade, serrated on one side. "It'll fit with the wounds. I bought this one down the street. You can buy 'em anywhere. A carving knife's not your typical weapon for a pro, but they don't all use twenty-twos. A bullet to the back of the head says assassination. That sends a message. It's cold. It's all business . . . but so's this." He laid out a photo of one victim, whose shirt was open to expose a wound where a stolen organ used to be. "Cutting out the heart—that's got some hate to it. It's personal . . . but *not* to your killer. He cuts 'em open. Only one wound—a stab sawed out to a long, straight cut. *Not* a rage attack." He held up a hammer. "This'll match tool marks we found on the broken ribs, the ones that would've been in his way. So . . . a slice, a few whacks, then snip, snip and done—like it's just stuff on a checklist. No passion, not even close. That says hate at one remove. He could be a real cold whack job . . . but I'd say he's getting paid for this."

And *that* would be Mallory's punch line.

ALBERT COSTELLO and his no-name guest smoked cigarettes companionably as they discussed the mugging on St. Marks Place. "He didn't get my wallet. The coward must've been scared off. I can't remember much. The doc said I should expect that with a cracked skull."

The stranger drained his beer. "I heard a blind kid went missin' that day."

"No shit? I ain't seen TV or a newspaper in days. What else did I miss?"

"The cops think the kid was on this street around the time you got mugged. You never saw him?"

Albert shook his head. And then, pressed to recall one more detail, he said, "A nun? Oh, yeah. I *do* remember her. I saw her comin' from half a block away, even with my bad eyes. Not often you see that kind of outfit these days—like a black sailboat floatin' down the sidewalk. So the nun stops at the bodega on the corner. She's lookin' at flowers, fixin' to buy some, I guess. She must've been at it for a while before I got hit. The doc said I could count on losin' maybe ten minutes or so. What's your interest in a—"

The stranger closed one hand on his beer can and crushed it.

4

In this place of white tiles and stainless steel, sharp-pointed weapons were on display alongside the home-repair tools of saws and drills, all put to the service of mutilating the dead—the pathologist's art. The most recently violated bodies were lined up in a row of four dissection tables. The autopsies had been completed, and the corpses only awaited removal to the morgue's cold-storage drawers.

Chief Medical Examiner Edward Slope said to the young detective, "As you can see . . . you're *late*."

Kathy Mallory had come without her partner, the peacekeeper. And so Dr. Slope braced himself for warfare. He welcomed it. What *fun*.

The gun in her holster was a jump up from the razorblades confiscated in her childhood, but not much else had changed. She was still cold of heart, assuming she *had* one. Edward Slope felt honor bound to love the child that his old friend had left behind. However, the doctor took pains to make it known that he had to *work* at this obligation. And, in that spirit—on with the fight; he anticipated knives and guns, trip wires and torture. At times like this, he always felt nostalgia for their first battle when she was only a baby card shark in the Louis Markowitz Floating Poker Game. The little girl had insisted that, if he could not *prove* cheating, she must be innocent. And her foster father, the cop of cops, had backed her up on this rule of evidence. That may have been the start of the bond between Lou and Kathy—that assist in stealing the doctor's money. And years later, Edward Slope saw payback when Lou got the heart-attack news that his little felon, a *born* thief, was quitting college to join the NYPD.

It *was* a balanced universe.

Today, doctor and cop squared off across the first dead body. Out of respect for the calling of Sister Michael, hers was the only corpse to lay under the protection of a sheet. He had arranged the cloth to cover all but the nun's wound, though every inch of her had been photographed for the police. But the detective had not yet seen those pictures, and it should have been predictable that Kathy Mallory would sense something hidden and—

She whipped off the dead woman's sheet to expose the snow-white skin—and a colorful aspect of Sister Michael. Inked red roses encircled her thighs in a spiral climb to the hips. "These cloistered nuns . . . they just get more interesting all the time."

"Kathy, that—"

"Mallory," she said, reminding him to keep the professional distance of her surname. She had *rules.*

And he always ignored them.

However, her interruption had spared him a point lost for mentioning the obvious thing—that the roses had certainly preceded a religious calling. Catholic nuns so seldom visited tattoo parlors. And now Sister Michael's apologist added, "It *is* rather beautiful work." Late in life, he had found that he was something of a romantic, and he had privately rechristened the dead woman as She Who Lay in Chains of Roses. "I can't name the tattoo artist. We've got nothing like this on file."

"She didn't have tattoos when she was arrested for prostitution." The detective raised her eyes in time to see his rare moment of confusion. Too pleased with herself, she said, "I'm sure that was *before* Sister Michael became a nun . . . but I could check."

Without rising to this bait, he said, "Red roses. That might suggest the lady fell in love."

"The *lady?"* Kathy moved to the head of the dissection table and picked up a photograph taken with his instant camera prior to the autopsy. "A Polaroid? You wanted a souvenir?"

Of course she would see no other reason for this archaic form of photography in an age of digital everything. However, she was actually right. She had nailed him.

Kathy stared at the picture. "The nun's smile. . . . That still bothers you, doesn't it?"

Yes, but he was loath to admit this. "It's rare, but facial expression *can* survive the primary relaxation after death." Sister Michael's smile had not survived the second laxity of rigor mortis passing off, but it had not vanished until he was done with her. The woman had smiled at him all through the brutality of her autopsy, the cuts that had laid her open from breastbone to Venus mound. And all the while, he had known that he was missing something here.

Something vital?

"Those stitches . . . that's *your* work."

"I always pitch in on high-profile cases." Did that sound defensive? Apparently so.

Kathy's eyes lit up—only an illusion of flickering eyelids, but a good one. She *had* something on him; she *wanted* him to know it. "No, this time it's different." In the sweep of one hand, she covered the length of his closing stitches. "This is almost like . . . embroidery." The detective looked up to catch him—at what? Now she was distracted by a line of stitches that intersected his autopsy cuts. "So my perp's a slasher."

"Not exactly. He cut her open and—"

The naked corpse was attracting sideways glances from a morgue attendant, who had entered the room all too quietly to collect the dead. Dr. Slope ripped the sheet from the young detective's hand, and he covered the body again to protect the nun's modesty.

A sign of weakness.

A game point lost.

Kathy watched in silence as the interloper was waved off and told to "Come back later." He knew the detective had long suspected this minion of serious leaks to the press, but then—she suspected *everyone* of *something*, including his pathologists and, of course, himself. When the door had finally closed on the departed attendant, she looked down to stare at a pocket of the doctor's lab coat.

Might she have a paranoid conviction that he was holding out on her? Oh, yes. Always. He looked down to see only a tip of the cellophane bag protruding from the suspicious pocket, and he had to wonder how many volumes of information she had extrapolated from that.

He pulled out this piece of evidence, properly tagged for chain of custody. The plastic identity bracelet bore the name of the nun and the hospital where she had been a patient. "Sister Michael was in town for diagnostic tests. I spoke to her attending physician. The day she went missing, she should have been in surgery to stem the leak of a brain aneurism. She was in pain, but she postponed the operation. She mentioned some pressing family business. Her doctor didn't get any details."

And Kathy said, "She wanted to visit her mother while she still had strength to deal with a crazy woman."

This added more depth to his collected lore of the dead nun—scientific and not. "Sister Michael checked herself out of the hospital on Friday morning. She was expected back in the afternoon." He was looking forward to playing his hole card, the one obvious aspect of the nun's smile that he could back up with evidence. Though the essence of the smile bewildered him. Something familiar. What had he missed? Sometimes he felt that he was close to grasping it—like now—and it eluded him again. As if to some guilty purpose, the thought sprouted legs and ran away.

Kathy Mallory had lost interest in the nun's corpse. She turned to the other dissection tables, the three bodies left naked and with less lovely *embroidery,* obviously the work of other pathologists on his staff. "What about them? Same cause of death?"

"By that, I assume you mean heart failure—due to the fact that their hearts were cut out of them."

"Trophies?"

So she had not yet spoken to CSU. This butchery was news to her. But the theft of body parts was a hallmark of the unbalanced killer, one who would leave the messiest tracks to his door, and this possibility should not have disappointed her—yet it did.

"The hearts have to be kept quiet."

"Not a problem." He had already gone to some trouble to ensure that no leaks would be made to the news media. "So . . . things in common. Except for the nun, they all had tape residue around their hands and feet. No food in the stomach. Signs of dehydration." He glanced at the row of tables beyond this one. "Those three had antemortem knife wounds. I can't tell you if the killer's sadistic or just impervious to suffering."

She examined marks on the arms of the middle-aged man, the purple bruises left by fingers and thumbs—upside-down handprints. The bodies on the neighboring tables had similar discoloring. "They were dragged."

"Yes, I was *getting* to that." Via a different avenue. "Three victims had abrasions in the leather at the back of their shoes. The fourth wore sandals. His abrasions were in the heels, and some broke the skin. So, for that one, you've got antemortem drag marks *and* postmortem."

"Still alive when he was dragged the first time. No defensive wounds. So he was drugged when the perp moved him to another location for the wetwork."

"Or only tied up hand and foot." Edward Slope's problem was with her logic. Did he not mention the tape residue on wrists and ankles? Her conclusions were too often right, as in this case, but for the wrong reasons. And he had yet to mention the—

"You found needle marks, right?" Score for Kathy.

"Except for the nun. The other three have scabbed injection sites. But no drugs showed up in any of the tox screens."

"You'll have to redo them. Add a few things to check for."

The *hell* he would.

She handed him a sheet of bloodwork with the letterhead of a New Jersey hospital lab. "Trace evidence from a live victim."

He scanned the text. "No point in retesting. These

drugs wouldn't survive my time frames for death and decomp. The first one's used on livestock. That might suggest injection with a medi-dart. Very smart. Your killer could inject his victim from a distance of thirty feet—assuming he's a good shot with a dart gun. I don't see the point in the other drug, the Rohypnol . . . unless he wanted to induce blackouts." But that would indicate a plan for catch and release—a plan that would hardly fit a serial killer. Well, that was confusing, and he could see by her smile that she was waiting for him to admit this—so she could humiliate him with a simple explanation.

Tough luck.

Instead, he fired off his best shot. "As I said, there were *no* needle marks on the nun . . . but then . . . she wasn't killed with a knife wound. That was done postmortem. And she was the only one with head trauma." Ah, something Kathy had missed. A clear win.

The detective returned to the nun's table to inspect the scalp, lifting the dark hair to expose the bruising of a bloodless wound.

"The weapon was a hand or an arm with a good deal of force." He smiled when she eyed him with suspicion, not buying this at all. And so, moving along to Kathy's second miss, he said, "Check the other side of her head. More trauma. I found crumbles of hard, reddish material embedded in the cloth that covered her head."

"Red brick." She walked to the other side of the steel table. "Crumbles? Old brick."

"CSU will have to confirm it." But that had also been his guess. "It appears that the first blow knocked her into a wall." Hence a hand or arm for the initial trauma.

Kathy inspected the second wound. "You found a skull fracture on this side, right?"

"No, not enough force for a fracture, but that's your death blow. It ruptured her aneurism. The cloth of her veil protected the impact site. So . . . no broken skin, no blood to nail down time of death by coagulation. She *might've* died on the spot, but she could've easily lingered for hours. A stroke from hemorrhage—"

"You told me she was dead when he cut her open."

"*Right.* With the first three victims, the killer came up behind them for the injection." He was inappropriately cheerful when he said this, for she had missed something else. "Look at the angle of the first blow to the nun's head."

Kathy hunkered down, eyes level with the nun's skull. "So Sister Michael was the only frontal assault. She *knew* the perp."

Oh, *please.* As a man of science, he preferred solid evidence over unsupportable inference. "Well, here's something . . . *factual,*" he said. Not *too* caustic. He held up the New Jersey hospital's tox screen for her live victim. "If the other three were injected with these same drugs, the doses would've been tailored to weight."

"So every time out, he worked off a shopping list of specific victims."

"It would seem so." He pointed to the first drug on Mrs. Cathery's lab report. "That one's got a paralytic component. It's used for tagging animals in the wild. Lethal in the wrong dose. The injected victims would've fallen down almost immediately. That would suggest a location that wasn't in full view of the public or—"

"No, it *doesn't.*" One hand went to her hip to put him on notice that he was venturing into cop territory. And where did *he* get off doing *her* job? "My perp could've done it on the sidewalk in broad daylight. Say a pedestrian passes by, sees our guy supporting a helpless victim, *helping* him. Fine. No need to stop. The good Samaritan moves on . . . while the victim gets dragged away and murdered."

"The *nun's* assault—"

"That one needed privacy. An indoor crime scene with an exposed brick wall." She lifted Sister Michael's right hand as if to kiss it. "I smell bleach. The perp cleaned her fingernails."

Damn. He had lost his last ace. "Only one hand was—"

"After she died," said Mallory.

"You can't *know* that. I *told* you! She could've lingered for—"

"*Logic.* She got a piece of him." The detective held up the doctor's personal Polaroid, the shot taken when the nun still wore a sly smile. "She had his skin under her fingernails. She wouldn't smile that way *after* the perp bleached out the evidence. So no DNA, but now we know he's got scratches."

"She marked him for you, that's *obvious.*" And, per the rules, no score for Kathy. "But you—"

Oh . . . fresh hell.

Edward Slope bowed his head as the other mystery, the most troubling one, came undone. He called himself six kinds of a fool. How could he have failed to *recognize* it—when the young cop beside him was the Queen of Get Even? The nun's smile that had so disturbed him—but affected him most while he had been cutting into her—it was Kathy's smile.

THE CHAIN-SMOKING STRANGER finished another beer, and now he considerately dumped his crushed can into the duffel bag at his feet, rather than mar Albert Costello's coffee table with a ring from the sweaty aluminum.

Well, somebody had raised this guy right.

The younger man's meaty arms spread across the back of the sofa—so at home here. It was like they had known one another for years. He had not yet tired of the mugging story, asking, "What was you doin' out there on the street that day?"

"Watchin' life go by," said Albert. "Every day I got a cravin' for it. So I go outside. But I got nowhere to go. I lean against a lamppost for a while. I watch the people walk past me . . . the ass end of life."

The last cigarette in Albert's pack had been smoked, and there was no more beer in the refrigerator. What food had remained over the past few days of his hospital stay was inedible now. And so he accepted the stranger's offer to share a meal with him, cold beer and smokes, too.

What a deal.

His companion led the way down the stairs. On the ground floor, the man turned his back on the street door to open the one for the rear of the building. "I'm parked out here."

When Albert stepped into the alley, the sun had gone down, though there was still lots of light left to a summer evening. The air out here was cooler, invigorating, and he was not tired anymore. No, he was coming back to life. Precious life.

WHO WAS ALBERT COSTELLO?

The commander of the Special Crimes Unit sat in Detective Mallory's chair, staring at one paper neatly aligned with the edges of her desk. It was a fax cover sheet for a report from the Lower East Side precinct, but where was the report? The information on this single page was sparse; it only told him that she had blown off the priority case to waste time on a days-old mugging.

The lieutenant opened and slammed every insanely neat drawer to no avail. And when he had checked the call history on Mallory's landline and savaged her wastebasket, he raked one hand through his hair, a bad habit that increased the bald spot at the back of his head.

Jack Coffey would credit most of his lost follicles to the stress of running a homicide copshop. Otherwise, he was the average physical specimen who could rob six banks in a day without a single witness able to supply one distinguishing feature. At the age of thirty-seven, what set him apart on a police force of thirty thousand was the early rise to an elite command position, *and* he would have to agree with his mom that he was one smart cop—because he always knew when Mallory was scamming him.

Her desktop was so clean that insects would not land here for fear of leaving incriminating prints in the fresh layer of furniture wax. Apart from the telephone, the report's cover sheet was the sole item on display, and he read it again—all four lines of text.

He called it bait.

Yeah, after sending all his calls to her voice mail, Mallory knew she could count on him to go through her stuff and go a little nuts over the one totally meaningless thing that was *not* there—the damn report.

He walked away from her desk, cover sheet in hand, with a plan to hunt down the missing report on Albert Costello's mugging and actually read it—a waste of *more* time—instead of following a better instinct to crush this paper into a ball, set it afire and spread the damn ashes all over her desk.

FROM BASEBOARD to ceiling molding, the walls of the incident room were lined with cork, and the pinned-up text and photos for the priority case were spreading virally. Jack Coffey quickly spotted the mugging report. It was fixed to the cork at two corners, and so it had caught his eye as the only sheaf of paper that did not dangle by a single pin. He knew that a carpenter's plumb line applied to one edge would find it in perfect alignment with heaven and earth. Mallory's contribution. Where was that neat freak now?

And "Who the hell is Albert Costello?"

"Mugging victim," said Rubin Washington, a broad-shouldered cop with thirty years on the job and an invaluable lack of charm that worked well on hard-core felons. Not a chatty man, he stood before the wall, pinning up the ME's preliminary. But now, with a glance to the side, he noticed that his lieutenant was still staring at him. "It was a bop-and-drop, boss. It went down on St. Marks Place a few days back. Riker and Mallory went over there to chase the old guy down."

Oh, and dare his boss ask, "What the *fuck for?*"

"Costello left the hospital, and he doesn't answer his home phone."

And that was so *not* Jack Coffey's point. "They're wasting time on a damn mugging?"

"Mallory says the nun won't fit the pattern, but the old man might."

There were times when Lieutenant Coffey believed that he was in charge of this squad. Today he was more in line with reality. He walked down half the length of this wall to read a spread of yellow sheets, the handwritten statements gleaned from interviews. He had sent detectives out to canvass the neighborhoods of their victims, in part just to make the point that Mallory could not get all the pertinent background data from a computer. But her theory was proving out from one sheet to the next in this information gathered by mere humans knocking on doors. There was a pattern—but it would only fit three out of four victims.

The first and most decomposed was Ralph Posey, forty-one years old and a resident of the Upper West Side. He never spoke to neighbors, and he had no job, no co-workers or family to notice if he was alive or dead. He was only known to the local grocer, who bagged his purchases every Monday at noon and professed no surprise at the man's murder because "He was a shithead." The oldest victim, Sally Chin, had lived on the Upper East Side. She had twice weekly hobbled to her chiropractor's office on crutches. If not for this habit, no one on her street would have recognized her photograph. And the very shy young Alden Toomey had worked from his home in the West Village, only venturing outside on Sunday to attend church services, the only service that would not make a delivery to his apartment.

Mallory was right. The nun would not fit the victimology, and neither would her nephew. They were the only two people who would have been reported missing on the day they vanished. Unlike his aunt, Jonah Quill did have a predictable routine, the daily route of a schoolboy, but he had not been following it when he was taken.

On the other side of the room, his expert on nuns, Father DuPont, stood alongside Detective Janos, a gorilla cop with a face of pure menace and a voice of surprising softness. Janos, a gentle, polite person, confounded everyone he met, and that made him the perfect choice for this assignment. Priest and gorilla faced the cork wall—the bloody one, with pictures of a woman's body laid open on the autopsy table, her innards hollowed out. For Jack Coffey's purposes, these shots were better than the crime-scene pictures of wounds that were too modest by comparison.

Though appointed by the Pope, Cardinal Rice was the town's best-liked politician in every election year, and he had more influence than God. And so his emissary, Father DuPont, had been shown every courtesy at Special Crimes. Rare was the civilian who was allowed into the incident room, though this man had been invited only to view this one set of photographs—to soften him up for the detective's interview. And the priest did seem paler now, sickened and so politely bludgeoned by the bloody ruin of Sister Michael's dead body.

MALLORY KNOCKED ON THE DOOR of the mugging victim, Albert Costello.

Riker leaned against a wall and read her copy of the old man's police report. It matched the date when the nun and her nephew had disappeared from this same street. "But this guy won't fit the pattern. The cop coded it as a straight up bop-and-drop."

"No, that's a training-day screwup." Mallory banged on the door one more time. "The partner, the *real* cop, signed off on it, but he let the rookie do the paperwork."

"How do you *know* that?" Who, apart from this precinct's desk sergeant, would *know* that? Riker could not ask if she was setting him up for a sucker bet. They had an audience.

"There's people been livin' here for years," said a woman from the first floor, "and they think it's an empty apartment. That's how quiet the old guy is."

"Oh, yeah," said the neighbor from an upper floor, when he looked at the photograph filed with the mugging report. "When I'm home on the weekends, I see him outside sometimes, just hanging out on the sidewalk."

Another tenant sniffed the air. "Cigarettes? A *smoker.*" Her face scrunched up. "Well, at least it doesn't smell like he died in there."

Mallory turned to this woman from the top floor. "You pass this door every day, and you never caught a whiff of cigarette smoke?"

"Hey, I would've noticed if it was *this* bad."

The jingle of keys bobbing on a belt loop announced the building superintendent, who was huffing up the stairs to unlock the apartment. When the onlookers and the super had been dismissed, Mallory opened the door and flicked on the light.

The odor of cigarette smoke was thick, and dust coated lampshades and tables. Riker hunkered down to touch a spill on the carpet. It smelled like beer. "Still wet. The old guy hasn't been gone long."

Mallory was staring at the only clean ashtray in the apartment. Others were in various stages of full to overflowing with cigarette butts. "Our perp's been here," she said.

"What?" Where was this coming from? Riker only saw evidence of one occupant in the beer cans that littered a small table next to an armchair.

"The perp's a smoker, too," she said. "He didn't just take his butts with him. He *washed* an ashtray. No DNA left behind, and we won't find any prints."

Riker picked up a week-old newspaper and uncovered another empty ashtray, but this one had not been cleaned in years. The detective recognized the crusted residue of every ashtray in his own apartment. He turned to look at the efficiency kitchen, rendered useless by dirty dishes overflowing the sink to cover the countertop and stove. That area's small patch of linoleum recorded a hundred sticky spills never cleaned up. The garbage pail was full of soiled paper plates and cups, a few plastic knives, forks and deli napkins that accompanied take-out food—and solved the problem of no clean dishes. The old man who lived here never washed *anything*. So his partner had zeroed in on one ashtray, clean and shiny, and now Riker was a believer.

"He's finishing up his original kill list." Mallory pulled out her cell phone and called in an all-points bulletin for Albert Costello, eighty-one years of age and last seen wearing a thick bandage on the back of his head.

Riker studied a framed photograph on the wall. The resident of this apartment was pictured here in younger days, standing with a gang of laughing people, and the woman beside him was his bride. There were other such pictures on every wall, a younger Costello among friends who, one frame by another, dwindled in number, and they were all dated to other eras by the clothes they wore. The most recent picture was at least a decade old.

This completed Riker's portrait of a loner to fit their victim profile. "You figure the kid and the nun witnessed the attack on Costello?"

"There's more to it. They *did* show up before our perp

could finish with the old man. But I think Angela Quill knew the killer. *That's* why he switched victims."

Riker was skeptical. There was only so much to be gleaned from one clean ashtray.

DOWN THE HALL, the squad room of Special Crimes was in chaos tonight, phones ringing, men coming and going, shouted words flying desk to desk.

The incident room was an oasis of silence—no phones in here, only the rustle of papers being pinned to the cork walls. Blood-red was the dominant color of one broad patch that now held autopsy photos of all four victims. The adjoining wall held the paper clutter of their vital statistics and the statements of people living close to three of them with no clue that those victims had ever existed. Lieutenant Coffey could not claim a lack of manpower on this one. Every cop in town was at his disposal to run down leads.

Detective Gonzales ducked his head in the door to say, "We got company. It's Lieutenant Maglia."

"Good." Just the bastard he needed to see. "Bring him in here." Coffey turned to a group of detectives gathered at the back wall. "I need the room," he said, and all of them filed out.

The visitor walked in.

No, that lieutenant *strutted* inside and slammed the door behind him. This was a departure from Maglia's go-along, get-along nature, but offense was always the best defense in Copland. He had also come armed with a better head of hair, a few more inches in height, and ten more years on the job.

Coffey waved his hand toward a group of metal fold-ing chairs, but the lieutenant in charge of Missing Persons would not sit down. Tony Maglia jammed his hands into pants pockets and faked impatience when he said, "Jack, I haven't got time for this."

Yeah, *right*. Maglia had refused to talk on the telephone, and this in-your-face visit was his own idea. His squad's major foul-up on the two missing Quills required privacy, and that was understandable. This was not the first time Maglia's people had mishandled a case, and this one would warrant investigation. Who knew how private a phone line might be, who might listen in—or what might be recorded?

And who was more paranoid than a cop? *Nobody*.

Jack Coffey walked over to the evidence table at the back wall. By a come-hither hand gesture, he invited the other lieutenant to join him. He gently laid down the nun's poster. Alongside it—*bang*—he slammed down the widely circulated photograph of a kidnapped schoolboy, the *other* missing Quill.

Point made.

He was pissed off.

"Tony, they even look alike . . . and your guys never made the connection?"

"The report was filed for Sister Michael, *not* Angela Quill. It was called in by a priest."

"No, it was made in person—and backed up by a doctor at New York Hospital." Coffey made a show of scanning the cork walls. "Somewhere in here, I got a copy of the doc's email confirmation. The nun's medical condition should've bumped her up to the top of your list. That's why the priest gave this—"

"There was *no* photo when we—"

"Your squad got the photo and all her bio material . . . including the name and address for Angela Quill's mother. It was personally handed to your guy."

"And that detective was out the door six seconds later—*huntin' for a missin' kid!*"

"A kid with the same last name . . . same face."

"I've got no *picture!* No bio and *no* right name for that damn nun! I *saw* the goddamn file. So . . . whatever you *think* happened—"

"Would a priest lie?" Coffey said this with a broad smile. "Father Dupont didn't think your detective was all that interested in his missing nun. And that's . . . odd. You see, *before* the report was filed, he went to Mayor Polk for help. He didn't want the nun getting lost in your paper shuffle." Following that visit to the mayor, the Catholic vote, in the person of the cardinal's man, should have guaranteed that Tony Maglia's detective was standing at attention and serving high tea when that priest walked in the door. "Oh, yeah, and Father DuPont was back at Gracie Mansion today—to ID his *dead* nun. Her body was on the top of the pile. I think he's still in my office. Should I invite him in here right now?" *No? Good choice.* In any conversation of evidence lost—or destroyed—it was probably best to keep the witnesses to a minimum. "The priest tells me he gave everything to—"

"Detective Fry." And now Tony Maglia decided to take a seat. He *needed* to sit down. "Fry remembers the priest coming in."

"Twice in one day," said Coffey—just being helpful. "First to report her missing, and then—"

"And maybe my guy got an envelope or somethin.' But it's not like he had time to plow through it. Like I said, Detective Fry was out the door, followin' up a lead on that blind kid. He's got no idea what happened to the damn envelope."

Jack Coffey had an idea or two. Early this morning, the nun's photograph and her personal details would have become an embarrassment to Maglia's squad, and the envelope had gone into the shredder.

His other idea revolved around a cover-up by the chief of detectives. That theory was born from Father DuPont's colorful account of Detective Mallory's interview style at Gracie Mansion. Added fuel was the absence of a complaint from Chief Goddard, who should have nailed her ass to a cross by now for insubordination.

She would never mess with that bastard unless she had something on him. Or maybe she had only played the chief of *D*s with that possibility. Mallory ran a good game.

ALBERT COSTELLO finished his take-out dinner in the stranger's van as they rode up the parkway along the Hudson River. The road ahead was bright with streetlamps, headlights and taillights. Lit windows in tall buildings were popping out like stars. The day was done. A damn shame. The old man wished it could have lasted longer.

The younger man at the wheel offered him another invitation.

"Yeah, great idea." An evening stroll by the water was just what he needed. A chance to walk off a heavy meal. A few smokes. A little conversation. "Oh, yeah, the bridge. Perfect." He might see some more boats. "I live on a damn island, and ten years ago—that's the last time I seen the water."

* * *

THE COMMANDER of Special Crimes turned off the noise when he shut the door to his office—and locked it. Next, he closed the venetian blinds on his wide window view of the hustle out there in the squad room. After killing the ringer for the landline, Jack Coffey sat down at his desk.

Head back. Feet up. Eyes closed.

There were no more distractions, but he had no peace. No one in this city would give a damn about three of the murder victims. Hermits died every day, and who knew or cared till the bodies got ripe and the maggots hatched? But the fourth one, the dead nun, was a threat in high echelons. Why?

Chief of Detectives Joe Goddard had not weighed in yet, and that was also strange. It was a rare day in a high-profile investigation when Coffey did not hear that thug's heavy breathing on the telephone.

Then there was the problem of Father DuPont's station-house interview. It made a liar of Lieutenant Maglia. The priest had asked for the mayor's clout behind a search for the nun. That was not in dispute. DuPont was the cardinal's man; a favor for His Eminence was political bedrock, a guarantee that Andrew Polk would light a fire under Tony Maglia's ass *before* the nun's missing-person report was filed.

But Maglia never got that phone call from the mayor?

And lie number two?

Maglia's squad had never owned the blind boy's case. A suspected kidnapping for ransom was not in their job description. So the story about Detective Fry running out the door to follow up a lead on Jonah Quill—that was bogus. Every squad in town had logged hours on that case, but not one single lead had come from Missing Persons. So why blow off the priest when he came calling, not once but twice, begging for help to find his lost nun? If Father DuPont had the full support of the mayor—

The lieutenant opened his eyes.

Shit!

Clarity like this could knock a man to his knees in prayer for his job and his pension. He was making a Mallory kind of a leap, and that worried him. Twisted? *Yeah.* But there was one explanation for Maglia's man not bothering to open an envelope with the nun's picture and bio inside.

What if the mayor *did* call Missing Persons—to *bury* the search for the nun?

Given every fact and lie, that was the only scenario that made any sense, and it made no damn sense at all.

5

Four and five flights of apartment dwellers lived private lives on the upper floors of the old brownstones. At ground level, the cafés, shops and bars were jumping, *manic,* and the crawling cars were helpless; foot traffic ruled here. Riker had stepped out of his partner's slipstream, and now he executed the New York step-and-glide to avoid an incoming tourist with a kamikaze way of walking, leading with the nose and begging to get clipped.

The street was jammed with people and humming with energy along these three blocks between Third Avenue and Avenue A, though it was not like the old days. Over time, even the air had been gentrified when the scent of weed had gone indoors. But the local headshop still sold gaudy feather boas alongside the bongs.

Passing a store where he could get a cappuccino *and* a tattoo, Riker looked up to see the mustard-colored words, *eat me,* written on a giant hotdog suspended over the sidewalk. That was new. Or was it? So many years had passed since he was last here. This narrow tree-lined stretch of nineteenth-century houses was more than a neighborhood to Riker. St. Marks Place was not a place at all. It was a *time.* Many a midnight in his youth had been a rock 'n' roll party for a stoned teenage boy, dodging cars to dance in the street that reeked of weed and thrummed with canned music from high windows and live tunes from his own guitar, played for dollars and change.

Where did the time go?

A middle-aged Riker stopped by a building as familiar as an old friend. Back in the eighties, Keith Richards and Mick Jagger sat on that stoop in a rock video to promote an album. He shook his head, squinting a bit, as if that might help him recall the name of the—

"The old Stones album?" Mallory had been watching him waste their time, and she had caught him in this struggle with his memory. "It's called *Waiting on a Friend.*"

Like her foster father, she was an encyclopedia of rock 'n' roll trivia. And though that music was Riker's religion, not hers, he knew she could even supply the album's release date if she wanted to get him for getting old, a drag that slowed her down. But she only turned her back on him and walked away.

He caught up to her as she entered a corner bodega with a flower stall out front, the one visited by Father Brenner while backtracking his lost nun. The detectives confirmed the day and the hour for a purchase of two red roses. The owner only knew Sister Michael as "My Angie." He had known her since she was a child, and—*bonus*—he recalled that she had been in a hurry. But that was at nine o'clock in the morning, and Mrs. Quill had not expected her daughter before ten. So, somewhere along this street, the nun had planned to meet up with her nephew, and a café was a likely fit.

Out on the sidewalk again, they retraced Angela

Quill's steps, but Mallory moved past the first café, showing more interest in the wares that a young sidewalk hawker had laid out on a spread cloth. She leaned down to grab a white baton and held it inches from the crouching teenager's face. "Were did you get this?"

There was no badge or gun on display, but everything about her said *cop* to the strung-out youngster. A drug addict was an easy call. The boy was way too thin and too scared. "I dunno. . . . I get lots of stuff from the trash."

"No, you *stole* it." Mallory held the baton by its ends, pulling them outward to telescope the short piece of fiberglass to the length of a white cane. "You stole this from a *blind* boy." And the words, *you cockroach,* were implied.

"No! I found it on the sidewalk up the street. I *swear.*"

"When?"

"Who knows," said the hawker. "Maybe a few days ago."

"Where? Exactly . . . *where?*"

The teenager's hand shook with a palsy as he pointed up the street. "You see that store with the big rental sign? I found it on the sidewalk . . . maybe a few yards past that building."

The detectives walked back the way they had come, passing Albert Costello's street door to stand before a dark storefront with a realtor's sign. This was the address where the old man had been found unconscious—a *vacant* store. And now Riker knew how Mallory had pegged the mugging report as a rookie kind of error. Obviously, the victim had been moved to this secondary location, and so the assault had not been a classic bop-and-drop and rob 'em where they fall. Oh, and the door was not locked—an open door in the most locked-down town in America.

Leaning over the threshold, Riker tapped the light switch. Two feet in, he looked down to see a bloodstain on the floor. "So that's where Albert cracked his head."

"In a fall," said Mallory. "That fits getting drugged with a paralytic—like the old lady in Jersey."

Even *if* she had a tox screen to say the old man was drugged, a fall was no sure thing. Costello's head might have been bashed into this floor. But Riker said nothing. He was accustomed to her forcing puzzle pieces to fit the picture she liked best. He turned to the window and its view of a tall silver pole dead center in the frame. That had to be what one neighbor had called the old man's favorite lamppost, his hangout spot for an hour every day. The hermit's fixed routine was another match with three of their murder victims.

Mallory stood on the far side of the room, leaning down for a look at the lock on the back door. "A few light tool marks. Nice job. This was jimmied in advance. It's a good lock, damn near pickproof. Our perp wouldn't leave it for the last minute." She walked back to the front of the store to stand by the window. "He chose this place because he knew he'd find the old man out there by the lamppost. That says stalking, planning." She opened her hand to show him a single red rose petal. "Found it in the doorjamb. The nun was in here, too. The perp must've taken her flowers with him, but he missed this."

It was a leap to pin the nun's presence on a flower petal, yet Riker would go along with her on that. And now the paralytic made more sense to him. "So our perp sticks Albert with—"

"A medi-dart. Animal Control uses that same paralytic

to bring down wild dogs. So the perp would've fired his dart gun from in here. He's nowhere near Albert when the drug kicks in."

"Okay." It was a stretch, but— "I'll buy that. So then he hustles Albert in the door before the old guy can hit the sidewalk." Just being neighborly. "And along comes the nun, lookin' to meet up with her nephew, and she gets this far."

Mallory glanced at the stain that *might* be Albert Costello's blood. "The old man's out cold on the floor. She can't see him. But she sees our perp through the window, or maybe he's standing in the doorway. She *knows* him. That's why he reaches out and drags her inside. And then, before he can kill her . . . she screams."

Riker grinned. "Yeah, sure she did." Hell she did. A lot could be gotten from the physical evidence, but, for damn sure, evidence made no noise, no screaming, not so much as a whisper. The sarcasm should have pissed off his partner, but no. Her eyes lit up like scary green candles, advance notice of his impending humiliation.

He would never learn.

Mallory turned to the open door. "Our guy goes to a lot of trouble to cover up what he's doing in here with Costello. Grabbing the nun, a witness who can place him on the scene—that's chancy, but she's right there. Reaching distance. Why would he risk going outside to snatch a *blind* kid off the street? And you know Jonah hasn't gotten as far as this store before something startles him." Arms folded, she faced her partner. "The boy can't see, but he *hears* his aunt scream. It surprises him, scares him. Nothing else fits with the kid dropping his cane out there on the sidewalk and *leaving* it there—yards away from this store."

Okay, maybe the evidence *could* scream. Riker nodded. "So . . . no cane in the kid's hand when he comes through the door, lookin' for his aunt. Maybe the perp doesn't know Jonah's blind."

"Or the boy can tie him to the nun. She *knew* her killer."

Maybe the nun knew their perp, but Riker let that part slide on the off chance that his partner was holding out on him, setting him up for another fall. A hard call. It could be that she just loved this theory enough to marry it.

The detectives left by the rear door to stand in the alley on a large square of cement piled with the store's discarded shelving and bags of trash. But there was room enough to park a car, even a van, and there was privacy for a double kidnapping. The rusty metal overhang would've sheltered the scene from the high windows, and a view from the lower ones would have been blocked by a dumpster.

"The perp cut out the nun's heart to match the MO for the other kills," said Mallory. "He figures we probably won't make a connection to a mugging victim, the original target, but why risk it? So today he came back to finish off Albert Costello."

TRAFFIC ON THE BRIDGE was light. The stranger walked ahead of him on the footpath, walking fast, and Albert was being left behind. Hey, he had not come all the way out here to take a stroll by himself. He had to hoof it to catch up. The younger man stopped behind a wide section of the steel framework, hidden from the passing cars. The brim of his cap was pulled low, and his eyes were going in all directions, everywhere but up.

"Smell that air," said Albert. "I think it might rain. . . . What're you lookin' for?"

"Cameras. They're everywhere these days."

"Yeah, it's gettin' so you can't take a piss without somebody watchin'." Albert raised his eyes to the high ironwork. "I don't see no cameras."

The stranger was on him, grabbing him. *Wait a blessed minute here!* Gripped by arm and leg, Albert was lifted upward.

Over the railing.

God Almighty!

He was in flight over night-black water.

Falling, *screaming*, Albert pawed the air, working his legs, as if he could climb an air-stair back up to the bridge. Reason was flown. Life was *everything*. Life was *all*.

He hit the water, landing hard, as if upon a bed of concrete. The *pain*. His legs. His back. Plunging down and down. Holding his breath. He would *not* give up his last bit of air. His arms flapped like wings. He flew up to the surface and filled his lungs. *Blessed be*.

Albert expelled a gulp of air as a wave covered him and he was sucked under, inhaling water, his chest in the grip of a giant fist. Back to the surface, and there his coughing ripped his innards. Drowning was lung-tearing, nose-searing, godawful hurt. The water torture went on and *on*—until, exhausted, he sank below the black waves and hung there. Motionless. Calm now, all the oxygen cut from his brain. Taking away the pain. No trace of him was left on the skin of the river. The last bubble from his mouth floated up and away to pop his final breath in the open air.

* * *

WATER?

Jonah Quill was slow to awaken in this dank room, sipping air fat with moisture. He could feel water all around him—taunting him. His throat was sore. His lips were cracked. One hand dropped to a cool stone floor. The other one touched down on a rubber surface, and he walked his fingers across it to find a wire that would plug an air pump into a wall socket. This was an inflatable mattress like the one his uncle dragged out for Jonah's sleepovers with friends.

The boy lay very still, listening to his own replay of an old soft-spoken reminder, his ritual for every awakening, *Open your eyes.* This had always been his aunt's first command of the day. Not till he was in kindergarten did he think to wonder—what for? Why lift up his lids for eyes that could not see?

"I'll show you." Aunt Angie had taken him up to Bloomingdale's to run his hands over a department-store manikin. A saleslady had lain one down for him, so he could reach and touch the lids of open plastic eyes, and the saleslady had told him it looked nothing like a living person. "But shoppers *feel* the dummies watching them, and they don't steal so much. We call it the spook effect."

And then Aunt Angie had said, "Open eyes, even blind eyes are useful . . . because you *might* be watching them, all those strangers out there with eyes that can see."

This was a gift she had given him, one that had increased him by guile, but it was not so useful now, not here. Still, he opened his eyes—for her.

The boy rose from the mattress, and it took some effort to stand up on cramped legs. He was nauseated, and his stomach hurt. Jonah kicked off one sneaker and, by light touch of toes, looked for obstacles in his path. His big toe hit cold metal, and he ran his hands over the stacked appliances, identifying the clothes dryer by its round door and inside drum. The object beside it was lower to the ground, smooth and—

A laundry room with a toilet?

Jonah was tempted to drink the smelly water in the bowl, but then his elbow hit something taller, and his hands found—what? Rough outside, smooth inside, a hole. A drain? A *sink!* A *big* one! His fingers traveled along the edge to find the faucet taps, and he turned on the water. Cupping his hands, he drank from a stream of cold, clean liquid.

All the while, he gave thanks for this manna, forgetting for the moment that God was his sworn enemy, He Who had stolen Aunt Angie—and then let her die. Jonah's voice was hoarse as he sent up another prayer to the Almighty *Bastard* Who art in Heaven, a suggestion for God to drop dead.

Next in the order of exploration, his one naked foot touched the source of a mildew smell, and his hands dipped low to identify a bucket with a mop inside. Then he let his fingers travel waist-high across the wall to find the ball of a knob and turn it. There was no give to the door—locked—but there was a growl on the other side. Low to the ground. Guttural. Ugly.

Given more water over the past few days, he might have pissed his jeans when the dog barked and raked its nails on the wood, scratching, pawing, clawing, *howling* now, *mad* to get inside—to get *at* him!

Jonah had never fainted before, and so he would not call it that, and he would not call it sleep. He—just—switched—*off.*

* * *

MALLORY AND RIKER remained standing, still waiting for a response from their boss, the *very* quiet man behind the desk.

Lieutenant Coffey continued to toy with a paper clip, unfolding it to a straight length of metal, a flimsy weapon at best, but he dared not unlock the drawer where he kept his gun. Calm enough now, he said, "Okay, *that's* a first. You want me to believe this freak, this whack-job serial killer . . . hired a *professional* killer . . . for the wetwork?" No doubt, bet money would change hands between these two when they realized that he was not falling for their bullshit. But Jack Coffey was not inclined to drag this out, and so he reminded them that "The freak takes trophies," and then yelled, *"He cut out their fucking hearts!"*

Riker nodded in agreement. So true. "Talk to Heller. He says—"

"No!" He was *not* going to play this out with the commander of Crime Scene Unit, a man with no sense of humor. The lieutenant turned his back on the detectives, swiveling his chair to stare at a street window never washed in this century, as if he could see through it. Good sport that he was, and with no rancor at all, he said, "Go away."

And they did.

KILLING A *NUN?* Snatching a *kid*? Had Iggy lost his mind? Their client was only paying for four *low-profile* kills. Oh, and a phone call, a lousy heads-up on this mess, that would've been nice—a professional courtesy.

Goddamn hell of a day!

Gail Rawly was not the one on the murdering end of this enterprise. He saw himself as more of a matchmaker, though his wife believed he was a freelance insurance investigator, and he was—on the side—but only for the sake of filing income taxes. He would never want to run afoul of the Internal Revenue Service.

If only his partner would be so cautious of the law.

He switched off the radio's gory news story when six-year-old Patty entered his home office in footed pajamas. Gail could see his own features in the little girl with his wavy brown hair and ocean-blue eyes. She was carrying a newspaper, helping Daddy, so he might overlook the fact that she was not asleep at this hour. He thanked her for the paper and laid it on his desk. "Back to bed, Princess."

No, she would stay. Her pajama feet were firmly planted on the rug to say so, and the lift of her chin said she went where she pleased, did she not?

Gail turned his eyes to the newspaper. He could not recall the last decade when the New York *Daily News* had published a late edition. This one had front-page photographs of the nun and the boy. Three of the four bodies dumped on the mayor's lawn were almost footnotes to this story. And there was no mention of the mutilation, not a line about organs cut out of the corpses.

What was the client doing with those hearts?

A phone rang. Before Gail opened his desk drawer, chock-full of cell phones, to see which one it was, he predicted that his caller would be the freak for hearts, wanting to carp about the *alteration* in the plan. He could almost read anger into the phone's chirp.

But there was pure joy in the client's voice. "Well," said Gail, "I'm so happy you're pleased."

He waved one hand to shoo the princess from the

room. Her Highness ignored him. "Yes," he said to his caller, "quite a splash in the news." Did the hit man still have the blind boy? "I'll check on that." He must do it quickly, and that little boy should not turn up dead or alive without further instructions. "Okay." A photograph? "That's not a problem." Now he received another instruction to carry out before the next sum would wind up in his offshore account. And their business was done.

Gail dropped the client phone into his desk drawer and picked up the one reserved for conversation with his business partner.

The little girl glared at her father, so impatient for him to read her a bedtime story because—*that was Daddy's damn job!*

Gail smiled at her. "Soon." He held up one finger to say, *Daddy has just one more thing to do*. And it might be best if she did not listen in while he discussed a little boy's murder with Iggy.

"No!" The princess would not be put off. She stamped her little foot. She had *spoken*.

IGGY CONROY cast a bulky shadow by lamplight as he lowered the boy's limp body to an armchair. The drug should have worn off by now. This kid ought to be wide awake. The man ran a hand over the stubble of his shaved head. Aw, he must have gotten the dose wrong again. He lifted one shoulder in a hell-with-it shrug.

For the first three hits, the ones kept alive for a while, it had been a simple storage problem. At the client's request, they had gone three days without food or water, and Iggy had no problem with details like that. They were not his pets.

He called them meat.

And he never talked to the meat. He had no need to know all its little hopes and dreams. But this kid was a wild card with no instructions. Iggy watched the boy's shallow breathing. Would it live or die?

The boy's head lifted. Fingers curled, and one blue-jeaned leg stretched out. The eyes were opening. What for? Why open its eyes if it really *was* blind?

"YOU LOOK JUST LIKE HER," said the man with cigarette breath.

Jonah had awakened in a different room. Not a basement. No dampness here, no smell of dank walls or mildew. Exploring fingers rounded the thick arms of an upholstered chair. One of his sneakers was gone, and there was carpet under the one bare foot. A wave of nausea came on with stomach cramps as the fog in his brain slowly cleared—and then she was dead again. Aunt Angie died every time he opened his eyes.

"Hear me, kid? I said you look just like the nun." The voice was raised, but not at the level of speaking to the hard of hearing. Jonah knew that pitch. It was like the man was talking on the telephone to someone in another place—where all the blind people lived.

You killed her, you freak!

Jonah, don't say that out loud. Don't take him on. That's what Aunt Angie would say. He could not believe that she would never talk to him again. It was too hard on him. And so he played her voice in his head, off and on like a radio—until the touch memory of her skin, so cold in death, just skittered away.

And now it was time for a little terror, a sound that did

not belong to Cigarette Man. It was low to the ground and nearby. Jonah's fingers dug into the padded arms of the chair, and he turned his face down toward the mouth-breather, the wheezer on the floor. "What kind of dog is it?"

"Pit bull. How'd you know it was there?"

The subtle heat of a hand waved in front of Jonah's face, grazing his nose. "I heard the breathing. . . . I know that dog smell."

Dogs like that—they can go off on you for no reason. Aunt Angie had said this before, when he was small, when she was teaching him to navigate the sidewalk with a cane. She had never wanted him to be afraid of the street, only wary of what he reached out to touch with his bite-size fingers.

"As long as I'm around," said Cigarette Man, "the dog won't hurt you. And if I'm not here? Don't move. That's important, kid. It won't attack if you don't move . . . if you're real quiet."

The dog was an *it*? Most people's pets were *him*s or *her*s. Cold metal was pressed into Jonah's hand. Round. A can. A tickle of carbonation in his fingers.

"It's okay, kid. No knockout drug this time. Just soda." He put something else on the palm of the other hand. "And crackers. Little bites, okay? Your stomach's been empty for days. You wolf 'em down, it'll make you sick."

Jonah traced the tiny bumps of crystals on the crackers, and he said, "Saltines."

"You see a lot for a blind kid. . . . What's it like? Is it all black . . . like when you turn out the lights?"

"I was *born* blind. I've got no way to know what black looks like." Aunt Angie would tell him to tone down the anger, and he tried. And he failed. Hatred ate everything inside of him. He loved her so much—and this freak *killed her!*

"Not a dumb question, kid. You gotta see somethin'. Even nothin' looks like somethin'."

This might top the list of stupid things asked about his blindness. What did nothing look like? "I can help you with that," said Jonah. "Close your eyes." *You freak!*

"Okay, they're shut tight."

"So tell me . . . what can you see . . . out of your *asshole?*"

Right about now, Aunt Angie should scream, *Shut up! Don't make him mad!* But there was no anger to the man when he said, "That's a good one, kid." The voice had moved to a different place in the room. Jonah heard a click of the cigarette lighter, and now a familiar static.

"Do blind people—"

"—watch TV? Yeah," said Jonah, his mouth crammed full of crackers, "all the time."

SHE WATCHED LIEUTENANT COFFEY enter the lunchroom to wolf down a late meal from a take-out carton. He ate fast, but a lot could be accomplished in fifteen minutes or so.

Mallory turned off the desk lamp in his office and opened the blinds by a crack so she would see him coming. When his laptop had been powered up, the detective entered the password, the one he believed would keep her out of his business. There were no new entries since she had last hacked in from her own computer.

She already had the stats for the lieutenant's cell phone and landline. The chief of detectives had not yet called to complain about her insubordination. No contact at all. Though there were other communications to interest her, some of them handwritten notes to read by the glow of the laptop screen. The desk phone rang. The chief's name and number appeared on a lighted bar of text. She picked up the receiver—and waited—and finally the caller said, "Jack?"

"Can I take a message?"

"Mallory." Goddard's tone conveyed more than disappointment. He did not want to talk to *her—anyone* but her.

Before she could lose him to a hang up, she said, "The mayor lied about the ransom demands."

"Forget that! It's a dead end. *Officially* a dead end. Got that, kid? So there won't be any more visits to Gracie Mansion."

With no emotion, no inflection, she said, "I know why the killer cut out the hearts. . . . They're not trophies." And by the silence, she could tell that the chief had no ideas of his own or he would have shouted her down. He was waiting on her next words.

She *let* him wait, let him *hang.*

Seconds ticked by. Close to a minute. The phone went dead, but not with the sound of his usual slam-down to end all his dealings with underlings. No, this call ended with the quiet click of a receiver gently lowered to its cradle, and she could read much into that.

Apparently, the chief had worked it out.

Did it scare him much? Oh, *yes.*

6

Riker remembered when this small space had been occupied by a Xerox machine, a supply cabinet, and one old glitch-ridden desktop computer that had been abandoned here after its last breakdown. Over years of invasion, this place had been packed with technology, most of it alien.

Now it was the geek room. One large monitor had pride of place on the back wall, and three small ones lined a console of switches, slots and a keyboard. The computer screens were dark, but there *was* light; tiny points of it winked and blinked from the walls of stacked electronic gadgets that Riker could not name. It was all he could do to keep up with new models of laptops and cell phones. He seldom entered this room alone, and this morning, working on only four hours of sleep, he could not lose the idea that the machines were watching him, talking about him.

This was Mallory's domain, hers even when she had been much shorter, when he was still allowed to call her Kathy and sometimes You Brat, Punk Kid and other terms of endearment for a child. This had been her playpen in the after-school hours until Lou Markowitz's workday ended and he drove his foster child home to

Brooklyn. The old man had thought it a bad idea to let his little darling wander among innocent people on the sidewalks of Manhattan—so many unprotected purses and pockets. One day, while Lou was on midget duty—cop lingo for watching the kid—he had thrown Kathy in here with a challenge to get the old crap computer back in working order. The city would give him no money for a good one, but the squad's slush fund might cover a few new parts.

This little room had expanded into a universe of potential for a child with a natural bent for computers and online robbery. According to her foster father, the baby bandit had been almost giddy that day. So appealing was the idea of stealing pricey toys from the police, brand-new computers, a gang of them, via bogus electronic purchase orders. She had freely given all her loot to Lou—or Hey Cop, as she had called him then—with no bills to pay, not on hacker's goods. *Surprise!* And so a little girl had hung the old man's pension out in the breeze for a few nervous years of awaiting a summons from Internal Affairs.

Riker had first heard of the geek room when Kathy was in elementary school. He had been a captain then and on his way to a falling-down drunk who would soon fall from grace and rank. He had come to Special Crimes as a visitor on that day, kicking back, feet up on his best friend's desk, just talking shop, when a detective had come in with a message for the squad's commander. "Lou? The kid wants to see you . . . in her *office*." And Lou Markowitz had laughed until tears squirted from his eyes.

Where was the grown-up Mallory this morning?

Riker read a line of digital numbers on one of her machines that gave him the time to the millisecond, and it was now five past nine. It was rare for the punctuality fanatic to be late by so much as a minute, and this put him on guard. And then he saw her. If not for her reflection in the dark computer screen, he would never have known she was coming up behind him to stop his heart with one hand, one poke of a finger or a word.

Not gonna jump this *time.* Without turning his head, he asked, "Whatcha got?"

"I found Albert Costello," said Mallory.

"Where?"

"Don't tell him." Lieutenant Coffey's voice came from the doorway. "Don't ruin it. He's gotta *see* it." Riker spun the chair around to face the boss, who now pointed to a computer, saying, "She found him in there."

TWO MORE DETECTIVES had entered the geek room to stand, shoulders squeezed to shoulders, behind Mallory's chair with Lieutenant Coffey and Riker.

"That's Albert Costello in the Hudson River," she said, as the image of a floating body filled the wide-screen computer monitor.

"He was pulled out by three kids on a speedboat," said Jack Coffey, for the benefit of the other men, who had not yet seen this feed. "Driving drunk out of their minds. One of them was so smashed he lowered the anchor. Then, the other two boys noticed it was slowing down the boat. So . . . up comes the anchor, and up comes Albert."

The video had not picked up any conversation from the high-school boys in the boat, but there *was* a sound track. As the detectives watched the corpse being pulled aboard like a great floppy fish, they listened to the a cappella lyrics of an old children's song sung in rounds,

"Row, Row, Row Your Boat." Albert's body was seated at the back, and, with help from his new friends, the dead man waved to the viewers.

"No rigor yet," said Detective Gonzales.

"That comes later," said Jack Coffey, "after the kids pose him at the other end of the boat. Albert was in full rigor when the ME's crew got to the pier. They had to pry the old man loose. He had a death grip on the steering wheel and a beer bottle in the other hand . . . while smoking a cigarette . . . while *dead.*"

"Well, that's the way *I* wanna go out," said Riker.

All the while, the voices on the sound track sang in the sweet, pure notes of young tenors, each line of lyrics riding over the last and the next, blending in perfect three-part harmony, the end of the song forever chasing its beginning.

"I bet their parents sobered 'em up real fast," said Gonzales. "No way those little punks could make that sound track three sheets to the wind."

All through the video, the boys sang, *"Row, row, row your boat—"*

They took turns posing for cell-phone pictures, mementos of each one of them with arms wrapped round their good buddy, the drowned man.

"—gently down the stream—"

One boy put a cigarette in Albert's mouth, and then the youngster thoughtfully relit it when the corpse lacked sufficient breath to keep the butt burning.

"—merrily, merrily, merrily, merrily—"

Another boy forced the old man's lips into a surprisingly lifelike grin. Finally, Albert Costello looked like he was enjoying the party, and they propped him up behind the wheel.

"—life is but a dream."

Now these ancient lyrics were followed by new and obscene improvisations that praised the stamina of the old man's genitalia and his ability to hold his liquor despite the infirmity of death.

"Ya know?" said Riker. "They don't sing bad."

"There's a reason for that," said Mallory. "These kids hooked up at their local church when they were ten-year-olds."

"Choirboys?"

"Yeah," said Lieutenant Coffey. "Ya gotta love it."

And Riker did. *Good for you, Albert.* Not a bad sendoff for a lonely old man.

"Here's the best part," said Mallory. "If our perp was only cleaning up a loose end, there were easier ways to kill Albert Costello. But he can't have another murder on that street, right? That won't fit the pattern. So Costello gets tossed in the river. A staged suicide gets an obit in the papers, and then it's forgotten. But now the old man's gone viral. Over a hundred thousand hits on this video."

Riker was liking this more and more. "If our guy's Internet-savvy, his head's exploding right now." And if he was a computer illiterate? No problem. A televised media circus was guaranteed. Then their killer could watch his mistake expand into a broadcast-news miniseries with a catchy theme song.

JONAH HAD FINISHED his breakfast of saltines, but with a spread of peanut butter this morning. His stomach was less queasy, and it was easier to keep his crackers down.

He sat on the couch across the room from the talk of traffic patterns on the television set. Now the volume was turned off, a cue for more conversation from the man seated beside him.

Early lessons of Aunt Angie: Sometimes people talked with only their faces and their eyes. *Be careful what you say to them with yours.*

He knew what she had meant by that. Back when they had lived with his grandmother, emotion would rearrange his face. He had tried not to give away his fear. Granny *liked* that too much. Whenever he had been left alone with the old woman, when he felt her hands on him, he would smile and say her magic words, *Pray with me.* And the meanness would turn to pain-free rants of *Praise the Lord,* while he waited for the sound of bells to climb the stairs, a jingling that would say to him, *Hold on! I'm coming!* Aunt Angie was coming to carry him away.

But not this time.

Jonah knew his face was showing only curiosity, and it was genuine. He wondered what *this* monster's magic words might be.

A click, a fume of smoke, a sigh, and Cigarette Man said, "I still can't wrap my head around the idea of *seein'* nothin'. How do *you* know, anyway? How *could* you know what nothin' looks like?"

Jonah found the man's voice calm enough, reasonable. There was nothing to be afraid of yet. "Ask me anything about eyes. Yours. Mine. I got it wired."

This was not quite true. There were still bridges to cross. In his preschool days, he had spent hours sitting on Aunt Angie's lap while she plugged all his questions into a computer at the public library. His curiosity had continued after she left him, but now he had a computer that could talk and listen. Sometimes at night, alone in his room, he would ask for a link, and his electronic oracle would guide him to a room in the ether were other explorers gathered, those who wanted to know what blindness was like—or what it was like to see. Building bridges in the night.

"I know how *your* eyes work," said Jonah. "They don't *show* you anything. They're a one-way road of data. They can only feed the brain raw information. Then the brain sends it to three different places and makes it into pictures of what's right in front of you. If the brain gets scrambled, so does the picture. Every day, every time you open your eyes, you're going on faith."

"Naw, I know what I see."

"You see in your dreams, right? You think that stuff's real? No, it's all lies from the same picture factory inside your head. It lies to you when you're asleep. And when you're awake? *Tell* me you never saw something that just couldn't be there."

Jonah could feel the silence. It was cold. It was bad. And this conversation was so over. He had said the wrong thing, but what?

Cigarette Man turned on the television's volume in the middle of a broadcaster's sentence about a drowned man. Then the TV voice was killed. And there was a sound of rapid tapping. Typing? Yes, the man was working at a keyboard on his lap and mumbling obscenities in the long stream of a single breath. The tapping stopped. The laptop sang.

Jonah knew that old tune. *Row, row, row your—*

"Damn it!" ended a string of curse words, and the laptop was closed with a hard slap on the lid. Heavy feet stalked away. The panting from the low-lying mouth-breather was dying off as the dog also left the room, toenails clicking, trailing its master over a patch of uncarpeted floor.

After a slow count of ten, a distant door slammed, and Jonah rose from the couch with a plan to walk the walls and find another door, one that would let him out of this place. His hands outstretched, only five steps across the room, the dog's toenails came clipping back to him across hard floor. Then only wheezing as the dog traveled over the rug.

The animal growled. The boy backed up to the sofa and sat down.

The pit bull was in front of him. Hot breath snuffing one of the sneakers. Slobbering on it. The jaws closed on it—and *squeezed.* Jonah stiffened. His crackers were creeping up his throat. He waited for the teeth to penetrate the leather, but now his foot was pulled straight out and shaken in the dog's teeth. Frenzied, furious, the animal tugged at the sneaker and pulled it free. Jonah's naked foot dangled in the air. He dared not move or draw a breath, though he followed the dog's heavy breathing as it trailed off, but not far.

And now the chomp-down noise of the pit bull biting into the running shoe that stank of a foot.

Chewing it.

Loving it.

RIKER LEANED against the door frame and said to his boss, "We got good news—and *good* news."

Mallory stepped into the lieutenant's office to lay a sheet of paper on his desk. "That's Albert Costello's bloodwork."

Suspicious, Jack Coffey stared at the report from the Medical Examiner's Office. "We got the old man's body back from Jersey? That was quick." Too quick.

"No," said Riker. "That's from an old sample. After Albert got mugged, he spent a few days in a hospital. They took a vial of his blood in the emergency room."

"But it was never tested." Mallory moved toward the television set in the corner. "Dr. Slope had the blood sample picked up last night. It's positive for the livestock drug—a match to the carjack victim in Jersey."

"There was no date-rape drug in Albert's system," said Riker. "But we figure that's 'cause the old guy was on the original hit list—before our perp screwed up and killed the nun. So Albert only got the injection to drop him. Nothin' to wipe his memory."

"And that's why he had to die." Mallory picked up the remote control for the muted TV set in the corner. It was tuned in to the city news channel. "We know the killer spent time with him yesterday. He'd want to know if Costello remembered anything about the botched hit." She pulled out her gold pocket watch, a hand-me-down from three generations of police in the Markowitz line. In times of trouble with the boss, she used this prop to remind him that she was from a family of cop royalty. But today she actually seemed to have an interest in the time.

Jack Coffey knew she was planning some kind of a bomb for him, and now his eyes were trained on the TV screen. "Very nice," he said. "In *theory.* So you got a tie to the carjack lady, but nothing connects to the body dump at Gracie Mansion. All four of 'em were drug-free."

"Sure they were," she said. "Three of them were kept alive long enough for the drugs to clear their systems. He didn't need any drugs for the nun. She died a minute after she met him." And now, in the tone of *Oh, and by the way,* she added, "We need a warrant to search Gracie Mansion."

Oh, *right.* "Not a shot in hell. I know what happened

between you and the chief of *D*s. So I'm guessing Goddard's behind a memo from the deputy commissioner." Coffey tapped his laptop, the source of the memo. "An email was sent to Heller, and he copied it to me. It says the mansion's interior is off-limits to the CSU." And this had surprised the man in charge of the Crime Scene Unit—since he had never planned to send his CSIs inside, not until he saw that keep out sign among his morning emails.

"That sounds like the chief's work," said Mallory, "but you won't be butting heads with Goddard anymore."

Riker chimed in with "That's the *other* good news."

On this cue, Mallory closed her pocket watch and turned on the volume for the television as an anchorman said, "—aired earlier this morning."

Jack Coffey watched a recycled news clip of reporters outside One Police Plaza, the headquarters of the NYPD. On camera, a reporter spoke to his anchorman, saying that the chief of detectives was unavailable for comment on the Gracie Mansion murders. "Chief Goddard is currently on vacation in parts unknown . . . for an undetermined time."

How dirty could the mayor be to run the chief of *D*s out of town? Well, *this* could open the door to Gracie Mansion. Just the smell of it would kill objections from higher-ups in the NYPD. "Okay, you'll get that warrant." Obtaining it would fall to the district attorney, an elected official, not a mayoral appointment—and the DA hated that little prick, Andrew Polk. "It might not happen today." It would still require careful judge-trawling to snag a magistrate who would sign off on a search of the mayor's residence.

* * *

IGNATIUS—call-me-Iggy-or-lose-your-teeth—Conroy stubbed out his cigarette. He stared at the cell phone in his hand, willing it *not* to ring. But then it did, and he held it to his ear, saying, "Yeah!" He detected happy-shit notes in his partner's voice, even before Gail Rawly got to the good part, the news that their mutual client had nothing but praise for Iggy's work. The nun was "—an inspired choice."

And Iggy relaxed his grip on the cell phone. Gail and the client had made no connection to the bizarre drowning party for Albert Costello, a man from the neighborhood of the nun's murder.

Even better, the client had promised Gail another payday, a big one—given certain conditions. "The boy?" Iggy covered the phone with his hand. *Steady.* He lifted it to his ear, and his voice was icy when he said, "Yeah, the kid's still alive. . . . Yeah, yeah. . . . How many days? . . . Okay, tell him it's doable." He was going to get paid for cleaning up his own mess.

Iggy walked back to the living room and found the boy on the sofa, eyes wide. Scared. Shaking. And the dog was chomping on one of the kid's sneakers.

Damn mutt. "Gimme that!"

The pit bull opened its jaws to drop the new chew toy on the rug. Now the old dog stared at its front paws, unwilling to meet Iggy's eyes, knowing it had done wrong. Iggy picked up the sneaker, wet with saliva. He crossed the room to grab the boy's right hand and jerk him out of his little trance of shock. "What did I *tell* you?" He slammed the sneaker into the boy's palm. "Didn't I tell you not to *move* if I wasn't around?"

This talky kid was flat out of words.

"You know what a pit bull can do to you? *Do* you? Maybe next time it'll go for your throat. Maybe your nose, or you lose an ear." And now Iggy was done with life lessons on blood and guts. "Lunchtime, kid. Enough with the crackers. Barbecued burgers. How's that sound?"

When he had led the boy out the back door to the patio, Iggy handed him today's newspaper with front-page photos of the nun and her nephew. "Just hold that for a sec, okay?" Iggy knelt down so the camera-phone image would give up no other background than blue sky.

Click. The picture was taken, proof for the client that Jonah Quill was still alive. And—*click*—it was sent off to Iggy's partner.

Even the photo of a dead nun had worked as proof of life—with her eyes open and that damn smile, a first in his career—dead meat that could smile at him.

These pictures he took, they had nothing to do with kidnap for ransom—so said his partner, who was too smart to ever touch a job like that. The photos only guaranteed a space of days between kills. And Gail Rawly had sworn that this murder scheme could never net a ransom payday for the client.

If that was true—what was the client's game?

Well, he had to be lousy with cash to pay for these hits, and rich dudes lived on different planets. Yeah, Gail was right. Who would pay good money to ransom strangers? The client had not picked out the targets. He had only named streets in four different neighborhoods, and that would rule out an insurance scam, too. All the other contract kills in Iggy's career could be put down to love, hate or greed.

But not this one—and that worried him.

His profession dated back to Shakespeare's time, and Iggy believed this because he had read it on the Internet.

Murder for hire was old, but the element of random kills—*that* was new.

Iggy distrusted all things new and different.

"BAD NEWS."

Samuel Tucker had just concluded a phone conversation with a former college classmate, a fund of *gorgeous* information from the District Attorney's Office. He spoke to the back of his employer's Armani suit. "The Crime Scene Unit's coming back." Andrew Polk stood before the library window overlooking the river and the freshly mowed front lawn. Gone was every sign that four corpses had ever matted down the grass.

The mayor's voice had only a trace of annoyance as he asked, "When?"

"Tomorrow. But this time, they have a search warrant. They want a look around *inside* the mansion." The aide said this to the air. The mayor had fled the room.

Tuck found his boss in the kitchen, standing before the open door of the refrigerator. No doubt His Honor had noticed that the ice cream was gone—and so were the four small parcels that had previously been in the freezer compartment, hidden beneath and behind other items that now lay scattered on the floor at his feet. The refrigerator door swung shut, and its shiny chrome was a funhouse mirror that enlarged Mayor Polk's gaping mouth to a wide screaming hole.

Totally understandable. The little boxes were missing. The searchers were coming and—

When the mayor turned to face him, Tuck could see that the man *was* excited—but not in a *bad* way. Well, that was unsettling, but any speculation might be akin to opening a trunk full of spiders and other crawlies.

The four boxes had accumulated in the mansion while Andrew Polk had been aboard his yacht in local waters. Only a call from Cardinal Rice's office could have ended that impromptu vacation. Otherwise—*oh, dear God*—those packages might still be wrapped and stacked on the desk upstairs—at *room temperature*. After opening the horrid little containers, refrigeration had seemed like the best idea—at least, until the return of the housekeeping staff, which was still days off. That other delivery, the four dead bodies, had killed a plan for the mayor's next escape to the open sea, a good dumping ground for unwanted mail.

"Tuck, tell me what you did with them," said Mayor Polk, disregarding his own recent instructions, his desire to wish away all knowledge of the packages and their disposal.

"Well, sir, you wanted them out of the house." And it was so convenient to have a great rushing body of water flowing by, only a stone's throw from the mansion. "So I tossed them in the river. It seemed like the—"

"Good job, Tuck. They're fish food by now."

As the mayor walked away, Samuel Tucker's head tilted to one side—lips parting, eyes rounding. What were the odds that some clever fish could open hermetically sealed plastic bags? He had not wanted to touch the contents of the boxes. Oh, just think of the germs. And so, in addition to the protection already offered by the thick plastic, and because bacteria were crafty little buggers, he had also donned the rubber kitchen gloves for the chore of hurling those . . . *things* into the water.

Well, no matter.

How buoyant could human hearts be?

7

Four hearts encased in plastic bobbed up and down among the waves. All of them were sucked into the wake of a cabin cruiser. They traveled against the current for a time and toward the open sea. The passage of a tugboat altered their course once more, sending them back to the northbound shipping lane of the East River, where they became the playthings of every passing tanker and garbage scow.

THE ARMS OF THE CHAIR were rough wood. The seat cushion was plastic. In the mix with birdsong, there were spits of grease on hot coals, and the tantalizing smell of cooking meat mingled with the scent of—her. This was real, not like her voice spun from memory. "What color are your roses? Are they red?"

"Yeah," said Cigarette Man. "What's color to a blind kid?"

They were my favorites, said Aunt Angie, *when I was alive.*

"Just asking," said Jonah.

"There's a good story behind my garden, but nobody

believes it. . . . I don't tell it no more." *Plop* went the flipped meat, and *spit* went the grease.

There were small things on the wing. The whine of a fly. The buzz of a bee. The only bugs in the wild that startled him were the quiet, mystery things that flew into his face or crawled up his body as silent attackers—like the one dancing on the back of his hand.

He smacked it.

"Congrats, kid. You just killed a butterfly."

The smell of cigarette breath drew close to him, and the rasp of a paper napkin wiped the squished mess from his skin. "Thank you," said Jonah.

Butterflies would always be problematic.

Caws in the sky. He recognized the ugly song of starlings.

And then—*click*—the cigarette lighter.

"That nun," said the man, "was she musical?"

"Huh?"

"A long time back, I remember a girl—looked just like her. I saw her in a pizza joint, grabbin' a slice after school. She had these bright red flip-flops on her feet . . . and little bells tied to 'em. She was just a kid back then, not much older than you are."

The jingle bells. Yes, she had always been musical.

The sun was hot on Jonah's face. He listened to the ritual sounds of a summer day. The meat sizzling. Plopping on plates. One burger. Two burgers. The rustle of wrapping. For the buns? A ping off the tabletop. Best guess—the cap to the ketchup bottle. Yes, it was followed by slaps at the glass bottom to get the thick juice running. A plate slid across the table. The smell of meat was under his nose. A few feet away, a chair scraped its legs on the flagstones. Then . . . nothing. The man was too quiet now.

And the dog's wheezing was gone. Where *was* the dog?

Jonah rushed to fill this panicky silence with "Jingle bells. They were old Christmas-tree ornaments." His aunt had worn them on her sandals in the summer months. In colder seasons, the little bells had been threaded into the laces of her shoes and, in winter, the fringe of her scarf.

"Yeah, jingle bells. . . . So that was your aunt, huh?" This last part was a string of false notes. This man had known the answer before he asked.

He—knew—her.

When the meal was done and thanks given to the cook, who had murdered the one Jonah loved best in all the world—*click*—a cigarette was lit.

"So, how long was your aunt in the convent?"

"The *monastery,*" said Jonah. "There's a difference. A convent has a mother superior. Her monastery has a prioress. . . . My aunt left me when I was seven."

"You never saw her again?"

"Once." When they had made that long trek upstate, his uncle had described an entry road thick with trees, but the centuries-old monastery was on open land, he said, with a crop field, and a barn to house a nun-driven tractor.

"Nobody can touch them. There's this big screen made of iron curlicues between the nuns and the visitors." Jonah had been silent during that visit, angry with her for leaving him—for loving God more. He hated God, her first abductor—for that had been a seven-year-old's early theory of the ironwork that jailed her. In later years he had come to understand it as her protection from the rest of the world—and from him, the burden of him. But on that day, he had punished her with broody silence, believing that there should be a penalty for desertion. And then, in tears, he had jammed his small hands through openings in the iron screen, calling out to her, begging to be touched. Uncle Harry had pulled him back, saying that there was no one there anymore. She was gone.

Jonah had carried that day around with him for a long sorry time.

There was a lean-back creak to Cigarette Man's chair.

On Jonah's own side of the patio table, he sat spinning this story, and, like a blind spider, weaving a scheme. "So I never got to talk to her that day . . . but now she talks to me *all* the time. Last night, she—"

"What did you say?" The man's chair legs scraped back. A slam hit the table and rocked it. Then its pedestal settled to ground with a thunk of wood on stone. The voice was rough, but there was another underlying tone when he said, "There ain't no such thing as ghosts."

Spoken like a true believer, said Aunt Angie.

NEAR THE SHORE, the curious fish of shallow waters watched the plastic bags float by overhead on the sun-bright surface. The bags were widely spaced, but all moving in the same direction, swimming in a school of hearts.

"THERE AIN'T NO GOD," said Cigarette Man. "No heaven, no hell—and *nobody* comes back from the dead. You been to too many horror movies, kid. All that haunted-house crap."

True. Jonah *loved* horror movies. "I don't think ghosts haunt places. I think people are haunted. . . . *I* am."

"Knock it off." Another cigarette was lit. Feet tapped the flagstones. "So . . . you got a granny, huh? What about her?"

"A long time ago, we all lived with Granny. When she was having one of her crazy days," she would hunt him in every hiding place, looking under beds, in closets and low cupboards, talking scary, but she never thought to look for him outside the window on the fire escape, where he would wait, scared out of his mind, listening for Aunt Angie's bells, the sound of rescue from the sidewalk below, "and that's why hide-and-seek was a different game at our house."

"Christ," said the man who did not believe in God the Father, much less God the Son. "That went on every day?"

"No, I spent lots of time in day care. Uncle Harry used to pick me up when his classes let out. When he left the apartment, he'd take me with him . . . when he could . . . or my aunt hung out with me. I was five when she got us another place to live, me and her and Uncle Harry. I never saw Granny again."

"Angie saved you."

Angie—not Sister Michael. How long had Cigarette Man known her?

"Yes, she saved me, and she always will. Today, she said—"

"I *told* you," said the man in low warning notes, "there's no such—"

"Listen." Jonah raised his hand to beg silence, and he faked surprise. "I hear bells," he lied, his eyes bugging out as he turned his face to the man who had murdered her, aiming for innocence when he asked, "Hear it? Jingle bells?"

"THAT'S BULLSHIT!" Iggy knew when he was being conned, and this kid was putting on a piss-poor act. "Don't even *try* that on me."

Ghosts were nothing like this kid's dime-store haunt. Iggy knew what they were. Leftovers. Old habits left over from life, like the way his mother had always waited up for him till all hours. Ma would run to the kitchen to cook him a meal the minute he set foot in the house, even if he came home at three in the morning. "Food is love," Moira Conroy used to say.

Years back, he had come home from an out-of-town job, dead on his feet from loss of sleep. After dropping his suitcase on the floor, he had fetched a beer from the frig. Beat to hell, too tired to pull off his shoes, he had lain his gun on the coffee table. Before sinking into the sofa cushions, he saw the shape of her hurrying across the wide mirror on a darkened room, right behind his own reflection, running into the kitchen. Unalarmed, he had called out, "Ma, I'm not hungry," forgetting in that moment that his mother had died the year before. His beer can held in midair, frozen there, Iggy had stared at his gun on the table. Never thought to touch it. Never thought to rise from the sofa. And *nothing* could have moved him to enter the kitchen—where *it* had gone.

A trick of tired eyes?

No, that lie told to himself a hundred times had never worked for him. But neither had *it* been his mother. Eight years ago, he had shut up that leftover *thing* in a room at the back of his mind—and bolted the door.

The boy should not come tapping at that door one more time.

AT THE WATER'S EDGE, a toddling child, slathered in sunscreen, emptied the treasures of a small red pail onto her mother's beach towel. The little girl had not yet learned to count, but there, at her mother's feet, lay four pretty stones that still had the shine of wetness—and one human heart sealed in a plastic covering that bore the indelible message: *proof of death.*

The child awaited praise for these finds, giggling now, unaware that Mommy was sliding into shock.

Farther along the sandy shoreline, other children were bringing their hearts to their mothers.

JONAH WAS LIFTED off his chair to dangle by one arm. He could name a gang of cells and nerve endings on his skin that sent messages of pain to his brain, but this rough handling was a jolt to every inch of him, inside and out—as if he had tumbled from a plane—fear in free fall. Then came a hard touchdown on the flagstones, and he was dragged across the patio. The pit bull picked up on his master's cue, growling and snapping jaws.

Don't show any fear, Aunt Angie would say. *Not when that dog's around.*

"I can tell you the story about the bells," said Jonah. "Her jingle bells."

The man's grip relaxed. The atmosphere changed with the dog falling silent and mooching off to lap water on the far side of the patio. Jonah knew he had cracked the code for Cigarette Man's magic words, *calming* words, when he was led back to his chair.

And the pit bull came back, too. Under the table now. Too close to Jonah's feet, the other monster panted and wheezed.

"Okay," said Cigarette Man. "The jingle bells."

"It started the summer she taught me to use the cane outdoors. I guess I was three years old." All through the lessons, Jonah had repeated the words, *side to side,* as a mantra, while lightly sending his cane this way and that in advance of chubby baby feet, testing the pavement for obstacles. "She tied bells on her sandals so I'd know where she was."

If he reached out for her, she would always take his hand, but he had to learn the cane so he would not be afraid on the sidewalk. "'Just listen to the bells.' That's what she told me. After a while, I could walk down the street without grabbing her hand even once. She said I had to know how to be alone. But I never was alone, not on the sidewalk. I could always hear her bells."

All that summer long and year after year, she had gone everywhere jingling. Jonah could hear her on the stairs up to Granny's apartment. That music would set him in motion, racing round every obstacle mapped in his head, *running,* flinging himself at the door just at the very moment when the knob turned, and he was swallowed up in her arms, her perfume and bells.

If love could make a sound—

A wind was coming his way, almost here. It was in the noise of a zillion leaves slapped together, clapping in waves of applause. Lots of trees. But no close neighbors? There were no barking dogs or shouts of children, and no singsong voices of women calling them indoors. Only occasionally did he hear a car passing by, a far-off motor on a distant road.

Jonah's hair was blown back as a warm scent of flowers washed over him. He would never believe that this garden was made by a monster. Some woman must have planted these roses. Where was she now?

I think you know, said Aunt Angie.

8

The archaic autopsy bay was the only one to survive modern-day renovations. Though it had not seen any human remains for more than half a century, it was intact, all its original furnishings and tools kept as historical mementos. Anticipating a special delivery, the chief medical examiner had selected this small room for privacy and secrecy.

"Gallbladders?" Dr. Edward Slope had found a snag in the paperwork for chain of custody. He removed four plastic-wrapped human hearts from a carrier cooled with dry ice. Still awaiting his explanation, he said, *"Gallbladders!"*

Detective Riker shrugged. "When I saw the Coast Guard bulletin, all it said was medical waste washed up on the beach. So I called and told 'em I was in the market for somethin' like that. They only asked how many body parts. I said four, and that's what they gave me. I signed off on gallbladders, so what? Those guys don't know hearts from hamburgers."

"And what about the labeling?" Each organ's wrapping was clearly marked with the words, *proof of death.* "The Coast Guard didn't find that . . . odd?"

"Well, they might think that was normal—for an animal-testing facility." Perhaps sensing that this falsification of documents was not going over well, the detective said, "Hey, nobody gives a shit about chain of custody. All I'm lookin' for here is containment. No media leaks." Riker did a slow revolve to admire his surroundings. "This'll do just fine."

The antique dissection table lacked even the sophistication of a suspended microphone, and Dr. Slope spoke to a conventional tape recorder, correcting the misidentification of organs. Scalpel in hand, he bent down to his work, cutting open the thick plastic that sealed each heart. "Excellent preservation of tissue."

The detective, lacking enthusiasm for the bloodier, smellier side of his job, faced a glass case at the rear wall and pretended an interest in the ancient instruments on display.

Done with recorded observations, the doctor consulted his autopsy photos, four close shots of severed vestiges inside heartless corpses. "You don't need to stick around for the tissue match. I'm dead sure these organs belong to your victims. . . . So where's your partner today?"

"I think Mallory went to church," said Riker, as if that might sound reasonable to anyone who knew her.

THE CHURCH OF ST. JUDE was small, though not modest. Tall filigreed spires *aimed* for heaven, but fell far short of it, and the flying buttresses that flanked the structure were a bit of architectural overkill, hardly necessary to support walls that did not tower. The buttresses had the look of stone legs bent at the knees, as if the church meant to rise up on tiptoe aspirations of becoming a cathedral.

Father Brenner's parish was not one that any ambitious churchman would take any notice of. Thus, he understood why the young detective felt that Father DuPont had been slumming when he had selected a simple priest, one closer to the streets, to go—*cop shopping,* as she had put it.

Kathy Mallory sat beside him in the first pew, staring at the great stained-glass window beyond the altar, an outsized wonder too grand for this space. While tipping back sherry one night, a parishioner, whose trade was interior design, had let slip a term for such a display—*Piss Elegant*—along the lines of a chandelier to light a closet. Father Brenner looked up to the vaulted ceiling and gaudy flights of angels painted there with insufficient room to fly. Sometimes, in Kathy's presence, he felt the need to apologize even for things beyond his control.

Her reason for today's visit was tattoos, though she would not elaborate beyond her need for a small, manageable venue to catch a particular mourner, one who might lead her to the lost boy.

Good enough.

Priest and detective had resolved the matter of the nun's mass being held here instead of St. Patrick's Cathedral, the first choice of Father DuPont, whose conduct and character she held in reproach.

"He went to the mayor *first,*" she said. "He wanted something buried."

"No, he didn't want to hide anything," said Father Brenner. "Quite the opposite. He wanted Sister Michael found. But it was his feeling that the mayor and the police wouldn't be of much help. He came to me because I've known him since he was a boy," though not an altar boy. It had come as a surprise when he was asked to write a seminary reference for a much younger DuPont, no one's idea of a candidate for the priesthood. "He trusted me to find someone . . . like you. Incidentally, he complimented me on my excellent choice. Let's see. How did he put it? Oh, yes. You beat the crap out of one of your superiors. Chief Goddard? I believe Father DuPont is a bit in awe of you."

"You told me the mayor knew the nun was missing *before* the report was filed. But he heard it from DuPont. You left that part out. You tricked me."

On the contrary, he knew this for a trick of *hers*. Rather than ask a straight question to clarify matters, she would always shoot first and *then* determine truth or falsehood in the screams of denial from the wounded. And he must admit that this had always been hideously effective.

"No trick," he said. "Father DuPont told me there was something in the mayor's attitude. Without putting it into actual words, Mayor Polk managed to convey that he already knew Sister Michael was missing, and that he . . . had it covered."

"You're telling me that priest does a good cold read on people. That's in the skill set of a hustler, a con artist, a pimp, a pedophile—just stop me when I'm getting warm, okay?"

Ah, obviously they had come to the real reason for this visit.

"Tell me, Father," she said, she *commanded*, "Where does DuPont hang out, when he's not running errands . . . like taking out the cardinal's trash?"

* * *

IT TOOK TIME to be blind.

At first, this new room was sketchy. There was only this straight-back chair. The smooth tabletop. And the man.

Then came the hum and ping of a microwave oven. A clatter of plates. The slam of a cupboard door. Chair legs sliding on the floor. Pizza. It smelled good, and Jonah's fingers found the slice on the plate in front of him. The man was eating. Teeth gnashing. The dog's jaws-open breathing walked under the table. A wheeze whistled up from the lungs. Was this a sick dog or an old one?

Pop. Fizz. The smell of beer.

Cigarette Man's voice had the mushy sound of a mouth full of food when he asked, "What's the worst thing about bein' blind?"

Jonah had a stockpile of smartass comebacks for that one, but he swallowed them all, and he said to the man, "Shins and knees." He crooked one leg into his chest and rolled up his jeans to expose a shinbone. "This is my best scar." He ran one finger over a raised welt. "Four inches long, thirty-six stitches. . . . It happened at a friend's house when I was nine. I tripped over a footstool and ended up breaking a glass coffee table. After my first visit, I thought I'd know where everything was. But Lucinda's mom moves the furniture around all the time."

"It's a great scar, kid."

"*I* like it."

"So, after you got stitched up—that lady—did she stop movin' stuff around?"

"No, she still does that," said Jonah. "We are who we are."

The man was chewing again. Somewhere behind Jonah's chair, a clock ticked off passing seconds. Minutes.

He rocked his body—just a little, a calming thing, a left-over habit of baby days. Waiting. Tensing. What was going on with Cigarette Man inside this emptiness of no words?

The boy turned toward the breeze of a window left open and the smell of flowers from the backyard. "Big garden out there, huh? I bet those rose bushes cost a pile of money."

All he got back from the man was the sound of a plate being pushed to one side. The click of the lighter. Smoke. Then nothing. So quiet. Too quiet.

"My aunt grew roses, but she started with seeds." Jonah had been her accomplice in the October harvests. "I was her bag man," when they had gone into city parks, seeking the bushes that had not been cut back, and every overlooked stem with a ripe ball of seeds had been the treasure of these hunts. Later, in the after-dinner hours at his grandmother's kitchen table, those balls were cut open and the seeds plucked out. "My job was cleaning off the hairy fuzz so we could soak them overnight. The floaters got trashed and the sinkers were keepers." The next night, the keepers were cleaned again with old toothbrushes. "If you don't get all the pulp off, they get moldy." After being rolled in wet paper towels that reeked of peroxide, the seeds were bagged and kept in Granny's refrigerator for a long time. "For months and months. Then we planted them in egg cartons full of dirt."

Jonah fell silent. The low whistle of lungs told him the dog was asleep beneath the table. Cigarette Man was still in his chair, but had he been listening? Did the man even care where rosebushes came from? What was he—

A grunt from the other side of the table was an invitation to keep talking.

"So . . . maybe a month and a half went by before they sprouted," and when they were a few inches tall, their next home was in tiny pots. They had filled up steps on the fire escape and the outsides of windowsills. "They need direct sunlight." Lots of time had passed before they earned bigger pots, and more time before the first yield of rosebuds. "My aunt said they're like children. Not exact copies of the ones they came from," and a rose made this way was a long, patient wait of loving care. "It's a lot of work."

And Cigarette Man said, "Yeah, it is," like he already knew how roses were born.

His garden had not been bought by the bush.

No, said Aunt Angie, *he watched me work at this table. I sat in the chair where you're sitting now.*

THE SMALL LOWER EAST SIDE hole-in-the-wall was a neighborhood restaurant with late hours and a liquor license. This was a priest's version of a cop bar. A number of tables and bar stools were occupied by men with notched clerical collars.

Father DuPont sat with a layman, a member of the city council, who would not be the first politician to hold court at this time of night with a foaming beer stein in one hand. The priest drank from a wineglass, and he was the better-dressed politico.

Detective Mallory and her partner loomed over the table and held up their badges. Councilman Adler's eyes popped, and his conclusions were easy to guess. Years ago, this was the way cops had made the public arrests of the pedophile priests, and now Adler was afraid that reporters were lurking nearby, waiting for a staged photo opportunity that would end his career.

The councilman could not distance himself fast enough, tossing money on the table and bidding DuPont a good night with the lying tagline, "I'll call you," the kiss-off to whatever business they had in the works.

With no invitation, Mallory sat down in the vacated chair. In lieu of hello, she said, "A monastery's a good hiding place. Who was the nun afraid of?"

"Afraid?" The priest shook his head. "Angie wasn't—"

"Angie?" Riker settled into the chair next to his partner. "Not Sister Michael? So you knew that girl when she was still workin' the streets."

Mallory held up the mug shot of a teenage Angela Quill. "Was that her first arrest for prostitution?" She watched DuPont's eyes drift to the side. Was he tossing a coin in his mind, heads for truth, tails for a lie?

"No," said the priest. "The first time, the arresting officer knew her family situation. He'd chased her down before for truancy. So when he caught her soliciting, he brought her to me instead of the police station. She was a child, only thirteen years old."

"And the cop brought her to *you,"* said Riker, faking incredulity. "You like 'em young, Father?"

DuPont should have shown some outrage here, but he let the accusation slide past him. "My degrees are in psychology. Back then, I was interning at a local clinic, counseling runaways—and she wasn't the first child prostitute to walk in the door. Angie told me she needed the money to keep her nephew in day care while she was at school. She didn't trust her mother to watch the baby. Well, hooking for day care. I'd never heard that one before. . . . But then I met her mother. No one would leave an infant with a monster like Mrs. Quill."

"Here's the problem." Riker flipped through a small

spiral notebook. "It's what you left out." He found a page he liked. "Here we go. Your internship was attached to Social Services. That made you Angie's therapist *and* her caseworker. One call from you and those kids could've gone into foster care."

"I've made that mistake before. There are uglier fates for foster kids than life with Mrs. Quill. So I found Angie an after-school job to keep her off the street. And I got her nephew into a day-care center. It was in the basement of a local church. I think that's where she became infatuated with nuns."

"But Angie kept working the streets, turning tricks," said Riker. "*Two* jobs. Busy little kid."

Mallory liked the stunned look on the priest's face. He must be wondering how many answers the cops already had *before* their questions were asked—and might lies be a bad option here?

Wondering done, the priest said, "Yes, family came first with Angie. She had a little plan to get her brother through a computer-science course." He stared at the mug shot on the table. "I didn't know she was still selling herself, not till I posted bail for that arrest."

"But that wasn't her last time out as a hooker." Mallory laid down the autopsy photo of the nun's naked thighs. "Check out the tattoos. She didn't have them when she was booked. You've already seen them, right? The pictures at the station house? And maybe you saw them before that? Do you like red roses, Father? Are they your favorites?"

"YEAH, YEAH." Cigarette Man had soured on the topic of roses. "What about dreams? You gotta see somethin', or what's a dream for?"

"The blind can see in dreams, but only if they had years of sight before they lost it. That's not me," said Jonah. "I was born this way, and I can't even tell day from night, not with my eyes. Some can. *I* can't."

"But when you're asleep—"

"I dream voices, other sounds." And there was a sense of place, even when he was dreaming of a plane in flight or being on a train to somewhere else. His dreams came booted up with maps inside his head. No need of a cane. "I smell things in dreams, touch them. And people touch me. The feel of—"

"Naw, you can't feel nothin' in a dream. It's like watchin' a movie."

"You only think that because the picture's all you remember when you wake up." Aunt Angie had once believed in that movie idea. She had no memory of touching anything in her sleep—or of anything touching her, not before Jonah had told her about his Granny dreams of pinches and worse things. After that talk, his aunt had discovered that her own dreams could hurt, and that had made him sorry for telling her his nightmares.

"Sometimes," said Jonah, "when you're asleep . . . you feel *pain*. Things can *get* you."

"That's nuts. I never got hurt in no dream."

Maybe you will tonight.

THE PRIEST would not look at the photograph of the nun's tattoos.

Mallory held it up in front of his face. "You don't think they're beautiful, Father? Our medical examiner does. His theory? She fell in love. The ME's seen a million tattoos. Hate and love are big themes on his dissection tables. We're looking for one of her johns, a freak with a thing for roses. Now, how bad do you want us to find that little boy?"

Father DuPont lowered his eyes and spoke to his wineglass. "I don't know how many men she— Angie was a prostitute till her brother finished school and got a decent job. Then she rented an apartment. Home and a job, that was the criteria for Child Protective Services. Without that, they'd never get the little boy away from Mrs. Quill. Once Harry got custody . . . well, then it was Angie's turn to have a life. She became a nun."

Another lie. She knew Harold Quill's first job would not have supported an apartment and a child. Angie had been the breadwinner for two more years before joining up with the nuns. "I checked out the website for her monastery. Angie didn't have the qualifications to—"

"No, they prefer a college background, and Angie didn't even finish high school. But the monastery's prioress was satisfied with the interview. And I provided references from very influential—"

"Let me get this straight," said Riker. "You politicked a *hooker* into a *nunnery?*"

"Detective, you overestimate me." The priest drained his wineglass and raised one hand to signal the waiter for another. "Monastic nuns are hardly swayed by church politics. Angie sold her body on the street to protect a child. And the prioress didn't see this as a contradiction to the girl's religious calling."

That shut Riker down for the moment.

Mallory was less impressed by the wisdom and compassion of some old prioress, a jumped-up *nun*. And she read the priest as a player. "You're not one of the banking DuPonts. You didn't come down from socialites. Your family wasn't even middle-class. Do you bother to mention that to your superiors . . . while they're moving you up the church ladder?"

"Yeah, your job had a few perks." Riker looked down at his notebook of illegible ciphers. "More than just the pretty hookers. You milked the church for a pricey education. Wound up with a Ph.D. from Columbia University. Is that why you signed up for the priesthood? The free ride?"

Father DuPont did not take offense, but he took his time. Running his options? In Mallory's experience, truth came quickly. Lies took longer.

"A free education—then ditch the church? Yes, that was my original plan."

It was rare for New York City detectives to be taken by surprise when it came to confessions. Well, *Riker* was surprised. Mallory was only suspicious. This was too damn easy.

"But Angie changed all of that," said the priest. "She changed *me*."

Mallory folded her arms in a silent comment of *Yeah, right*—just to let him know that charm and bullshit was not a good game plan tonight. The priest sat up a bit straighter to say he got her meaning, clear as a gunshot to the head. A waiter appeared at his side to exchange the empty wineglass for one that was full. Fresh anesthetic. DuPont sipped it—leisurely. Stalling again.

"Here's something your research won't tell you—because I never got caught. I wasn't a very nice guy in my younger days." All the nicely modulated tones of higher learning had fallen away. "Tell me about the worst screwup you ever knew, and that was me. Selling dope, snatching purses, you name it. Breaking commandments was like a hobby with me. . . . I was no virgin altar boy when I entered the seminary."

"You slept with her," said Mallory, as if he had *fed* her these words. *Had* he?

"Not when she was a kid," said DuPont. "I never touched her then. Did I love the girl? *Yes.* But Angie and me . . . we were a twisted pair. She never loved one man she screwed. By her code, she could only do it for money. . . . So I paid her . . . because I loved her."

"She seduced you?"

"No, it just happened. . . . In psych circles, we call it transference. . . . But that's not it, not all of it. I was the one who came on to *her* . . . when she was seventeen."

Finally, Mallory was surprised. What was the priest's angle for this confession?

EIGHT YEARS AGO, a large flat-panel television had replaced the long mirror on the wall of Iggy Conroy's front room. The matte material of the plasma screen reflected nothing but dull points of light when lamps were lit.

Tonight, he stood before the mirror over his bathroom sink, the only one left after the purge, a wild night of breaking every looking glass in the house. Instead of destroying this one eight years ago, he had blacked out his reflection with a coat of paint on the medicine cabinet's door. Mirrors were traps for *things*—like the thing that had once passed for his dead mother. On the shelf above the sink was Ma's old plastic compact for face powder. Its round mirror was so small it could only capture his own skin when he shaved—nothing behind him, nothing scary.

Iggy passed through the doorway to enter his bedroom, and he raised the window sash to let in the breeze from his backyard. When had he ever been so tired? He had little red pills to keep him awake, but he would not trust any drug to make him sleep, no pills that could dull his brain to noise of an intruder, nothing to slow down his reflexes. Ah, but the mistakes, the loose ends that had cost him sleep were all behind him now. The reporters were pitching the old man's drowning as a suicide. The cops had nothing.

He closed the window and locked it. The scent of roses remained in the room with him as he laid himself down on the side of the bed that was closest to the door. Angie had slept on the side by the window. In those days, the girl had her own key to the house so she could come to him when she needed money—and go away again days later, or only hours afterward, whenever she had earned enough to suit her.

Not his typical arrangement with whores.

Sometimes she had shown up late at night, off the last bus out of New York City. Over time, she had dulled his instinct to reach for a gun when the mattress dipped on her side of the bed. And maybe he could backtrack all his mistakes to that first one—giving her a key, putting that kind of trust in a whore.

PEOPLE LINGERED in the restaurant after closing time. The manager pulled down the shades on the street window, and ashtrays were carried to the tables that were still occupied, signaling that the smoking lamp was illegally lit. Little fires from matches and lighters flared up all around the room. The priest, solidly behind this outlaw activity, fired up a cigar and then handed a credit card to the waiter, saying, "A round of drinks for my friends."

Riker pulled out his pack of cigarettes and lit up, always happy to smoke, happier to drink.

Mallory left her listening device under a cocktail napkin as she rose from her chair. She walked toward a customer seated at a nearby table, a man whose three-piece suit outclassed even the priest's fine tailoring. And Charles Butler had other outstanding features. The small blue irises afloat in the whites of a frog's eyes, heavy-lidded and bulging, gave him a perpetually startled look. Oh, but the large hooked nose was incomparable. It could roost a pigeon.

He saw her coming and gave her the wide smile of a simpleminded loon, belying his huge brain and a long string of graduate degrees. That unfortunate smile was another accident of birth. Charles's face was simply made that way, and so he was forced to play the fool each time they met. He rose from his table, unfolding his well-made body to a height of six-four, and the quintessential gentleman pulled out a chair for her.

He was also a psychologist, but one with better skills than DuPont's. Charles played the liars' game of poker once a week, and it was only his famous blush that genetically kept him from winning by telling lies of his own. But no one in Mallory's acquaintance was better at reading the poker tells that told Charles who was holding and who was running a bluff.

He pushed back his curly brown hair on one side to remove the earpiece that had allowed him to listen in on her conversation with the priest. In the role of police consultant, he had been invited here tonight because Mallory thought it might take a shrink to catch a shrink.

* * *

CHARLES BUTLER glanced at the table where Mallory's partner drank and smoked with the suspect. Father DuPont, a fellow psychologist, had abandoned that profession years ago and without making any significant mark in the field.

"I read one paper he published. The subject was juvenile runaways, but nothing on child prostitution. It centered on—" He could see that he was losing Mallory's interest. So on to the fruits of his eavesdropping—all that she really cared about. "I'm sure he did love Angie Quill. That part seemed very real to me. He covers the notch in his clerical collar when he's being less than credible." Even if he had not caught this gesture twice with Mallory's early trip-up questions to net lies, it would have been a noticeable tell.

That priest would be dead meat in a poker game.

"I already know he lied about the girl's age the first time he raped her," said Mallory. "Too convenient that Angie Quill was seventeen."

"Because he hesitated too long on that one? That's not a liar's tell, not for him. He also did that when he was being truthful. He was just trying to figure out what you wanted to hear. I guessed that when he confirmed every bad thing you thought of him . . . so you'd believe the truth as well." That had not been a good strategy for dealing with Mallory, who also practiced the art of mixing truth with lies. Her toolkit for deceit was extraordinary. Poor priest, he had no idea with whom he was dealing.

Though it was always risky to oppose her point of view, Charles said, "I suspect DuPont of behaving decently. Nothing carnal at all. I think he lied about that part. I *do* believe he cared for the girl. But apparently, Angie Quill only loved God."

Mallory gave him a look that said, *No sale.* "You're feeding me the saintly priest routine? That's as bogus as the hooker with a heart of gold, and I didn't buy that one, either."

"Too cliché?" He would concede that a one-sided love affair for the priest had been perhaps too fanciful. Charles had fashioned it upon his own scatterbrained heart that had never loved wisely. "You're right. Obviously DuPont's no saint. He's ambitious—that's in the career track he's chosen."

"And he's a liar," she said. "What's his plan here?"

"The *child*—finding that little boy. He's playing to your sympathy." Poor fool. "Toward that end, he would've told you anything you wanted to hear. Not necessarily the truth, but what you *wanted.* So he painted himself in the worst possible light. Not a bad strategy if he—"

"He's worked with lots of kids," said Mallory. "If he wanted to be convincing, he would've told me Angie seduced *him.* Even the baby hookers barter that way. She wanted help from him, and she got it. I say the girl was thirteen years old when she made the first move on the priest."

"I see the problem." Charles smiled. "You're faulting the man for lying badly. Well, that's fair. He *is* a pretender. But he only lied at his own expense—never hers. I'm sure, at some point, she did come on to him. Sex was currency for her. Nothing to do with transference. He lied about that. During counseling, her advances would've been a problem for—"

"Count on it. When Angie Quill checked into a monastery, who do you think she was hiding from?"

"Not the priest. He didn't register any off notes on that point." He could tell that she did not care for this observation. Always a mistake, when choosing up sides, to pick any side but hers. She seemed withdrawn for a moment, and so he was unprepared for the sudden anger. Mallory pulled a photograph from the pocket of her blazer and slammed it down on the table. Now Charles was staring at front and profile poses of a girl's police mug shot. The bruised bare shoulder spoke to the violence of Angie Quill's life on the street. The thick mascara was running. The girl had been crying when—

"I interviewed the mother," said Mallory. "When Angie was a kid, there was no after-school job. DuPont lied about that, too. So this kid's hustling johns for close to seven years. Her first arrest was a freebie, that much was true. An idiot cop just handed her over to the priest. She wasn't much older in that mug shot—the *only* arrest on record. She never gets jailed again? Any idea of the odds on that? That's how I *know* Angie had a steady customer. Half her brother's college tuition came from a church scholarship. Angie paid the rest in cash. Then there's the free day care for the nephew. Not a bad haul for a kid hooker."

"So the steady customer could only be Father DuPont?" Yes, he could see that she was wedded to this theory. Unlike sainted clergy and hookers with golden hearts, a child-molesting priest was one cliché she was willing to believe in, and never would Mallory own a blind spot—her bias against the church. "All right." He raised both hands in mock surrender. "Let's say Father DuPont left out the part about ravaging a little girl."

Oh, Mallory *liked* that.

"Right," she said. "But if he really wanted sympathy

for a hooker, he would've thrown that in. It's not like a dead nun could file a police complaint."

Excellent reasoning. But now for the caveat that would anger her again. "Would you ever believe he'd confess to child molestation . . . unless he was hiding something worse . . . like a link to her murder and a kidnapped boy? That priest might be a better liar than you think."

Better than *she* was?

No, that was definitely unacceptable. He could see that in the slight jut of her jaw, but before she could speak, Charles said, "DuPont's not shielding anyone, least of all himself. *Logic*, Mallory. Take his whole sorry story, truth *and* lies. This is his game—every word out of his mouth to one purpose. He can't have you believing Angie was a trashy fit to everyone's idea of a prostitute . . . even if she was. He needs you to be on *her* side . . . and the boy's. So he made a false confession of bad acts—because he's a man of deep conscience."

Mallory stared at Charles, as if she had just found him guilty of all the priest's supposed crimes. "You *like* DuPont. . . . I have to wonder why."

Oh, fine. Now *he* was suspect in a conspiracy to thwart her. Did this surprise him? Well, no. It took suspicion on the grand scale, a truly gifted paranoid, to make such a leap. She was all that and more—so cold when she rose from the table and walked away, the back of her accusing him.

Of what?

CHARLES BUTLER punched an inoffensive down pillow.

The hour was late, but his eyes were wide open, and a book lay on the far side of the room where he had flung it in a bibliophile's act of heresy—and frustration.

He turned out the light.

Over the course of a lie-awake night, he mangled his bedsheets and gave more thought to all the evidence Mallory had laid out for him. On balance, he considered his own counterpoints, which contained no such factual basis, only supposition and poker tells. And then, upon reconsidering paranoia as an aspect of her final words, he sat bolt upright in bed.

She *knew!*

Mallory had worked it out, but how?

Before setting him up for her parting shot, there must have been a point when she suspected him of—

No, wait.

Perhaps he was only being paranoid.

THE MOON WAS RIDING HIGH over Iggy Conroy's house. Ma's old knee-high troll crouched in its place on the front lawn. It was not like other people's garden gnomes. The eyes were dark sockets, the mouth set in a snarl, and its pose was a forever-waiting game, waiting for the thing to spring at him, to *get* him. Only one garden shop sold them on special order from a twisted artist, who must believe that there was a market for tense, ugly lawn decorations.

Armed with a sledgehammer, Iggy came up behind the little stone man and—*Bang!*—the head went rolling off to his left. *Bang!* The torso broke into pieces, dropping an arm here, an arm there. Lowering his hammer and holding the handle like a golf club, he made a mighty swing, and a crooked leg broke in two, half of it flying across the grass. He should have done this years ago, after Ma was dead and long past missing the scary little dude with the pointed ears.

Iggy laid himself down on the dew-wet lawn. No sooner had he closed his eyes than he felt a great weight on his chest. Hard to breathe. His ribs hurt so bad.

The troll was on top of him, whole again, straddling him, squeezing his sides with stone thighs. But Iggy could not lift his hands to fend it off; he had gone to stone himself. He could only watch. Ribs aching, close to breaking. Heart beating wild. Sipping air, all that he could get, then nothing, not a breath. Panic time! And then—

Everything changed.

He was back in his bed. The pain was gone. *Pain* in a damn *dream!* Gone was the garden gnome. Only a nightmare. That little stone freak was still out there on the front lawn, still all of a piece and crouching in the dark.

Iggy rose from the mattress and walked through the rooms of his house, turning on all the lights.

9

The shingled red roof sloped down to eaves of floral lacework. Tulips were carved into the window shutters and the front door. And the air was thick with the scent of roses. Iggy Conroy's house of flowers was neither too big nor too small, but just right, as Ma used to say, parroting *Goldilocks and the Three Bears.* Most of her old sayings had come from scarier fairy tales, and the land was decorated with small statues of creatures from his childhood nightmares. They crouched behind bushes and trees, lying in wait for bad children, so said Ma.

He had no firm count on the number of garden gnomes she had acquired. All these years later, he could still be surprised to find one hiding in the foliage. They looked alike, evil little bastards with nasty mouths, and they were widely spaced around the property to create the illusion that there was only one ugly stone man who moved about on his own. And so, this pale-yellow stucco house would have fit well in the neighborhood of the Brothers Grimm.

A long driveway wound through encroaching woodland, and it was a fight to keep the creep of foliage from reclaiming that dirt road. Every summer, Iggy fought back with a machete, hacking off new growth that would scratch the paint on his van if he allowed it to live. Most people in the area hired out this work, but he liked his privacy.

Like mother, like son.

Even before the move to the country, Ma had always favored pit bulls to ensure her own peace and quiet. One day, while out walking, she had met fellow churchgoers, the elderly couple on the next plot of land. They had stopped her on the road to ask the name of her dog. "Silly question," she had said to them. "Who names a weapon?" After that, all the neighbors had learned not to stop by. Separated by acres of land, they probably believed that his mother still lived here, though her church attendance had slacked off in the nine years since her death.

Angie had been the only visitor in all that time—and now her nephew, who sat in an armchair only a few feet away from the discarded machete that oozed with the blood of young plants. Iggy wiped sweat from his face and sipped his beer as he watched the boy's blind fingers tracing the raised pattern on the chair's upholstery.

And when the kid had figured it out, he said, "A tulip."

"Yeah, they're all over the place." In every room, there were vases holding plastic tulips and wooden ones, and some were made of silk. "My mother was never much good with live flowers." They had always died on her. With the onset of dementia near the end of her days, Moira Conroy had believed that this was her dark power over all living things. "But Ma was a fool for tulips."

And with Angie it was roses.

Any burglar to survive the dog's welcome might believe that a woman lived here. This feminine construct was more than shelter to Iggy—this illusion of the women and their company.

The boy was real, but he would not live long.

Neither would the dog. It was aging badly, its breathing labored. That mutt should have been put down years ago, but Iggy was resistant to change.

•

KATHY MALLORY disliked change of any kind. Riker watched her struggle with the new position of her desk telephone. A clerk had just moved it in order to set down a stack of files, and now Mallory was stalled, just staring at it. Or was this an act? Did she know her partner was watching her, waiting for her to put the desktop back in crazy-perfect order?

Still waiting?

She was the grand master of tension in all things, large and small. It pissed him off, and it fascinated him. Most mornings, hungover and sick, Riker was tempted to follow his old dream of alcohol poisoning by too much bourbon for breakfast, but Mallory was his reason for showing up to work sober and wondering what she would do to him next. He could also give her credit for keeping him alive during her childhood of driving him up the walls.

On *this* morning, he reached across his facing desk to pick up her telephone and restore it to the corner position, neatly aligned with the edges of the wood.

She rewarded him with a smile that said, *Sucker*.

And *now* the day could begin.

Detective Janos ambled past them, followed by three children—a gorilla leading a parade of baby ducks.

* * *

DETECTIVE JANOS had given some thought to this venue. The lunchroom of Special Crimes had a twelve-tier snack machine, a magnet for kids—but not *these* three. They were not in a candy kind of mood today, nor were they cheerful about escaping their morning classes. This was Jonah Quill's hangout crew, nice enough kids, not a bratty bone among them, and this spoke well for their kidnapped friend.

The room was warm, but the two boys and the girl had not removed their school blazers or even loosened their neckties. They sat up straight in their chairs, the very picture of well-behaved innocence—as if they already knew that they had been caught doing something wrong.

"I know you kids talked to a dozen cops uptown," said the detective. "But sometimes you remember stuff later on." He looked down at his notes on their previous interviews. "So . . . your friend Jonah ditched school at the front door? Just turned around and left?" The trio of twelve-year-olds nodded in unison, which told him this question had been asked and answered more than once before.

"Here's the problem, kids." They were *liars*. "The janitor saw Jonah leave school that morning. So I guess he made it through the front door, huh? Maybe I only think that 'cause he was last seen wearing a red T-shirt, jeans and sneakers. His school clothes were stuffed in his locker . . . and *somebody* left a note on the secretary's desk." He opened a manila file and plucked out his copy of the typewritten text. "This says Jonah was home sick on the day he disappeared. It's got his uncle's signature—but the uncle never signed it." And this excellent forgery had provided all the weight necessary for a kidnap theory on day one. "We don't suspect Jonah. Blind kids—they're not much good at copying signatures."

The two boys were toughing it out, but the little girl with a thousand freckles cried. Janos, a sucker for little women in tears, handed her a tissue. So ladylike, the small redhead dabbed her face dry and then blew her nose—a great honking blow, not at all dainty, and the detective rather admired it. But Lucinda was not the prime suspect. Janos favored the smallest child, who would not meet his eyes, and now Michael, called Mickey, cracked wide open.

"*I* did it! I *had* to. If Jonah didn't show up for attendance, the school would've called his uncle, like, six seconds later. Mr. Quill's a total freak for security."

"It was a very *good* forgery. That's what I hear from our guy in Documents." And this eased Mickey's distress even before Janos said, "You're not in trouble. So what did Jonah tell you about—"

"I don't know where he was going that day. I *swear* it."

"Okay, I believe you." And the other two had ceased to squirm. He also believed all three of them when they said that Jonah had never mentioned Angie Quill. His best friends never knew he had an aunt? This fact was worth a quick line in the detective's notebook, and he underscored it. Now, on to a fast game of show-and-tell. Holding up a wand of white fiberglass casing, Janos flicked his wrist to extend it to the full length of a white cane with smudge marks where it had been dusted for fingerprints. "How well does Jonah get along without—"

"Most of the time, he keeps it in his knapsack," said Garth, the tallest one, who already had the solid build of the man he could one day become.

And the small forger chimed in. "Jonah mapped the

whole school." Mickey tapped his temple. "Mapped it in his head. He can find his locker in a hallway full of them. *Never* gets the wrong one."

"He's good at tricks like that," said the girl. Lucinda was so obviously Jonah's girl. "First time you meet him, you can't tell he's blind. He fooled every substitute teacher he ever had."

The detective jotted down a note. "Does he do that all the time—pretending he can see?"

"No," she said. "And he doesn't pretend for the subs. It just takes them a while to catch on. He doesn't wear dark glasses, hardly ever uses the cane. And he's got no trouble finding his way around the classrooms."

So . . . an independent kid. Janos tapped his pencil on the tabletop, wondering how to phrase the next question. "Would you say he's a smart kid?"

"Real smart." Lucinda said this with a pride that brought out her smile.

"But does he have a smart *mouth?*" By that, Janos meant a mouth that might get the boy killed if he ran it the wrong way.

Oh, they knew what he meant. He could see by their eyes that they had followed his trainwreck of thought. The girl's smile was gone, and she streamed the tears of a little widow. All three children slumped low in their chairs.

THE FAST SHUTTLE from anger to fear and back had worn him down and worn him out. In this moment, Jonah was almost comfortable with the threat of sharp teeth.

He sat at the kitchen table, zeroing in on a wheeze, keeping track of the dog. Behind him a cupboard door opened. Then came a rattling shake to answer the question of how much cereal was left in the box this morning. Not much, but enough. It was poured into the bowl in front of him, and, by the peppering of little chinks on china, he correctly guessed Cheerios before he touched one. This had been his game with Uncle Harry, who sometimes swapped out the Cheerios for bran flakes—a crunchier pour.

On the other side of the table, chair legs scraped back and forth as Cigarette Man sat down. No cereal for him, only coffee, *strong* coffee, a deep rich aroma, and—*click*—a smoke. "What was your aunt doin' in that neighborhood?"

"I was supposed to meet her there. We lived on that street when I was little. I guess she thought it was time for me to make peace with Granny." Or maybe she had wanted him to see that the bogeyman was just an old lady. Not so big anymore. Not so frightening. "I guess I'll never know what Aunt Angie wanted that day."

Because you fucking killed her!

SAMUEL TUCKER sprawled on the divan, happy as a dog only recently allowed to bed down on the furniture. This antique was the highly prized, personal property of His Honor Andrew Polk, as were other furnishings of this private office on the upper floor of Gracie Mansion.

The mayor's aide spoke to his cell phone, thanking his friend, his snitch, in the District Attorney's Office. After goodbyes were said, Tuck waved the phone in a wide circle of *Hurray!* "The search warrant has restrictions. They're treating the mansion as an expanded crime scene—*not* an investigation of you, sir. So they can examine computers on the premises, but they can only look at emails and print out what's germane to the murders."

"Sweet!" Mayor Polk had finished shredding papers that had been scanned and copied onto a flash drive, a tiny one that could be walked out the door on a key ring. All the seriously embarrassing computer files and emails of his first and only term of office had been deleted from the computer. The tired politician sagged in the chair behind his desk. "Tuck? You're sure they can't get at this stuff?"

"What you erased? They could—if the police took your laptop to Tech Support. But they can't take it anywhere. You're perfectly safe." He checked his watch. "You have time to catch a nap, sir. They won't be here for hours." Without leave from his employer, Tuck put his feet up on the antique divan, and he was not yelled at to get *off* the furniture.

MILK STREAMED into Jonah's cereal bowl as Cigarette Man said, "I didn't mean for you to wake up in that room with the bodies. Never had to figure a dose for a kid before. Tell me what you remember about that day."

"I remember getting on a downtown bus. . . . Not much after—"

"That's a long trip for a blind kid. You live way uptown, right? Anybody come with you? Maybe your uncle?"

He knows where you live with Harry, said Aunt Angie. *He must've read it in the paper . . . or maybe you're on TV. If he thinks someone came with you the day I died, well, that's a problem.*

"I don't need help to get around. I've got my cane and

a cell phone with a GPS that talks to me." But now his phone was missing from his pocket, and he had only the memory of a dead woman's voice for guidance.

"Sorry, kid. That phone went out the car window. I never saw no cane. I guess you dropped it somewhere?"

Was this a trap? "I can't remember."

"Nothin' between the bus ride and wakin' up in that room?"

He's looking to tie up loose ends, said Aunt Angie, *before he—*

—kills me? Jonah's hand shook. The spoon dropped into his bowl. Milk splashed on his skin. The pit bull's toenails were clicking across the kitchen tiles. The dog was excited, panting.

THE CRIME SCENE UNIT was not due for another hour. Samuel Tucker passed through the back gate at the jog in the brick wall. Best to cut through the park and avoid reporters camped out on East End Avenue. He strolled along the woodland path to emerge on the sidewalk a block from Gracie Mansion.

The mayor's dirty paperwork, condensed to a small flash drive, dangled from his key ring, and a letter of lawyer's instructions was safely tucked into a breast pocket. His current errand was a visit to Andrew Polk's attorney, who would vault these goods beyond the reach of the police.

Oh, happy day. He would never fly coach again—only millionaire class all the way.

Tuck put up one hand to hail a taxi, and—almost magic—one materialized at the curb. His life was truly charmed from now on. The yellow cab carried him off and away, though the driver had not yet asked for a destination. As the car rounded the corner, Tuck reached into his breast pocket for the envelope that bore an address line for the lawyer's firm.

Why were they slowing down?

He saw the detective on the sidewalk, and she was wearing another beautifully tailored blazer. What was her name? *Mallory.* The car stopped, and he saw her up close, too close, as she slid into the backseat beside him.

Up front, the cabbie removed his sunglasses and smiled in the rearview mirror. Tuck recognized the crinkled, hooded eyes and the voice of Mallory's partner when the man said, "Hey, pal. How's it goin'?"

A rhetorical question.

Everything had suddenly gone into the crapper, and he was already saying goodbye to his job.

IGGY CONROY watched the boy's two-handed search of the tabletop to find the sugar bowl.

The kid's shakes had passed off, and now, hands steady, three heaping spoons of sugar were sprinkled over the cereal. It occurred to Iggy to repeat his mother's automatic snap that too much of that crap would rot a kid's teeth, but this one did not have long to live—maybe today and tomorrow. It hung on a phone call. "I can almost see her as a nun. It makes sense. Angie was never into the game."

The boy's spoon was suspended in the air above his cereal bowl. "What game?"

The kid never knew his aunt was a hooker? "Life," he said, "life out here in the world with the rest of us. No safety net—*that* hairy game"—instead of the game she had played with the men. With her eyes shut. With the lights out. "How long was she in that monastery?"

"Five years before she took her final vows. That's when she got married to Christ."

Iggy sat very still. His cigarette went out.

The kid tensed up. He always did that when things got too quiet. And now, maybe just for the sake of some noise, the boy asked, "Do you go to church?"

"No," said Iggy, "not since my mother died. That was nine years ago. I used to take the old lady to mass on Sundays. She was a good Catholic. Me? Not so much."

The kid looked down as he dipped his spoon into the cereal, *acting* like he had eyes that worked, and he was good at this. "Did you ever make confession?"

What? Where was this going? "I used to," said Iggy. "But not for a long time now."

"I never did. I was too young to make confession the last time I was in church."

"Little kids got nothin' to confess."

"How does it work? With you and the priest in the—"

"The confessional? Well, you tell him all the crap you've been up to. The priest gives you a string of Hail Marys to say, and, presto, you're clean."

The boy raised his eyes from the cereal bowl. His spoon made little circles in the air while he considered this. And now, in the tone of talking sports or weather, he asked, "How many Hail Marys for killing a nun?"

10

On the ground floor of the SoHo station house, the prisoner in handcuffs and a bow tie stood accused of lying to police. Samuel Tucker did not balk at this or the next offense, obstruction of justice. And so, just for the hell of it, Riker tacked on a few more. There was no evidence to support any charges, but that posed no problem. The District Attorney's Office would never hear about this arrest.

When Riker was done reading the list of constitutional rights from a Miranda card, Tucker did not have *all* the signs of a recent lobotomy. His eyes were glassy, and his mouth hung open—but he did not drool.

"Do you understand your rights?" No, Mallory could see that this question was too difficult, and so she said, "Just nod," and Tucker did.

Riker removed the cuffs and gave the mayor's aide a pen. When the signature line at the bottom of the card was pointed out to him, dazed Tucker signed it—thus waiving his right to an attorney—which might not be all that clear to him.

Good boy.

Now for the sanctioned robbery by cop, their suspect's

pants pockets were emptied by Cantrell, the uniformed officer in charge of property, a man one year away from retirement. A key ring clinked into a metal tray, and the officer moved on to the higher pockets.

Tucker's voice was small, almost a squeak, when he asked, "Don't you need a search warrant?"

"No!" Officer Cantrell had explained this a thousand times to hookers and gangbangers, rapists and now this sniveling idiot. "We can't put you in lockup till we confiscate your weapons." He held up the key ring with a flash drive now in plain sight of the detectives. "Keys can be used as weapons. You get 'em back after the arraignment—*if* you make bail."

"That shouldn't take long." This was Mallory's first lie of the morning. "You get one phone call. Maybe you'd like to call Mayor Polk and tell him where you are?"

That suggestion scared him witless, speechless. He could only manage a shake of his head to say, *Hell no!*

Mallory watched the officer pull a sealed envelope from Tucker's breast pocket. "Oh . . . just think of the paper cuts. You'd better log that, too." She turned to face the mayor's aide, saying, "That's standard," while calling his attention away from the officer, whose expression said that keeping prisoners safe from the threat of paper cuts was *not* standard protocol, and damned if he was going to log—

"Hey, Cantrell? Never mind that," said Riker. "If the guy's not lawyering up, this might be a waste of time." The detective picked up one of the large property envelopes and dropped in the key ring and the letter. Handing it off to his partner, he said, "Just hold on to that, okay?" With one avuncular arm wrapped around Tucker's shoulders, Riker turned him away from the table for a word in confidence. "I get it, pal. You're worried about your job, right? Maybe I can fix it so the mayor never finds out you were here. Tell you what—we'll go over what we got on you. If there's nothin' there to make the charges stick, you can forget the arraignment. Then—if you want—we can just burn the paperwork on your arrest. Sound like a plan?"

Tucker's face lit up to say that this was a very good plan indeed.

"I don't have time for this," said Mallory. "Here." She gave her partner a sealed property envelope, not the *same* envelope but one that had the convincing bulge and jingle of her own key ring. "If everything shakes out, just give it back to him."

A GORILLA may sit wherever he chooses, but the polite Detective Janos remained standing until Samuel Tucker selected a chair at the table. When they were both seated and facing each other, the detective smiled, though this was only reassuring to children, who were more inclined to liken him to something they could pet. Adults found his first show of teeth to be frightening.

A folded newspaper and a fat manila file hit the tabletop with a thud. Oh, dear, did the suspect find that jarring? "We got people crawling all over the mansion right now."

"Yes, the Crime Scene Unit," said Tucker, answering a question never asked, so eager to be helpful—to get this over with—to get the hell out of here.

That response was only interesting to Janos because the CSIs had not made their surprise visit until *after* the mayor's aide was taken into custody. "They're looking for pieces of mail connected to the murders." As yet, nothing tied Andrew Polk to any of the victims, and ransoming strangers was an insane idea. A *stupid* idea. But who among his fellow man was perfect? No one. Thus, Janos was seldom critical of serial killers. "We figure at least four letters were delivered to the mansion over the past two weeks."

"The mayor was out of town," said Tucker. "He wasn't there to open any mail. And I never saw—"

"Careful," said Janos. "You want all the paperwork on your arrest to disappear. Am I correct?"

The man's head bobbed up and down.

"Good. We'll start over. I *know* the mayor was in town. I got the duty logs from the guys on his protection detail. Oh, and where'd the housekeeping staff disappear to? We need to talk to them."

"The mayor was on his yacht for the last two weeks. The staff's still out on paid furlough."

Janos pretended to scan the contents of his file. "Naw, there's no paperwork on furloughs. And Polk for damn sure wasn't on his boat all that time." He laid down a sheet with a telephone company logo. "See here? We got calls between City Hall and maybe twenty people. The ones we talked to never got through 'cause Polk was jammed up in meetings uptown and down. That accounts for the—"

"There were *no meetings!* . . . I covered for him, handled all the calls myself. And those furloughs were off the books."

"Hey, I got logs from three shifts of detectives on the mayor's protection detail. You're telling me *all* those cops lied about—"

"Only two of them were on the yacht," said Tucker. "The other four got the time off—just like the mansion staff. The mayor does this a lot. Call the harbormaster. He'll tell you."

No need. Janos had already made that call. "So all that time, it was just you in the mayor's private office at City Hall."

"Yes, sir."

"Just you answering phones at the mansion. Trucking in mail from downtown."

"Only the personal mail. And nobody opened it."

"Till the mayor got back on dry land. Well, I guess that explains a lot. Now I see why the bodies were dumped at the front door. The killer got pissed off . . . waiting for his ransom."

"I'm not aware of any ransom demands."

This time, Tucker's words did not have the ring of panic that Janos found so reliable. No, it was the sound of something read from a script. Mallory's ransom theory was gaining traction.

The detective unfolded his newspaper and pushed it across the table. The photograph of Jonah Quill was on the front page. "That kid's still missing. You really *do* wanna help us. I think you read those ransom notes. I'll tell you why. The mayor knew about the nun's kidnap before we did—before he ever met Father DuPont. Polk didn't get that news from ripping into two weeks of mail—like a secretary. That leaves you."

The whites of Tucker's eyes got wide in the way of frightened horses. *Lovely.*

"I *never* open his personal mail. If the address is handwritten—"

"Any of those envelopes stand out?"

"I just stacked the letters on his desk. He'd been gone for—"

"But *you* got ahold of him . . . when the nun and the boy disappeared. A ship-to-shore call was made from the mansion, and you were the only one there. No staff, no dicks. Just you." The detective sat back in his chair, admiring his work—this look of dumb surprise spreading across Tucker's face. "There had to be communication between our perp and the mayor," *if* Janos bought into the cracked theory of kidnap for ransom—and now he did. "But the yacht captain killed the idea of cell phones and email. At sea, they gotta be wired for that. And *you* placed the only ship-to-shore radio call."

Tucker sat with this last bomb for a few nervous seconds. Was he counting up his lies and the trip wires of facts?

"Let me help you with this," said Janos. "The captain tells me the boat was parked six miles offshore when—"

"I called the ship to tell him that Father DuPont was coming. That's all I said—all I *knew*. And the mayor *did* read his personal letters. That was the first thing he did when he got back. I never—"

"So Polk hauls ass to get back to town in a hurry . . . *and read the mail*? Now, that's where you're losing me, kid. The cardinal's man is on the way—and the mayor takes time to rip into bundles of letters? No, that's your job. And it was a *big* pile of mail. I know the mayor gets around fifty handwritten letters a week, mostly from whackos—like our perp. Here's what the mayor's secretary tells me. Friends, family, people like that get a four-digit security code. If you don't see those numbers on the return address—*you* read the letters. I figure you opened a *lot* of envelopes, maybe packages, too . . . and you saw something hinky."

Like a human heart.

Janos could not ask about the hearts. That information had to be volunteered or it was useless.

ON THE OTHER SIDE of the one-way glass, Lieutenant Coffey sat in the dark of a watchers' room that was the envy of copshops everywhere. While other squads made do with cramped standing room, this space had three tiers of cushioned theater seats—the anonymous gift of a grateful city politician—or so the fable was told.

And the real story? No one knew.

In one rendition, Lou Markowitz had dropped his jaw and clutched at his heart when the contractors rolled in to revamp this room—*gratis* and zero paperwork—a terrifying miracle in Copland. Kathy Mallory would have been fourteen years old at the time, though no blame had been laid on the little wizard of *irregular* requisitions. That would have been a leap too far and unfair, given a child who only ripped off electronics. But there *had* been speculation that Lou's kid might have a sense of humor, and maybe she thought a peepshow should have the look of one—replete with whorehouse-red velvet chairs.

The lieutenant leaned toward the wide glass window on the room next door, and he turned down the volume on Janos's interview with the mayor's aide. He had questions for his fellow eavesdropper, the psychologist in the next chair.

He wanted to ask what kind of freak cuts out human hearts, but Mallory had cited a conflict of interest as her reason to narrow Charles Butler's access to case details. She had offered no evidence against this man, only suspicion, though Jack Coffey could think of one solid reason. She had to know that Charles, a dead honest man, would never support her hit-man theory of the crime, and that alone was enough for her to place him in the enemy camp.

Though she *had* magnanimously allowed the use of her pet shrink as a human polygraph machine, and this interview was netting more than a stall for time. Kidnap for ransom was now solidly on the table. The lieutenant nodded toward the window on the interrogation room. "Gimme something on that clown. Can you see him in a conspiracy?"

Charles shook his head. "I can only tell you he's holding back on *something*. I know he's more afraid of the mayor than Detective Janos."

The lieutenant tuned out the shrink's lecture on alpha dogs versus subordinate personalities, only politely waiting for this man to stop talking, but then Charles asked, "What was that business about ransom notes? The newspapers call it a spree killing."

Jack Coffey waited a beat before framing a lie for this walking-talking lie detector. "Janos was only jerking him around. But we gotta figure—with a psycho like this one—there'd be some communication between the perp and the mayor."

"Well, there was. That's obvious from Tucker's reaction to—"

"Okay, thanks." The lieutenant meant to end this before Mallory's wall between Charles and every case theory could fall down.

"But if the mayor did hear from the killer, why wouldn't he—"

"We're done here. Gotta run." He had no problem leaving Charles alone in the watcher's room. No more useful information was likely to come from the ongoing interview, a ruse to kill an hour while Mallory had a look at what was taken from the mayor's errand boy. But Janos had, at least, confirmed her not-so-paranoid ideas about ransom and a mole in the District Attorney's Office.

This had not been a total waste of time.

Jack Coffey glanced at his watch, as if it could tell him how many days had passed since Jonah Quill had gone missing.

THE PIT BULL padded up to the sofa to snuffle the sneakers again, and Iggy swatted the air to send the animal away.

The boy pulled off his pricey running shoes, tied them by the laces and strung them around his neck. Well, that was not too bright—risking the feet to keep the sneakers safe. This kid had no way to know that the mutt smelled blood on them. The T-shirt and jeans were also stained with Angie's blood.

"You got her eyes," said Iggy. "Me, I got my dad's eyes." And one look from his father had scared the shit out of people. That should have been a drawback, what with Dad selling shoes for a living. But no. Folks would come in to the shoe store for one pair and leave with three. Long as he lived, Dad could never stop at selling just one pair. And the customers—they did *not* want to disappoint the scary shoe salesman.

"But you got the nun's eyes for sure." Unforgettable. Silvery gray, bright and shiny as dimes. Iggy waited for the boy to say something, anything about Angie.

"Why do you have a toilet in your laundry room?"

"Ma's idea. . . . Old legs. Sometimes, near the end, she just couldn't make it up the stairs fast enough to pee. Then there was a day when she couldn't go nowhere on those legs. Spent the last month of her life with a bedpan."

"What did you do with her . . . after she died?"

"Hey, a little respect." Damn kid. "You think I dumped her body by the side of the road? This was my *mother.* I buried her like everybody else does. She's in a real nice cemetery. Once a week I bring her roses."

"I thought she liked tulips."

"Flowers is flowers. I go with what I got."

"What did you do with my aunt's body?" The boy turned his blind eyes to where the rose garden would be if he could only see through walls and doors. "Is she out there?"

"No, kid."

"But she's nearby, isn't she? I can *feel* her—"

"Knock it off! . . . Don't play me one more time." Iggy got up from the sofa and walked to the kitchen to get another beer. As he reached for the refrigerator's handle, a cupboard door swung open. *Not* the work of a ghost. The catch was worn, and the house had a tilt that made spilled water run downhill on the kitchen floor. The bedroom's other-way door had the opposite habit of closing itself.

The exposed shelves were full of mismatched glasses, coffee mugs and one cup that was special. Every morning when he opened that cupboard door, there it was, the girl's favorite cup. Just sitting there, waiting for him. And there was weight to it, like an anchor that kept her close in his thoughts. Even dead, she was unfinished business.

There was no sound at his back, but he was so well attuned to every space he occupied, he could sense that the boy had come creeping, barefooting up behind him, and Iggy spun around.

He was alone in the kitchen.

He turned toward the arched opening on the living room. The kid was out there, sitting on the sofa. Could a blind boy move that fast? That quiet?

There was no way to test this idea, and so it nagged at him until he resolved the problem of skewed senses by the sleep he had lost, the pills he had taken to stay awake in the daylight hours. He liked this solution better than a cracked-up brain, better still than *things* from mirrors stepping out to follow him through the rooms of the house.

But maybe he should break that last one, the painted-over mirror in the bathroom.

DETECTIVE MALLORY waylaid the lieutenant in the hall outside the geek room. "I've got proof," she said. "The mayor's not just a liar. He's a thief."

Ah, one of your *people.*

Jack Coffey did not bother to suppress a yawn. The mayor had made his wealth as a stockbroker, and damn few of those Wall Street boys did not belong in jail.

His detective was holding a cream-colored envelope. Her proof? It was an expensive piece of stationery. He held out one open hand to take it, and she pulled it back, unwilling to give it up. His first instinct was to protect himself by walking away from what had to be fruit of the search through Samuel Tucker's pockets. The uniformed cops downstairs tended to gossip like old biddies. Cantrell, the property officer, was the worst of them, and this envelope fit his description of the dangerous personal item that might cause—paper cuts.

Oh, what the hell.

Now in the mood for jumping from high windows, he snatched the unsealed envelope and opened it to read the first sheet of paper. It was printed on cheaper stock, and the letterhead belonged to the Securities and Exchange Commission, the federal cops of Wall Street. At the bottom, there were signatures in blue ink. When had the tree-killer feds ever printed *any* document on a single sheet of paper? This alone was grounds for suspicion. The SEC agreement gave only a case-reference number as the cause for a penalty. Might that indicate something hidden? Yeah. The nondisclosure clause could only mean embarrassment to both the mayor *and* the government. The second sheet, printed on stock to match the envelope, was a personal letter with an opening salutation of "Hi, Arty." No title but— *No!* This was Polk's instruction for a lawyer to vault a flash drive and a federal document. He pointed to the single line written on the envelope. "You didn't check out the address—*before* you opened it?"

Mallory declined to respond, and this was her gift to him, assuming he would prefer to believe that she had *inadvertently* steamed open a client letter to an attorney. He tallied up the day's damage. One, two—yes, *three* violations of civil rights.

Beating her to death was not feasible, not in a police station. Maybe later.

Jack Coffey's head lolled back, as if she had ripped out every bone of support. Could his day get any worse? "And the other thing?" By this he meant the letter's mention of a flash drive. Cantrell had left it out of his paper-cut story, and Coffey doubted that the property officer from the old-fart generation would even recognize a flash drive.

Mallory stepped to one side to give the lieutenant a

clear view through the open door of the geek room. Seated in there was Charles Butler, an antique lover with an aversion to any gadget manufactured after 1900. Yet this man was staring at a computer screen of rapidly scrolling text. Poisonous fruit of the flash drive? Definitely. And some kind of punishment for this man? Absolutely. Mallory was shielding everyone in the station house from this illegal scanning—*except* for Charles. What terrible crime had this poor bastard committed against her? She had the use of a world-class shrink for a set of sick kills, but she only used him as a walking file cabinet that could store everything in a freakish memory and spit it out on command.

Poor freak.

The lieutenant kept his silence as he backed away from the door. With one crooked finger, he commanded his detective to walk with him, and when they stood at the end of the hall, Mallory said, "So . . . the other thing," the flash drive, which, of course, neither of them would have any knowledge of, "I think it's the mayor's idea of smoke. He didn't want Tucker to get too curious about the sealed envelope. That SEC doc was all Polk cared about, and he couldn't destroy his signature copy."

The lieutenant gave the federal document a last glance, then folded it into the envelope. "Okay, Polk did something outside the law. He admits that to the feds." And normally a broker would have to rip the face off a newborn baby to lose his license. "But the crime's not spelled out. Unless you've got a snitch in the SEC. . . . No? Well, then I guess you've got nothing."

Mallory shifted to a boxer's stance and grabbed the purloined envelope. "*This* nets me a suspect. You *know* the feds caught him in a stock scam. So Polk did some financial damage to our hit man's client, and that guy wants payback."

She was spinning theory from air again. Four people had their hearts cut out, and Mallory only saw a money angle, but now she had layered on the imagined element of revenge—another favorite of hers. And she was going to run with it. Run where? Into whose computer?

And why was she smiling?

Coffey held up both hands to say that he was in collusion with all three wise monkeys of *see no evil, hear none, and know* nothing *that you do behind my back*. This surrender attitude had originated with the former commander of Special Crimes, that late great cop Lou Markowitz. Hacker's goods could not be used in court, but they could be useful.

So . . . need he have any worries on this account?

All the time.

The monkeys were heavy; they weighed on his back; they fed on his brain. He would take them to bed with him tonight and get damn little sleep. And *that* was why she smiled.

FOR THIS OCCASION of a home invasion by the Crime Scene Unit, the mayor expressed an appropriate amount of stress, though he felt none. And Sunday's discovery of four dead bodies on the lawn had not quickened his pulse by one beat. This was nothing like the old days on the trading floor, all hell cracked wide open, the heat and the screams and the *pain*, the roof coming down, the ante jacking up. Wall Street *knew* how to do up a bloodbath. A serial killer was somewhat tame by comparison.

Once the CSIs were done with the laptop in his personal office, Mayor Polk sat down in the leather chair at his desk. Its seat was perfectly molded to receive his backside, and now, relaxing in cushioned comfort, he smiled at every cop to pass his way, and he posed with one of them for a cell-phone-picture souvenir. His own phone vibrated in his breast pocket. He pulled it out to see that it was just the lawyer texting to tell him that Tuck had been delayed in traffic, but now everything intended for the vault was accounted for.

And all was right with the world of His Honor Andrew Polk.

The phone pulsed again. This call could only be from his nitwit aide. It was predictable that Tuck would grovel for being late to the lawyer's office and— No, not Tuck.

He stared at the image on his cell-phone screen—a picture of young Jonah Quill holding a newspaper and posed against the backdrop of a cloudless blue sky. The companion text was short, only three words, *proof of life.*

Well, *this* was different. The previous ransom demands had come by snail mail of more expansive text accompanied by printed photographs. Each stamped postal date had preceded one for packaged proof of a murder. This electronic dispatch indicated urgency of lost patience and imminent death for a little boy. Yet the mayor only contemplated his list of those with access to this cell-phone number—a short list—which made this new demand rather risky.

And exciting.

The kidnapper was obviously coming undone and rushing his play. Or maybe—even better—this guy *knew* that Gracie Mansion was full of investigators from the Crime Scene Unit, some of them only a few feet away.

So delicious—like going naked in public.

Given only television ideas of police procedure, Andrew Polk was certain that this cell-phone communication could be traced, and the child could be brought home safe with his heart still beating inside him.

It was an exquisite moment, one to be savored.

And then—*click, click*—the photograph and the text were deleted.

11

They should not call it a bell. It did not ring—it shrieked like an alarm for a house afire.

Charles Butler stood at the epicenter of Jonah Quill's milieu. *Pandemonium!* He pressed his back to the guidance counselor's door as children poured out of classrooms to jostle one another, jockeying for the fast track along the hallway, their shouts and conversations all around him. Up and down this corridor, the metal doors of lockers opened and slammed shut. There was a jailbreak energy in the air.

He imagined Jonah in this swarm, tensing, anticipating the last bell and flight into summer vacation. *Freedom.* At this day's end, they would all hightail it out of here and into the sunlight. Places to go. An endless afternoon, and they could not use it up fast enough.

Reverie broken, a door opened behind him, and a little red-haired girl left the guidance counselor's office. Oh, so many freckles. And tears.

Dr. Eunice Purcell invited Charles in—and out of the fray.

This morning's interview had been scheduled at the

behest of Detective Janos, who believed that this woman might be more forthcoming if a fellow psychologist asked the questions. Thus Charles, a man with a boxcar line of Ph.D.s, shook hands with Dr. Purcell, thin and gray in her sixtieth year. Her dress was conservative, her posture ruler-straight, and her face was stern—until he smiled. And then, confronted with the tall frog-eyed man who grinned like a halfwit, she smiled, too, albeit against her will, for the lady was on the defensive once they were seated at opposite sides of her desk.

"I *did* cooperate with the police. I answered all their questions . . . *twice*." She handed him a thick manila folder. "I only refused to give them a copy of Jonah's file. Feel free to leaf through it, but I can't allow you to take it with you."

Charles was already pilfering the file, committing each line of text to eidetic memory. Only pages in, he knew the boy was intelligent, not a genius IQ, but most children had a genius for something or other. They were *all* brilliant liars. However, there was not enough here to make an assessment of survival skills. Most important was Jonah's behavior under stress, and there was no clue to that, either. Perhaps the most intimate things were not written down. "Dr. Purcell, his uncle is the only one listed under family contacts. Did he ever speak to you about—"

"The nun? Before Jonah disappeared, I didn't know his aunt existed."

The boy's file logged numerous visits to this guidance counselor, but he never confided in her? Or was this woman protecting a child's privacy? Trolling for his answer, he asked, "Did Jonah *ever* come to you with serious problems?"

Correctly inferring an insult, she put some ice in her

voice. "He's seriously in love with Lucinda Wells. The girl who just left. I give him tips for staying on her good side. It's a bad day for Jonah when they have a falling-out."

The boy was clearly a favorite of Dr. Purcell's, and yet, "Here it says he's spent a lot of time in detention."

"Yes, our new headmaster is humorless, and Jonah writes a humor column for the school newspaper—so they're natural enemies. But here's where the boy gets into trouble. He doesn't think Mr. Keller's smart enough to pick up on a twelve-year-old's idea of double entendre. Half the time, he's right about that. And the other half—Jonah does detention."

"When you say they're enemies—"

"Well, no one *likes* the headmaster. He's an authoritarian ass. I think most of the children would like to get rid of him—if they could only get a gun past the metal detector."

Dr. Purcell was nothing if not candid—in some respects. However, in regard to what he needed from her, she was a vault.

Charles closed the file and set it on her desk. "I don't suppose you'd care to tell me why Lucinda Wells was crying?" When the woman shook her head, he knew the little girl had not wept for the obvious reason—missing Jonah. On to the next most obvious thing, he said, "If she's keeping secrets, holding something back, something the police would—" Yes, he had gotten that right. Dr. Purcell made no response as she rose from her desk.

He was being dismissed.

AH, A FUGITIVE.

The little redhead was perched on the middle step between the school's front door and the sidewalk below, perhaps trapped there by indecision. Should she stay till the final bell of the day—or run like mad?

"Miss Wells?" Charles smiled, but the girl never saw this, his most winning trick. Her head bowed with some great weight as he sat down beside her to offer his card. It identified him as a police consultant to the NYPD.

"It should say you're *Dr.* Butler." She pointed to the line of academic credentials following his name.

"I never cared much for titles. Call me Charles." And then he learned that, like himself, she had no nickname. Just as he had never been a Chuck or a Charlie, she was neither Luce, nor Lucy, but always Lucinda, and this was followed by a comparison of notes on the downsides and upsides of being two of a kind—outsiders.

He plucked a bit of data from Dr. Purcell's memorized file. "I understand you're Jonah's designated walker."

She nodded. "But he doesn't need anyone to get him to classes. He had the whole school mapped out when he was nine years old. . . . You know, there's a lot more to it than counting steps. His maps aren't like yours and mine. They're *three-dimensional.* Everything has height, length, width. All the rooms in his life are stored in 3-D memory—three dimensions *he can't see.*"

Charles already knew how the blind repurposed the brain's visual cortex for sense perception and spatial relationships, and it was fascinating, but so was Lucinda. She was a rare one. Few people could grasp that paradox as she did, and it added to his understanding of her bond with Jonah. "You're still listed as his designated walker. So . . . sometimes you find that useful?" It would allow the two children to spend more time with each other. He could see them holding hands in the halls, their desks always side-by-side in class, two heads leaning close together in a covert exchange of whispers.

"I use it to do detention with Jonah."

Charles now learned that this forced attendance on Saturday mornings could be very tedious without a friend along for company. And still, she would have him know that the hours passed like years. Phones and tablets were confiscated at the door by the headmaster, who personally, *joyfully* presided over these gatherings of at least ten children doing penance for the smallest infractions of rules. And one boy was condemned to do more time in this hell of boredom than any other student.

"I think Mr. Keller had a real hate on for Jonah. But detention petered out after the thing with the spider." She raised her face to his. "Did Dr. Purcell tell you about the tarantula?"

"No, she didn't." There were probably many things Dr. Purcell had failed to mention. "I rather like spiders myself."

"So does Jonah. Well, he likes old Aggy. She lives in the science lab. She's really very sweet. In spider years, Aggy's in her nineties. Slow. Harmless. But the headmaster's new. He didn't know that. So, when Jonah walked into detention . . . with the tarantula on his head, Mr. Keller was petrified." Lucinda slapped a concrete step to the beat of "He—could—not—*move*." The little girl was smiling now, reliving a particularly happy moment. "When that big hairy spider crawled down Jonah's face, the headmaster wet his pants." And apparently she had so enjoyed that great dark stain spreading on Mr. Keller's crotch. "Detention ended early that day."

Her smile faded off. She looked down at her hands.

Somber again.

And so was Charles. He now had a portrait of a resourceful boy, a planner, a plotter and, worse luck, a—

Lucinda stood up, eyes shiny, watery, and she stepped lightly down to the pavement, saying over one shoulder, "I hope Jonah's behaving himself." The little girl ran to the subway entrance at the end of the block and disappeared down the stairs below the sidewalk.

Evidently, she foresaw the same grave problem of a child who would take on an adult opponent.

IGGY CONROY killed a little time in an East Village plaza bordered by traffic lanes and famed for a giant black cube that stood on point, attracting tourists and homegrown roller boarders. There were no police in sight, not that they would take any notice of him today, though he hardly blended in with this crowd.

In a reversal of fashion sense, he had dressed up to visit the summer scene of T-shirts and sandals on St. Marks Place. He wore lace-up shoes, a white linen shirt and a tie. Dark glasses hid his eyes, his most striking feature. And so his old-fashioned straw boater would be the only stand-out memory of witnesses as he made his way along the first block, checking names posted by intercoms on the street doors. His outfit was almost cop-proof. The police were so busy looking for hiders lying low and acting shifty, he would have been invisible to them if he had worn a clown suit today.

This was the neighborhood where Angie Quill had grown up, so said the boy. She had lied about bedding down in an Alphabet City squat, one she had claimed to share with her hooker buddies and the roaches. All her free time had gone to the kid, keeping close to home, keeping him safe from his fruitcake grandmother.

Iggy climbed ten steps to stand on the stoop of a brownstone and read the names posted on a panel by the street door. He pretended to push a few buttons, and he mouthed words to no one on the silent intercoms. The bag of religious pamphlets slung over one shoulder gave him the perfect cover for this kind of reconnaissance. Few New Yorkers would buzz in a stranger peddling God off the street, and no one would find it odd if he never entered a single building. Four doors away, he found the buzzer labeled for Mrs. Quill, and his search was over. But then he went on to the next building, and the next, because there were cameras everywhere these days—and the cops *might* be watching.

DETECTIVE JANOS COULD ONLY LISTEN. His eyes were on the clock as he patiently heard out Charles Butler's lengthy report on what he had learned at the school. It was not good news for Jonah Quill.

Funny kid.

Good as dead.

Janos needed to end this conversation before his favorite shrink could ask any questions. He did not want to be the one to tell Charles that Mallory had locked him out of case details. "I gotta hang up. Thanks."

Oh, *more* trouble. Jonah Quill's girlfriend was hovering on the threshold of the stairwell door. Lucinda, a paragon of perfect attendance, was ditching class on the last day of school. By the looks of her, she carried a world of worry into the squad room.

The girl walked toward the only woman here, wrongly

believing good things about that cop's whole gender. And before Janos could sing out, *No, don't,* Lucinda sat down in the chair by Mallory's desk, announcing that she had come to make a confession. Janos hurried across the room to stand behind the schoolgirl, looming over her like a great hulking nanny.

After Mallory had made a cool appraisal of the twelve-year-old's watering eyes and fidgeting signs of guilt, she asked, "Do you like chocolate?"

Yes, Lucinda did.

Janos trailed the two of them down the hall to the lunchroom, home of the snack machine and every kind of chocolate bar known to God and the NYPD. Mallory and Lucinda sat down at a table—for two. And he was not slow to take this hint that his company was unwanted. However, with great discretion, he made repeated walks past the open doorway.

Just checking in.

Over time, candy wrappers accumulated on the tabletop, and the young visitor was showing no indication of stress. No tears.

Janos went off to rethink Mallory for a while.

Another half hour passed before cop and child reappeared in the squad room. Lucinda was walking taller, even smiling as the two of them approached the stairwell door, where a uniformed officer waited to take the little lady back to school.

Mallory watched the girl and her escort descend the stairs, and when they were out of earshot, she said, "You wondered why the kids didn't know about Jonah's aunt? His uncle told him not to tell anyone, but never said why. The boy only knew it was a secret. . . . But Jonah tells that girl *everything.*"

"The uncle's holding out on us?" Well, this shored up the theory that Angie had known her killer. Who hides having a nun in the family—unless the nun is in hiding? Harold Quill had become a constant fixture in the squad room. Janos and other cops had shared meals with the man, sympathized with him, all but held his damn hand while that miserable little *bastard*— "Excuse me. I have to go shoot a guy." The detective was on his way to the lieutenant's office, where Quill was making himself at home, watching the news channel on the boss's TV. No one had ever seen Janos lose his temper. That was not his way. But *today,* this *minute*—

Mallory's hand was on his arm, feather light but weight enough to restrain him. "Not now," she said. "Let me pick your moment. We'll do Uncle Harry up right. I know a way to carve out his guts and make him screaming crazy. . . . You'll like it."

Janos inclined his head, almost a courtly bow to her, the squad's undisputed champion of retaliation.

"YOU'RE RIGHT, KID. Girls don't play fair." Foot-long hotdogs sizzled on the barbecue grill, and Iggy rolled them for an even burn. "Makes a guy nuts when they won't even say what you done wrong. But when she called you a jerk? Hey, that's just another way of callin' you a guy. It ain't a bad thing. It's the cold shoulder that bugs *me.*" Done with his condolences on the issue of girlfriends, Iggy moved on to the other woman in the boy's life. "So, what about your aunt? She ever make you nuts with the silent treatment?"

It took the kid a while to come up with an answer to that one. He hung his head, just like the dog, a sure sign of guilt when he said, "No, she always talked to me. . . . But I don't remember her laughing much. Even after we left Granny's place, she was never all that happy. I think it was my fault . . . because she had to take me with her."

For the first time, the boy did not seem anxious about silence. He only sat there with his thoughts, sad ones by the look of him. And then came a surprise to end that lag in the conversation. The kid was done with the subject of what girls want, and he was on to the next mystery of life—sudden death.

"What's it like to murder people?"

LIEUTENANT COFFEY stood at the center of the squad room, counting noses. Only one no-show. Damn Mallory. He had seen her in the building just a few minutes ago.

"Okay, guys." Such tired guys. Some of them held their heads up with both hands. "We started out with a sick freak and random kills. Now we got four hearts labeled *proof of death*—big, bold letters." And those hearts had surely passed through the mayor's hands before they hit the water. Down at One Police Plaza, another squad, the one that *should* handle every kidnap for ransom, was disputing the whole idea that proof of death might have been preceded by proof of life and a demand for cash. "Major Case bowed out after we tied the kid to the body dump at the mansion. No help there."

Candy-ass bastards. Those downtown dicks would never ruin a perfect record for bringing every kidnap-for-ransom victim back alive—their house specialty. No, four corpses would have marred their scorecard. *Pricks.*

Some of his men leaned on walls or furniture, but

most of them sat at their desks, the easier to lie down their tired heads if their commander would only shut up.

"We're still working the background check, boss." Sanger was the only cop on the squad who wore diamonds. His earring and the pinkie ring were the bling of early years working undercover in Narcotics. And sometimes it seemed like this detective was competing with Mallory's wardrobe, outshouting her expensive threads with loud colors like today's war of a purple necktie and a green shirt.

And his hair was longer than hers.

"We still got zero connection between the victims," said Sanger. "And none of them tie back to the mayor."

This must be why Mallory had failed to show up for the briefing. She would not want to answer the question left hanging in the air: *Who pays ransom for strangers?*

Gonzales the Doubter sang out, "I say the perp's targeting the city." This young man was the best set of muscles in the room, but his value to the squad was an ability to poke holes in every scenario for a crime. This made him Jack Coffey's favorite whenever one of Mallory's theories was on the table. "Hitting the city up for the ransom, that's a good fit with killing random taxpayers."

"Nice," said Coffey, "but the mayor wouldn't have any reason to keep that quiet, and he's been holding out on us. So what else have we got? Any luck with the tattoo artist?"

"Yeah," said Gonzales. "Me and Lonahan found the place where the nun got all that ink. We flashed Angie Quill's old mug shot and the ME's photo of the rose tattoos."

"The guy who did her tats is Joey something," said Lonahan, barrel-chested and better known as Bullhorn.

His normal speaking voice could be heard in the city's outer boroughs, and now everyone in the room was awake. "Joey hasn't worked there in years. But we know Angie didn't get all those roses in a day. Maybe one tat a month. So . . . forty roses. The guy knew her that long."

"Good. A customer he'll remember," said Coffey. And maybe the tattoo artist moonlighted as a hit man. "Any leads on where Joey is now?"

"Naw," said Gonzales. "Our guy was long gone before the new owner bought the place. And no Joeys in the old employee records. We figure he worked off the books for cash." He handed the lieutenant a police artist's rendering of what Joey might look like, him and a million other lean young men with long hair and beards.

In the drawing's margin notes, Jack Coffey read a list of all the tattoos that other employees remembered seeing on the arms of this artist. "Okay, maybe we'll catch a break at the nun's mass tonight. Joey might turn out for her."

One detective slouched in his chair, facing the only unoccupied desk.

"Riker, where's your partner?"

THE SQUAD'S MOST ENDEARING NAME for her was Mallory the Machine. He found her in the geek room, melding with the technology, plugged into it for all Riker knew. It was hard to tell in an age of wireless computing. Her eyes were fixed on a glowing screen of text when he came up behind her with no illusions that she might be surprised. One of her electronic gadgets would surely rat him out. They were kin to her.

"Riker, it's time to dust off one of your old snitches.

After you cut him loose, Chester Marsh got a job as a lawyer with the SEC."

He looked down at his shoes. Confidential informants were sacred names that carried curses. Cursed was the cop who burned his snitches by speaking their names in the wrong company.

Fourteen years ago, he would have preferred to shoot Chester Marsh in the head instead of bleeding him for information on a criminal client. But Riker had been blindsided by an agreement between Marsh and the District Attorney's Office. Such deals were standard currency, done all the time, but this one had been done behind Riker's back, and the stench of it would never go away.

After that case had been wrapped, one of Marsh's honest clients died—a suicide. The lawyer had embezzled an old woman's money and cost her a berth in an upscale retirement home. A backroom agreement with the DA had allowed that thief to skate on restitution, and so Nora Peety, left with nothing and no one to take her in, jumped down to the subway rails and into the path of an oncoming train.

Before choosing the A Train to take her life away, she had mailed a letter to the *nice* policeman, the sympathetic one, who had held her hand for days and days, while gathering dirt to turn her thieving lawyer into a snitch. The lady's goodbye note to Riker had no salutation or signature, only eight words written in a faltering, spidery script.

One line.

It had destroyed him.

Nora had *loved* James Taylor. She had played his music all day long, and maybe counted on Riker to recognize the final line of a refrain, lyrics to a song of fire and rain.

"I always thought that I'd see you again." That was all she wrote.

When her suicide train had come and gone, it left a stain on Riker. He called it murder. He took all the blame. And he had lost three days to binge drinking before unpacking his guilt for Lou Markowitz, a man who could be counted on to keep secrets.

Kathy Mallory, a child in those days and an eavesdropping brat, had listened in and made off with the name of his snitch. The kid had later invoked Chester Marsh, just testing the value of her goods, when she tried to extort Riker for coins to feed the lunchroom's snack machine—*literally* blackmail for peanuts.

The little girl had picked her moment well—his first day out of rehab for cops who saw the spiders of delirium tremens. Riker had never been more vulnerable—and yet he had held the advantage in that short negotiation. He had a store of holy kid words like *rat*. "Okay," he had said to her then, "do it now. Tell everybody what you got on me. Tell 'em all how Nora Peety died. You know why they don't already know that story? It's 'cause I'll never rat out a snitch, not even that sack-a-shit lawyer. *There—are—rules.*" Then he had spread his arms wide, saying, "Take your best shot, kid."

Kathy had quietly slipped away from the lunchroom. On toward the close of that bad day, Riker had found a bag of peanuts lying on his desk.

A peace offering.

An understanding.

And she had never again mentioned Chester Marsh, not till today. So, all those years ago, he had taught her nothing lasting. Kathy the child had only saved away the snitch's name in her little toolkit of useful things. This sad thought was writ on his face when he raised his eyes from the floor to see his partner smiling at him. But it was not a *gotcha* smile, and that threw him for a moment.

"Riker, is there anyone you hate more than that cockroach lawyer? . . . You want payback for the old lady?" Mallory turned to her computer and scrolled back the text to show him the logo of the Securities and Exchange Commission. "Marsh got a severance package when he left the SEC. He can't practice law anymore. That was part of their deal to get rid of him. But they gave him a government pension."

Oh, this was so wrong. "You gotta do twenty years to qualify for a—"

"Right," said Mallory, "Unless the feds were worried about blowback on a dodgy case—like Polk's. So let's call it payment to keep Marsh's mouth shut. But if he talks, his deal gets rescinded. He was only there for ten years, so the pension isn't much, but it's all he's got. You can take it away from him—rob him just like he robbed the old lady." She swiveled her chair around to face Riker. "And you won't be burning a snitch. Nothing to do with that old business. This is a *new* game. He's just a material witness—no deals, no protection."

Mallory was offering him another present, something bigger than a bag of peanuts.

"WHAT'S IT FEEL LIKE TO KILL PEOPLE?" Iggy stabbed one of the grilled hotdogs with a fork. It was like that. But, to answer the boy, he said, "You get used to it. Just a job." He slid the cooked meat from his fork to a bun and laid it on a plate. "There you go. Dig in, kid."

The boy wanted all the details of doing murder. He was soaking up every word—just like school.

"I keep it simple. No noise, no witnesses, nothin' the cops can track back to me."

Iggy saw no need to mention that he had been caught his first time out. An insurance-company investigator had found the neighborhood bar where that first deal was done, where the money had changed hands. Then he had followed the breadcrumb trail out of that place and down the street to the apartment Iggy had shared with his mother. Gail Rawly had pushed his business card under Ma's door and, later that same day, over a few rounds of beer, Iggy had learned a lot from that insurance man.

"Every job's got rules, I guess. I never hire out to nobody I know." Digging up business was Gail's job. But the big rule? Never *kill* anybody he knew. Well, that one was shot to hell. And so was another one: *Don't talk to the meat.*

Iggy rarely talked to anybody. For these past five years since the girl went away, his longest conversation had been with the old man who owned the garden shop down the road, but they only talked roses. He sure as hell never thought of socializing with Gail, that smug asshole, who never got his hands dirty, who fancied himself a damn businessman.

After sitting down to his hotdog and beer, and with his mouth full of meat, he gave the little boy more pointers on contract killing. "Oh, yeah, there's the surprise blitz attack." That one was a staple of the trade. On the subject of the murder kit, he said, "You don't wanna get too fancy. For most of it, you buy cheap, untraceable stuff." Iggy was a Walmart shopper.

When the boy was one bite into his second helping of hotdogs, he asked, "So everybody has the same rules?"

"No idea what the rest of 'em do." He had never even

met another one of his kind. Ah, kids and their cop shows. "It's not like we all get together and exchange secret handshakes. No exposure. That's the key thing."

But had he somehow given everything away to Angie? Did she know how he made his living? The girl had never asked. That was the upside of hookers—no nosy questions. Even so, after coming home to find that the few belongings she kept here were gone, he had spent many a night camped in the woods, watching for cops, wondering if his house was safe—and what *had* she known?

Why had the girl gone away?

Tonight, he would get answers from Mrs. Quill. He was owed an explanation to jibe with what Angie had done on the street that day, the last day of her life.

The kid raised his hand—just like school. He had another question about murder.

12

The detective pulled out a chair at the heavy oak table, and he sat down with his back to the wall of a saloon that he called home, though his apartment was upstairs. Riker would not call himself an alcoholic, nothing that grand. He owned up to the lesser title of Garden Variety Drunk, and he had this in common with his former snitch, Chester Marsh. Short on cash these days, Marsh would shop a baby for body parts just to buy more booze. Most drunks would stop short of that, but Riker held a lower opinion of lawyers.

The bartender, a retired cop, stood behind the long plank of mahogany that spanned one side of the room. Off-duty police drank here, and civilians were made to feel unwelcome—with one exception tonight. A former government attorney sat at Riker's table.

Marsh's silk suit was showing its age, and it no longer fit him, nor did his cleanest dirty shirt. "So what's it been? Fourteen years?"

"Give or take," said Riker. "I hear you landed a job with the SEC."

"Yeah, but I quit a while back."

You weasel, they fired your ass . . . but let's pretend.

Riker set a paper bag on the table, and he lowered the brown wrapping an inch at a time, a striptease for a bottle of single-malt whiskey beyond the purse of a pensioner who lived in one-room squalor. Marsh smelled like he had gone days without a bath, though he had shaved for this sit-down, and there was evidence of the shakes in every nick of the razor. The disbarred lawyer stared at the bottle just beyond his reach, and his eyes had the shine of true love.

The detective pulled the brown bag back up around the capped whiskey and held it hostage in both hands. If called upon in court to swear to a snitch's sobriety, the bartender could easily testify that this cockroach had not been served liquor in the presence of police, nor had he been intoxicated when he entered the bar. Though Marsh had tremors in his hands, there had been no weave to his walk.

"I had nothing to do with Andrew Polk's case. No idea why that guy's not in jail," said the thief who had all but pushed the elderly Nora Peety in front of a subway train. "I never saw any paperwork for a settlement."

"Fine. . . . You got nothin' for me." Riker rose from his chair, cradling the bagged bottle in one arm.

"Hang *on*," said Marsh. "I do remember the buzz around the office . . . gossip, mostly."

Riker settled down in his chair and set the bottle on the table. "Yeah?"

"Maybe I handled some paperwork—busywork, stuff like that. But it never went to court. No corroboration. Polk's victims never had a bad word to say about him."

"But the feds had something on him," said Riker. "What was it?"

"Hey." Marsh, spread his hands to say, *How should I*

know? "I'm only guessing here, okay? Let's say Polk copped to a breach of ethics. A pansy charge, but at least they get to pull his license and knock him off Wall Street. From Polk's point of view—that beats a trial, even one the SEC can't win. He'd figure that was too messy, too public. It was election time. But I'd bet my pension Polk strung them along—wouldn't sign till after he took office. Then maybe our new mayor gets amnesia. Settlement? What settlement? He might need that broker's license if he can't cut it in politics. But now? Polk's going after a second term. He *has* to sign. So I guess he surrendered his license."

Mallory was right. This man had read some early form of that settlement. And the recent signature date explained why the SEC document was walked out of the mansion in the pocket of the mayor's aide—one hour before the Crime Scene Unit came knocking on the door. Dicey timing, but all high rollers loved high risk. They *lived* for it.

"So," said Chester Marsh, "you can bet Polk's settlement was loaded with a nondisclosure clause. No formal court filing, nothing to mess up the next election."

The ex-lawyer reached for the bottle.

Riker held it back. "We need a list of Polk's victims. Pare it down to the ones with open wounds. Who hates the mayor most?"

The lawyer pulled back his hand, as if Riker had burned him—and he *had*.

"Oh, *right*. Tell me you don't have Polk's client list in your pocket. I'm not buying it, Riker. I *know* what you're doing. You need details on that scam. The big losers on the list, they still won't rat him out, right? And the SEC won't give you squat."

Close enough, though all Riker needed was confirmation of a suspect list that his partner already had. And to pass the smell test with a judge, only a federal witness would do. The list of scammed investors had to come from a source who was not a cop—and sure as hell *not* Mallory.

Marsh folded his arms against the detective. "So you have to milk dirt from an insider. Like *me*. Like I'm gonna break my severance agreement, lose my pension 'cause I love you so much? How stupid do you—"

"So Polk only burned his own clients—not all of 'em, just the big losers on one stock swindle. That's my victim list?" Oh, damn right. He had nailed this little bastard on that score. He could see it in that sudden *oh-shit* expression on the ex-lawyer's face.

And—*bonus*—Chester Marsh felt obliged to reiterate this aloud, saying, *"Shit! Shit! Shit!"* accompanied by table pounding. He was *so* loud that heads were turning all around the room.

"So that's a *yes,"* said Riker. The mayor's former clients were on the public record, and now their likely implication in murder was also on record. He pushed the bottle toward Marsh. "Enjoy."

Payment for a snitch.

No need to further wreck the cockroach's night by disclosing the fact that the detective was wired for sound. Riker had what he came for, a documented, pared-down list of suspects with cause to be insanely get-even angry with Andrew Polk. He also had a witness on a sound track that would back up any warrants they might need for one of those angry people. And with the first warrant served, Chester Marsh's government pension was good as gone.

Payback for an old lady who took the A Train.

* * *

"THE FIRST STAR." Iggy Conroy leaned back in his patio chair. "And it ain't even half dark yet."

"First mosquito." The boy smacked his arm, but not quick enough. He must be tired. He was flat out of questions to keep a conversation going. The kid's fingers tapped the arms of the chair, and he rocked himself like a cradled baby, not liking the quiet.

"Some things about the city I don't miss," said Iggy. And the boy stopped rocking. "More stars out here in the sticks. They look like weird little matches floatin' up there. Flame but no heat. Too bad you can't see 'em." He lit a cigarette and watched the smoke drift until the rocking started up again on the other side of the table. The kid *needed* noise, and so Iggy said, "Nothin's *gotta* look like somethin'. I know it's no good askin'. If you can't tell dark from light, then maybe you're walkin' around in white soup. But *somebody* should've figured this out by now."

"Someone did," said the boy, "someone who could see. Try this on. When you close your eyes—"

"Yeah, yeah. I see black."

"No, I *told* you. You don't *see* anything—not with your eyes. They only take in what the brain needs to make up a picture inside your head. With your eyes shut, the brain's got nothing to work with. It has no idea what's going on out there. So when you close your eyes? When you *think* you see black? That's the brain lying to you. It's telling you the story about what life looks like when the lights go out. It's a trick. But *your* brain knows what black looks like. Mine doesn't. It can't fool me that way."

"So how the hell would you—"

"Just close your left eye. . . . You don't see black with that one, do you? No, your brain doesn't need to make up a story for that eye. A stream of real data's coming from the one that's still wide open. . . . It's the *closed* eye that shows you what nothingness looks like."

With one eye open, Iggy saw everything, even a shadow on the bridge of his nose, but no lights-out blackness in the eye that was shut. He saw *nothing* from that one. The closed eye might as well not be there. "I get it."

Now he knew what death looked like, too. Nothing. And so he knew where Angie was and where the boy was going.

FLORAL OFFERINGS for the dead nun were enough to fill a cathedral, too many for a neighborhood church like St. Jude's. The inspired sexton and his helpers had wound the overflow into garlands that hung from the walls in natural wonders to rival the stained glass.

It was rare for this house of worship to be visited in great numbers at this time of year. Summer was a fallow season for Father Brenner's trade.

Tonight, there was one more wonder to behold. Should he live to be a hundred, he would never see this spectacle again. His chief suspect in the working of miracles was Cardinal Rice's emissary, Father DuPont, who had declined a place in the first pew to sit in the last.

Father Brenner turned his eyes toward the raised tier of the altar, so like a stage, where church history was in the making—all for the love of a woman.

By unprecedented permission granted by the cardinal himself, a prioress and ten cloistered nuns stood there, wearing the long black robes and veils of their order.

They had journeyed many a mile. No longer sheltered by far-off monastery walls, they bravely stood exposed to a public gathering. In a further breach of centuries-old tradition, they formed a choir and sang Sister Michael to her rest. Their songs were old, but their voices were new to this world. Imperfect performers, they cried as they sang, creating wavers in notes here and there that broke heart after heart in row upon row.

DETECTIVES WORE WHITE CARNATIONS in their lapels and played the parts of ushers strolling to the organ music. Moving down the rows of pews, they searched faces for one to match a rough drawing, and they also scanned all the summer-bare skin for identifying marks.

Beyond tall wooden doors, left open to the night, a crowd filled the church steps, the sidewalk and the street, and everywhere out there were candles and cigarette lighters and matches held high. Amid that gathering of standing mourners, one upraised arm was covered in tattoos of snakes, hearts, daggers—and a twining vine of red roses to match every cop's camera-phone image of a dead woman's naked thighs. This skinny arm was grabbed by the large hand of a uniformed officer, who sang out to nearby detectives, "I *got* him!"

IGGY WATCHED the TV news coverage of the church interior, and he described it to the child beside him on the living-room sofa. "There's a shitload of flowers. And the *people*—big turnout, kid. Angie would've loved it."

The boy held up one hand to shush him, the better to hear the priest introduce a speaker, Harold Quill.

"Hey," said Iggy. "That's your uncle?" Sure it was. The guy even looked like the kid.

The boy left the sofa to stand close to the TV screen on the wall, his hands cupped to catch only that voice in the church. When the uncle began to speak—to beg for help—the boy hugged himself, bending at the waist, as if he had taken a hit, and he slowly folded to the floor. Head low, arms wrapping round his legs, he was all knees and elbows now. When the uncle was done talking, the kid's voice cracked on the words, "I want to go home."

Ain't gonna happen, kid.

At that moment, the boy lifted his face, his attention called to an empty chair, and he nodded to no one there.

"Stop it!" Damn kid and his games. The boy turned to stare at him, *glare* at him with Angie's big gray eyes, like he could *see*—or she could.

Jesus. What the— Iggy heard the tiny muffled sound of bells. From the hallway? *Naw.* He turned back to the TV. A *church.* Yeah, churches had all kinds of bells. But still, he pressed the mute button on the remote control, and he strained to catch that sound again. All he heard was the dog's heavy breathing on the floor at his feet. No jingling.

WHEN THE CHURCH had emptied of all but the clergy, the monastery choir gathered in the nave with their small bags of belongings, saying their good nights and preparing to leave under the protection of the teaching sisters from the parochial school. The visiting nuns would be their guests tonight. A small child of the parish approached the gathering, not on the run, which was her nature, but stepping softly on best behavior. She reached up to give Father Brenner a folded paper, and he opened it to see the letterhead of Cardinal Rice.

The priest thanked the little girl and shooed her away to join her parents, who waited on the steps beyond the doors. Turning to the monastery's prioress, he said, "Reverend Mother, the *cardinal* is here." Father Brenner pointed to the confessional, a small, freestanding structure with three doors. A light glowed above the center compartment in invitation to the Sacrament of Penance. "He'd like a word . . . in private."

The prioress nodded and excused herself from a conversation with Father DuPont, asking, "Wait for me? I have a few more questions."

HER BLACK ROBES flowing, she walked to the end of the aisle and opened a door to enter a closet-size enclosure. Arthritic legs were slow to bend as the prioress lowered herself to the cushioned kneeler. Before her was the metal weave of a lattice, all that separated her from His Eminence, but the prioress kept Custody of the Eyes, looking down at her veined and wrinkled hands clasped in prayer upon a worn wooden ledge. She began the ritual words that must open every conversation in this intimate space, "Forgive me, Father, for I have—"

"The cardinal's busy," said a woman's voice, and a gold badge was pressed to the lattice. "But there *will* be a confession."

13

Mallory leaned close to the metal grille and spoke softly so her words would not carry beyond the flimsy wooden door of the confessional. "I know your family was loaded with money . . . and you got a law degree from Georgetown."

"That sounds a bit like an accusation, my child. So my background doesn't fit your idea of a monastery prioress?"

The old woman was a backlit shadow, but her voice gave away attitude, and the detective could hear a smile on the face of this glorified nun.

"No," said Mallory, "it *does* fit. Thirty-five years ago, you were a public defender. Your caseload would've been heavy on street trash. Lots of hookers like Angie Quill. You don't want to lie to me. I've already talked to DuPont."

Hesitation? Was the prioress still smiling? The detective thought not.

"Sister Michael had a difficult life."

"I've already heard that story," said Mallory. "My interest begins when she was just a hooker knocking on your door. No education—rough trade for a monastery. DuPont says you signed her up as a nun because you thought she had a true calling. *I* say you gave her sanctuary."

"Can't both things be true?"

"Don't jerk me around." There would be only one warning.

"From our point of view, Sister Michael's life began when she entered the—"

"I don't have *time* for this!" Mallory pounded the grille.

Oh, too violent?

The silhouette of the prioress went rigid, tensing. Feeling less protected now? Mallory whispered a little poison through the metal screen. "Angie's nephew is just a little boy. I have to find him before a freak cuts out his heart—while it's *still beating*."

The prioress lowered her head, and her form in shadow appeared to be cut down in size—not quite chopped off at the knees yet, but given time—

"I know the girl didn't trust cops," said Mallory. "But you *better* trust me. I'm all that boy's got. Angie loved him—that much I believe. Now you tell me something that isn't a lie. Were you *hiding* her? Was she *scared?*"

"My first impression of Angie . . . she was beaten down by her life and very tired."

Too tired to run. Too tired to fight.

"Go on," said Mallory, and the prioress did go on—and *on*.

WAS HE LOOKING at Angie Quill's killer? Probably not. Riker sat down next to the suspect and gave him a hey-how's-it-goin' smile.

The cop on the other side of the table did not pull up a chair. Detective Washington liked the advantage of looking down at the young man, who was surprisingly clean-cut from the neck up, lacking the beard and long hair of their sketch for the tattoo artist. Washington had taken the lead, though he had yet to say one word. He only sneered while eyeing the suspect's torn jeans, the raggedy T-shirt—and tattoos that covered both arms.

Joey Collier was quick to guess that he had just been assessed as lowlife scum, and now he wanted it known that, sure, he made the punk scene by night, but he wore a suit and tie in the workday hours. "When I quit inking skin, I went back to school for my CPA. I've got a job in a big accounting firm. Lots of corporate clients. I'd rather the news media didn't—"

"No worries, pal," said Riker. "When you got grabbed off the street, all the reporters were inside the church." He stared at the accountant's arms of red roses, snakes and daggers. "Bet that wouldn't go over well at the office. So you gotta wear long sleeves to work all summer, huh? Damn."

"Am I under arrest?"

"I haven't decided yet," said Washington, a genius in the game of Bad Cop, a rough-talking, I'm-gonna-getcha, *bastard* of a cop.

And Riker, a friend to all mankind tonight, asked, "How long did you know Angie Quill?"

"Three years, maybe a little longer," said Joey Collier. "She came in once a month for a tattoo. But that was years ago."

"How'd she pay?" Washington looked like he was about to crawl across the table and do some damage. "Did you get that girl to spread her legs?"

"No, she wasn't like that. Angie was a nice kid."

Riker laid the old mug shot on the table, the picture of Angie Quill punked out with purple streaks and goth-black fingernails. "She was a hooker. You know it. We know it."

"She never came on to me."

"Yeah, right," said Washington. "And you never made any moves on *her*? Gimme a fuckin' break." Alongside the mug shot, he set down the medical examiner's photographs of the tattoos on Angie Quill's thighs. "So she's standing there, her skirts hiked up. *Great* legs."

"She wasn't *like* that," said the former tattoo artist to the angry cop facing him—disbelieving him.

"Okay, Joey," said Riker, the smiling detective. "I'll buy that. How'd she pay for all those tats? You didn't say."

"Cash. But she didn't pay for the first one. That time she came in with this guy. He paid for the first rose." Joey pointed to the roses on one arm. "She liked my tats. So the boyfriend told me to start a vine on her thigh. That's why I think he bankrolled the rest of them."

Riker pushed a pad of yellow-lined paper across the table. "We need a name and address for this guy."

"Are you kidding me? I only saw him once, and that was ten years ago."

"When Angie Quill was fifteen," said Washington, "a minor *child*." And his face said, *I got you now, you little pervert.*

"We can work this out." Riker lightly rested one hand on Joey's shoulder. "You didn't screw her for the roses? Okay, we find this guy, he backs up your story, and you're outta here." The detective tapped his watch. "You need your beauty sleep, pal. You don't wanna show up for work tomorrow with bags under your eyes."

"I never got his name, but he's the memorable type—a bruiser. And he pulled out a big wad of a cash—big as my fist." The tattoo artist jammed a thumb in Washington's direction. "Big as *his* fist. . . . After that, Angie came in alone, always paid cash. Brand-new bills, just like the boyfriend's money. My guess? Every time he got laid, the guy marked her with another rose."

"But she never screwed *you.*" Washington was playing thick with disbelief. "Not even a blowjob to save herself some money?"

"That was never gonna happen. The boyfriend scared me shitless. It wasn't anything he said. It was the eyes, I guess. Like he could go medieval on me any second."

"You're doin' good," said Riker. "You remember if the boyfriend was a smoker?"

"Oh, yeah. Chain smoker. Hard to forget that part. The guy lights up a cigarette, and he looks at me—scary cold. I figure he's waiting for me to tell him to put it out. He's standing right under the no-smoking sign on the wall. But I wasn't about to say anything. Not to him. I figured that might be worth some broken teeth."

IGGY CONROY drove through Alphabet City, east of St. Marks Place. He kept a lookout for a parking space in the old neighborhood. His white van rolled by the apartment house where he had once lived with his mother. It had not changed. Same old crack on the second step. But next door was a dry cleaner, and that was not right. The old pizza parlor had closed up shop and gone away. Iggy took this loss personally.

That was where he first saw Angie, his come-and-go girl, the one with the jingling red flip-flops. That day, she had been jailbait in schoolgirl braids and blue jeans. How old? Not old enough. But so pretty. He had not been the only man in that place to watch her for the length of the line to buy a slice and a soda, but he had never thought of approaching her. Only fools and perverts messed with kids.

Half a year later and late at night, he caught sight of her again. No bells, no flip-flops or braids that time. She wore red lipstick and a trashy skirt the size of a low-slung belt. She was otherwise the same kid—until the moment when his van slowed down, when the girl knew his eyes were on her, and *snap*—that fast—the girl grew up. One hip swung out as a high-heeled shoe stepped off the curb. And, curbside, she had negotiated money and terms like an old pro.

Years after that, there were still times when Angie would walk out of his bathroom, her hair damp from a shower, no makeup on, and all alone for all she knew. And then he would see the other girl, the jingling one, but only for the few seconds before she sensed him nearby, watching her, and then—*snap*.

She would come and go like that.

ANGIE QUILL's former counselor stood in the hallway. "Sorry I'm late," said Father DuPont. "I thought you might've gone to bed. It's very quiet in this building. It feels so—"

"Empty? Well, I don't have many tenants. None on this floor." Charles stood aside to usher the man into his apartment.

At the end of the vestibule, the priest paused to take in the front room of antique furnishings and paneled walls.

"I love the windows." Tall and arched, they were an architectural detail from a time when this old apartment building had belonged to the factory age of SoHo. The interior had since been remodeled to resemble more elegant private rooms of the same era. And now DuPont focused on the tray of whiskey and glasses set out on a small table between two armchairs. Taking this cue, he took his seat.

When Charles had poured their drinks, he said, "I'm glad you could make it."

"I'm flattered that you remembered me. There were so many psychologists at that convention."

"And you were out of uniform," said Charles. "You wore a gray sports coat over a T-shirt. Faded jeans, right? It was winter in Chicago. You were carrying a topcoat. Camel hair, I believe."

"Impressive." The priest made short work of his whiskey. "There were at least a hundred people in the room. After you read that brilliant paper, I'm sure half of them had a word with you."

"But I only heard one confession that night." Charles raised the bottle. "Refill?"

IGGY LIKED TO TRAVEL by rooftop in New York City, where security cameras only watched the streets, and the only light tonight was a waxing moon. Mindful of high windows on the other side of St. Marks Place, he crouched to keep his silhouette low. There was no need for him to pick the crummy lock on this roof door. He turned the knob hard, forcing it until he heard the mechanism break, and then he was through the door and down the stairs to the top-floor landing, where music played in one apartment. Across the hall, there was no sound at all behind Mrs. Quill's door. The kid's granny was probably in bed, and now she could kiss her nighty goodbye. His résumé included accidental deaths for insurance money, and he favored bathtub drownings.

But first—a quiet little talk with the lady. In Iggy's experience, nobody ever screamed when the point of a knife was an inch from an eyeball. It never failed.

Gently, so gently, he worked two bits of metal in her locks. The door was opened slowly with no giveaway squeak to the hinge. Guided by the thin beam of a key-chain flashlight, Iggy passed through one room and another to find beds with bare mattresses holding piles of old clothes and cardboard boxes. The bed in the last room had sheets and pillows, but no Mrs. Quill. He checked the closets and every space that might hide her. No luck, but he did find enough crucifixes and rosaries to stock the gift shop of St. Patrick's Cathedral. Where was Angie's mother tonight? The church service had ended hours ago.

There was no toothbrush in the bathroom. Maybe she went home with the kid's Uncle Harry. Or could Mrs. Quill be in protective custody? No, that would only work if the cops were onto him. And how much could Granny tell them, anyway? Nothing. Fat chance that Angie would give a God freak like this one any details about her johns.

So what was he doing here? If there had been a good reason for the risk, he had forgotten it, and he blamed this on the drugs he took to keep his eyes wide open. If Granny or the uncle had a name and address to give up, the cops would have come for him days ago. So why the—

A reason for coming after Angie's mother popped into his head. He had a question. Why had the girl gone away?

He returned to the front room and its reek of incense. Everywhere he flashed his beam of light, it hit a plaster saint or a plastic one, and Jesus Christ was framed on every foot of wall space. What was it with all of this zany, hair-on-fire-for-the-Lord crap?

Oh, *idiot!*

He smashed one hand into his forehead, as if that might fix a loose connection and restore common sense. He was surrounded by all the evidence he could ever want that Angie had not known what he was—what he did. She had not been running scared, not running from him. Angie had left him for God.

YES, FATHER DUPONT would very much like another drink to top off the second one. Charles Butler refilled the priest's glass and waited for the real conversation to begin.

"I should've spoken to you the other night at the restaurant."

Ah, finally. "But I was talking to Detective Mallory," said Charles. "I can see how that could've been awkward. I gather she made you rather uncomfortable."

"Understatement," said DuPont. "I ran into her once before . . . at Gracie Mansion. Maybe she mentioned it? I take it she's a friend of yours."

"I've known her for years." And he had no intention of sharing any business of hers. He knew how to keep a confidence as well as the clergy. Shuttling the priest to another track, he said, "I've been to Gracie Mansion for a few charity events, but that was a long time ago. Never met Mayor Polk. What's your impression of him?"

"He's a flimflam man."

"Like your father."

"Two of a kind—except for the obvious things." One would have to discount the fact that the priest's father had never lived in a mansion, and he had died in a prison cell. "That makes Andrew Polk the perfect politician. Me, too. I guess it's in my genes, and maybe it shows. I don't think your friend, the detective, believed a word I said the other night." He smiled, as if this meant nothing to him.

Yes, there was definitely a touch of paternal genes. The priest was charming. People would like him on two minutes' acquaintance, and they would open up to this man. In respect to Mallory's distrust, DuPont was obviously expecting a confirmation or a denial. And now Charles had his own trust issues.

He glanced at the priest's glass, nearly drained of whiskey. He recalled his first meeting with this man. On that long-ago night, the priest had nursed his drink, only one, but this evening he was bolting down the liquor. Was he self-medicating his recent angst? Or had he become an alcoholic?

"I'm not a therapist anymore," said DuPont. "I quit the profession. You may remember giving me that . . . suggestion."

During the ensuing silence, Charles gathered that this man did not plan to tell him how many years had passed before following that good advice.

The priest's dilemma, as Charles had seen it then, was not one of keeping his oath as a psychologist. That had been violated, though Father DuPont had sworn to him that he had never touched the girl. On that long-ago night, the priest had given a very different version of his confession to Mallory. The Chicago recital had been sugared with poetry and irony when DuPont had told him that Angie Quill could only have sex for money or favors, never for love, and the priest could not bed her for any sort of currency—because he *loved* her.

Certainly favors had been granted to the girl, and Mallory had rightly called that currency. However, on no account could he see this man through her eyes. DuPont was surely no molester of children, though now Charles was less certain about the priest's position on vulnerable girls nearer the age of consent. "I make excellent coffee. You know what goes nicely with that?"

And, yes, Father DuPont thought a cigar would sit quite well with him tonight.

Charles walked down the hall to his kitchen, a place of high tin-ceiling charm and warm ochre walls racked with copper-bottom pots and spices. While the old-fashioned percolator on the stove brewed a custom blend of coffee, he turned to see Father DuPont standing in the doorway. "Come in. Sit down." Most of his guests eventually gravitated to this room. Mallory had once told him that she favored kitchens over station-house interrogations. Understandable. People were less guarded here in this place of perfect peace, chairs padded for comfort and a table to accommodate elbows.

The priest did seem more relaxed. And planning to stay awhile? Yes, he sensed that DuPont was not done with the expedition into Mallory's affairs, though this might be only a show of concern for the missing boy. But there was another possibility.

When the two men faced one another across the table, and praise had been lavished on the coffee, they were enveloped in a pleasing cloud of cigar smoke, an opportune moment for a bomb to go off. "You have to tell the police what you know," said Charles, "for the boy's sake."

"I *can't.*" DuPont fumbled with his cup, spilling a bit of coffee as he set it down. "And there's not much point to it. The newspapers say all four of the murders were random. Reporters couldn't find any connections between those people—not ties to each other or anyone else. You see? Angie wasn't killed by someone from her past. That's just too far-fetched."

Charles nodded, but not in agreement. So the priest had someone in mind for the murder of Angie Quill—if not for the complication of three other killings. "Go to Mallory. You don't want her coming after you one more time." Charles took a sip from his cup. And another. Then he ceased to wait for a response from the other side of the table. "It *is* far-fetched. I'm sure you're right. Once you talk to her, she'll see that. Mallory's nothing if not logical."

"I *know* what she is. . . . So do you."

"I won't discuss any personal issues of hers." Nor would he force Mallory into the neat cookie-cutter framework of a sociopath. He placed her in a realm all her own, and inside its borders, he had fashioned a ruthless government—no mercy, no compassion—and every night was poker night, as she figured the odds and took down the players.

In any contest with her, this priest was surely toast.

"Charles, when you talked to her in the restaurant, did you mention that you knew me?"

"I was surprised that she knew *you,*" and this was the truth. There had been no warning, no name mentioned beforehand. "No, our meeting in Chicago—that never came up in conversation. That would've been . . . inappropriate." Charles pushed his empty cup to one side. "I believe, at core, you're a man of good conscience. Otherwise, you'd never have asked for my counsel the first time we—"

"I can't tell Mallory anything. It's not that I don't want to."

"Seal of the Confessional?" Perhaps he had underrated Father DuPont. The therapist's oath was blown to hell, but a priest's vows might be left intact—and at stake.

MALLORY STEPPED into the shadow of a doorway. The cobblestones of this SoHo street wore a wet shine, though it had yet to rain. Drops of water hung in the air as fine mist.

Hours had passed and the priest was still here? That would explain the lack of a phone call.

A few drops fell as Father DuPont stepped out on the sidewalk, caught with no umbrella and looking skyward, maybe wondering if he could beat the rain to a taxi. He hurried away.

The detective stayed to watch the lights of the fourth-floor apartment—waiting for her cell phone to ring, giving Charles a last chance to confess. But his windows went dark one by one. He had no plans to tell her about this covert meeting.

The priest had reached the end of the street, where cabs were more plentiful, but Mallory had no further interest in his travels tonight.

She turned her eyes back to Charles Butler's darkened windows.

What have you done?

And now the rain came down—hard-driving, *punishing* rain.

* * *

THE REPORTERS held umbrellas as they kept vigil on the sidewalk.

The mayor stood by the corner window in the Susan B. Wagner Wing. He waved to the press corps. That always excited them. They were so hungry for any activity, and this was his version of feeding pigeons.

He turned around to speak with the two men in shirtsleeves and shoulder holsters. "Why don't you guys take a break? Give us a few minutes." He nodded toward Samuel Tucker, indicating the need for some privacy with him. When the bodyguards had withdrawn from the room, he said, "Tuck, about those four packages. How many people saw them before you did?"

"Sir, you told me not to—"

"Well, now I need to know." Deniability was hardly an option anymore.

"Postal workers, I suppose," said Samuel Tucker. "It wasn't an outfit like UPS or FedEx. . . . You *saw* the—"

"Who gave them to *you?*"

"The kid who comes around with the mail cart."

"Good." That teenager was a stoner, half his brain cells gone to drugs. Those very special deliveries could have been given to the mail boy as still-beating hearts in the hand, and that kid would remember nothing useful to the police.

Tucker was straightening a bow tie that was not crooked. Nervous? Had this fool screwed up somehow?

"Go home. Tomorrow you work downtown, the desk in the lobby. If another package gets dropped off, call me." No chance of that. Deliveries would be intercepted by cops before they got through the door to City Hall, but this chore of busywork would solve one problem. "Good night, Tuck." He could not get this idiot off the premises fast enough.

The aide left the room, leaving Andrew Polk alone for the first time all day. The damn protection detail, recently turned zealous, would sleep with him if he allowed it.

Thanks to the news media, everyone in the city knew he was a virtual prisoner in Gracie Mansion. The next package would surely come here. The Post Office would be too risky. Would the killer make a personal appearance? The patrol on the surrounding parkland had been doubled, and this time there would be no opportunity to blind security cameras with paint balls. How would the delivery be managed?

No matter. It was going to happen.

Anticipation gave him an adrenaline rush that he could not buy. No drug could do this for him. He was flying high, smiling broadly, as he faced the window to see that the rain had stopped. He watched the street of reporters.

And the street watched him—while he waited for his heart.

IGGY CONROY turned off his windshield wipers as he made a left turn into his driveway. The van's headlights illuminated the muddy roadbed through woods. Despite the curves, he could drive it in his sleep with no fear of hitting a tree. A temptation to close his eyes was—

His right foot slammed the brake pedal. Full stop.

The twin beams were trained on one of Ma's garden gnomes where he had never seen one before. Its ugly face peered out of the foliage. That last time out with the machete, he must have gotten carried away and, eyes blind with sweat, he had cut back ferns that had hidden this one for all the years since his mother's death.

Thank you, Ma, for this nasty little surprise.

He drove on to the garage at the top of the road, and there it was again. The same little man, but this one had always crouched in plain sight. It was the first one Ma had bought. Others were hiding in the woods, and one in back of the house had the cover of rosebushes grown up around it.

Even in her last years of oncoming dementia, Ma had continued to order them from the garden shop. Sometimes he would come home from a trip and the see the track of a new one, the rut left behind after she had dragged it across the lawn to hide it among the trees and thick undergrowth. How many were there? He had never understood her love for the trolls. Child catchers, she called them. Ma never did like other people's kids much, most of them *damn* kids to her. How many of her little men were out there? An army?

On this so tired night, he could almost believe that there was only one. This one on the lawn. In the woods. Down the driveway. And sometimes among the roses.

14

Good Dog knew only one trick, a fast game of fetch. By taps of a keyboard and a double click, Mallory sent her software creature through a back door, a pet flap of sorts, and into the databank of the Securities and Exchange Commission, a vast circuitry of twisty electronic halls, silver chambers of chips and deep pits covered over with the twigs and branches of burglar alarms. Through this labyrinth of data, mega-billions of bytes, the Good Dog virus followed her command to bring home any bone attached to a case-reference number for Andrew Polk.

The dog ran merrily through the federal network, easily skirting familiar firewalls and making great leaps over known trip wires, crawling under others, and then—out of nowhere—a zap laid him low. Oh, the *pain!* One leg gone and dripping blood from the stump, loyal Good Dog came limping back to his mistress with no bones in his teeth, only scraps of data. The case itself had been deep-sixed in the basement vault of a sealed computer sector.

So the feds had a new hiding place. Fancier weaponry, too.

Well, this was how her dog learned.

The Queen of Good Housekeeping gathered her electronic buckets and mops to clean up the bloody paw prints so the feds could not follow her dog's tracks home.

Bless the feds for hobbling their field agents with triplicate paperwork. Sets of reports had survived the sweep to bury interviews with some of the mayor's victims from his Wall Street brokerage days. Other bits of the case lived in private email chains of Andrew Polk's former clients, angry outcries of foul play. These civilians had flimsy firewalls, safeguards that a ten-year-old child would spit on, and a nondisclosure agreement had surfaced in the open book that was one investor's home computer.

She so loved the fools in their glass houses.

Her intercom buzzer announced an expected visitor. Compulsively punctual Mallory would be late for work this morning.

IN CHARLES BUTLER'S ESTIMATION, *living* room was a misnomer here. Mallory's environs of stark white paint, black leather, glass and steel had the feel of a domicile forever stalled in transition, each bare wall and clear surface either anticipating the mementos of personality—or suddenly bereft of them, and the furniture only awaiting the moving men.

The psychologist sipped his coffee in tense silence and with the tacit understanding that he was sitting in the open jaws of a trap. The recent strain in their friendship had not dissipated any; he had known this the moment she trotted out the good china cups. More generous ceramic mugs were reserved to her friends, the trusted few. Not him. Not anymore.

Cups emptied, he followed her down a short hallway and into another room, one with not even the pretense of hearth and home. This was where the machines lived, and the offending warmth of hardwood floors was covered by a rug of battleship gray. Electronic equipment sat on steel tables, and more was stacked on shelves. A far cry from the claustrophobic geek room at the station house, here her mechanical slaves could stretch out, reach farther and steal more.

A good portion of one upper wall was aglow with a gigantic computer monitor, her best-loved toy, and onscreen were small pictures of file holders. As she touched one of these icons, it responded to her body heat and opened in a flurry of cartoon documents flying across the screen's surface to line up in a row of perfect symmetry. Judging by the labels, some of this information once resided in government computers and those of financial institutions in the private sector. Her stolen goods on open display might show a new level of trust in him—or disdain for his honesty. It was a coin toss.

Mallory touched the first image in the lineup. "This one has dirt on the mayor's old brokerage house. Lots of questionable transactions, but one scam stands out. He gutted his own clients to pull it off." She tapped an arrow in the margin, and the page changed to a long roster of Polk's former investors. "My suspects."

Great financial losses *might* work as a motive, though it strained credulity to place money at the core of four insane murders. But her world was all cause and effect with no tolerance for random acts of unhinged minds. Money motives had neat figures, and she was good at math—not so good with the chaos of madness. There must always be logic in the State of Mallory, and she would even make it up to make it so.

"The mayor's scam was a variation on a pump-and-dump," she said. "He hyped a drug company that was going public. The whole thing hinged on a lie about a vaccine for Alzheimer's. Polk's lie—fobbed off as insider information. That's why his clients believed a mediocre stock offering was the deal of the century."

"I remember that old rumor. It was years ago." He could recall the exact date of the stock's dazzling rise and more spectacular fall, but that would be showboating. What he could not recall was any link to Andrew Polk. "That story spread like a virus. Why do you think Polk was the epicenter?"

"I *know* he was. The feds know it, too." Mallory turned to her list of names. "Ten of these people started a stampede of investors up and down Wall Street. The public was lining up to buy in on a bad deal." She pointed to another document on her screen. "This is Banter Capital. They placed casino bets with every big brokerage house in town. Foreign markets, too."

"Stock futures?"

"For the performance of one stock—on one day. They bet it would tank on the first day of trading. It did. The bets paid off in long-shot odds when Polk's rumor was killed on the trading floor."

"And the stock was downgraded."

"It was in the toilet," said Mallory, more succinctly. "Polk lost money, too. That kept him off the feds' radar for a while. He got a job at Banter Capital, and a year later, he left with a severance package worth five hundred million dollars. His golden parachute."

"That was his cut on the betting?"

"No, more like extortion—go-away money. Banter Capital needed to sever ties to him when the SEC opened an investigation. I think Polk deliberately triggered the feds' interest so he could jack up the fear—and his parachute money."

Charles *could* follow her logic, but he would rather not. That way lay a massive headache. But rather than point out that this was maniacal beyond belief, he only said, "Seems a bit risky."

"But Polk likes risk. The criminal case hung on what he told clients before they invested. Insider trading, even for bogus information—that's jail time. Polk's ex-clients wanted him dead, but they wouldn't help the SEC investigators. I figure he promised them hush money, maybe some payback on losses. That's the only way he could've gotten all ten of them to sign nondisclosure agreements. *Idiots.* They risked prison when they lied to federal agents, but Polk's agreements locked them into a criminal conspiracy. There's no way out for them now. They're stuck."

Charles nodded his understanding of legal flypaper.

"They'll never cooperate with us," she said. "But they might talk to you. Then you can pick me a likely psycho—a killer."

Well, this was progress. At least she acknowledged an element of insanity in four murders. He read the list of badly damaged investors—her suspect pool. Among them, he recognized names of people he knew, two of them old friends of his parents'. That elderly couple could never have been a party to anything like this. "How many of these—"

"I'm only interested in ten big losers for one transaction." She tapped the document again. The page changed to her pared-down list, and his parents' friends were still there. "One of them hired out four kills."

What? Murder for hire? "So the spree—"

"*Not* a spree killing. Forget what you read in the newspapers," she said for the hundredth time in their acquaintance. "Here's what the papers can't tell you. Our perp paid for those murders over a two-week period . . . and his hit man cut out the hearts."

That made *less* sense. "A serial killer's not likely to pass up the joy of hands-on murder. And the hearts, the trophies, wouldn't provide any pleasure, either. If someone else cut them out, they couldn't give him a tactile—" Oh, he was telling her something she already knew. He intuited this mistake by her folded arms and a warning in her eyes that said, *Don't. Seriously . . . don't.*

Aloud, she said, "Rich people. They hire out raising the kids, walking the dog *and* murder. But you'd have a point—*if* the hearts were trophies."

And what else might they be?

Ah, now he understood. They were clearly into her sport of the day: finding new and different things to do with human body parts. It took him two seconds. "That would only work with kidnap and extortion. . . . Ransom. . . . The heart of one victim prompts payment for the next one?" When she smiled, he knew this was the correct answer—even though it could not *possibly* be right. "But it's my understanding that the four victims were selected randomly." Again, her smile was his confirmation, and he said, "So . . . no apparent reason to *pay* a ransom."

Her smile held.

And before his head could spin around three times upon the axis of his neck, she changed the subject, turning away from him to face her shortlist on the screen. "I matched some of these people to the Social Register."

He counted three names from the old families of the New York Four Hundred, and he recognized others from the charity circuit. "I can tell you some of them are dead."

"But they had heirs." In Mallory's reckoning, the love of money would be in the DNA of their descendants.

Would she ever return to the matter of random murders and stolen hearts? Certainly not. No sport in that. There were subtle rules to be observed in this game of hers, chief among them, *no begging*. And so he could only continue on the topic at hand. "Why do you think any of Polk's former clients might talk to *me?*"

"Because you have lots of money, Charles."

She classified him as one who was not on her side, but one of *them*, the silver-spoon suspect class. This should have given him a hint of things to come, but he was startled when both hands rode her hips as she said, "So you and Father DuPont . . . what did you talk about last night? Catching up on old times?"

Ambush by appointment. How original.

Now it was her turn to be surprised. She was studying him, waiting for the telltale blush of embarrassment, a genetic defect that programmed him to be honest in all things. A sudden cherry-red complexion made deceit impossible, and so it was said that his face could not hide a thought. Untrue. He *could* keep a confidence with no intent to deceive. However, the blush's loophole of all things pertaining to principle seemed to escape her.

She failed to read his mind. It pissed her off.

Well, too damn bad.

No—just a trick. Her half smile set off warning bells in his brain, great swinging gongs sized to fit a cathedral.

Was it just possible that he had already given up everything?

Yes. And was this witchcraft on her part? Well, no. Mallory's logic was good, but she also had a lexicon of silences to work with. And what had she gleaned from his?

Oh . . . everything.

Obviously, last night she had followed Father DuPont from the church and confirmed her suspicion that he and the priest had met before. Though, the previous night in the restaurant, neither man had acknowledged the other. Charles's failure to comment on their acquaintance, both then and now, had given her *two* silences, enough to infer the rest—up to a point, but *what* point?

Pressure, pressure—almost a race to outrun her galloping paranoia.

Well, she could deduce that he had first met Father DuPont in the context of a psychologist's trade, or else he would have mentioned this man quite naturally in passing, but he had not—and Mallory made a feast of things unsaid. More damage: Since he had no private practice, she could guess that his first meeting with the priest had been a one-off therapy session for a man in deep distress.

"Here's what I *don't* know," said Mallory. "The first time DuPont came to you for help, was he was still counseling Angie Quill?"

At least, that part she could not tell. And he *would* not tell. Though, when she was done probing *this* silence, he felt like a shopworn virgin with little to nothing saved for the marriage bed.

MALLORY HAD BEEN WORKING late last night.

Lieutenant Coffey stood at the center of the incident

room. Every cork wall was so orderly now, but this was more than compulsive neatness. She had also pruned evidence, shifting attention to her own focus points by taking down all the paperwork and pictures for every victim that was not a nun or a schoolboy. Even Albert Costello had disappeared from the walls, his hour in the media spotlight used up and gone. Albert and the other three hermits had been relegated to file holders stacked on the evidence table—should anyone care to look at them, and he guessed that no one ever would. Mallory only saw these people as clutter. Cold as that was, he could not argue the point.

The lieutenant pinned up Joey Collier's sketch of the boyfriend who had accompanied Angie Quill to the tattoo parlor. How reliable could this drawing be?

Almost a decade had passed since the only meeting of the tattoo artist and their prime suspect. A thick head of hair had been roughly sketched in, probably not a well-recalled detail, and neither was the mouth of faint lines that were almost not there. But he knew the drawing had gotten one feature right—the eyes of a predator in that moment right before the lunge. Tension, *tension*—waiting for the strike. Waiting to be dead.

The boyfriend had kept close watch on the artist for maybe an hour while the first rose was tattooed on young Angie's thigh. Not exactly a hit-and-run memory.

Alongside this drawing was a blowup of the tollbooth photograph taken on Sunday. Computer enhancement had raised finer detail—a waste of time for a picture of nothing. The driver's face was hidden by the pulled-down brim of a blue baseball cap—not one visible feature. But there *was* a departure from the sketch—no hair to be seen, not a single strand stuck out below the rim of the cap. Short hair or no hair? He could not tell. If the driver in this photo was completely hairless, shaved-head bald, that would fit with a killer evolved over time into a forensic-savvy pro, who wanted no DNA left at his crime scenes.

The lieutenant bit down on the tip of his tongue. The pain kept him from tumbling into that Mallory mind-set, a kind of black pit where evidence, based on *nothing*, mushroomed in the dark. Even when she was not in the room, she could still get him.

But, unlike Mallory, Jack Coffey would not bank on anything quite this flimsy. He was for damn sure *not* going to alter the artist's sketch to shave a head he could not even see.

CHARLES BUTLER trailed Mallory into her favorite interrogation room, and this should have given him pause, though it was nothing like his own kitchen, no warmth, no charm to make a suspect less wary. It was all stainless steel with mechanized utensils like the computer that passed for a mutant coffeemaker. She was the antichrist of Luddites, but her brew *was* rather good. When they were seated at the table, she poured their coffee into brown ceramic mugs, and he took this as the warm-up for a deceptively cozy chat. He knew she would begin with casual conversation, something innocuous and only one rung above a comment on the weather.

"Picture Angie Quill as a kid hooker," she said, "a little girl getting raped every night by five or ten men."

Oh, a *gut-shot* warm-up.

She leaned toward him. "Or maybe just one man, a priest, her counselor, someone who's supposed to protect kids like her. She's only thirteen years old. She's got no way out. I've heard of younger hookers slitting their wrists, but not this one. Angie Quill knows how to wait. Now imagine that little girl all grown up and full of hate. She tells this priest she wants to be a *nun*. Well, Angie can hang him out to dry. He knows it—and she works it. She forces him to get her into a monastery. Then she's off the street, out of reach. No one can ever touch her again. Better than that—she gets revenge. Every day that goes by, DuPont's going nuts. What's she confessing to the local priest? And what about the nuns in that monastery? How many people know what he's done to her—what he *is*—this man you *like* so much? The one you *protected, defended.*"

Charles dropped his head. He was helpless to—

"But that's not what happened," said Mallory.

On this cue of hers, his head jerked up.

"Did your good friend DuPont ever rape that girl? I guess we'll never know, Charles. He's such a damn liar—but he wasn't Angie's steady john."

When would this *end*?

"I had a little talk with the prioress of her monastery," said Mallory. "What she said backs up my theory that Angie had one regular customer for years. So . . . one day, she must've realized that her rent-money john was a pro, a hit man. If he ever found out what she knew, she'd be dead. Hookers are usually so good at reading men. They're better than you are at figuring out who's nuts, who's likely to go off on them—*cut* them—*kill* them. But here she is, sleeping with a killing machine. When she finally figures out what he is, it gives her the shakes. Cold-sweat fear. She knows she can't hide that from him. She *has* to run."

"Why wouldn't she go to the—"

"The police? Prostitutes are dirt to cops. So she went to Father DuPont for help. The monastery was *his* idea. That's the only way it all fits. I didn't just take the Reverend Mother's word for it."

Of course not. A trustworthy nun? Not on Mallory's planet.

She looked down at his coffee mug—cooling, untouched. "I could've sorted this out a lot earlier, wasted less time on the priest's lies."

He anticipated her final salvo before she said, "Maybe Jonah would be home by now . . . if you'd been straight with me."

And—*bang*—Charles was truly shot through the heart. He had done nothing wrong. Logic was not on her side. And yet he sat there calmly waiting to find out what his punishment would be. There would always be payback. Though the biblical quotation must be paraphrased to spell it out as such—*Vengeance is mine, sayeth Mallory.*

SO, LATE LAST NIGHT, she had been in here, too.

Jack Coffey set a mug of freshly made coffee on his desk beside an envelope addressed in Mallory's machine-perfect printing. It was marked for his eyes only, and this was rare. Normally, if she wanted case details kept secret, she just held out on everyone, even her own partner. Inside the envelope, all he found was a standard background check on members of the Quill family. *Standard* was the key word here. Any civilian could have gotten the same data by running a credit check, and there was nothing among these dry facts that could further the investigation.

But who had not already seen them? For days, these

pages had hung on open display in the incident room. What was the point of secrecy now?

He could not ask for enlightenment. Giving her that satisfaction would be like taking a direct hit in their never-ending boxing match.

Lieutenant Coffey smiled at his own private joke on her. It would destroy Mallory to know that, perverse as it might be, one of the high points of his job was going round and round with her. She had a fight style that fascinated him. His wins were few, but they got him through all the down days. So many times he had wanted to turn in his badge and gun, to bail on the political hell, the power plays and the squeeze of higher-ups—the crap side of his career. And then along came Mallory, and he would be up for a battle, *on* his toes and *back* in the fray. Most of the time, he wound up bloodied, beaten, and yet he reveled in it, and she always left him wanting more.

Following protocol, he locked her envelope in a desk drawer. Mallory's data of no significance continued to bother him, and he figured that was the object here. He *knew* how her mind worked. There had to be something in that envelope that he should have caught, some item that would make him feel foolish after she explained it to him.

A sucker punch.

Hours would pass before he realized that he had guessed wrong.

15

"Sorry, Miss. I've never seen him before." The owner of the bodega returned the tattoo artist's sketch to the detective. "But don't go. Not yet." While the old man worked a crank to lower an awning over his sidewalk flower stall, Mallory endured a lecture. His subject was roses.

He dipped into a silver bucket of water and fresh-cut flowers to pluck a red one from a cellophane-wrapped bouquet. "Take this rose, for instance. Commercial trash. No scent. Looks pretty for a day, and then it droops. But that little girl's roses? *Perfection.* Ah, my Angie." He blew a kiss up to the sky.

Upon their first meeting, he had not been told that Angie Quill was among the dead of Gracie Mansion, and now, days later, he was deep into grief. His eyes were shot with red from long crying jags, and he looked to be on the verge of one now. The elderly man was also moving more slowly this time, his face fixed in an expression of sad surprise. She recognized it from other homicides, that look that asked of everyone he met, *How could she be dead?*

For the first time in this case, Mallory said the customary words that were normally reserved for family members, "I'm sorry for your loss."

He thanked her and held out the rose—a gift. "A bribe. Don't forget my Angie. You find the one who killed her."

"I'm working on it, but Angie changes with everyone we talk to. It's like she was three different people. So . . . you were close."

"I watched her grow up. If you hear things about her on this street—dirty things—pay no attention. She was a wonderful kid—sunny, happy. But then later . . . I think she was maybe twelve or thirteen. . . . Well, next thing I know, she's lugging a baby around everywhere she goes."

"Her nephew."

"My Angie stopped being a little girl that year. You could see it in her eyes. Like she was my age, looking back at life the way it used to be. Kids, they're always looking for what's up ahead, but not her. It killed me to see that happen . . . but I can't blame Jonah."

More likely he blamed her baby-hooker life. He *knew* what that girl was—he knew a lot. "Did you ever picture her growing up to be a nun?"

"Never. When I saw her in that nun's habit, I couldn't believe it. I still don't. Kids raised by religious freaks, they go the other way. And nobody's got more reason to hate God than my Angie."

So he could tell her more, but never would he volunteer any stain on that girl's memory. The old man was so vulnerable right this minute, showing her his underbelly, exposing his heart for her best shot, and this could be such easy short work. But instead of laying him open and making him cry, Mallory held up his rose, nodded her thanks and moved on down the sidewalk.

* * *

"THE PUBLIC STILL THINKS we're dealing with a spree killing," said Lieutenant Coffey. The better story of a serial killer kidnapping taxpayers and cutting out their hearts—this had not yet occurred to the very imaginative news media. "But that won't last long."

He stood behind the lectern in the incident room, addressing a squad of detectives slumped in their chairs. Half of them should be sleeping in the bunkroom down the hall.

Only one man was on his feet, and the tall psychologist's back was turned, his attention focused on the evidence pinned to the cork walls. Mallory had finally allowed Charles Butler full access to the case—except for the dry details she wanted locked away in a desk drawer.

Jack Coffey stared at an empty chair. Mallory was late.

"Between forensics and the autopsy reports," and one insane theory of the crime, "it looks like we're chasing a hit man." Well, that woke up one cop in the back.

Other detectives only stared at their boss in disbelief, none of them wanting to buy into the idea of a contract killer, a pro. If this was true, they stood a better chance at catching lightning in a pisspot.

Lonahan's voice boomed from the back of the room, where he had been napping. "You mean a hit man gone nuts, right?" He seemed to like this idea for good reason. It might give them an edge. Lunatics were easier to bag.

"Good logic," said Coffey. "But, no, that's not it." And now, since Mallory was a no-show, he presented her theory. "A serial killer may have hired a hit man for the wetwork." At this point, no lynch mob was forming among the ranks, but maybe they were only too tired to fetch a rope. "So we'll start with the hit man's client."

His eyes were on two empty chairs, side by side. Riker was on Granny duty, but where the hell was his partner?

RIKER STOOD on a Brooklyn sidewalk not far from where he had grown up. This location had been his own suggestion. It was not on the NYPD list of safe houses. It was safer.

He smoked a cigarette and read the writing on the tall gray walls of stone. The graffiti gave no passersby a clue that nuns were cloistered here. No one in this neighborhood had ever seen one. Aside from delivery people, visitors were rare, though the way had been paved for one very special, very crazy houseguest.

There were no worries for Harold Quill's safety. He slept in the station-house crib, surrounded by detectives on bunk beds, and he had become so shabby and in need of a shave, he was beginning to look like them. His weird mother had been the problem, refusing to go anywhere with the men sent to fetch her.

But the batty religious fanatic *liked* Mallory. Go figure.

And the old lady had gone for the bait of a hideout with more crucifixes, rosaries and candles than she could fit in her East Village apartment. Then all that had remained to Mallory was to hold a gun to the head of an elderly priest, who had closed this deal with the mother superior for a bed with the Brooklyn nuns.

The door in the convent wall swung open, and Father Brenner escorted Mrs. Quill to the waiting car. Her insane majesty was ushered into the backseat, and the white-haired priest rode up front with Riker. Father Brenner was anxious, nerves shot, though, apart from dropping the old lady off at the door and collecting her again, he had ridden shotgun during their comings and goings.

So much damage from so little contact.

As they pulled away from the curb, Riker glanced back at the convent, wondering what kind of shape the nuns were in this morning.

WHERE THE HELL WAS MALLORY? She had promised a profile of the investor crowd, her pool of likely suspects for a hit man's client.

Jack Coffey's attention was called to the back of the room, where the civilian in the three-piece suit raised his hand to volunteer. *Damn Mallory.* She had fobbed off this duty on her pet shrink, a bad choice, considering all these catnapping cops.

"Okay, Charles, can you brief us on a Wall Street kind of perp?"

"Of course." As the obliging psychologist walked toward the front of the room, he said to the surrounding detectives, "Money makes people mean. The sudden loss of money makes them *crazy* mean."

In his role as a police consultant, Charles Butler did not usually deliver lectures with such punchy opening lines, and this spoke to coaching from Mallory.

The lieutenant surrendered the lectern to this speaker best known for lulling his audience to sleep. And Charles said to the gathering, "I can't even give you an age range. As you all know, criminal profiling is largely junk science."

That was a crowd-pleaser. The men were happy to

know that voodoo would be kept to a minimum this morning. Personally, they liked the man. Professionally, they spat on all of his kind. But when Charles held up a sheet of paper and announced that Mallory's list had only ten suspects, the detectives came back to life, eyes open all around the room. *Now* they were getting somewhere.

"I have a few markers that might be helpful in singling one out," said Charles, "Hiring killers is done all the time in every economic group—by husbands, wives, even their offspring. Frequently, it's a low-level connection. A bartender knows somebody who knows somebody. It might also be a family member in need of quick cash, or any acquaintance with a criminal record who'll do the job on the cheap. These amateurs usually get caught. And so do the people who hire them."

Trouble. Charles had gone off Mallory's script to brief detectives on their own store of information. He was in danger of losing these tired men to comas. And so Jack Coffey called out to him, "But this time it's different, right?"

"Oh, yes," said Charles. "Sorry. I only wanted to make the point that *your* suspect is willing to pay a lot more so he can distance himself from the killing. It's a pattern with him. You see it carried out in the randomness of the victims and their far-flung neighborhoods. None of those deaths will ever tie back to him or the mayor. You can stop looking for those connections."

The men were nodding, agreeable to chopping routine hours off this chase.

"Hiring a professional killer leaves less chance of things going awry. And you can count on a third party to broker the murders. The middleman and the hit man might live out of state. *More* distance from the crimes."

Oh, if only Charles knew when to stop. They already understood why a pro was hell to catch.

"All ten suspects lost fortunes in a high-risk venture. We might extend that trait to other forms of high-stakes gambling and a tie to bookmakers. Or, given market losses in the millions, the suspect may owe large sums to loan sharks. He's likely done business with *someone* who had access to your hit man. Andrew Polk was the stockbroker who engineered crippling losses for your suspects, and the government *could* back that up, but I doubt that they're so inclined."

Whoa! Where did that come from? Not the sketchy SEC document. And now Jack Coffey knew why Mallory was supplying information via ventriloquism. She was another one who liked some distance from bad acts.

Charles held up the suspect list. "These ten people have more than enough money left to cover the hit man's fees. Given the . . . extra work . . . the kidnapping, the mutilation, delivering hearts and corpses and such, you can figure each murder at approximately a hundred thousand dollars."

The lieutenant could almost see Mallory with her calculator, coolly cost-estimating the time and trouble of cutting out a human heart—times four.

Detective Washington stood up. "So we're lookin' at bank withdrawals, stock liquidation, stuff like that . . . to cover a *hit man's* payoff." His sarcasm begged the question: *Isn't that just too damn easy? Oh, yeah, and hasn't Mallory already hacked into the suspects' accounts?*

"You needn't waste time on that," said Charles. "Too many ways to separate oneself from offshore assets. Names become just numbers on a spreadsheet in a foreign bank."

So . . . the short answer would be *yes,* Mallory had already looked into that. Satisfied, Washington sat down.

"And that does it for the investor who paid for the murders. Now we move on to the hit man." Charles held up the tattoo artist's drawing. "An efficient killing machine . . . up to a point. He *can* be rattled. He made a mistake murdering the nun instead of his intended target. Then there's the highly publicized drowning of Mr. Costello. And stealing a child? Huge blunder. Your hit man is under enormous pressure. Too many errors. You *know* he's unraveling."

"Then it's over." Gonzales, the house skeptic, rose from his chair. "When a job goes sour, the pro goes underground. There won't be any ransom demand for Jonah. No heart this time, either. The hit man's a million miles from here, and we'll never find that kid's body. You gotta know Jonah's dead."

Backfire! *Oh, Mother, make up my bed and turn out the lights.*

The other detectives could fill in the rest—every last shot at catching the hit man in one more screwup was gone. They all had a dead-end look about them. But, after the first forty-eight hours had passed, who among them had held out any hope for Jonah?

"I have good reason to believe that child is alive," said Charles.

Well, that was not from Mallory's cheat sheet of lecture notes. She knew better.

ONLY ONE LOCK out of three required finessing. When Jonah had gone missing, his security-conscious uncle must have left home in a hurry. Mallory saw no blinking lights on the wall panel by the front door. Harold Quill had not even taken time to set the alarm. Daylight penetrated the draperies enough to see her way across the front room of upscale furnishings and deep-pile carpet.

She walked down a hallway and stopped by the open door of a bedroom. Discarded jeans lay on the floor. A sneaker here, a child-size T-shirt there. An unmade bed. She approved of the state-of-the-art audio equipment and speakers. The shelves held thick books with raised dots of braille on the spines, and a computer sat on the desk. Detectives from this Upper East Side precinct had already passed along the store of files, kid stuff, nothing useful. But the laptop should have been confiscated. Something new might have come in. She tapped the power button. The screen glowed, and voice-recognition software responded, "Hello, Jonah."

When Mallory said, "Email," an argument ensued between the detective and the robotic voice that did not recognize her as one of its people. And so she killed it. After tapping in a change of settings, she stole into the boy's mail the old-fashioned way and found nothing recent apart from ads and one short love letter from Lucinda: "If you die on me I'll KILL YOU." Unlike everyone else on the contact list, this little girl held out hope that the boy might log in—any minute, any second now—to read his messages, but Jonah was gone.

Dead and gone.

"THE BOY'S ALIVE. *Please* hear me out." The psychologist had fallen into the begging mode. "There's something very personal in the nun's murder. That's how you'll catch the killer. She's your tie to the hit man."

Jack Coffey was willing to believe that last part, but the boy was certainly dead, and every face in this crowd said so.

"The nun's likeness to her nephew is so strong," said Charles. "That may be why he stole Jonah. Nothing else fits quite so well."

Poor guy. He was sagging, dragging now. He must realize that he had lost credibility with his audience of detectives. All those sorry eyes. *Pity* from *cops.*

"You read the autopsy reports," said the man who did *not* know when to quit. "You know the killer kept some of those victims alive for days."

"Not the nun," said Gonzales the Doubter.

"No, she was the anomaly, a mistake. So look at the broad scheme. Such a public exposure of the murders. From the beginning, the hit man was on board with publicity—lots of it. And now the whole city's on a first-name basis with Jonah. They're all captivated by a *living* boy, and they want him brought home alive. And I know that's what you want. Some of you have children of your own."

Yeah, a lot of these men were fathers. Well, that part was pure Mallory, pulling heartstrings by remote control.

Cheap shot.

Well placed.

"The tension is building by the minute," said Charles. "The news media's keeping a round-the-clock vigil on the mayor. Andrew Polk's on every TV channel, millions of watchers. He can't step outside the mansion without facing the mob. The pressure's rising. It's over the moon. Could anything be more irresistible to the hit man's client? You have to know he doesn't want Jonah killed. *He hasn't gotten paid yet!*"

Gonzales was about to stand again, but thought better

of it. Maybe he didn't want to bludgeon the man at the lectern. Or was this detective weakening? He had two kids at home.

"Never underestimate the power of greed," said Charles Butler. "People *will* make stupendous gambles for the love of money. They'll bet on a big win, *knowing* it's just too good to be true. And then they grieve for the money they lose. Look at what one of Polk's victims has done to get it back. Can you really see him giving up something so precious—worth so much money?"

Charles had ceased to be boring. Mallory must have written that closing shot. Greed was her favorite call for every criminal act on the books. But this idea that avarice would save the boy—these men would never have bought that spiel from Mallory. And she would never have begged them to believe in her.

The lieutenant walked among the seated detectives, passing out copies of the tattoo artist's drawing, and he noticed a change in his men. Kudos to the shrink in the nice suit. Charles had created doubts among these cops in slept-in clothes, who traded glances with no roll to the eyes. In twos and threes, they got up from their chairs and marched out the door to hunt for Jonah, all of them believing that the boy *might* be alive.

But not Jack Coffey.

The plea had come from Charles Butler's heart, genuine—and not. This man had been infected with a Mallory pathology, generating theory from spit. And though Charles could only have spoken to truth, it was a Mallory kind of a lie. What better way to refuel these exhausted cops than to dangle the beating heart of a living child?

She had only wanted fresh horses.

Well, she got them.

* * *

RIKER WAS ENJOYING a quiet time-out from Mrs. Quill's ministry of religious rants and grievances against whores she had known and raised. A civilian aide had volunteered to guide the old crone to a restroom, where she might drown in some freak toilet-bowl accident—if there *was* a God. Though not a churchgoing kind of a cop, he liked his odds.

The detective's moment of perfect peace was ruined by the sight of Charles Butler leaving the lieutenant's office. So much was on display in that poor bastard's expression as he crossed the squad room to Riker's desk. The psychologist folded his tall body into the visitor's chair and slumped there, his face stuck in a comical look of surprise, like a giant frog poked in the eye—by Mallory, though she was miles way.

Jack Coffey must have ratted her out.

Only seconds after "Hello," Charles asked the predictable question in the tone of *Say it ain't so.* "Mallory believes the boy is *dead?*"

Riker nodded. "Her and every other cop on the squad—till you tuned 'em up for us. And thanks for that."

"She *played* me?"

"What a world, huh?" The detective killed off a smile in the making. Charles was also known as the Man Who Loved Mallory, and her playgroup of friends was not extensive, not if he discounted her machines. So now it fell to Riker, this chore of mopping up after his partner's carnage. "You know her history with hookers."

When Kathy Mallory had been much smaller and more feral, a homeless child whose theme song was "Gimme Shelter," she had milked prostitutes for money, food and even a roof when she needed one. Crafty little kid, she had chosen hookers as the only patsies who would not give her up to social workers. And she had played those women, taking them for all she could get.

"One of the hookers even fenced the kid's stolen goods. Kathy was a *great* street thief." Whenever the late Lou Markowitz had spoken of his foster daughter's felony childhood, he had been damn near bragging. And Charles had been the old man's friend, his best listener. He would have heard many a story, but only bare bones, nothing that stank or bled.

"By the time Kathy was ten years old, she'd been to school on whores—the *stink* of whores. The cum from the johns on their skin and their skirts. The vomit when they were dope-sick or drunk. . . . What hookers smelled like when they were three days dead, ripe and gassy. So you'll excuse her for not buyin' into that pretty story of a whore who *saw* the light, *found* the Lord and turned into a damn *nun*. But here's how really twisted Mallory is. . . . She doesn't give a shit about nuns. Take 'em all out back and shoot 'em—she won't mind. But the second she saw Angie Quill's old rap sheet for prostitution? Mallory was on *her* side. Mallory's the engine on this case, not Jack Coffey. *She* drives it. Whatever it takes, she's gonna get the freak who cut out Angie's heart."

Almost done, Riker splayed his hands and shrugged. "So she played you, *lied* to you. Why do you care if she's on the side of the angels . . . or the side of the whores?"

MALLORY MOVED ON to Harold Quill's bedroom, lit by airshaft windows, shadowy—and so she knew that the man loved the boy. For no sane reason, this fool had given up the better light of the *blind* boy's room around the corner, where the sun shone for nobody.

The other contrast was the adult neatness here, everything in its place, her guarantee of a quick search. This was where she would find all the hidey-holes that civilians thought were so clever. The wall safe behind a hinged bureau mirror was a disappointment, holding only valuables. More promising loose floorboards were in the predictable place under the only scatter rug.

The hole in the floor held a gun.

This was a surprise, and not just because the Upper East Side squad had failed to note it in their report on the search of this apartment. Perhaps they had seen a homeowner's weapon as all too common a thing, one with no relevance to their case of a kidnapped child. Stashed alongside the gun was the paperwork for purchase and registration. It was dated to the year Angie Quill had entered the monastery.

What else had that local squad left out of their report?

Mallory opened the closet. Given the neat spacing of clothing grouped by color and the regimented placement of shoes on the floor, she could tell that the messy upper shelf had already been ransacked by other detectives. When all the contents of that shelf had been pulled down, she held an ordinary shoebox in her hand, and the moment she lifted the lid, its importance was obvious. Yet this was something else found unworthy of mention by local cops, who had not even bothered to write a damn line about a hidden gun—an item that said the homeowner was not just scared, but very secretive about his fear.

She returned to the front room and pulled the cord for the drapes that spanned one wall. Beyond the glass, the balcony was at least twenty feet wide and filled with mature rosebushes growing in large ceramic pots and long wooden troughs. Mallory recalled a tossed-off line from the prioress in the confessional, an afterthought of her dead nun: *Everywhere she goes, the roses grow.*

The detective sat down on the floor and, by this better light, spread the contents of the shoebox across the rug. One old photograph instantly had her attention.

And held it.

With no idea of how much time was passing, Mallory was lost in two dimensions of glossy black and white.

16

Harold Quill was officially in protective custody, but no one had found it necessary to apprise him of this.

Days ago, he had ceased to haunt his own Upper East Side precinct, and now he was a round-the-clock guest of the SoHo station house. Given a shower in the downstairs locker room, he smelled better today, and a clean sweat suit had been found to fit him. But he was still unshaven. Razors were too difficult to manage just yet. The poor rich man, with no coins for the snack machine, had been fed from deli bags, and he was always wide-eyed, jazzed on cophouse coffee.

With no knock on the door, he entered the lieutenant's private office, lured there by the glow of the television set. Ignoring the man behind the desk, Quill pulled up a chair in front of the screen and flicked through the channels. Apparently, even zombies could work a remote control.

It was always a mistake to let him watch TV, but Jack Coffey never sent him away.

Quill found a channel for what passed as network news, and today's guest for bullshit and coffee was a fiction writer touted as an expert on kidnapped children.

This was not a great improvement over the star of an FBI shoot-'em-up movie, who had appeared in yesterday's segment as the voice of law enforcement.

The lieutenant turned to face his second visitor. *Finally,* Mallory had decided to put in an appearance. She stood in the open doorway, holding a shoebox in her hands and staring at the back of Quill's head. Clearly, she wanted that man squashed underfoot and swept out like a bug.

Something had changed.

What was in that box? The lieutenant would not ask, in hopes that his lack of interest would spoil her fun. Without a word said, *no* explanation for showing up late to work, she turned and walked back to her desk in the squad room, where she handed the shoebox off to Janos.

Quill looked away from the TV screen to ask, "It's true? The more time that passes, the less chance I've got of getting Jonah back?"

Yes, the idiot onscreen had gotten that part right, but Jack Coffey said, "He's full of shit," and that was also true. "Sometimes years go by and the kids come back." Every rare once in a while, such things did happen, but this time there could be no happy ending.

Harold Quill was suddenly drawn to the window that looked out on the squad room. Coffey followed the track of the man's startled eyes to see Father DuPont carrying a suitcase toward Mallory's desk.

"You know that priest, right?"

"No, I've never seen him before." Quill turned back to the TV set, missing the surprise on the lieutenant's face.

Maybe it was not in the nature of zombies to tell convincing lies.

* * *

FATHER DUPONT set his suitcase on the floor. "I've been reassigned to a little town in North Dakota. I'm told the Catholics are wildly outnumbered by buffalo. . . . Can I *stand* the excitement?"

"So you screwed up," said Mallory.

"I did." Yet he smiled as he sat down in the visitor's chair. "Cardinal Rice seems a bit fuzzy about granting permission for the nuns to leave their monastery. Also, he can't recall slighting their bishop, leaving him out of the chain of command. That caused a few hard feelings between them. And the cardinal has no memory of chartering a bus to bring the nuns to the city, but he did authorize me to pay the bill . . . as my last act in his service."

"I was wrong about you," said Mallory. "You never had the makings of a good con artist."

"My father was terrible at it. He got caught, too. Dad went to prison when I was a kid . . . but I'm sure you already knew that."

She did. "Even the prioress was onto you, but I don't think she ratted you out." Mallory had dug his pit for him, but he had fallen in without so much as a push. Like father, like son. She had counted on incompetence, knowing from the onset that this scheme could end no other way.

"Well, Detective, was the prioress at all helpful?"

"Yes. Now I'm damn sure our killer was a john from Angie's hooker days. . . . But you already *knew* that."

During her time in the confessional, the prioress had not been able to supply anything as useful as a name or address. Angie Quill had never given up details like that—

or how the dangerous man in her life made his living. But the girl would have told everything to this priest. And, *still,* DuPont would give up nothing helpful.

Bastard.

"What's left of Angie's family . . . I'll keep them safe," she said. A deal was a deal: a promise of protection in exchange for the no-questions-asked delivery of a prioress.

That must have been an interesting ethical dilemma for a priest. He *had* to know why she wanted to get at that old woman outside the shelter of monastery walls: The prioress might say what he could not. And Mallory could have tortured that frail nun all night long if she had wanted to—while the priest's vows remained unbroken. *That* was integrity? No, and they both knew it. And the prioress—she knew it, too.

"Do you think the boy's still alive?" Quiet seconds later, Father DuPont was subdued by the understanding that, if he anticipated hope—from *her*—he would wait forever. He rose from the chair and picked up his suitcase.

They were done.

And he was off to do penance among the buffalo.

JANOS ENTERED the interrogation room with the shoebox found hidden in Harold Quill's closet. He removed the lid to show the man what was inside, and asked, "You got any more of these stashed away?"

Surprised, Harold Quill shook his head. "No, that's all I have left. I hid them under my mattress when I was a kid—so my mother couldn't butcher them. They were *mine.*" He reached out for the stolen shoebox, but Janos set it down on the other side of the table.

Were the contents still precious to Quill, or did the man understand what this covert stash of family snapshots said to the police? "So you were the family photographer, huh?"

Quill nodded and resumed his study of the other photographs, the ones in the album retrieved from his mother's apartment. He turned the pages of mutilated faces stabbed away with scissors and knives. "Crazy old woman. I was lucky to save anything." He pointed to a figure in the background of one picture. "This guy used to follow Angie around the neighborhood. She called him her puppy." He glanced at the tattoo artist's sketch of their suspect. "But he was nothing like that guy."

Janos doubted that they would identify Angie's steady customer this way. The squad had counted on Mallory to beat the living crap out of that priest until he gave up what he knew, but evidently she was off her stride. And so, on to the fallback game, the torture of Uncle Harry. Janos had been looking forward to this. "Mallory says you got lots of photographs on your walls. Mostly pictures of you and the kid. All the shots of your sister were hidden in the closet."

Quill kept turning album pages, pretending not to hear this.

Janos emptied the shoebox on the table and sorted the loose photographs into a timeline. Every face was still intact, rescued from Mrs. Quill's knife work. In one sidewalk shot, a schoolgirl posed with a baby in her arms. By the age of the nephew, he knew this was a portrait of Angie at thirteen. She looked so tired. Was she already selling her body on the street? A very pretty kid. In the background, the eyes of grown men were fixed on her. The little nephew figured in most of the pictures. By

Christmas trees and haircuts and tricycle rides, the boy grew inches taller, shot to shot, too heavy for her to carry anymore. He would have been five years old when the backdrop of St. Marks Place disappeared from the shots. Two more years were pictured here before his aunt vanished from the family photos, and Jonah posed alone.

"I don't see any pictures of the monastery here." Janos's face expressed curiosity, though he already knew the answer when he asked, "Maybe you got some on your phone or your laptop?" Mallory had already checked the man's electronic picture galleries and come up dry. "I looked at the nuns' website. I know they got visiting days. You took the kid up there to visit his aunt, right?"

Uncle Harry, the camera bug, had recorded every missing baby tooth and even Jonah's visits to the dentist. Yet now the man looked up at him, dumbstruck at first, as if this absence of monastery photographs might be hard to explain. "Well, we only went up there around the holidays."

Yeah, sure you did.

"Funny thing," said the detective, "I talked to Jonah's friends. They didn't know his aunt was a nun. They didn't know he *had* an aunt. You told your nephew not to tell anybody. Is that right?"

Quill squirmed.

Janos leaned across the table. "That was your scary little secret for years, wasn't it? You knew about that hit man all along. But you don't tell *us*? Do you know how stupid that is?"

FATHER DUPONT sat at the airport bar, drinking a glass of wine. While awaiting the boarding call for his plane to North Dakota, he knitted an imaginary hair shirt as a component to self-flagellation.

He had known that girl for years, and he had never known her at all.

Who *was* Angie Quill?

She had acted her age only one time—for the cop who had brought her in for that first counseling session. As the officer was leaving, pulling the door shut behind him, her childlike affect had slipped away. That first time alone with her, what the priest remembered best were her full lips. Wet. Licked in anticipation. What did he have that she might want? And she had given him a knowing smile that day, a hooker's understanding of what any man might want in return.

For their next meeting, Angie had brought Jonah along as her living proof of hooking for day-care money, and all her words had been softly couched in kindness, no tones or looks of seduction that might taint the infant on her lap. He could still see her wearing that Madonna face of motherlove.

On days reserved for family counseling, Angie's mother had never bothered to appear. But the brother had shown up once, a bit late and sullen, a generic teenager. Though Harry was the older sibling, he had minded Angie in matters of cussing and sitting up straight in his chair. She had been Harry's drill sergeant of good manners that included a thank-you to the priest for scholarship money.

She had been someone else again, another stranger, when she opened the door for his home visit, his interview with the monstrous Mrs. Quill. Angie had played asylum-keeper that day, so skillful at ducking smacks and thrown objects, diverting the religious zealot's tantrums into sane responses for the priest's questionnaire. His mission that afternoon had been to determine the fitness of the home.

Father DuPont winced, drained his glass, and asked the bartender for another.

Angie's survival had depended on splitting herself into fraudulent pieces—like the time he had appeared with her in court to request that another arrest for prostitution be set aside. That time, she was fifteen years old and acting the part of the clean-scrubbed young penitent, a winning act for the judge.

Poor fractured baby, going nowhere on a carousel of ever-changing personalities. Had there been even *one* that she could have called her own?

It would not be the persona that she had created for her interview at the monastery. That day, her face had been radiant with false piety. Years of reports from the prioress had yielded nothing but praise for the young acolyte, and so he knew that Angie had been stuck with that face until—

She must have been so tired when she died.

MALLORY ENTERED the interrogation room and settled into a chair beside Janos. Eyes fixed on Harold Quill and faking curiosity, she said, "If word got out that Father DuPont knew about the hit man, he'd be dead, right? That's why you lied to Lieutenant Coffey—told him you'd never seen that priest before? You were protecting DuPont?"

This gave Quill a plausible out, but he only sat there shaking his head, playing the baffled idiot who knew nothing of priests or hired killers.

And that was going to stop. *Right now.*

"When your sister was in the monastery, she had one family visit. *One* . . . in five years." Mallory banged her fist on the table, just to see the man jump, and he did. "Everybody lies to us! You *want* your nephew to die!"

"No! God, no. When Angie said she was going to be a nun, I-I—"

"You didn't believe her," said Detective Janos. "Because she was scared? Maybe packing her bags on the fly?"

"Yes. . . . What was I supposed to think? After my sister left, months went by. No letters, no phone calls. I knew she was still tight with the priest, so I went to Father DuPont. I told him I'd tear down the whole damn church if he didn't tell me where she was. He wouldn't say anything, but he made a phone call. And then he drove me and Jonah upstate to the monastery."

"So Angie could tell you not to shoot off your mouth anymore," said Janos.

"Yes, but not in front of Jonah. She put it all in a letter. I had to read it and give it back to her before we left. That's how scared she was. So . . . no more visits. That was *her* idea. We moved after that, me and Jonah, when I came into money. Nicer building. Good security." His voice cracked. "We should've left New York. Maybe left the country. It's all my—"

"Never mind that," said Mallory, all her anger switched off as a reward. "What else can you tell us about Angie's—"

"Did my son tell you she was a *whore?*"

Harold Quill turned to the door as Riker escorted his mother into the room. "Shut your goddamn mouth! She put *food* on your *table!*"

"And she earned the money on her *back*, legs in the

air." The harpy's loud laughter finally tapered off into giggles and coughs. "Oh, Lord," she said. Out of breath now, Mrs. Quill graced her son with a malevolent smile. "My *daughter* . . . the *nun.*"

Her laughter erupted again. The fun just went on and on.

JACK COFFEY turned to Charles Butler, who sat beside him in the watchers' room. "Mallory says Mrs. Quill is bat-shit crazy."

"Based on what? A lack of maternal instinct? Did you know that researchers believe they've isolated a mommy gene? It's triggered by ER alpha waves in the preoptic area of the brain. A genetic marker for good parenting—in *mice.*"

"Okay, Mrs. Quill has no mommy gene." The lieutenant made a rolling motion with one hand, silently begging this man to get *on* with it. "And?"

"And neither is she a mouse. So far, I'd say she's just . . . ugly mother material."

"HELLO, DEARIE." Mrs. Quill sat down in the chair beside Mallory's, singling out the young detective as the one best liked in this company, which included her son. "What can I do for you?"

"We have some pictures for you to look at." Mallory arranged a slew of old sidewalk photographs into a neat display, *too* neat, each one perfectly aligned and equidistant from surrounding shots. She did this as fast as her partner could deal from a deck of cards.

Riker knew a ruler would tell him that the first row of

photos were lined up exactly an inch from the edge of the table. Was Mallory even aware of doing things like this? At times, he thought it might be a parlor trick, played to a purpose—like now. He could see that Detective Janos was suppressing an urge to applaud, but he was also spooked by her, and so was the crazy lady's son.

Mallory invited Mrs. Quill to look over these old pictures in a spread of years on St. Marks Place. "Tell me what you can about the faces in the background. Just the boys and men."

Mrs. Quill's hand moved across the display, fingers spider-walking, and then she clutched one photo. "This boy—he *wanted* her. You can see it in his eyes." She pointed an accusing finger at another snapshot. "And that man there? Pervert. You *know* what he was thinking. Angie, too. That *slut*. That *whore*." Her son laid down his head on folded arms, and she said to him, "Oh, poor thing. Tell the nice police lady you had no idea how Angie bought you that fancy education. Spreading her legs for every damn—"

"Enough!" Harold Quill stood up too fast, knocking over his chair and jolting the table. "Okay, Mom. Why don't I tell them what you did to Jonah." He turned to Riker. "Mom favored old-fashioned diapers. She liked the *pins*—the *screams*. Angie and me, we couldn't watch the baby every minute."

Riker nodded. "So you needed somebody else to change Jonah's diapers when your kids were in school." And Angie had worked the streets to pay for it. Was that how it started?

"You're a smoker, Mrs. Quill?" Mallory opened a dog-eared file, and a photograph lay on top of the city paperwork. Riker and Janos stared at the five-by-ten image of a little boy with marks on his back in the shape of a cross. Each angry red sore was the size of a lit cigarette. "That's your work?" By Mallory's tone of voice, she might be asking about the evil old bat's prowess in needlepoint.

Harold Quill answered for his mother. "Damn right. A social worker took that picture . . . so I could get custody of my nephew."

His mother leaned toward Mallory, speaking low, confidentially. "Nobody'd give little Jonah to Angie . . . 'cause she was a *whore.*" Grinning, she lowered her head to more closely admire the photograph—her handiwork on the skin of a five-year-old child. "Ah, Gabby's boy. The son of *another* godless slut." One finger traced the cross of cigarette burns in the picture, and her voice was so maddeningly reasonable when she said, "It had to be done."

Previously, it had never occurred to Riker that he might come to a point in life where he wanted to break a woman's teeth with his foot. He smiled at the monster and gently covered one of her hands with his own. "Take another look at the pictures, ma'am. See any more faces you know?"

MALLORY PRESSED THE PHOTOGRAPH of a tortured child to the one-way window. On the other side of the glass, Charles Butler could not look away as Lieutenant Coffey said, "The day it happened, Angie reported her mother. That picture was taken a few years before she went into the monastery."

"Why didn't Mrs. Quill go to jail?"

"The police never saw a complaint on Jonah. It was investigated by Child Protective Services. Maybe they figured the kid's grandmother was just too crazy to stand trial."

The door opened and Mallory walked in to sit down beside Charles, and he said to her, "Angie Quill probably saved her nephew's life."

"Don't." Her tone was a warning to pick his words carefully.

What had he done now?

"Angie was no saint, no hero," said Mallory. "She ran away to save her own life, and I don't blame her for that. But don't build her up, not to me." That was an order. "Angie was the family meal ticket. Mrs. Quill and Harry always knew where the money came from. The crazy mother's just more open about it."

Mallory stared at the window on the interrogation room, where mother and son sat in testy silence. "They might as well have pimped her out on a street corner. You think Angie's brother went up to that monastery because he was *worried* about her? No. He hadn't made his big pile yet—just a working stiff wage. His sister was probably paying the rent right up to the day she left town. That's what worried him—losing the meal ticket."

"His feelings for his nephew are genuine," said Charles. "All the pictures he took of Jonah—that's what doting parents do."

"Right," said Mallory. "The hell with Angie. I'm talking to myself here." And now, she only spoke to the glass window on the room next door. "That weasel *knew* his sister was hiding from a hit man. That's why he's been sticking close to the police. Not because he wanted updates on the nephew he loves so much. . . . He was scared, but he left his own mother hanging out in plain sight on St. Marks Place. What a *good* man. What a *decent*—"

"I only meant that not everyone has a money motive for—"

"Not your buddy, Father DuPont. He only wanted access to Angie. He should have had the kids taken away from that old bitch." She leaned toward the window and stared at the Quills. "Those two and the priest, I'd put them all away if I could."

"Father DuPont *told* you why he—"

"Yeah, he wanted to save the poor kids from the horrors of foster care."

"A very reasonable—"

"*Angie had two living parents!* . . . I knew that five minutes into my first interview with Mrs. Quill. Then I ran a trace on her ex-husband."

"The background check," said Jack Coffey. "That's standard. When a kid goes missing, we always look at family, the *whole* family. But the uptown cops didn't even know about the mother. Harry told them he was an orphan. He was afraid they'd give the old lady his address."

Mallory was accurately reading Charles's stricken face when she said, "You wonder if Angie's dad would've been a fit parent. . . . I'll never know. DuPont didn't even *try* to contact him when the kids were young—when the *sane* parent was still alive and sending support checks. You see . . . the father lived in Canada."

And DuPont would have lost his access to a little girl, the object of his obsession.

One bit of knowledge could be so—

Charles's head moved slowly side to side. What a sorry fool he had been. He well understood why Mallory had not trusted him with that detail, not after sensing his past association with DuPont. That night in the restaurant, he had played the role of the priest's apologist and defender.

He had unwittingly taken up sides with a man who had once been infatuated with a thirteen-year-old child—obsessed to the point of sabotaging any measure of childhood that might have remained to her.

And Mallory was the only paladin that Angie Quill ever had.

There were just a few moments to absorb all of this before Detective Lonahan entered the room to announce, "The investors are here."

"Good." Jack Coffey clapped Charles on the back. "*More* sick bastards. Ready?"

Charles turned his sad eyes to Mallory, but he only saw the back of her as the door was closing.

Well, what could he have said?

MALLORY HAD NOT been at her desk to receive a cry for help from an airport bar. She played the message left on her landline and listened to a recording of the priest's slurred words, his plaintive question, "Who *was* Angie Quill? You *know*, don't you?"

Yes, she did. And now she had DuPont's confession that he put no faith in the Sister Michael façade. The now famous portrait of the nun was still on the front page of every newspaper. Angie did seem at peace in that pose, but the same could be said of the dead.

The detective pulled an envelope from a drawer and addressed it in care of the New York Archdiocese so that it could be forwarded to the land of the buffalo. She slipped in a photograph that Harold Quill had saved from his mother's knives and scissors. Next, she penned a brief note to answer the priest's question.

The subject of the enclosed snapshot was a child, only

twelve years old, laughing for her photographer in the year before her life ceased to be worth living. Why Mallory had stolen it, she could not say. She was not inclined to keep souvenirs. But now there was a get-even use for it—even better than spending a bullet. This would only work on a man of conscience, schooled in guilt and drowning in it—*drunk* with it. And she was going to *kill* him with it. This was a version of Angie Quill that DuPont had never seen. It was a picture of a little girl who believed that she had something to look forward to.

The companion note in Mallory's neat script said, "This is who she was." No need to add a closing line to say, *Have fun in purgatory. Send postcards.*

After licking the seal of the envelope, she laughed. And Detective Janos, in passing, seemed to find that odd, but he was in the camp of those who believed that Mallory had no sense of humor.

17

The cobblestone street took on the flash and the bling of a red-carpet event with reporters and photographers, stretch limousines and town cars. As each luxury vehicle pulled up in front of the SoHo police station to disgorge passengers, the camera crews acted like lovesick groupies, and uniformed officers kept them from mobbing the murder suspects and their attorneys.

Once inside the station house, the lawyers were separated from their clients and herded into a waiting area on the ground floor. There they passed the time outshouting each other to be heard on cell phones. All of them remained standing, eschewing the hard wooden bench, where two felons sat handcuffed and scratching themselves, putting the uptown attorneys in fear of bedbugs and lice. Windows and doors were penetrated by screams of reporters demanding quotes from the officers outside as more news vans arrived to block traffic and drive a dozen horn-honkers wild. And this cacophony of street noise was chorus music for a naked schizophrenic, who slipped his keepers to run about the room, shouting Bible verses for the coming apocalypse.

Just another day at the zoo.

* * *

UPSTAIRS, THE ERSTWHILE CLIENTELE of Andrew Polk's defunct brokerage firm congregated in the more luxurious lunchroom, which boasted a vending machine, a half-size refrigerator and a microwave oven. More chairs were brought in for the investors and their spouses, but some preferred to stand in small conspiracies of twos and threes. A few of them stood by a window, pretending not to know one another as they whispered to the grimy glass. Others were seated around the small tables, and Charles Butler had one to himself. He could follow conversations on the other side of the room by expressions of puzzlement and hands raised in the gesture for asking, *Why*? And he could pin the moment when they discovered the common denominator of Andrew Polk. Discourse quickly died, and faces turned sour.

Between his own knowledge of personal acquaintances and Mallory's notes on the predilections of others, the majority of these people were hardly of good character, and so he was disturbed by the presence of Jonathan and Amanda Wright, who were deep into their retirement years. How had they landed here in such bad company?

These old friends of the family crossed the room to speak with him, to ask if he thought their former broker, Andrew Polk, was under some new investigation. Charles stood up to pull out a chair for Amanda, saying, "I'd rather not discuss it . . . if you don't mind." Even if he could lie without a blush, he would not deceive them.

"I don't blame you." Jonathan Wright sat down beside his wife. "Who wants to admit to losses like that, eh? So, tell me, Charles, how are your parents?"

Jonathan's wife gently rested one hand on the old

man's arm. "Charles's parents died a long time ago, dear." And her husband had attended both funerals. A moment later, Jonathan had also forgotten about his stock-market losses. He asked why they were all here—and *where* exactly were they? He was astonished to learn that this was a police station.

No doubt these symptoms of dementia had set in before Jonathan's introduction to Andrew Polk. Previously, this man had been an ultraconservative investor and a wealthy one, but now his wife informed Charles that they had been forced to decamp from their old apartment. With a promise to stop by for drinks one evening, Charles wrote down their new address, still a good address. "But we're renters now," said Amanda.

He already knew that their fortune, generations in the making, had been decimated in a single day of trading. Dotty old Jonathan must have been such easy prey for a con artist like Polk. But Charles's greatest concern was for Amanda, still so clear of mind, so aware of what had been done to them—and fearful of how this day might end. She wore a false smile. He thought she might cry.

Another Social Register blueblood sat down at the table. The atmosphere changed. The flesh crawled. Zelda Oxly's coal-black eyes fixed on Jonathan Wright, who retained enough of his sensibilities to recoil. And his wife, a woman of grace and good manners, refrained from making the sign of the cross as she led the old man away.

Now they were two, Charles and the Vampire of East Sixty-ninth Street.

Zelda did her best to live up to this legend begun on a playground when they were both ten years old. All these years later, at the age of forty, she was as unwrinkled as the undead; her lipstick and summer frock were her favorite color, that of freshly let blood; and her eyes still mesmerized in the sense that one dare not look away for fear of fangs to the neck. Still scary as hell.

Early into their conversation, she recalled the funerals of Charles's parents. "Lovely people." Zelda Oxly was not. Malicious lawsuits were the source of half her wealth. She seldom had legal grounds for litigation, but she always won. She had staying power for the drawn-out court battles and a knack for tying people's guts into knots. It was rumored that more than one of her victims had been killed by the stress.

In an all too obvious ploy to seek common ground with him, Zelda confessed to fantasies of a slow death for Mayor Polk, though she had less reason for spite than most of these people. According to Mallory, this woman was hardly down to her last million or two, and definitely not feeling the pinch of last season's designer shoes. Her detractors claimed that her handmade stilettos were fashioned to conceal cloven hooves, but Charles stuck with the bloodsucker analogy, a better fit.

However, she would not fit in with this crowd of bilked investors—not if he believed in Mallory's theory of hush money, and he did. He could never envision Zelda settling for restitution of losses at nickels and dimes to the dollar, not when she could sue. Litigation for a bad investment had not been an option for others, the ones who had ensnared themselves in a conspiracy of silence. But a lack of corroboration would never have stopped the vampire. Might a test of this idea raise a blush in his face to give up a bluff? No, he thought not. He was on sure ground when he looked about him, and then turned back to her. "Do the rest of them know about your out-of-court settlement with Polk? They only got a pittance. But *you*—"

When Zelda abruptly stood up, he had his answer. She must have signed her own agreement of silence. Only the forfeiture of a great deal of undeclared money would trump this opportunity to gloat. She left the table without another word, leaving no doubt that she had recovered all her stock losses. And so, though she met the standard for a sociopath who could cheerfully sanction the murder of innocents, Charles eliminated her as a suspect.

And now for the rest of this group, rather than weed out the least likely, one by one, Charles did his gardening en masse, cutting out those who showed anxiety. These people had broken federal laws and taken terrible risks to do it, but not all of them were comfortable with the risk of criminal acts.

He pulled out his pen to make a few notations and then folded his newspaper just before Riker entered the room. The detective paused at Charles's table, glanced at the names scrawled above the front-page headline and walked away.

Ten minutes later, the best candidates were called. Charles and three others were led down the hall to the interrogation room, where they were directed to take seats beneath sputtering tubes of fluorescent light and facing the wide mirror on the wall. Mallory sat alone on the other side of the table, her eyes cast down as she opened one of four manila file holders.

Among those voted most likely to hire out murder and mutilation was Susan Chase. The brunette had switched to a less expensive hair salon, so said Mallory's notes on this woman, and Ms. Chase was doing her own nails these days, but she was otherwise keeping up appearances at charity functions and other important network sites for investment bankers. She nodded to him, for that was the sum of their relationship, their only mode of congress in passing one another's tables in the dining room of the Harvard Club. He had intuited enough about her psyche to avoid any closer association. The banker had a bit of a slither to her walk, and his feelings for her were akin to a phobia of snakes.

The man seated next to her was Charles's age, but he looked ten years older, a side effect of excess in all things. Martin Gross's source of money was tied to his extreme good looks and the art of fleecing wealthy women, though his boyish charm had begun to sag at the jawline. But narcissism would never allow Gross to see any flaws as he admired himself in the mirror, a looking glass for him and a window for the watchers in the next room. The man straightened a tie that had gone out of fashion.

One thing Charles shared with Mallory was an eye for the sartorial faux pas.

In a bizarre psychological twist to financial reversals, those who still held multimillionaire status had made cutbacks in small areas of personal spending, which did not extend to limousine service. None of these people had arrived on a bus. And Mallory had ascertained that, like Susan Chase, Gross's credit rating was still triple A.

The third suspect was the anomaly. The heir to the Brox Mills fortune was two years out of Yale and still unemployed. He lived on credit, lacking sufficient funds to pay outstanding debts, never mind the cost of murder for hire. Yet he was spending freely and cutting back on nothing. He wore a suit of fine white linen with lines in the style of the season, and he owed his blond highlights to the salon where Mallory said he had bought his suntan as well.

Charles, a devout pacifist, wanted to smack this young man. But they had met before, and this was nothing new.

Only an urge. It would pass.

Dwayne Brox's head was held a bit higher than need be, and so he could not help but literally look down his aquiline nose at everyone present. And last, he took notice of Charles, an acquaintance of his late parents'. Brox nodded an acknowledgment and stared at the psychologist for too long with eyes that had ceased to recognize him anymore.

Unsettling? Oh, yes. Way past that.

Dress up an insect and style its hair, and there you are.

All three had a look of boredom about them, and this was not affectation; it fit their pathology, the need to fill time with stimulation. Quiet minutes dragged by as fingers fussed with items of clothing and hair. In a collective breach of self-absorption, furtive glances were cast in Mallory's direction.

The detective ignored them, only showing interest in the paperwork on the table. The suspects were invisible to her. And when two of them voiced grievances, she was deaf to them, outclassing them in utter disregard for her fellow man. Next came their silent appraisals and nodding approvals of her costly attire and tailoring. How confused this gang of sociopaths must be, for she was so obviously one of them—and *not*.

THOSE WHO HAD NOT been singled out for interrogation, the lunchroom escapees, stepped into limousines. Only Zelda Oxly waved off her own driver. She lingered on the sidewalk steps away from the entrance to the SoHo police station, waiting for the chosen four to emerge. Charles Butler was the first to come through the door. Ah, he saw her. His head inclined a bare inch in his idea of a bow, and then he turned toward the curb, maybe hoping to get away from her with that minor courtesy.

"Not so fast, Charles!"

He stopped on command. Such a gentleman. Even as a little boy he had always displayed good manners under torture. He turned around to show her a sad face of resignation.

"They let you go—and so quickly." She made a wide show of bared teeth, not *exactly* a smile, when she asked, "Were you the police mole . . . or the Judas goat?" As if she had already caught him in a lie, he blushed. "I pick . . . the *mole*," she said. "I'd bet my portfolio that you never invested with Andrew Polk. That firm was strictly for high-risk players, the kind who were *hoping* that Andrew was dirty. That's *so* not you, Charles." He walked away from her, and she called after him, "I'm *insulted* that I didn't make your list!"

After he had disappeared into the delicatessen across the street, Zelda remained near the door to the police station. Charles Butler was not the one she had wanted. She waited for the other one.

RIKER SAT DOWN beside Jack Coffey in the watchers' room, and he turned up the volume for the interrogation on the other side of the glass, where Susan Chase, tired of being ignored, had just demanded to know why Charles Butler was released.

"He's been cleared," said Mallory, without looking up

from her paperwork. "He had his accountant fax us five years of tax returns. No FBARs. We don't think he was hiding offshore assets."

Jack Coffey turned to the detective beside him. "No *what* bars?"

"*F*BARs," said Riker. "*F*, as in, you're fucked if you didn't report an offshore account. Mallory says, if these people wanted to hide Polk's hush money from the SEC—and they did—that cash had to spend at least six minutes in undeclared accounts."

"Why are they smiling at her?"

"They think cops are stupid. It also means their accounts were in countries with no U.S. tax treaties. By now that money's somewhere else, maybe three shell corporations removed from their names."

In the next room, Mallory was saying, "It's amazing how many ways there are to distance yourself from your money. Some are even close to legal. Offshore hedge funds, trusts. But let's say you had an offshore account of your own . . . and you lied about it. A lie to a federal agent—about *anything*—that's jail time. So before we invite the feds in," she said, as if that would ever happen, "would any of you like to volunteer undeclared assets? . . . No? . . . Your attorneys are still downstairs. Would anyone like to lawyer up?"

Three hands were raised.

In the watchers' room, Riker said, "That means everybody's dodgy."

"Okay," said Jack Coffey, "I'm losing the drift. Didn't the feds interview the investors?"

"Yeah, all of 'em, years ago."

"If they'd squeezed hard enough, one of them should've caved by now and implicated Polk."

"Well, the feds didn't try all that hard. Polk ran a sweet scam, smart as they come." Because Riker knew his boss played the ponies, he opted for racing parlance. "Say that old stock deal's a nag in the Derby, okay? Polk's been juicin' that horse to make it run real fast, and now it's a favorite to win. But him and his buddies at Banter Capital, they got long-shot bets against that win. So Polk's horse is outta the chute, and he tips off the feds on the fixed race. Then the government boys show up . . . and shoot that nag before it crosses the finish line."

"That's why the SEC let him skate with that settlement deal? He embarrassed the crap out of them?"

"Oh, yeah. He couldn't have done it *without* 'em. . . . Polk could only win with a dead horse."

THE LAWYERS FILED INTO the interrogation room to pair up with their clients, and the peepshow was over for Jack Coffey.

He walked down the hall to the incident room, where, only this morning, every bit of paper had been fixed to the cork in neat rows of perfect alignment. But now lopsided notes, photos and layered sheets of text gathered by the rest of the squad had spread around the walls. *Mallory's* walls. Oh, the horror. The lieutenant watched her move from one crooked sheet of paper to another, righting every wrong-hanging thing in her path.

Quiet, stealthy, he crept up behind her. "So the investors—where did that get us?"

Unsurprised, she never lost her momentum of pins and papers. "If Polk goes to jail for insider trading, those people go down, too. It's all about complicity in bad acts. He lied to the feds, but so did every—"

"I *got* that. And this ties to murder and kidnapping . . . *how?*"

"The hit man's client is using Polk's own playbook. If the perp goes down, he takes the mayor with him in a plea bargain. That was probably spelled out in the ransom demand."

Coffey nodded, as if this made sense—as if he did not plan to nail her for a money motive based on a probability shored up by a string of ifs. "So . . . *if* the killer is one of those investors, and *if* he gets caught hiring out the kills—"

"He—can—take—down—Andrew—Polk!" Her last pin was *stabbed* into the cork wall. "And *that's* how I know the hit man's client is one of the investors . . . because Polk doesn't *want* him caught."

Very nice—almost a perfect fit for the mayor's lies and lack of cooperation. *Almost.* The lieutenant tapped the picture of Dwayne Brox. "So what's *he* doing on the list? Polk can't be worried about this one. Riker told me Brox's parents were the only ones who could've signed the nondisclosure. And they're both dead. So their kid's got no leverage on Polk—unless Mom and Dad put a confession in writing. What are the odds on that?"

Riker joined them at the wall, maybe sensing that he was needed to referee. The giveaway clue would be the way his partner and the lieutenant were squaring off as Mallory said, "That logic only works if the mayor knows *which* investor's doing this to him. You think those ransom notes were *signed?* Give me *those* odds."

Good one. Totally humiliating. But Coffey was up for a counter-strike. "Even if everybody's got offshore accounts—what's *that* worth? Nothing. We'll never know if a ransom gets paid or who—"

"A ransom can't get paid that way." Mallory ever so slightly raised her eyebrows.

And he knew—HE KNEW—she was asking if he had given up all hope of shielding himself from her forays into other people's computers. This time, he would have to *agree* to be punched in the teeth. And so he said, "Okay, talk to me."

Riker wisely drifted away from this conversation.

Mallory picked up a glass jar from the evidence table and emptied more pins into her right hand, a lot of them, a messy nest of sharp points. "The feds still want to get Polk on *something,* tax evasion—anything at all. It's a vendetta with them. They watch every online keystroke he makes, every dollar he's got."

"But they can't track offshore—"

"Onshore, offshore—bank secrecy's eroding all over the planet. Polk cleaned out the hinky accounts years ago . . . and he *probably* mentioned that to his lawyer." She idly hefted the ball of sharp pins in her right hand, perhaps waiting for her boss to pursue the *probability* that she would know that for a fact.

No way in hell. He did *not* want to—

Mallory tightly fisted the hand that held the nest of stick-out pins. *Christ,* that had to hurt like mad. He could not tell by her face, and he could not tell her to *stop that.* He would not own up to being freaked out. But she knew it. She *loved* it. And she did have his focused attention, a guarantee that there would be no need to repeat herself one more time. She *hated* that.

"Polk's got the profits from his stock scam, all of it legally laundered and invested," she said, so calmly, as if she had not been stabbed at least forty times by the fisted pins. "Now the mayor's set for life, and the feds can't touch him. So he *could* open a new offshore account. That only takes twenty minutes, but—"

"If he moved a large chunk of cash, the feds would catch it." And they would have all the access numbers to follow that electronic breadcrumb trail. "The SEC might be real happy to share that with us."

"*Right.* And Polk knows he lives in the goldfish bowl."

Coffey cadged a quick look at her fist. No blood yet, but he half expected a pin to poke through her skin. "Then there's no way our perp can get his payoff from the mayor."

"Oh, I wouldn't say *that.*" And she would not say more. On this last tantalizing note, Mallory turned back to her work on the wall, jamming pins into paper and cork, so happy to leave him dangling.

She cheated! Those pins had never been in her fist. They rested, unbloodied, in the palm of her other hand.

His chance to wring her neck was lost as more detectives entered the room to see Mallory's improvements on the walls—and something new. One wide, insanely neat swath of paper had been added for the hit man. Two items had center place, the tattoo artist's sketch and a large map of New Jersey, though the carjacking of Elly Cathery was hardly proof of the hit man's home state.

Coffey stepped up to this patch of the wall to stand with Riker and two other men.

Lonahan was reading Mallory's profile notes. "Our guy smokes cigarettes?"

"Yeah," said Riker. "He policed his butts in Albert Costello's apartment." And when it looked like he was up for a challenge on this, he said, "The perp polished an ashtray, one ashtray out of ten. Costello never washed anything—ever."

"Okay, good enough," said Gonzales. "But what makes you think he owns a pit bull and a Jaguar?"

A sag to Riker's shoulders told all of them that his partner had held out on him.

"I got that from the monastery's prioress," said Mallory.

Jack Coffey did not recall that witness statement crossing his desk, and might there be a reason for that oversight? Should he ask Mallory how much ugly pressure it had taken to get that head nun to snitch on one of her own kind? No, perhaps not.

"The prioress told me a pit bull wandered onto the grounds. Very sweet dog. No aggression. Angie Quill was the only one to run away. She wouldn't go outside for days after that. Always at the windows. Watching the woods. Then the nuns got a call from the pit bull's owners, people on neighboring land. So the dog's still on the property, but now Angie thinks it's safe to go outside. . . . I say she *knew* our hit man, and the minute she saw that dog, she thought he'd found her."

Gonzales nodded to admit that this was strangely plausible. "And the Jaguar?"

"The nuns grow their own food. Not a little vegetable garden. A crop field. When Angie volunteered to run the tractor, she told them she learned to drive stick-shift in an old Jaguar. That gets more interesting if you know that Mrs. Quill and her son had no idea she could drive or where she'd get her hands on a car like that. Works nicely with a prostitute's steady customer. She'd never mention him, either."

"No way." Gonzales shook his head. "There's gotta be a million Jags in New Jersey." And, based on something so flimsy, he was sure as hell *not* going to—

"Pastrami on rye?"

Charles Butler walked in with a large brown paper bag from the delicatessen across the street, and Gonzales was distracted by the sandwich held out to him. As the deli bag was passed among the others, the psychologist mentioned running into an investor on the sidewalk, though not one from their shortlist. "Zelda Oxly all but confirmed Polk's scam. Actually, that's more of an inference drawn from—"

"Close enough," said Coffey. "We can use that to lean on her."

"I doubt it," said Charles. "Zelda's fearless beyond imagination. You have no idea how frightening that woman can be."

"Right," said Mallory, as if she might think that worth jotting down. "So, after talking to you, did this woman leave? Or did she hang out on the sidewalk, maybe waiting for someone else?"

"I HAVEN'T SEEN you since the funeral," said Zelda Oxly. But when Dwayne turned her way, he was looking beyond her or maybe around her, as if she merely blocked his line of vision. Weird—but he had always been an interesting little shit.

Young Brox stood at the center of his front room, one of seventeen. Zelda knew every detail of this apartment, the square footage and every amenity. The view was incomparable. She approached a wall of floor-to-ceiling window glass to admire the panorama of Central Park. At her feet, there were depressions in the rug that would fit the legs of a missing grand piano. On one plaster wall, large rectangular shapes of lighter paint had picture hooks at their centers. So Dwayne had sold his parents' art collection, too. And had he burned through all of their restitution money from Andrew Polk? Or was he simply at a loss as to how he might liquidate an offshore hedge fund?

She could help with that.

Zelda gave the young orphan a benevolent smile. "You're behind on your mortgage payments. Such a *big* mortgage. . . . I keep tabs. Did you know your father and I were in a bidding war for this apartment? When he lost all that money, I was rather hoping he'd put the place back on the market."

"So you dropped by to discuss real estate?"

"No, dear. I came to talk about the *unspeakable* things."

18

Zelda Oxly was in a rare good mood as she passed by the liveried doorman for Dwayne Brox's apartment building. Smiling broadly, she stood on the sidewalk and—

Ah, there he was. Her chauffeur, Leaman, waited by the rear door of the limousine, holding it open. There was no word of warning, and he would pay for that. She had one foot inside the car before she saw the uninvited passenger, a young woman who was too preoccupied with papers in hand to even acknowledge the *owner of the damn car!* Everything about this stranger spoke to money—even the designer blue jeans, dark blue, obviously dry-cleaned. And her hair—the cut was fabulous. Zelda made a mental note to get the name of the stylist.

But first, "Who the hell *are* you?"

The young blonde raised her face. Such cold eyes—electric green, *machine* green. The interloper reached out to tap the intercom below the wide panel of privacy glass.

Lovely manicure.

"Circle the block," said the blonde to the chauffeur, and though there was zero inflection in her voice, Leaman was all too eager to please her, pulling away from the curb on command. Turning back to Zelda, she said, "That's all the time I'm giving you. Once around the block." And now to answer the question of her identity, she pulled back her blazer to display a very large gun in a shoulder holster—a calling card of sorts.

"So you're a cop. And what should I call you?"

"Mallory, just Mallory." She handed over a sheet of paper. "So, Zelda—"

"*Miss* Oxly," she said, correcting the young— *Oh, bloody hell!* This was a copy of Andrew Polk's nondisclosure agreement. It was neither signed nor addressed, but—

"I'm sure Dwayne Brox has one of those sheets," said Mallory. "Part of his parents' estate. So it's not binding on him. That made Dwayne a weak link in the restitution deal. And that worried you, didn't it . . . *Zelda?*"

Yes, but no more.

Not until Mallory said, "But Brox isn't a problem now. When you came out of his building, you were just too pleased with yourself. Before his parents died, they didn't tell him anything about Polk's problem with the SEC, right? Nothing in writing?"

No, and even if Dwayne had read their nondisclosure agreement, it covered only a year of client conversations with his parents' broker—neatly protecting the one conversation that could hang Andrew Polk. So this cop was running a bluff based on nothing more than a satisfied smile after leaving Dwayne's company. What damage could this possibly—

Zelda's musings came to an abrupt end.

In answer to no question voiced aloud, the young mind reader said, "I've been going over Polk's old brokerage transactions. All those hinky tax dodges he told you were legal? . . . They're not. They're called Dodge by Custom. IRS customarily ignores them. You think that'll save you if you lie to me the way you lied to the feds?"

Another bluff? It was not a very good one. There was a reason why God made so many tax attorneys.

"You declared a loss for the stock scam—even though you got full restitution. But never mind tax fraud," said Mallory. "My favorite charge is conspiracy."

Instantly deflated, every sip of air sucked out of her, Zelda waited for the blonde to demand details of the crucial broker's conversation. When no such thing was asked of her, she began to count up her misdeeds in earnest. What else might this cop already know? And what interest could the police have in tax matters—unless that old swindle tied into something bigger, uglier. Zelda took a tentative step outside a world that revolved around only her own concerns, and—crash!—she smashed up against murder and kidnapping. And like any accident victim, she felt a clammy knot in her chest and a sudden coldness on a warm summer day.

The limousine had completed its circuit of the block, and the detective pressed the intercom button to say, "Leaman, pull over." And to Zelda she said, "Your chauffeur tells me you have an appointment with Andrew Polk. *Cancel* it. *Now!* . . . You're not going to feed the mayor any insider information about today, nothing on Brox or anyone else. Don't cross me. I'll know if you do. A little boy will die. . . . I'll come after you. . . . Any questions?"

Noooo, not a one.

* * *

THE BOY had to die tonight. That part of the conversation was plainspoken.

"Yes, I can fill that order." While Gail Rawly talked back to his cell phone in code words and tones of dry business, the little princess sat on his desk, pouring invisible tea into tiny plastic cups. "Huh?"

A catch? A change of plan? *Of all the idiotic—*

A bonus! "How much?" The promised amount would put him close to his figure for retiring to the bolthole in Costa Rica. *Beach house, I hear you calling me.* "Sure. That's doable." Gail winked at his daughter and set down his little teacup to write out the new drop site for the heart of another child. "Got it."

And—*click*—the conversation was over.

Gail waited with endless patience until Princess Patty grew tired of pretend tea for two and wandered out of his den, dragging her favorite doll by its hair. After dropping the client burner in the top drawer of his desk, he picked up the one used exclusively for calling his partner.

Iggy Conroy answered on the first ring with the same old salutation, *"Yeah!"*

"Do the kid tonight." Gail counted ten seconds of silence. "This isn't a problem, is it?" Had the boy become a pet—or was he already dead?

"Naw, no worries," said Iggy. "Hold on. I'm lookin' for my smokes."

Gail heard the reassuring click of a cigarette lighter on the other end of this conversation. All that anxiety for nothing. Iggy was no born-again child lover. Jonah Quill was just another piece of meat.

But when Iggy heard the details of the client's change in plans, he yelled, "And you went along with that! . . . Are you fucking crazy?"

* * *

THE TV NEWS LADY SAID, "And now for coverage of a limousine parade in a SoHo police precinct."

"Just a sec. I gotta tape this." But then Cigarette Man turned off the sound, wanting only pictures. After the remote control clattered to the coffee table, he continued their disturbing little talk on the theme of things that Jonah had never done.

A bucket list?

Uncle Harry had the DVD of a film with that title, a story of two characters fulfilling a list of last wishes. One of them had also played movie roles as the Almighty, so true to Jonah's idea of God—an *actor.*

"C'mon, kid. There's gotta be *somethin'* you always wanted to do. Somethin' like—"

"Aunt Angie said she'd let me drive the car when I could reach the pedals. But I was only six or seven at the time."

"She had a *car*? What kind?"

"A two-seater, low to the ground. It wasn't hers. Sometimes she'd borrow it, and we'd go driving up the Henry Hudson Parkway. She liked the lights on the river. I liked the speed. The wind. Top down. Music blasting."

IGGY GRABBED THE BOY by one arm and yanked him off the sofa to walk him through a kitchen door and into the garage, a generous space with room enough to hold his white van, a sports car and a workshop. Beyond another door, hidden in the false back wall, was a table laid out with tools for modifying pistols and rifles. The walls were racked with an array of knives and other items for a murder kit. A cabinet held his drugstore of potions for sleep and forgetfulness. And there were paralytics for the dart gun that he favored above all other weapons.

But out here in the garage area, in plain sight, there were only tools for working on the old engine of his car, his first love. He ripped the canvas tarp from a restored 1960 ragtop Jaguar. He had taught Angie how to drive in this car.

When she left him, she had ridden out of his life on a bus.

If this was the car the boy remembered, then Angie had taken it for joyrides while he was out of town. But she only had a house key. How would she have gotten past the premium locks on this garage? What else could she have gotten into? The hidden room? His murder kit? And how many people could tie that damn whore to his car?

Iggy placed the boy's hands on the classic hood ornament of a lunging cat. "That car you rode around in—did it have one a these?" Not waiting for his answer, he opened the door and guided the boy into the front seat on the driver's side, where curious fingertips explored the dashboard. Iggy turned the ignition key, and the engine came to life with the purr of maniacal maintenance. "Did it sound like that? And what about *this?*" He reached past the boy, turned on the radio and pushed a button for the customized iPod dock.

Yeah!

The kid's face lit up when he heard the song at the top of Angie's play list. The music boomed and bounced off the walls. The boy's hands slapped the steering wheel, keeping time to drums and a keyboard and the beat of a bass guitar.

* * *

THE ABANDONED AIRSTRIP was ten car-lengths wide and flanked by green fields of scrub grass. The sky was so big out here, all smeared with sunset pinks and gold. And there was no one for miles around to hear the music screaming, drums banging, rocking out heavy metal. Iggy could hear wheels churning in the rhythm of old road songs.

God bless rock 'n' roll.

The boy in the driver's seat had mastered the configurations of the stick shift and the pedals. Smart kid. The engine was idling when Iggy said, "Okay, you're good to go." And off they went. "Open 'er up! Knock yourself out!"

Pedal close to the mat, the fast straightaway tuned into zigzag patterns. Maybe the kid just liked the feel of the curves, but the last one put them close to the grass. And now they made a circle. Any tighter on the next loop and it would roll the car.

"*Easy,* Jonah!" *Jonah.* When had he ever called the meat by name? Talked to it? Or taken it out for a spin?

"Was I going to hit something?" The boy corrected the wheel in time to keep them on the asphalt, and he yelled to be heard above the crash of drums and cymbals. "Tell me where stuff is! I'll know to go around it!"

Iggy had a good instinct for all the off notes and the cracked ones. Was the kid scared? Oh, yeah. Sweaty scared. "There's an airplane hangar up ahead! A slow count to ten and you're there! So you wanna turn the—"

The boy gunned the engine, opening it up to the limit of the speedometer, not changing direction by a hair. And when he had passed that ten count twice and realized there would be no crash, the car slowed. The boy had a stunned look about him.

Disappointed?

Iggy reached over, turned the key and cut the engine. The car rolled to a stop, and then he stopped the music. "No, kid, you didn't miss it. . . . If there'd been a wall there, you would've smashed right into it," at a hundred and eighty miles per hour. And now they sat there, man and boy, in the quiet of the middle of nowhere. There was no need to talk about what they both knew. Jonah had tried to kill him—at the cost of his own young life.

Life-for-a-life revenge, and the boy had given it his all.

Iggy's head lolled back. The sun had set, but the light still held at the close of this summer day, and he watched a blackbird circle in the air above. The wind was warm. His voice was calm. "Good try, kid. . . . Good for you."

THE SPRINKLER SYSTEM took care of thirsty roses for most of the garden, but Iggy favored a hose for the ones lining the patio. "Up till today, my only enemies were weeds and aphids." He trained the nozzle's spray on plants growing near the boy's chair. "It's a big mistake to water flowers when the sun's up. Water drops act like tiny magnifyin' glasses. They make the sunlight hot enough to burn holes in the petals. If you spritz 'em after sundown, you get the bugs off, but you don't cook the flowers."

The boy's eyes moved as if they were not broken, as if they could take in all the roses. "It's a big garden, isn't it?"

"Yeah, I guess." Iggy twisted the nozzle to cut off the stream of water, and he laid down his hose. "Whadda *you* care?" He knew the boy was frightened and just filling in the silences until it was time to die. “What’s roses to you?”

“Soft petals. Ragged leaves. Skinny stems. The thorns are sharp. . . . What do *you* see?”

Iggy carried a can of beer to the edge of the patio. “I see red. You prick your finger on a thorn, and that’s the color. It jumps out at you. Grabs you by the eyes. Blood-red . . . fresh blood. It’s alive. It’s a color with a pulse.”

The kid shifted in his chair, lips pressed together, his head turning this way and that.

Lookin’ for somethin’ to say? Afraid I’ll kill you in the space between the words?

“You t-*told* me,” said Jonah, “there was a story behind the roses.”

“I don’t tell it no more.”

The boy’s body sagged.

In a pity offering, Iggy said, “It’s hard to raise roses from scratch. I know all the shit that goes into it. All the time, the *work*.” He saw Jonah coming back to life—a touch of hope in the lift of his head. “There’s a garden shop up the road. This old guy who owns it, he knows everything in the world about roses. So I tell him the story. Well, he gives me this smirk . . . and I know he takes me for a liar.”

But the boy might believe him.

Iggy popped the tab on his beer can and tipped it back for a long swig. “Five years ago, it was just a patch a flowers alongside the house. Then one day, I come out here and killed all the roses.” *Her* roses. “Pulled ’em up by the roots and stomped ’em to death. There was a bag a seeds in a box by the back door. Not the store-bought kind—they was cut from the garden flowers. I ripped that bag to shreds, and the wind took the seeds. Come next summer, hottest one on record, there was rosebushes all over the damn place, a dozen of 'em. It was a drought year, too. I never gave 'em any water. Just left 'em to the heat and the weeds and the bugs. . . . But they wouldn't die. . . . I got me some more seeds."

19

Cigarette Man yawned. Tired. The laundry-room door closed, and then came the familiar slide of the bolt—only the slide. It had not been shot all the way home to its slot, no click to the metal.

And that changes everything, said Aunt Angie.

Jonah had no plan to test the bolt, not while the dog was awake out there. The man was climbing stairs, so heavy on his feet. Then footsteps crossed the floor overhead. Another door opened and closed. Did he leave the house?

Soon the pit bull would be asleep. The old dog liked its naps.

The boy crouched beside the bucket in the corner, the source of a mildew smell. His fingers explored the strands of the mop inside, seeking that place where it attached to a pole, and he found the lip of a seam. This would be easy. He ran one hand up the length of the mop handle. A flick of one finger and the answering ping told him this rod was hollow. With a twist, he loosened it, and then unscrewed it from the mop, freeing it to heft the length of metal twixt fingers and thumb.

Not as light as a fiberglass cane.

Rising to a stand, Jonah grazed the floor with the tip of the mop handle, guiding it, side to side, from the wall to the mattress, and metallic vibrations traveling along tendon and muscle told him the difference between rock hard and rubber soft.

It would do the cane's job.

When the dog went to sleep—

No! No! No! Cigarette Man was *still here!* Upstairs there was banging, metal-crunching, glass-breaking anger. And the pit bull came wide awake with a yelp. Agitated. Nails clipping on cement, moving back and forth just beyond the door. Lungs wheezing in distress. Howling now. It was like listening in on the thoughts of the dog's master.

Dark, insane thoughts.

The banging went on and on. The dog wailed. Crying now. Almost human.

REPORTERS WERE STILL camped out on East End Avenue, and so Samuel Tucker walked along the riverside promenade. Carl Schurz Park was in sight when he answered the ringtone assigned to his boss's cell phone. The mayor had a few questions.

Tuck walked as he talked. "Yes, sir. It's exactly like the others." He was mildly distracted, seeing every pedestrian on the promenade as a potential threat. He decided on the parkland route to Gracie Mansion, seeking the cover of foliage. "Yes, sir, almost there."

A uniformed officer appeared beside him on the tree-lined path. "Evening, Mr. Tucker. Just hold up a minute." The officer spoke into a handheld radio, announcing the visit from the mayor's aide, and Detective Brogan's deep voice said, "Let him through."

Grinning, Tuck ran down the path.

The officer called after him, "Use the back gate!"

As if he needed to be told that this was the after-dark entry for *all* the mayor's whores. He was approaching the water fountain in the clearing, half the way there, when he caught a movement in sidelong vision, lamp-lit blond hair, a woman moving through the trees. Where did she—

Tuck stumbled. And stopped.

Detective Mallory stood on the path up ahead, blocking his way.

What a crap surprise. Awkward, too.

There was no salutation, no sign from her that they had ever met before, that she had ever arrested him, *handcuffed* him. The woman was looking in his direction, if not exactly looking *at* him. It appeared that he had no significance at all, not for her. So, *thank you, God,* she had not come to arrest him again.

Yet she stood in his way. What for? The detective could not possibly know what he was carrying, not unless she could read minds.

She smiled, but not at him. No, this was an *aha* expression. Meaning what?

Oh, *God,* he must look guilty as hell. *That* was it. But why would—

And now, time out for a frightened flight of fancy. Might this cop have X-ray eyes to see beneath his clothing—or, more rationally, did something show through his shirt in stick-out fashion? He glanced down at that place of concealment, but his shirtfront revealed nothing and—

The path was clear.

The detective had vanished.

* * *

IT WAS LIKE A DEATH.

Every car window was smashed, all the metal dented, and the beauty of the classic Jaguar destroyed.

Sweating, eyes closing, so tired, Iggy touched a pressure lock, and a panel opened in the garage's false back wall. The hidden room needed preparation before he cut out the boy's heart. Moving slowly, he knelt down on the gray cement to lay out a plastic sheet. It covered enough of the floor to catch the blood fly.

Christ!

Out in the garage, the wrecked Jag came back to life with the boom of a rock band on the radio. Iggy stood up ramrod straight, his heart pounding out a million beats a second.

The song stopped.

He sighed. The music was put down to frayed connections and wires crossed. Iggy turned to look at his collection of wall-mounted weapons. First, he pulled down the serrated knife for the deep cut. Now a hammer for the boy's rib cage.

MUSIC! *Fucking music!*

The radio was alive again with drumbeats and piano rolls. Frenzied, furious, Iggy ran back to the car and attacked it with the hammer's claw side, prying the radio from the ruined dashboard. When he had ripped out every wire, when all was quiet, he turned his back on the Jag.

Steady now. *Deep* breath.

And—*BANG!*—went the drums. The guitar screamed in high-pitched electric chords.

Hammer raised, he leaned down to the front seat littered with broken shards of window glass. His eyes fixed on a small rectangle of white plastic sitting in the dock that connected it to the radio speakers.

Oh, stupid, *stupid*.

It was not the car radio. A dock connection must be loose. That would explain the erratic music. When the last wire had been torn away, the old iPod had worked off the juice of its own battery. He smashed it into plastic bits, hammering beyond the need to only break it and MAKE IT STOP!

He pulled back from the car. The hammer fell from his hand. His eyes closed. Loss of control was new to him. Just tired is all. Yeah, that was it. In his pocket was a small vial of pills for times like this.

Or maybe a nap before the wetwork? Yeah, sleep was what he really needed.

He left the garage by the door to the kitchen, and he locked it behind him. Then he checked all the other locks in the house. After setting an alarm clock, he lay down in the dark, but sleep would not come. This was the fault of all those pills taken over the last two days. How could he have botched every hard-learned lesson on drugs?

His eyes opened.

There was something in the room with him. Old houses had noises of their own making, but had there been any sound? No, only a feeling, a prickle and shiver of flesh. He switched on the bedside lamp to find himself alone. His legs were lead-heavy when he shifted them off the mattress. Bare feet slapped the floor as Iggy clomped through every room, turning on all the lights, checking the locks *again*. Even the windows had locks that required a key to open them from the inside—a recent precaution of turning his home into a meat locker for the boy.

When every light was burning, he stayed his hand before double-checking the lock on the last window. And he said to no one, "This is crazy."

Only crazy people did this, or scared people, and that was never him. The jangled nerves and the misfire of his survival instinct—that was the pills. And so, as he walked back to his bed, every odd thing was explained away one more time.

DETECTIVE BROGAN, the senior man on the protection detail, stood between the mayor and his aide.

Andrew Polk watched the detective frisk Samuel Tucker, going first for the pockets, and then running his hands down Tuck's pant legs in the little joke that this dorky kid might be carrying a weapon. The aide was pronounced clean and allowed to accompany the mayor up the grand staircase.

When they had climbed to the upper floor and the door to the private office was closed behind them, Tuck unbuttoned his shirt to reveal a square brown envelope taped to his chest, the one area that had not been patted down in the search. So this kid had a brain. Who knew?

Tuck handed over the envelope, still sealed. "Someone put it under my door."

That might be true. There were innocent explanations for the faint stink of fear that rose off Tuck's skin and the damp of his shirt. Maybe this fool had raised all that sweat in a fast run to the mansion—so eager to lick the hand that fed him.

Andrew Polk tore the seal open to find a note that said, "I'M WAITING." There were no samples for comparison. The previous notes and package wrappings had been burned in the fireplace. These block letters could have been printed by the same hand—or just as easily by someone else's. Should he rethink his aide's idiocy? Was this note a ruse of Tuck's to get back inside the mansion? Or could it be something cooked up by cops?

Did he care? No. The mayor nonchalantly struck a match and set it afire.

There was no knock before Brogan and his partner entered the private office. And what had prompted this sudden boldness? The smell of smoke? That suggested that they had been standing outside the door. Ears pressed to the wood?

The unhappy detectives stared at the envelope turning to ash in the fireplace.

Andrew Polk winked at them. "Old love letter from a hooker." Did they believe this? No, they were probably not that stupid. Were they likely to admit to superiors that something else might have gotten past them? Absolutely not.

ALL WAS QUIET on the floor above Jonah's head. On the other side of the laundry-room door, the only sound was a low, rhythmic whistle of a wheeze. The pit bull was asleep. *Finally.*

Dog and master were so in sync, Cigarette Man must have gone to sleep, too.

Slowly, gently, Jonah turned the knob to open the door.

Resistance.

He knew the bolt had not gone into its slot, but it must be overlapping the door frame. By how much? Jonah pushed harder and heard the bolt move, grating against the wood. He stopped. He held his breath the better to listen, but the dog's breathing was unchanged. The boy exhaled. He reached out to try the door again, but it had swung open of its own accord.

His sneakers dangled by the tied laces strung around his neck, and the mop handle was in his right hand. In barefoot silence, he crossed the threshold, turned to a position of ten o'clock and softly padded the sixteen paces across the cool cement floor. Before reaching out to touch the banister, he knew he was at the foot of the stairs leading up to the kitchen door. The fourth step would creak and so would the ninth. He must step over them or the dog would be on him, shredding his skin in a bloody horror fest.

Go for it, said Aunt Angie. *Life is so worth it. Life is everything. I wish I could've stayed a little longer.*

20

His favorite bar was dismally unsuccessful and delightfully uncrowded, assuring him of attention at the crook of a finger. He liked that *so* much.

Dwayne Brox sipped brandy as he read the final passage of a novel by Franz Kafka, a rare German departure from his love of Russian classics. When his regular cocktail waitress returned, he planned to impress her with his critique of the author as a comedian of sadism. She would flatter him and smile, as if his affect did not repulse her, thus earning herself a generous tip. And this was his idea of a date. Like most attractive women of his acquaintance, she would never go out with him—never go home with him. But that was a call girl's job, not hers.

He closed his book and turned to the window on the street. Out there at the curb, a familiar asshole was exiting a taxi. Dwayne had detested him since they were boys. Oh, *really.* For this occasion, the fool wore a tie with the colors of their alma mater, Fayton Prep. The former classmate approached the street door, all nerves and tics, jerking his head this way and that, as if he suspected that someone, *anyone,* might care to follow him around town.

Upon entering the bar, he walked toward Dwayne's table, extending a hand in the spirit of schoolboy camaraderie. So needy. Always begging for a sign of acceptance.

Not in this lifetime.

"Hello, Tuck."

And goodbye?

Samuel Tucker's outstretched hand fell to his side as he took one step back, and then he ceased to move at all.

Mildly curious, Dwayne waited for the man to blink.

Oh, my! There was Detective Mallory standing outside close to the window and looking in—at Tuck. She pointed no gun at him, nor was there anything disagreeable about her, but she evidently had a Medusa knack for turning fools to stone.

Good *job*.

Tuck came alive again—nearly alive. Oh, dear, so pale. He spun on one heel and raced for the door. At a slower pace, Dwayne followed him out of the bar to linger on the sidewalk. He watched Tuck run down the street, calling out to a slow-moving cab, and chasing that car down as dogs were wont to do.

The pretty cop now stood beside Dwayne, and her eyes were on the car chase when she asked, "Friend of yours?"

"I don't have any friends."

Detective Mallory stepped off the curb and rounded a small silver convertible to slide in behind the steering wheel. A Volkswagen? Well, that make of car would not work with her wardrobe *or* her psyche. No, not at all. Now, *that* was interesting.

JONAH COUNTED HIS WAY UPWARD, his bare feet passing over the two cellar steps that creaked. He stopped to concentrate on the wheezy whistling of the sleeping dog below. He had no faith in the light mop handle as a weapon against a pit bull.

Next step, last step.

He reached out for the knob, but the kitchen door was wide open. Was this more of Cigarette Man's carelessness? Or did he always leave it that way so he could hear the dog bark? Jonah entered the kitchen. Five steps to the table. He skirted it and turned left to face the living room. His feet remembered the way, and, ten steps in, he rounded an armchair, continuing on to the far wall to graze it with fingertips and find the way out.

One hand closed on the ball of a doorknob, and it turned easily, but the door would not open. So there would be a deadbolt to undo—just like home. His fingers lightly climbed the frame to find a small piece of rounded metal that would open the bolt at a twist. This done, he tried the knob again. No good. Uncle Harry had three locks, and now Jonah searched for another bolt. Higher up the frame, he touched a thick plate with a protruding chunk of metal—nothing to twist, no chain to slide. Fingertips sensitized to reading dots of braille traced the shape of a ragged crease in the metal.

An opening to fit a key? Yes, he would need a damn key to unlock this door from the *inside.*

Abandoning that escape route, fingers traveled along the wall in search of a window. His hand brushed over curtains to find the glass, the frame, and now two metal handles near the sill. Hard as he pulled, he could not raise the sash. His hands slipped up the glass to undo the catch at the top, and he found another key-creased bit of metal like the one on the door. This was not the way out. Breaking glass would wake the man—and the dog.

But right this minute, a ringing telephone could rouse them both and end all his chances.

Jonah leaned the mop handle against the door. He did not dare to use it as a cane, not where he was going. It might connect with something hard and noisy. He made his way around the room, searching the floor by touch of toes. Guided by memory of the dog's toenails clicking on a hard surface, he knew the hallway would be on the other side of the television set and past the edge of the carpet. Hands outstretched, he found the opening. Arms wide now, his fingers grazed close walls on both sides of him. He found a door and opened it. Only a closet of shelves. A few steps farther down the hall, he heard light snoring. The bedroom? Was this door open? Panic was a fluttery thing in his chest, ice in his heart, his blood, and he was scared stupid.

Reason kicked in.

If Cigarette Man should wake, his eyes would tell him nothing at this time of night when the lights were out.

Back home, Jonah always left his wallet and keys on the nightstand by his bed, and he guessed that Cigarette Man would also keep such things close by. Bare feet found a slight rise of wood, and toes grazed it to recognize it as a threshold. The boy lightly dropped down to hands and knees on a hardwood floor. He moved forward in an awkward dogtrot, one arm extended, fingers reaching out to where a bed might be, and he found one thick leg of furniture.

Above his head, he heard the squeak of mattress springs. The snoring stopped. The man—so close—was turning in his bed. Waking? Jonah stopped breathing.

The snoring started up again. The boy drew a breath and crawled on to find a shoe. A bit of cloth. A rug. Moving slowly on this softer surface, he reached out to touch a thinner leg of furniture. The nightstand? Up on his feet now, feather-light fingers explored its surface, and felt *the heat of a lightbulb.*

The lamp was lit! If the man should wake—

Jonah fought down the urge to run, to crash through a window and run for his life. Hysteria was climbing up his throat, and—

Then his fingertips picked out the shape of keys on the nightstand.

THE CAB HAD NOT DROPPED him off at Gracie Mansion, as expected. Instead, the mayor's aide had gone home, that place of retreat to lick wounds. The address was on a bleak side street at the fringe of money, where no one went walking long after dark. Samuel Tucker's small apartment was one window up from the ground. He could not afford the higher floors where the light lived.

It was trash night in this neighborhood, and all along the curbs, garbage bags writhed with the slitherings beneath their plastic skins as rodents ate their innards. Kathy Mallory *hated* rats. This old grudge was a holdover from a childhood of cutting them with broken bottles and banging them with bricks, enraged because the bolder ones were too stupid to be afraid of her, a little girl who could not bed down without her shoes because rats liked the taste of toes.

The car windows were rolled up, but she could still hear them, the mechanized peeps, high-pitched and alien.

She watched her dashboard computer and waited for the first signal blip of an active cell phone or the track of a landline call to the mayor. Her keystroke bug on Tucker's laptop had yet to give up any messages sent out by that route. She turned her eyes to his unlit windows. Black. Not even the glow of a TV screen.

What was he doing in there—in the dark?

The street door opened, and Tucker walked out. He stood by the curb, lifting his face, as if to count stars—then bowing to cracks in the pavement. Now the man paced the sidewalk, never straying far from his apartment building. He paused to raise a hand and hail an oncoming cab. But then that hand was jammed into his pocket in a change of heart.

He went back inside.

To hide?

No report to the mayor?

No, of course not. Tucker could hardly admit to his runaway abortion of tonight's mission. How would he explain police interest in him, a cop *following* him? Just the sight of her had frightened him even more than the bogus arrest, and he would never want Polk to find out about that station-house interview—the trip-up questions asked and the *screwup* lies he had told.

No more surveillance on Samuel Tucker was necessary. The mayor's errand boy would not be reaching out to any other bilked investors. His fear worked better than handcuffs and leg irons.

So Mayor Polk was working off her same pool of suspects, and the shortlist had not been supplied by Zelda Oxly. If the mayor was using the aide to do reconnaissance on Dwayne Brox, this could only mean that Zelda was no longer a player.

And it was time to go home.

While reaching for the ignition key, Mallory felt the

cell phone vibrate in her pocket, and now its earpiece connected her to the small voice of a schoolgirl.

"You said I could call you."

"Anytime, Lucinda. Did you remember something?"

"I'm afraid to go back to sleep. I had this awful dream. . . . Jonah's *alive*. You believe that, don't you?"

"Yes, I do." Mallory turned the ignition key.

"You wouldn't lie?"

"No, never," said the consummate liar. The engine idled. Garbage bags quivered as rats scrabbled in and out of chewed holes. And she listened to Lucinda's long recital of a nightmare—until all the detective could hear was the breathing rhythm of a child who had fallen asleep with a phone on her pillow.

As the car glided into the street, Mallory had questions of her own. When would proof of death turn up at Gracie Mansion? Was that dead boy's heart in transit tonight?

JONAH SAT ON THE GRASS just beyond the door and tied up the laces of his sneakers. This plot of land in front of the house was an unknown country of crickets. Now an owl. He waited for his compass point—and there it was—a distant car engine traveling down a seldom used road. Where was the driveway that would lead him to it? Earlier, when the man had taken him into the garage, they had passed through a kitchen door, but where—

Dead opposite the door for the basement.

He had his bearings now.

On their way to the driving lesson, there had been a spit of pebbles from a rough surface beneath the wheels before they reached paved road. So that dirt driveway was a ninety-degree turn to his right. He picked up the mop handle and rose to a stand on the soft cushion of sneakers on grass. The makeshift cane moved back and forth over the lawn. *Side to side. Side to side.* It picked out an obstacle that was soft, no vibrations, but some yield to it. A bush? Yes. He touched the leaves as he circled round it. *Thunk.* The mop handle tapped an object. A hard vibration, harder than wood. Before he touched it, he knew it would be stone like the sides of buildings on sidewalks, a different sound than the metal feet of city mailboxes and lampposts. Was this a wall?

No. His free hand reached out to touch a bearded face. Arms. Legs. A little stone man.

Jonah walked around it and ran out of grass loam. He knelt down to sample the harder ground of packed dirt. The driveway. The way out.

He walked as fast as he dared, the mop handle moving across the dirt, knocking pebbles. *Side to side. Side to side.* He knew the long driveway would curve twice before he tapped pavement. Up ahead, no more cars were heard. But when he found that road, another driver would come along.

He was going home.

THE ALARM CLOCK had not yet sounded, but Iggy Conroy awakened—terrified. Eyes kept closed, he feigned sleep. Bright lamplight was a red stain on his eyelids.

There was someone or some *thing* in his bed.

He had felt the movement on the other side of the mattress, Angie's side. This was no dream, but he did not reach out for the gun on the nightstand. Paralyzed by fear, he could not lift a hand, and he would not open his eyes.

It might only be the dog, risking a kick to come up from the basement, looking for love. Iggy felt another movement on the mattress, the roll of a body beside him. Closer now. He waited for it to touch him. Inside his head, he was screaming, but he scrunched his eyes shut—because it *might* be the dog. *God in heaven, please, it might be only that.*

The air was warm. The man shivered. The alarm clock shrieked, and Iggy stiffened like a corpse.

The dog barked.

IT WAS NOT MUFFLED ANYMORE. The dog's barking was outside the house, and coming closer, coming on fast. And the man's feet pounded the dirt behind him.

Jonah dropped the mop handle, no time to stop and find it. He ran with hands outstretched. He ran with a prayer that his feet would find no rock or root to trip him. He plunged into an unmapped world. All sense of place was lost, yet he flung himself forward, legs churning. One hand touched foliage as it reached out to scratch him with long fingers of branch and twig. The dog was close. Closer. Jonah could hear the animal's labored breathing between the barks.

Right behind him.

Almost here.

TEETH!

The dog's jaws clamped down on Jonah's leg, teeth sinking into flesh, biting down to bone, and the boy hit the ground, his head smashing into an object hard as stone. He felt the warmth of blood coming down his face. He could smell its coppery scent, and now the taste of it streaming into his mouth. Jonah's fingers found more of his wet blood on the rough feet of a statue. Tiny feet. Another little stone man had been hiding in the brush, waiting there to get him.

The dog was on Jonah's back.

Hot breath on his neck.

The last thing he heard was the man yelling, "Get *off* him!"

The whole world went quiet. One thing by another, every sense of it ebbed away. No more pain. No fear. He was weightless as a balloon, letting go of the earth itself and—

IGGY CONROY walked up the driveway, carrying the torn and bloodied boy in his arms. The dog lagged behind, keeping its distance, not wanting to be kicked again.

And then it barked.

Iggy turned on the pit bull. "What now, you crazy mutt?" He had no more patience for the stupid dog. It should have died years ago.

Its snout was raised. It barked at the moon.

"Shut up!"

The dog fell silent for a moment of shame told by the hang of its head. Now it sat down on the dirt and regarded Iggy with deep apology.

"What the hell are you—"

Bells?

Iggy raised his eyes to the sky, the source of the jingling.

It stopped.

So now he was *hearing* things. All those pills, those uppers downed like candy.

No! That was *not* it. The dog had heard the jingle bells, too.

Any other night, he would have chased down that sound. Everything *must* have an explanation, and he would have turned the whole world inside out to find it.

He dropped to his knees, holding Jonah tighter. Iggy's eyes were still fixed on the sky—only stars and a cockeyed moon. No flights of angels. No ghosts to ring bells for him. Yet he spoke to the sky, childhood's old idea of Heaven's address, that place where Angie might be hiding, *still* hiding from him. "It wasn't never supposed to be this way." His breath was stuttered, and he was slow to rise. The boy's body weighed more now.

21

The two detectives sat in the dark of a parked car on Fifth Avenue. For this shadow detail in Money Country, they had selected a drug dealer's Lexus from the impound lot, so as to blend in with other upscale models. Though the average New Yorker might have recognized it as a stakeout vehicle by the backseat accumulation of coffee cups and take-out cartons. "I don't get it," said Gonzales. "A serial killer who hires out the kills?"

Lonahan shrugged. "Rich people."

His partner nodded. That actually would explain a lot. Gonzales pointed toward the doorman building. "There's our boy. Check out that getup." Their suspect had spiked his hair in stick-out strands, and he had changed his very nice suit for a ratty pair of jeans and a retro T-shirt of psychedelic colors. "Looks like he rolled an old hippy for those clothes."

"That's one butt-ugly T-shirt." Lonahan started up the car. "So whadda ya say? He's slumming tonight, or that's his idea of a disguise?"

"No," said Gonzales. "He's gonna make the downtown club scene." This theory worked well with the outfit and a waiting limousine. Customers who arrived in limos always made the cut with doorkeepers for the hottest nightspots in town.

A chauffeur opened the car's rear door for their suspect. And a minute later, they were all on the roll as the detectives followed the black Lincoln toward the river, onto the parkway and then down to the dingy commercial district near the docks. And there they watched the passenger bid the chauffeur good night. Dwayne Brox stood on the sidewalk, looking around, but paying no attention to his shadow cops. The detectives' stakeout car worked even better in this crummier patch of the city. Who looked for cops in a Lexus?

Their man walked half a block to enter the office door of Bargain Rides, and, after a short wait, he emerged from the wide mouth of the garage, sitting behind the wheel of a rented piece of crap that Gonzales would not be caught dead in, not even on a stakeout detail in an auto graveyard. The detective shook his head, saying, "Rich people."

And his partner nodded.

THE CLIENT had favored a toilet this time. What an idiot. But Iggy had withdrawn his objection. He had his own change of plan for this night.

The restroom would ensure privacy and anonymity in this busy truck stop. Lots of foot traffic passed through that door to the toilet. Not bad—providing the drop sight was not also used by local drug dealers. That would pose a complication. Luck was with him when he lifted the heavy ceramic cover of the toilet's water tank and found it to be virgin territory. The scum around the interior had not been disturbed in years. After leaving a red plastic box afloat in the tank water, he replaced the lid and opened the restroom door to hear the encore of a country music song on the jukebox. Some brokenhearted trucker had fallen in love with lyrics for faithless bitches.

The diner was a double-wide, lots of space filled with Formica tables, plastic chairs and aromas of coffee, chilli dogs and smelly men. The span of window glass gave Iggy a view of the customers' rides. They had ridden in on every damn thing. Cars and motorcyles were parked in the narrow slots up front, and the big rigs were at the back of the lot near the highway.

Heading for a stool at the counter, Iggy checked out the crowd for newcomers. He saw none of the people featured in a TV news clip of well-dressed civilians entering a SoHo station house with police escorts—the rich bastards branded as persons of interest to the Special Crimes Unit. So the client was not here yet. Gail Rawly must have impressed the fool with the importance of not showing up early, possibly running into the hit man, pissing him off—and, of course, getting killed. Tonight, Iggy was the one to break the rules, chief among them: Never get within a mile of the clients. Never give them a face to remember, should they get caught and feel the need to cut a deal with the cops.

For this occasion, Iggy wore eyeglasses, and his shirt bore the logo of a moving company to help him pass as a long-haul trucker for one of the big rigs in the lot—though his van sat in the tall weeds behind the diner, keeping company with two abandoned wrecks—good as invisible. When he sat down at the counter, he was positioned in line of sight with the restroom and every taker of pisses and dumps. He also had a view of the parking spaces near the door, those sized to fit cars.

He ordered a burger and fries. The waitresses were hustling stacked trays of food, deaf to shouted complaints from some of the tables. So many customers. Too many. He could count on slow service. Timing was everything.

Forty minutes passed before he pushed his empty plate away. A junker with rental plates pulled up to a slot near the entrance. The driver emerged in jeans and a bright-colored T-shirt. Sunglasses at night? He might be the client. The age was right for the youngest one on the news clip, though the guy's hair was spiked and he had a stubble of beard. Crappy jeans. Low-rent sneakers. This one definitely lacked the polish of the crowd hauled into the station house. But the new arrival's first stop *was* the restroom.

Iggy turned his eyes back to the parking lot, where another car had just pulled in. A Lexus, a *very* nice ride. But the driver and the passenger did not get out. The two men just sat there watching the long span of window glass.

Well, this was promising.

When the customer with the spiked hair left the restroom, he had a brown-paper bag in one hand.

Oh, you moron.

That bag must have been folded up in a pocket when the guy went in there, but now it certainly contained the red box from the toilet tank. There were dark brown wet spots on the brown paper.

The two men parked outside must have noticed that, too. They stepped out of their car as the fool with the paper bag left the diner, his identity confirmed—by *cops.*

The idiot client was being bent over the hood of his rental as they handcuffed him.

Iggy raised one hand to signal the harried waitress for his check. So far, everything was going well.

THE RED PLASTIC BOX had been dusted for fingerprints and then opened. The suspense was over long before the lawyer's arrival.

And the lawyer's laughter.

Dwayne Brox was not so cheerful. Judging by the pouty mouth, his arrest and detention had inconvenienced him, and worse—the surrounding detectives annoyed him. He resented every question that pulled his attention away from Mallory. Despite the fact that she had yet to even glance at the suspect, he was fixated on her.

Lonahan followed Gonzales out of the interrogation room. The partners were in a grim mood for good reason, though their stakeout had not been a complete waste of time. They had singled out the right suspect, and now the squad could end surveillance for the other investors on the shortlist.

Riker stared at Brox's cheap clothes and cheaper sneakers. The last time he saw this young man, it would have cost him a year's rent money to buy the creep's outfit. But here and now, if he shut his eyes, the detective could imagine gnats circling the guy's head. He christened the suspect as Bug Boy, but he called him "Dwayne . . . where do you get your disguises? A flea market? Is that where you shopped for your hit man, too?"

Brox looked up, as if he had just discovered Riker in the room with him, and then he glanced at the less interesting contents of the red box from the diner's toilet tank—*a goddamn ham sandwich.*

The lawyer, dubbed Shifty Little Bastard, also eyed the red box. He smiled at his scruffy client and then, since expensive suits always preferred to speak to equally good tailoring, he ignored Riker and said to the cop seated across the table, "Detective Mallory, if you can't make a case for ham on rye as contraband, my client and I will be leaving."

"Not yet," she said. "Your client's not very tidy. He didn't wipe *all* his prints off the toilet-tank cover. We know he was expecting to find something else . . . proof of death."

The attorney waved one hand to say that he could not be bothered with trivialities of life and death. "Since you had no cause to take my client's prints for comparison—"

"*Wrong*. I've got this." Mallory laid a warrant on the table. "I had a government witness talk to the judge who signed it."

Technically true—though Chester Marsh had lost his government job, and all the talk had been on tape. Riker had gone shopping for a newly minted assistant DA to play that snitch's interview for a judge on the cusp of senility. The kidnap connection to Andrew Polk's former clients was tenuous, but the judge was up for election this term, and the old man had wanted to be seen as a candidate who came out on the side of kidnapped children everywhere, but especially the blind ones. The judge had signed three warrants, one for each suspect on the shortlist, and the powers granted were so broad that they were damn near embarrassing.

"I can take your guy's fingerprints," said Mallory, "his financial statements—anything I want." One red fingernail trailed down the lines of the warrant's text. "Oh, and here? It says I can take the little weasel's blood if I want it."

Taking no offense on the part of *the little weasel,* the lawyer smiled at her and said, "But you had no cause for arrest—or we'd be discussing charges and an arraignment. So far, you have nothing but—" His eyes strayed back to the ham sandwich in the red box. "Well, actually nothing at all . . . We're leaving."

"But first," said Mallory, "a little blood."

DWAYNE BROX arrived home, yawning, wearied by the tedium of waiting hours for a lab technician to draw a blood sample from his vein. The lawyer had balked at this, insisting that a DNA swab would do, but the warrant had spelled out *blood,* and only blood would satisfy Detective Mallory. However, all in all? *Great fun!*

Upon entering his bedroom, the light switch would not work. How tedious—but a burned-out bulb could wait till tomorrow. Dwayne found his bed by the crack of light from the hallway. Too tired to undress, he flopped down on the mattress and—

"It's about time," said a rough voice from the dark. "I've been waitin' for the cops to let you go."

Dwayne's eyes were open now and blinded by a low ball of light as bright as the sun. He shut his eyes but the light persisted, burning through membrane. "Who's there?"

"Who do you think? . . . Did the cops *like* the ham sandwich?"

No, this should *not* be happening. He had an *agreement!* Dwayne raised one hand to shield his eyes before he opened them again. He could see nothing of the man beyond the light, nothing but the afterimage of a sun. "You can't *be* here! You're not even supposed to know my *name!*"

"And I wouldn't . . . if you weren't such a fuckup. You made all the news channels, kid. I was watchin' TV when the cops hauled you in the first time, you and your rich buddies. You know why they gotcha again tonight? You're an idiot."

"Are you insane?" No, actually the intruder displayed rather good cognitive reasoning, as evidenced by the ham sandwich. If not for that substitution— "All right. The toilet-tank thing? Bad idea. But police might be parked outside right this minute."

"Yeah, they are. Good thing they wasn't watchin' the roof. So what'd you tell 'em?"

"Get *out!*" Ah, that might be the wrong tone to take with a hired killer, not exactly the servant class. More politely, Dwayne said, "You should leave . . . *now.*"

"So you don't want this?"

The plastic bag came flying at him from the dark side of the light, and it landed on the bed. Dwayne had come to recognize a disembodied human heart on sight. This one was smaller than the others.

The heart of a child.

22

Dwayne Brox, bound hand and foot, sat on a kitchen chair as Iggy covered his eyes with a black silk necktie.

"Is this necessary? You probably burnt out my retinas with that damn—"

"That'll wear off." Iggy sat down to read files on the client's laptop computer. "You'll see just fine when you pay the balance on the kid's heart." The procedure for shuttling funds from one account to another was chimp-simple. Gail Rawly had introduced him to online banking, but Iggy still insisted on cash in the hand. He had no faith in his partner's guarantee that some offshore banks were still cop-proof.

"So, Dwayne, you and me, we got time for a talk. . . . What's your game?"

"You don't need to know. I'm paying extra to avoid stupid questions."

A bonus? Gail must be skimming even more than usual.

Done with the probate file, Iggy leaned back in his chair and lit a cigarette. "This was your folks' apartment? My condolences, kid, 'cause they didn't leave you much." The place was heavily mortgaged. A balloon payment had come due and gone unpaid. "So that offshore account—that's all the cash you got? Damn." He had opened that file with a password obligingly supplied by Brox. *Moron.* What was the point of a complex foreign account number, if it could be accessed with a name? And who the hell was Chekhov? The balance line had him worried. "Three hundred *K*. That's it? And what've you got left after you pay for the kid and the bonus, huh?" He said this with a sneer in his voice, as if he already had the answer.

"A hundred thousand."

That would net Gail Rawly a bundle of money in addition to padded commissions for every hit and heart. "A hundred *K*. That's chump change—a working stiff's idea of money. But you keep spendin' like you own the whole town." According the credit card accounts, this ditzy twit went everywhere in limos, and he was probably running a tab with a bookie. The sports pages of his newspapers were inked with notes on point spreads. "Big spender. That tells me you expect a windfall. Or maybe you plan to off yourself when you hit bottom. Which is it?" The most dangerous client was one with nothing to lose.

"I'm not suicidal. Does that cover it?"

It bothered Iggy that this guy had no fear at all. This was hardly normal behavior when a hit man came calling. "Can't be a life-insurance payoff. The hits were random targets. So . . . you got a beef with the mayor?"

"You could say that." This was the tone of a tease. "But you'll have to be content with the money." The little creep had the kind of smile that would beg perfect strangers to smack him.

"Wadda you do with the hearts?" Iggy thought he knew.

* * *

MAINTAINING THE RAWLYS' happy marriage required sleeping in separate rooms. Mary slept soundly and snored loudly.

Gail was a light sleeper, frequently awakened by the baby monitor on the nightstand. It was a lifeline to his daughter's bedroom. The listening device reassured him that she was still breathing. He had faced the terror of her asthma attacks too often. Though most incidents were controlled by her inhaler, some had required the mad dash to a hospital. And Daddy's girl was heir to other horrors of the night. He was Patty's hero, the one who rescued her from every bad dream. Gail was compulsive in his daddying, and when he detected the amplified whine of a mosquito, he would leave his bed on the run to vanquish the invader before it could touch her.

Who was that?

Gail threw off his sheet and sat bolt upright in alarm mode. He heard it again, a man's voice, a whisper. "Gail, we gotta talk." He switched on his bedside lamp. There was no one in the room. The voice had come from the baby monitor. In seconds, he was at Patty's bedroom door. A gun in his hand. Turning the—

What the hell?

Illuminated by the tiny bulb of a bunny nightlight, Iggy Conroy sat in the chair next to the pink canopy bed of the sleeping princess. "I didn't wanna wake the whole house with a phone call."

How polite.

Biting back anger, Gail lowered his revolver and issued sign-language commands to *shut the hell up!* Iggy silently followed him out of the bedroom and down the hallway to the den, where a long wire trailed from each of the French doors to prevent a break in the electrical circuit for the burglar alarm. Iggy was brilliant at breaking and entering. He had also defeated the motion detectors in the baseboards.

Gail walked to his desk, laid down his gun and rested one hand on the cover of his laptop. Warm to the touch. So Iggy had spent some time in here tonight—a waste of time without a password and a thumb drive.

The dangerous guest sat down, not at all contrite. This most even-tempered man was angry, though it only showed in the tension of his face and his fists. The baby-monitor stunt must have been revenge for something.

"What's up?" Gail's measured tone implied that having his house broken into might be a common occurrence. Was Iggy wearing cologne? *Now* Gail was frightened. The odor of cigarettes was bad enough, but all perfumes were the princess's enemies, possible triggers for asthma, and this man *knew* that.

No, hold on. Easy now. It was only a trace of scent, not Iggy's cologne; he never wore any, but it smelled like trouble. A familiar brand. Expensive. Who had this man been hugging tonight?

Iggy reached out to drop a cell phone on the desk. The plastic back was missing and so was the battery. "That's the client's burner."

"Please tell me he's still alive."

"Yeah, but I had a little chat with him. I know about your—" Iggy spat out the words, "*—bonus money.* That's why you let that idiot call the shots tonight. The toilet drop site? Of all the stupid— Well, he got his heart delivered in person."

"A change of plan. Smart move," said Gail. *How fucking crazy are you? A face-to-face with a client?*

"I watched him move the fee into your account," said

Iggy. "Pay me now. And then shut everything down, the account, too. I don't want no tracks. We're done with that little prick."

"No problem, nothing easier." Gail did not want this man's voice raised in anger that might wake the princess. He sat down at his desk to search a drawer for the thumb drive. Once it was inserted into the laptop slot, he was able to open the account in the Cook Islands. The client's payment was indeed there on the screen as a recent deposit. "I'll get your money before the end of the week. You could've had it in three seconds if you'd let me set up an offshore—"

"Cash. Get it *now.*" Iggy turned to the painting that concealed the wall safe. "It's all there. I counted it. But I didn't take any. That would've been . . . rude."

Gail opened the safe and stared at his emergency stash, what he kept on hand for the road, should the need to run arise. Reluctantly, he removed the banded packets of bills and put them into Iggy's hands. "So . . . you followed the client from the truck stop?"

"Naw. After the cops cuffed him and took him away, I knew I'd have lots of time to kill. Hours and hours . . . *Relax.* They let him go."

Inwardly flapping like a duck, outwardly calm, Gail settled into the chair behind his desk. "How did you know where—"

"I saw his mug on TV. That was the first time the cops hauled him in, him and his rich friends. I got all their names off follow-ups on the Net. Addresses, too, but those came from a society blog."

Gail had always known that Iggy was fanatical about the details of his job, but never would he have guessed that this man followed the doings of the socialite set. "It's a *nice* address, Iggy. I told you that. The guy's obviously loaded."

"Seventeen rooms on Fifth Avenue. I read the foreclosure notice. That offshore account? That's all he's got, and Brox owes six times that much, but he spends like he just won the lottery. He's outta control—a freak, a whacko, and *you* let him change the plan tonight. How could you suck me into a deal like this? And what's the guy's damn game?"

Gail had no idea. An up-front bonus had been paid in exchange for asking the client no questions like—*was he sane?*

"He's lookin' for a payday outta this. Gotta be kidnap for ransom."

"Iggy, you can't believe that. You're the one who made the hit list. Nobody pays ransom for strangers."

"Brox is a nutcase. . . . I don't expect this to make sense."

"Okay, we cut the cord," said Gail. "I'll lose the other burner, the one I use to take his calls."

"How do you know he didn't write down that phone number and leave it someplace where the cops can find it?"

"Wouldn't matter if he did."

"If the cops get your number, they can track every call you ever made on your burner. Location, too. Cell towers and satellites and—"

"Iggy, stop spending so much time on the Internet. Most of that crap on cell-phone tracking is urban myth."

Gail had never relied on anyone to follow instructions like—only use your burner and NEVER write down my number. Holding up the client's stolen cell phone, he said, "*I* sent this to Brox. Even if the cops had found this one, it would've been useless to them." He unlocked the top drawer of his desk and pulled out a phone of his own. "This is the one I used to call him. You see? It's just like his, a dinosaur—no GPS capability. And cell-tower triangulation? Not out here in the country. There's just one tower—an omnidirectional antenna. Let's say the client *gave* my phone number to the cops. It's a burner. They'd only have records of my calls to Brox, but not my name. And a ping off a tower out here only nets them a six-mile radius for a location." Bless crap technology.

The sky was lightening. The sun would be up soon. "Go home. No worries. I know what I'm doing."

Iggy Conroy took his leave just in time. Gail could hear the sounds of his household stirring to life with the first flush of a toilet down the hall.

His wife screamed.

She appeared in the doorway with their child clutched tight and riding on her hip. Mary held an asthma inhaler in her free hand. Empty? Or no use? His little princess was struggling to breathe. Lips turning blue. Eyes closing. Head dropping. Dying?

"Call nine-one-one!" yelled his wife. "Don't just stand there!"

He dropped the cell phone on the floor and ripped the child from her arms. Now he ran for the front door. It was still early for commuter traffic. He would make good time on the road to the hospital.

Gail was settling his daughter on the front seat of the car when his wife tore out of the house on a slipper-foot run, yelling, "Stop! I called nine-one-one! There's an ambulance coming!"

Smart. The EMTs would get Patty breathing in three minutes. His wife's brain worked much better than his in emergencies like this one. Fear for his child always clouded his thinking. He looked down at the tiny limp body. *Don't die, don't die, don't die!*

AN HOUR INTO DAYLIGHT, little Patty was doing just fine, and the small family was on the way home. The sleeping princess rode down the hospital corridor in Gail's arms as he walked alongside his wife.

This was Iggy's doing—the scent of cologne he had tracked into Patty's bedroom, that and the smell of cigarettes in his clothes. The miserable—

The red exit sign was in sight when another thought occurred to Gail, and he hid the dread from his wife when he asked, "Mary, when you called for the ambulance, which phone did you use?"

"The *nearest* one. What does it—"

"Mary? Was it the landline on my desk?"

"Uh-uh. Not that one." She walked ahead of him, passing through the glass doors as she opened the flap on her shoulder bag.

Gail wanted to scream!

But that would wake Patty.

He followed Mary across the parking lot and caught up to her at the car. He held his daughter tight, maybe too tight, and watched his wife riffle through the contents of her overcrowded purse. She laid a day planner on the hood of the car, then her own pink smartphone, Patty's juice box, an old stuffed toy that their child had outgrown and all manner of *crap*.

"I grabbed the cell phone you dropped on the floor," said Mary. "It's a real old one. I don't know why you— Here it is." Search ended, she held up his burner, the one used exclusively for his calls to Dwayne Brox—and, more recently, a 911 operator.

23

Gail Rawly stared at the cell phone used for making and receiving client calls. It lay on the desk blotter, gutted and dead—but too late. Its call history would now contain a link to a 911 emergency—a name—and an address. Had Dwayne Brox written down this burner's number on a scrap of paper left somewhere in one of those seventeen rooms on Fifth Avenue?

If only this problem could be fobbed off on his wife. Mary had a genius for the life-and-death crisis. Princess Patty had survived this day by her mother's wits, not his. And so he asked himself what Mary would do.

First, she might get rid of all the other burners locked in his desk. He opened the drawer that held his collection of outdated cell phones for contacting clients—and one hit man. *The drawer was empty.*

So Iggy had returned to clean up more loose ends. Had he been watching the desperate scene of the medics reviving Patty? Had he orchestrated that rescue mission to clear the house? Damn right. Iggy had planned it with the smell of smoke and cologne in Patty's bedroom.

Wait. This was a good sign. His partner could easily

have killed the whole family, but he had settled for wiping out cell-phone tracks—except for the burner that Mary had carried away in her purse. By now, Iggy had ditched his own phone to become invisible, unreachable. No skip-trace tactic would ever locate a cash-and-carry man who left no paper trails. After the Conroys, mother and son, had moved out of the city, Gail knew their names would have been jettisoned for new identities—because Iggy was paranoia incarnate.

He stared at the empty drawer of lost connections. What now? Beyond the glass of the French doors, he saw Mary and the princess out back, sitting on the edge of the swimming pool, dangling their legs in the water. The family landline rang at the front of the house, and he ignored it.

Second ring.

What would Mary do?

Third ring.

Gail was slow to rise, not caring much who might be calling that number, and his feet dragged on the way to the living room, where he picked up the receiver and said a listless, "Hello."

And Iggy said, "Your burners are dead and buried, but not all of 'em. I checked the numbers, Gail. I know you still got the one for calls to Brox. Get *rid* of it! And then, you and me? We're done."

"Wait! One minute, okay? . . . Iggy, I know you don't trust the technology. If you want to go back to the client's place . . . just to make sure he didn't write down my burner number. I understand. I really do. You got a pen on—"

"I already got that number, Gail."

Of course he did. That number would be the only one

listed for outgoing calls on the phone he had stolen from Dwayne Brox—a number that cops could link back to a 911 tape of Mary supplying this address for the ambulance.

“There’s no way to track that number back here.” Was he believed? Could Iggy hear him sweating through the telephone line? “But I know how you feel, and I’m okay with it. I’m not worried about you going back there to look for the—”

“So . . . you screwed up.”

The click of disconnection was terrifying. But Gail’s first calming thought was that Iggy was not lying in wait near the house.

Gail believed this because he was still alive.

MAIL CARRIER MARKO PATRONE zipped up the bulky blue bag on his cart and left it on the sidewalk to enter an apartment house. This building was always trouble. He inserted a key in the lock of a long metal plate, then swung it down on its hinges to expose the row of open slots for tenant mailboxes. One was jammed up with catalogs and junk mail from previous visits. That old lady *never* cleaned out her box without a reminder from him. *Bitch!* And there she was, waiting for the elevator only steps away from the interior door that his key would not open. He banged on the glass. “Hey!”

When his lecture had been delivered to the old bat, and all his letters dropped into their boxes, Marko passed through the street door. *Ah, jeez.* His mail cart had fallen into the basement well below the sidewalk. Had he forgotten to zip up his mailbag? Yeah. Banded letter bundles were lying on the cement floor where the trashcans were stored. He scrambled down the steps and righted the tipped-over cart.

If this had happened around the next corner, he'd be in deep shit for sure. All those reporters were still hanging around Gracie Mansion.

Marko wiped dirt from the bundles. Good as new. But when he returned them to his bag, he saw the cardboard corner of a package that should not be there. He parted letters and magazines to dig it out. This box was small, but not sized to fit a standard mail slot. It should have gone out on the parcel truck. The block letters addressed it to Mayor Andrew Polk. After twenty years on this route, a package for Gracie Mansion was not likely to slip his mind. And, sure as hell, he had *not* packed this one.

Damn supervisor. Back at the Post Office, he had seen that bastard poking through the bag, double-checking mail screened by the cops—so he said. Nothing had been said about *adding* one more to the carrier's load. The boss had no right to cram last-minute shit in a carrier's bag. And it was jammed in deep so it wouldn't get noticed until Marko was out the door.

More outrage—not one damned postage stamp on the box and no metered sticker, either.

Maybe supervisors and big-shot politicians thought they could just ignore postal regulations. He had a mind to go back there right now and raise a stink. *Or*, instead of filling out the paperwork for a package with no return address and no postage, he could forgo the satisfaction of reaming out his jerk supervisor, fun as that might be, and just drop off the damn parcel. Why not? For a package with postage due, maybe he could meet the mayor—and maybe get himself on TV.

* * *

ANDREW POLK walked down the passageway to the Wagner Wing, where space expanded into a grand ballroom of tall blue walls and white trim, bronze urns and crystal sconces. Crossing to the far corner, he entered a small tucked-away reception room, the one with the yellow walls and a view of East End Avenue, though only a snatch of sidewalks and road could be seen between the trees on either side of the driveway. He was watching the reporters watching him when the mail arrived. The postman, having passed muster with uniformed guards, was escorted into the park—*holding a small square box.*

Just the right size. And it was his birthday! *What* perfection.

There it was, hanging out in sight of a dozen cameras for all the world to see. Oh, this was almost too orgasmic to be endured.

Not waiting for the postman to reach the gatehouse, where another guard would surely confiscate the box, the mayor flew into the wing's entryway, down a short flight stairs, and he was out the door on the run to accept his small package in full view of the street. He stopped near the foot of the driveway, and then, with one arm around the civil servant's shoulders, Andrew Polk smiled and waved to reporters.

He looked down at the little carton addressed to him in familiar block letters. No stamps? *Bravo!* It had bypassed the screeners who opened his personal mail at the Post Office.

The mailman was paid the estimated postage due—and assured of five-seconds' immortality on the evening news. With a final wave for the cameras, the mayor retreated up the driveway to enter the Wagner Wing, silently singing, *Happy birthday to me—*

Would he make it back down the passage to the mansion before his protection detail noticed that he had slipped away?

—Happy birthday to me—

He was half the way across the ballroom when he met a worried Detective Brogan coming toward him. Good reason for worry. The man in charge of guarding the mayor of New York City was late to notice that His Honor was no longer upstairs in his private quarters.

And where was this bodyguard's partner? Napping?

Brogan looked down at the small square package—a brand-new worry.

—Happy birthday to meeee—

Andrew Polk pressed the addressed side of the box against his chest. "No problem. The mailman says they're screening everything at the Post Office. Oh, but you already knew that." Grinning, the mayor walked away with a song in his heart and a heart in his hands.

THE CALLER ID on Mallory's desk phone gave up the name of her pet reporter, Woody Merrill, who was part of the throng of watchers at the gate to Gracie Mansion. Media leaks were currency in Copland. In exchange for her promises of insider tidbits, Woody had agreed to update her on traffic in and out of the gate, as well as her keenest interest—any *odd* thing.

She trusted him more than the mayor's bodyguards.

That protection detail had been pared down to two men under house arrest in the mansion, where they awaited department hearings on charges of fraudulent furloughs and faked reports to cover up the mayor's many vacations at sea. The police commissioner might assume that this would scare Detective Brogan and his partner, Courtney, into hyper vigilance. But Mallory took them for cops with very little left to lose—only going through the motions of the jobs they had thrown away.

Tapping the keyboard on her laptop, she let the reporter's call go on ringing. On the fourth ring, she picked up the receiver, aiming for annoyance in her voice when she asked, "What've you got for me, Woody?" There had been no reason to pose this question. She was already watching the reporter's camera feed on her screen.

"Check this. I sent you a photo op with a mailman. The mayor almost kissed the guy. Is that—"

"Yeah, *right!*" Mallory slammed the receiver down on its cradle, leaving Woody to assume that this was her comment on his waste of her time.

Far from it.

She froze the video and zoomed in on the small square package cradled in Andrew Polk's right arm—held close to the chest—something precious. The mayor's police bodyguards were nowhere in sight. Those detectives had never been told what a serial killer was using as proof of death, but they had been under orders to report everything coming into the mansion. As yet, neither of them had phoned in the receipt of this parcel.

It was the right size to contain a human heart, proof that the boy was dead.

Riker was just sitting down at his desk when she said, "Have somebody pick up Dwayne Brox. Tell him we're bringing him in for a handwriting sample."

Before her partner had a chance to speak, she was on the move, car keys in hand. Crossing the squad room, she pulled out her cell phone to contact another detective on duty at the Upper East Side Post Office. Rubin Washington had been entrusted to open and read all of the mayor's incoming mail. Over the phone, he confirmed that the batch released for delivery to Gracie Mansion contained only letters, very dull ones, and a slew of birthday cards. "No boxes. . . . What? . . . No shit!" he said, when she explained why he needed to track down the mayor's local mail carrier, a mule for a contraband heart, and scare him, break his fingers—maybe shoot him a few times.

"Whatever it takes," said Mallory.

ANDREW POLK had stepped away from his mansion office only a moment ago. As long as a minute? Surely not. Yet this young cop had a sense of permanence about her, as if she had been lounging in the chair behind his desk all day, leisurely reading his copy of *The Wall Street Journal.*

With no hello or even a glance to acknowledge him, Detective Mallory asked, "Is there something you'd like to tell me? Anything the police should know?"

"Not a thing," he said.

"Really." She had just called him a liar, if only by inflection. The detective laid down the newspaper to plug a small device into her cell phone. "Mr. Mayor, you're being recorded." When she was done with a mention of the date, the time, the parties present in the room, and, best for last, a reading of his rights, she said, "Now let's try this again. Have you had any recent communication from the killer?"

Was she running a bluff? "No, nothing at all." He smiled, daring her to contradict him.

She idly turned a page of the *Journal*, saying so casually, "I've come for the heart."

He *liked* her style. After taking a seat in the facing chair, the one reserved for people seeking an audience with *him*, he crossed his legs, folded his arms and asked, "What heart?"

The detective continued to read the newspaper, *her* paper now, thus inspiring him to name this game Who Would Twitch First?

She did.

Leaning forward, holding out her cell phone, Detective Mallory showed him a picture of his pose with the mailman, and then she offered the proviso, "Don't play me. Just get it."

"There *was* a package delivered. . . . I haven't opened it yet." He looked around the office, as if he expected to see it lying around in plain sight. "Where *did* I put it?" He gave her an apologetic smile. "It was a small package. Such a big mansion, so many rooms."

She leaned back in the desk chair and stared at the bookcase lining one wall. "Get it."

This cop had an eye for detail. She was looking at the middle row of volumes, no doubt taking interest in the five books that had been hastily replaced upside down. Searchers from the Crime Scene Unit had also found this hiding place, and within only minutes of entering his office, though the CSIs had found it empty on that occasion.

A gracious loser, he removed the small safe that was disguised as a fused block of volumes and sized to fit numerous dirty documents—or just the one human heart. After removing the contents, he was startled by the quick flash of a cream-white hand. Red fingernails. Long ones. And now the small cardboard box was hers.

"It's been opened," she said.

"Must've happened at the Post Office. They're opening all my mail. I didn't look inside yet. I was going to hand it off to—"

"The mailman told us the package was sealed with tape when he gave it to you. We have his sworn statement."

"Well, then . . . one of my bodyguards? Maybe after I—" Oh, why bother? It took a player to know one. He made a slight bow of appreciation.

She pulled up the loose cardboard flaps and, with no show of surprise, looked down at the blood-red heart in plastic wrapping that was marked with the words, *PROOF OF DEATH*. "What about proof of life? Where's the ransom demand?"

"No idea what you're— That *hurts!*" His right arm was jammed up behind his back as she bent him over the desk.

MALLORY MARCHED THE HANDCUFFED mayor down the stairs to see Courtney, the younger detective on the protection detail. He stood before the front door on the other side of the foyer. He avoided her eyes.

She ignored him, turning with her prisoner to enter the hall leading to the Wagner Wing, her planned route to East End Avenue. The senior man, Detective Brogan, blocked her way down this narrow passage. His face was grim, his arms folded to put her on notice that he would not be moved from his post. Polk smiled at this bodyguard and gave him a nod that said, *Good doggy.* But Brogan seemed unaware of the mayor of New York City standing there in irons.

Brogan's eyes were locked on Mallory.

Showdown.

But why? He had to know there was a squad of reinforcements one phone call away. It was a fight he could not win. Mallory held up the small cardboard box. Each word carried equal weight as she said, "This is the bloody body part of a little boy. . . . Step aside."

The man had no bristle to him, only the tired stance of a cop who did not take orders from her. He was already saying goodbye to his shield and his pension. He might not mind if she shot him. Too many rules broken, too much gone past him, and now this. A piece of a dead child had been walked in the door on his watch. And—he—had—missed—that.

"Proof of Jonah Quill's death." She opened the box flaps to show him. "It's his heart."

Brogan looked sick.

He held his ground.

"This is the deal." His eyes were on her again, and he spoke cop to cop. "There's not gonna be any perp walk through that media circus out there. And no handcuffs, Mallory. This goes down real quiet. Me and my partner, *we* bring him in, not you. Where the mayor goes, we go with him—that's the job description. That's *our* job. It *sucks,* but—" His eyes drifted back to the small box.

Brogan's arms unfolded and dropped. The man's career would end today or tomorrow. That was a sure thing. But this, his last stand, was left hanging.

And his dignity.

In Lou Markowitz's confrontations with politicians, feds and cops, the old man had always shown great generosity to the losers. Mallory was more inclined to treat this detective like the grafting screwup that he was. Yet she unlocked the mayor's handcuffs—and stepped aside.

IGGY CONROY stood near the edge of the roof, his binoculars trained on the sidewalk across the street. Dwayne Brox was leaving his apartment building in company with the same two cops who had made last night's arrest at the diner. No handcuffs? The little twit was grinning, having his fun with them. That could only mean the police had no evidence to charge him—not today.

When the unmarked Crown Victoria had pulled away, more cars of the same make were double-parking along the street. He counted six men in suits—*more* detectives. A search party! Would they find a cell-phone connection? If Gail was suddenly worried about the burner number, that meant the cops *could* backtrack Brox's calls.

Gail, you shit!

How many more loose ends could there be?

THE UNMARKED POLICE CAR had reached its destination. Dwayne Brox heard the double click of lock releases and a clear invitation to "Get out!" But he waited in the backseat until Detective Gonzales was forced to play chauffeur, opening the rear door for his passenger.

At his leisure, Dwayne climbed out to stand on the sidewalk in front of the SoHo station house. Reporters were corralled behind wooden sawhorses, no doubt invited here by the police. He grinned and waved to every camera lens.

Detective Lonahan pointed him toward the entrance

to the police station. At the top of the stone steps, Dwayne waited until a uniformed officer finally stepped forward to do butler duty and open the door.

For all this, he was still invisible to Detective Riker, who stood only inches away, leaning back against the brick wall and taking a long drag on a cigarette. All the reporters and every camera turned to this cop. In response to a shouted question, Riker said, "No, Mr. Brox isn't being charged. He's only a *person* of *interest*." And that last phrase was every TV cop's code for *He did it! He's guilty! We got him!*

Glorious.

It was all the pressure that anyone could ever ask for. Oh, dear God, could the day get any better than this? Dwayne laughed as the door closed behind him.

THE DETECTIVES had finished with the filing cabinet that held only the detritus of two lives, the dead parents. Even the pile of junk mail and unpaid bills were addressed to the late Mr. and Mrs. Brox. No scrap of paper could be found with any helpful notation—like maybe a phone number for a hit man.

The suspect seemed to have damn little use for paper. Better luck was had by Detective Sanger, the most computer literate among them today, as he scanned the files of a laptop computer. "The guy's an idiot. I don't even need a password. Dwayne never logged out."

Sanger clicked the icon that would give up an address book of contacts, and he recognized one name. It was an old movie title for his girlfriend's favorite chick flick. "I dunno," said Sanger. "Our hit man *might* be Anna Karenina. Or maybe he's one of these guys." He pointed to the given names, Dmitri, Alyosha, Ivan and Pavel, each followed by the initial *K*. Given a bias from his days in Narcotics, he liked every tie with a Russian-mob flavor.

Janos, who favored books over movies, leaned close to the screen to read that segment of the contact list. "What a showboating jerk. He screwed up, too. Pavel's last name begins with an *S*, not a *K*. He was the old man's bastard."

"Oh, yeah." Sanger diddled the keyboard as he waited for someone else to jump in and say, *"WHAT?"*

"WELL, THERE'S NO reporters in the house," said Jack Coffey. "I want him cuffed before Mallory brings him up here." The lieutenant ended his call with the desk sergeant, having settled the downstairs argument with the mayor's protection detail.

Appearances were important today. He had arranged for the two men to meet in passing. Dwayne Brox was seated at a desk in the squad room, one that had been moved to face the stairwell door. He was filling a sheet of paper with samples of his block lettering. One line might match the box that contained the child's heart, though printing was only the next best thing to no good in handwriting identification. But that was busywork while waiting for—

The stairwell door opened, and there was Mallory, holding the arm of the handcuffed mayor of New York City. For this historic interrogation, no lesser lawyer than the Manhattan DA was en route to the station house.

When Brox looked up to see Polk in handcuffs, the lieutenant anticipated fear and anxiety. What he had not expected was their exchange of smiles, each man so happy to see the other—*in custody.*

This was fun for them?

The lieutenant turned to the tall psychologist beside him, saying, "What's up here?"

Charles Butler looked worried. "I should've guessed. . . . I'm so sorry."

THE SOLE OCCUPANT of the interrogation room, Mayor Andrew Polk, was smiling at some little joke he had told to himself.

Next door was District Attorney Ambrose, who had arrived with no entourage for this special occasion of bringing down a political enemy. Best to gloat alone.

And so there were smiles on both sides of the one-way-glass window when Riker entered the watchers' room to say, "We're just waitin' for the mayor's lawyer to get here." After that, if need be, the detective would spin a few lies to explain any further delay, while Mallory sat with Charles Butler behind the closed door of the lieutenant's office.

"TALK FAST."

This psychologist was prone to carefully considered wordy responses, and Jack Coffey broke the long silence, saying, "A little faster than that, okay?"

"I've never set eyes on the mayor before today," said Charles, "But still . . . I should've seen it. Polk and Brox, they're *both* high-risk sociopaths. *Dueling* sociopaths. You might call this the ultimate game of chicken. Neither of them is going to back down. It's not about money anymore—if it ever was. It's the power play, the *game*. All along it was headed this way. I should have realized . . .

given who they are, *what* they are. It could only have ended badly . . . and now the boy is dead."

Charles might be the saddest man in New York City. He was taking on all the guilt and responsibility for Jonah's murder. And the lieutenant could see that this man's self-inflicted torture was just fine by Mallory.

She was so quiet. A bomb with no tick. Could she be any angrier?

Her cell phone rang. After reading lines of text on her screen, Mallory was out the door and gone. And, yes, she could be and *was* a damn sight more angry.

DR. EDWARD SLOPE dropped his cell phone into a pocket of his lab coat. Kathy Mallory was on the way here, or so she said.

She damn well *better* be.

There had been an improbable, inexplicable error, and someone was going to answer for it, but he was determined that no one in the Medical Examiner's Office was going to take any blame. Well, maybe one person. Yes, certainly one. It was predictable that she would first blame him. What were friends for?

24

Gail Rawly quelled the urge to yell, to flap his arms and bang his head against a wall.

Perhaps it was a mistake to let Mary believe that they were going on a surprise vacation. She had wasted precious time securing every window's hurricane shutters to protect the house from summer storms while they were gone—never to return. And she had given Gail his own list of chores. Insanely enough, he had done them, though *speed was everything today.*

Mary and the princess were packing bags—*still* not ready to go!

He should've just tossed his wife and child into the car. One small mercy on a bad day, Mary and Patty could not see outside the shuttered windows as Gail lay flat on the driveway, opening the garage door with his remote control in one hand—and a gun in the other—checking to see that there were no feet hiding behind the two cars parked in there.

* * *

"MY PEOPLE *don't* make this kind of mistake!" said the chief medical examiner as he led the young detective into the old autopsy room that had been repurposed for secrecy. No keys to the door were held by janitors or morgue attendants. A single archaic lightbulb was trained on the dissection table, another artifact from the infancy of forensic medicine. Only the half-size refrigerator belonged to this century. Dr. Slope had wheeled it in here himself, and now he opened it to extract a small metal tray, one of five. "The chain of evidence is indisputable. It's got *your signature* on it." When he turned around to face an angry Kathy Mallory, he held a child's heart in his gloved hand, but "It's not Jonah Quill's heart."

And gone was her best evidence.

He gently placed the organ on the table. "It has the bio markers for a male, but it came from the body of a younger boy, six or seven years old. And there's one more departure you might find interesting." He nodded toward the small refrigerator, his makeshift morgue of hearts. "The other four were well preserved by the vacuum-sealed bags. No air to oxidize the tissue, and carbon monoxide was added to keep them red."

"Like meat from a fresh kill," she said. "That's what the hit man's client expected to see."

"And the grocer's customer, too. Gas flushing—that's a meatpacker's trick. Your killer shows an insane attention to detail." He looked down at the tray that held the child's heart. "But this one's a bit *too* red. It wasn't wrapped within hours of death—but days afterward. That's why your killer bathed it in red food coloring. Smell it."

Always game to sniff body parts, she bent low to the table and inhaled the odor of the heart. "Sour," she said. "Spoiled meat."

"Spoiled before the packaging, and it wasn't nicked by the cut to open—"

"But there *is* a wound," she said, as if he might have missed that gaping slice, so different from the cuts needed to sever the heart from the body. Every other appendage was a stub.

"Your butcher might've been in a hurry this time. Or—back to insane detail—he was trying to hide the fact that *this* child had an artificial valve." He saw the challenge in her eyes, a look that said, *Prove it!* And, as she well knew, he could not identify what was *not* there. She was always annoyed when he played detective, and he seldom missed an opportunity to irritate her. Now for his best shot. "If there was no artificial valve—maybe there should have been. The boy needed at least one. I found a congenital defect in another valve."

Take *that*.

"A damaged heart? So this boy died of natural causes."

And now it was his place to be annoyed. She was always making leaps with no foundation. "I can't make that call with only the—"

"*I* can," she said. "The hit man's *got* Jonah. It would've been a lot easier to take *his* heart."

Excellent point. If the killer had not slaughtered and mutilated twelve-year-old Jonah, what were the odds that he would murder a younger child for a heart? "So . . . let's say it's a death by natural causes."

"Right." She could pack so much sarcasm into a single syllable, but then she layered on a bit more. "Let's *say* that."

"Then your killer went shopping for corpses. There was no embalming, but you can rule out hospital morgues. They refrigerate the—"

"I would've done that anyway. Too risky for my guy. Too many security cameras, and they're staffed round the clock." By tone alone, she managed to convey that he should stop this cop kind of speculation. All she wanted from him were facts.

Well, too bad.

"Funeral homes," he said. "The boy might've been Jewish Orthodox. There wouldn't have been embalming for the—"

"And no stolen body parts. A relative or a family friend would've stayed with the corpse till they put it in the ground."

Kathy had done that service for her foster father, a not-so-orthodox Jew. The vigil had not been required for Louis Markowitz's death, and no one had asked this of her. But that ancient custom had been her story to the rabbi on the night when he had gone to the morgue and tried to coax her home.

However, Edward Slope, her greatest detractor, was not so easily gulled. He had always seen that observance of ritual as a liar's cover story for a long goodbye. Stubborn Kathy, neither ready nor willing to give up her dead on that night, had only grudgingly surrendered the body to a casket come morning. And so it was the doctor's theory that she had loved Lou Markowitz more than that good old man ever knew.

UPON WAKING, Jonah obeyed the old command of Aunt Angie's to open his eyes—to no purpose. Only his fingertips could see the bandage that covered his head like a helmet. More gauze was wrapped around his swollen leg.

Both wounds throbbed, but there was no pain. He was only groggy. Drugged again?

There was moisture in the air. He was back in the basement, and an antiseptic smell overpowered the stink of the mildewed mop.

Upstairs, the man's feet were heavy as hammer falls, pausing only for the slam of doors and the lighter bangs of cupboards roughly closed. Objects dropping, breaking on the floor overhead. And now an outcry, a long strung out *Ah!* from the gut that spelled out Cigarette Man's despair.

The dog was agitated. A bark. Panting. Wheezing. Toenails crossed the cement beyond the door, on the way to meet the man's footsteps stomping down the stairs.

Was Cigarette Man coming to beat him to death? Was he that angry?

The bolt on the door slid back. The smell of cigarettes walked in.

And Jonah said, "Before you do this . . . tell me why you killed her."

The footsteps came closer. The rubber mattress sank on one end as the man sat down, and his voice had no anger to it when he said, "Sure you wanna hear this?"

"Yes . . . please."

"I don't *know* why she died. . . . I set out to kill an old man that day." The lighter clicked. A sigh. The smell of exhaled smoke. "I was inside an empty store, waitin' for this geezer. He's like five feet away when I shoot him with a dart. His knees give out, and I'm right there to catch him and take him back to the store. So I'm halfway in . . . and I see you comin' down the sidewalk . . . with Angie's face. I dump the old man on the floor, and I lean outside.

I'm lookin' at you, kid—when she comes up behind me, *jumps* me. She's *on* me. We roll into the store. Her on my back. Fingers goin' for my eyes. *Screamin'!* I get her off me. Backhand her and knock her into a wall. *Now* I see her face. *Angie. . . . ForthelovaGod,* it's Angie. . . . She's slidin' to the floor when you come runnin' in. But she's already dead. She didn't hit that wall hard enough to even knock her out, but she's—"

The dog sent up a wail of pain, and the man yelled, "Shut up!" In a softer voice, he said, "And I see you standin' there, eyes real wide. Scared. Lookin' right at me. . . . I started that day with a clockwork plan, and it all went to shit in half a minute. . . . I don't know *why* she died."

"She died to save me. She's *still* trying to—"

"Naw, they don't come back, kid. Ghosts. They're not like you think. They're more like echoes of people."

"You heard the bells in the sky. I *know* you did."

"You were awake for that? I thought you was out of it. For a while there, I thought you was dead. . . . Okay, the jingle bells—that wasn't her. Out here in the country, sound can travel a long way."

"From the *sky?"*

"She's gone, kid. She won't never come back." Cigarette Man got up from the mattress. His steps were slow to cross the floor. The door closed on the man and the dog. Outside the laundry room, the pit bull whimpered and thumped to the floor, breathing ragged as if it had run a fast mile.

Jonah lay back on the mattress, falling in love with his own game of ghost. The jingle bells had sold him on it, and now he whispered, "Aunt Angie?"

The boy waited for a sign from her.

He waited so patiently.

* * *

DETECTIVE MALLORY was nowhere to be found, and all her calls were going to voice mail. Rather than wait any longer, District Attorney Ambrose decided that the commander of Special Crimes should do the interview. Rank should speak to rank—and not one, but three of Andrew Polk's lawyers.

Jack Coffey entered the interrogation room, mindful that the mayor was a control freak. He followed Charles Butler's advice to ignore the man—a sure way to piss him off and off-balance him. The lieutenant spoke to the first attorney in the string, the youngest one who seemed least at home in a police station. "We pulled the erased information from your client's cell phone."

The lawyer, just a tad apprehensive, turned to his client.

Coffey shot a glance at the mayor. He could translate Polk's smile as *Nice try, but no way.* True, there was nothing incriminating on the phone taken from the mayor's pocket. In a show of clarifying things for the least experienced lawyer, the lieutenant leaned toward this young man to say, "I'm talking about the other cell phone, the one with Jonah Quill's proof of life." This was only a bluff, but, "That bookends nicely with proof of death." And those last three words were made hideously clear as he laid down a photograph of the bloody organ and what was written on its plastic wrapping. "That heart was cut out of a murdered child, Jonah Quill. Maybe you've heard of him?"

All three attorneys were taken by surprise, even the eldest one at the end of the table. Coffey enlightened them. "The mayor was keeping it in his safe. Maybe a sick souvenir. Who knows?"

The two younger lawyers must be new hires, virgins in murder and mutilation. Their faces were that pale shade that preceded projectile vomit. But the old man at the table, Arty Shay, was famous for being able to stomach every damn kind of carnage, and so he was beloved by criminals uptown and down. Shay was not inclined to fold early, if ever, and he said, "About that phone. We'll need to see evidence of the—"

"You don't get zip," said the lieutenant. "Not till your client's been charged and arraigned for conspiracy kidnap and murder."

The other two lawyers acted as alter egos for the mayor, getting antsy on his behalf. Andrew Polk only sat back and enjoyed the performance. He must know that they would never find a second phone or any other tangible evidence against him. Jack Coffey's second thought was that the mayor was just not in touch with reality.

Either way, no sense of fear.

"Charge my client, Jack. Or cut him loose," said Arty Shay.

Very ballsy. Bluff called. Game over? No, not with one charge left on the table. "Okay, Arty, let's start with the appetizer—obstruction of justice. You're welcome to a witness statement for the kid's heart." Jack Coffey pushed the photograph of the disembodied heart in the lawyer's direction. "You can keep that if you like. I got my own copy for the judge at his arraignment. Hell with pictures, I can bring in the damn heart. We gave your guy first shot—as a courtesy, but now we're done."

The lieutenant turned to the youngest lawyer. "If you don't know the drill, when we got two perps, we give them a chance to roll on each other. First one to rat, that's our winner. House rules." And now he faced the mayor. "You saw Dwayne Brox when you came in, right? Sitting at a desk . . . writing out his statement. Hey, you had to wonder why the guy smiled at you. So, as far as a deal goes, it's his turn now. Oh, and the feds asked for a crack at him, too." He wanted to put his fist through the mayor's maddening grin.

At least Arty Shay seemed rattled, a small victory. And Shay's young associates took a cue from their boss's startled face, running over one another's words to say that they would need some privacy for a conversation with the client.

ALL THE PLAYERS had changed. Dwayne Brox was seated at the table with his own attorney when Riker walked into the interrogation room and announced that "Anna Karenina's a whore."

That might be harsh.

A phone number found on Brox's laptop had connected police to an escort service, but call girls were one up from whores in a prostitute's pecking order. And the lady's professional moniker, Kitty Kat, was not to be found in any Russian novel. So Bug Boy had created an alias for an alias for a woman whose real name was Su Ling, a recent arrival from Hong Kong.

"We had a talk with Kitty." It had been a short chat under threat of deportation. "She says you got a tiny weener, kid. Skinny, too. Her escort service has you down as Needle Dick on their client list, and that explains a lot."

Well, finally—an expression that was not smug. Dwayne Brox was leaning into it, angry and showing it.

The attorney rested one hand on his client's arm, a subtle warning not to react to the provocation of a dick shot, and now the lawyer favored Riker with an imperious glare. "Detective, I think we can dispense with remarks like that."

"Okay, Counselor, let's move on to *The Brothers Karamazov*." He smiled. "Yeah, you heard me right. Your client knows 'em all on a first name basis. He's got their phone numbers on his laptop. Just dumb luck we got a cop who's read everything by Dostoyevsky. One of the Karamazovs—Dmitri, I think—his number connects to what might be the last phone booth in America." Riker turned to Brox. "It's inside your bookie's favorite bar. Dmitri's real name is Bernie Mars. He's old-school. Doesn't wanna know from cell phones. Bernie says you don't know squat about sports, and you bet like a little girl. Pansy, that's what he calls you."

"Detective," said the attorney. "I warned you about deprecating remarks."

Yeah, like that ever worked. "Time to do a deal, Counselor. I got three more Karamazov brothers. You don't wanna wait till we finish tracking their numbers. We might find the hit man before your client pleads out."

That was a lie. Detective Sanger had already checked out the remaining book characters, Alyosha, Ivan and their bastard brother Pavel. Two of the cell phones had pings in areas of heavy drug traffic, and he figured them for dealers. For the third number, Sanger had gotten lucky with a call history.

Detectives Janos and Washington were on the way to visit a cell-phone owner, who had so generously left a name and street address on the tape of a 911 call—when a frantic woman had begged the operator to send an ambulance for her asthmatic daughter.

* * *

THE DETECTIVES from Special Crimes drove along a forested road in the neighboring state of Connecticut. Widely spaced mailboxes were the only indications that there were houses nestled deep in this expensive acreage. They found the mailbox they wanted, but they could go no farther. An officer in uniform was stringing yellow crime-scene tape from tree to tree on either side of the driveway. The two New Yorkers sat in their unmarked car and watched a medical examiner's team hoist a zippered body bag into a meat wagon.

Janos threw up his hands. Oh, shot in the dark—maybe they had arrived too late to question their suspected hit man, Gail Rawly.

"Well, that sucks," said Washington, indicating that he was not up for an interstate jurisdictional war over that corpse.

When they stepped out of their car, they had the full attention of the officer guarding the driveway. He examined their badges and ID cards very carefully—he was *that* young. "I can't let you in." So apologetic, he nodded toward the foot of the driveway. "The detectives are back there with the Crime Scene Unit."

"Not a problem," said Janos. There was no chance that those locals would give them anything useful. "You might be just the guy we need. I bet you were the first responder. Am I right?"

The rookie policeman's smile confirmed this. Janos could also depend on the fact that the hometown detectives had treated this youngster like he was unfit for anything beyond handmaid's duties. "Officer, if you got the time, we need some help on this case we're working back in New York."

Right again. The kid responded well to simple respect.

According to Officer Sacco, Gail Rawly was the victim of vehicular homicide. "In his own driveway." And this cop had other inside information as well, the only perk of being invisible to "those pricks in charge," when the grownups were talking. "They got a suspect. Mrs. Rawly had her bags all packed. The little girl's, too. So, she was planning to leave her husband, right? The detectives figure there was a fight, and that's why she ran Mr. Rawly down in the driveway. Then, I guess he was still breathing . . . because she backed over him and parked the car with one wheel sitting on his chest. That's how I found him—under the wife's car."

At Janos's request, the uniformed officer used his cell phone to call the local detectives at the other end of the driveway—to tell them that two New York cops had information on their victim. Always best to turn up with gifts when visiting another jurisdiction.

Officer Sacco put away his phone and pulled one end of the crime-scene tape free. As Janos and Washington walked up the driveway, they passed CSIs who were dusting a car's steering wheel for prints. Playing nice with this crew, the detectives held up their badges, and they were careful in giving wide berth to the blood pool on the ground. Up ahead, a man with a suit and badge stood outside the front door to the house.

This local cop was wary, unhappy to see the foreigners from out of state, and now he introduced himself as one of the detectives who owned this homicide. "We already know the guy's an insurance investigator."

"Of course you do," said Janos. "And I'm sure you

know Mr. Rawly's credit card was used to book *three* plane tickets north of here. We figure the guy paid cash for the real destination. Is that how you see it, too?" No, he could tell this was news to the hometown cop. "So you knew the whole family was planning to blow town . . . not just the wife and kid." He leaned around the detective to see suitcases stacked in the foyer. "I'm guessing when you checked those bags, you found Gail Rawly's clothes in the mix?"

No, again. What had these fools been doing with their time?

"We got more on your vic," said Washington.

The man from Connecticut stepped to one side, and the New York detectives pulled on latex gloves to make a cursory walk-through. They avoided the bedroom with its door ajar to show them the child-size furniture and pink walls of a little girl's room. An older female was also in there. They could hear her crying.

On their return to the front room, Washington handed over three passports pulled from a duffel bag found in the den. "Forgeries. Brand-new names for the whole family. So you gotta know Rawly's not your average insurance investigator. We figure him for a hit man. He must've known we were close to nailing him, but he didn't plan to leave the wife behind. That tells me they got along pretty well. We don't like Mrs. Rawly for this murder."

The younger Connecticut man took a hands-on-hips stance that said, in sandbox lingo, *Oh, yeah?* And his partner said, "Well, if she didn't do it—who hit the hit man?" And his smirk told them that he expected no snappy answer for that one. Evidently, these two liked their own theory of the crime, holes and all, and they were sticking with it.

* * *

TWO HOURS LATER, Janos and Washington sat in their lieutenant's office, making a full report. They had gotten as far as the driveway murder when Jack Coffey said, "So our hit man's dead."

"No," said Janos. "You didn't get our message?"

"Yeah, I got the gist of it." Lonahan had taken that call and relayed the bare-bones information that the Connecticut suspect was dead. The lieutenant had yet to read the more detailed account. "It's been a busy day." A bitch of a day. So much time had been lost to being reamed out by an irate district attorney.

"We figure Gail Rawly for the middleman." When Washington was done with the details of their walk-through, he said, "On our way outta there, we talked to the CSIs working on the car. They pulled fingerprints and matched 'em up with the wife's. Hers were the only ones on the steering wheel. . . . Mrs. Rawly really loves her car."

"Real *nice* car," said Janos. "The steering wheel's mahogany, and the spokes are covered with *gorgeous* leather. The lady keeps them oiled so they won't dry out."

"Those CSIs are Mrs. Rawly's biggest fans," said Washington. "Cleanest car they've ever seen. That's how they picked up on the smudges in the oil, smudges thick as fingers on the steering wheel's spokes. They stuck out 'cause of the cotton fibers."

"Gloves," said Coffey. "Could be gardening gloves, but even so—"

Janos finished this thought for him. "Who steers a car with the spokes of a steering wheel?" The wife would not go to that trouble to preserve her own fingerprints on the wooden rim. "That's how we know our hit man's still alive and—"

"Hey, what gives?" Washington was facing the window on the squad room, where Dwayne Brox walked solo toward the stairwell door. "We're kicking him loose—*now?* We got him tied to Gail Rawly."

"Who *might* be involved. That's not enough to hold Brox. But Riker *did* point out that the hit man might see him as a liability." Jack Coffey watched the stairwell door close on their prime suspect. Good as dead—given the murder of Gail Rawly. "But the little creep didn't seem to care."

"What about the mayor?"

"He's already gone." Detective Sanger leaned in the doorway with that finish to the day's update for Janos and Washington. "The arraignment was quick. It's a done deal on the charge of obstruction, but Polk's under house arrest at Gracie Mansion."

The other two detectives looked to their lieutenant, silently asking, *What? What did he just say?*

"That's the judge's call. We can't keep Polk in custody for a bailable offense." Apparently, there was nothing in the criminal code to cover receiving a child's bloody heart from the mailman. They could only slap his wrist for holding on to it, lying to Mallory and obstructing her case for an hour.

And now Jack Coffey could count on his squad taking the blame for a hit on Dwayne Brox and maybe a mayoral assassination because—*that was just how this fucking day was going so far!* But his demeanor was laid back when he said, "Okay, next assignment. Mallory's not taking any calls. Find her. Drag her back. . . . Handcuffs would be a nice touch."

* * *

SHE LOWERED HER EYES to stare at the open pocket watch in her hand. Time would be crucial in one special scenario, and Dr. Slope's voice was subdued when he said, "You think Jonah Quill's alive."

"Not for long. My perp's a killing machine. It's not like a hit man enjoys his work. It just doesn't bother him. Adults, kids—it's all the same to him. . . . So why don't we have the right heart?" Kathy was so still as she looked down at the old-fashioned timepiece, watching time get away from her.

On a note of hope, the doctor said, "Maybe Jonah escaped and took his heart with him."

"Maybe."

Edward Slope read defeat in her voice and the bow of her head. "If there's anything I can do to help . . . *Anything*."

She raised her face to his. He recognized that smile. And so he knew that she had already prepared a list of things that he could do for her—since he had asked, sucker that he was.

25

Chief Medical Examiner Edward Slope likened it to an invasion. An hour ago, this private office had been a fortress of tranquility with a dragon of a secretary to stave off intruders. Now it was full of staff, excited crosstalk and machines, as his own people—*traitors*—tapped keys for computers and cell phones, hunting down data on heartless cadavers. Kathy Mallory had altered the very atmosphere to copshop air that reeked of bad coffee.

The doctor sat at his desk, which had not yet been commandeered, though she *was* crowding him, sitting beside him, working at a computer perched on the credenza—*his* computer. The door opened, and another console rolled in, piloted by one of his pathologists *cum* furniture movers. The young detective had also recruited his own investigators, and it troubled him that they were so quick to follow her orders, never questioning her authority.

Her own tapping stopped as her chair rolled back from the credenza. "This is a dead end." After running the heart's DNA through data banks, she had come up with no leads.

Well, *good*. The I-told-you-so moment was upon her. "I *told* you the boy wouldn't be on a transplant list. The kind of surgery he needed—"

"There's too many surgeons who do valve replacements," she said. "And *you* wouldn't give me a time frame for the damn operation."

Dr. Slope sucked in his breath for a ten count. Something about her voice made it clear that he had been derelict in his duty, incompetent in her eyes—as if he should be able to look at a bloody hole in a defective disembodied heart, a hole that *might* have been the location of an artificial valve, and tell her exactly *when* that *theoretical* operation had been done.

Was his blood pressure rising? Undoubtedly. On that account, he must compliment her, though not just yet, perhaps on his deathbed. And he was *not* going to respond to that *ludicrous*—

"Got another kid!" Grinning ME investigator Bill Farley shot up one hand like an old lady on bingo night, and then he bent down to the work of circling another name on his printouts of registered graves in the tri-state area. "Best one yet. I got a seven-year-old who died in New Jersey. Jewish Orthodox—no embalming. He was buried yesterday morning." Farley turned an expectant face to Kathy Mallory.

Expecting what? A smile? A reward? Was he delusional?

She only nodded, not yet prepared to toss her new dog a treat. "And the follow-up?"

"I talked to the doctor who signed the death certificate," said Farley. "No valve replacement surgery, but the kid *did* have a heart defect. The parents had an appointment with a cardiologist right before their son died."

Edward Slope wondered if he might have scored a

point here for prescience—a surgery that *would* have been performed if only—

"Here's the bad news," said Farley. "We can't use the parents for a DNA match. The boy was adopted."

"That shouldn't be a problem," said Dr. Slope. "The child's personal items—"

"No such luck." Farley turned away from Kathy to face his boss, belatedly recalling which of them *was* his boss. "The mother was a wreck. So the family decided to—"

"They took away the dead boy's things," said Kathy. Her foster father had endured the attempted kindness of such thieves upon the death of his wife, Helen. "They didn't want the mother to see reminders of her son when she came home from the cemetery."

"Right," said Farley. "Even the mattress. Toothbrush, hairbrush, dirty laundry, everything with DNA—they bagged it all and trashed it. But here's the good news. With a little cooperation from the locals, we can get a crew to the city dump."

"Dumpster diving could kill a few hours. But a whole dump? No, this is all about time. I haven't got any." She turned her attention to the computer on the credenza. "Quicker to dig up the body."

"No way." Farley spoke to her back. "You'll never get consent. Mallory, these people are very religious. I got that from the funeral director. He says a family member came in with the body and stayed with it the rest of the night. So the hit man had no chance to cut out the heart while the body was in the funeral home. But if this is the right kid—"

"He died at *night*? The night before the burial?" Her chair spun around to catch the investigator's nod. "Good. No time for an obit in the local newspaper. If we've got the right kid, the perp didn't read about that death. He *saw* the funeral, the child-size casket. Then he came back and robbed the grave." The detective was smiling when she turned to the medical examiner. "A heart with no body. That's a suspicious death. You wouldn't need consent for an exhumation."

"*If* you had the dead boy's DNA match to the heart . . . which you *don't*."

"*If* I could make that connection, I wouldn't *need* the kid's body! I'd know I had the right funeral service, the right cemetery—the right section of the damn planet!" She turned back to the computer and opened a file to show him a daunting list of dead and missing boys spread out over three states. "I don't have time to rule out the rest of them with DNA matches. . . . It's all about *time*."

And pure conjecture.

Edward Slope rallied with a point of law, an actual *fact*. "You can't exhume a likely corpse on just the theory that—"

"Care to place a bet? . . . *I'll* take your money."

THERE WERE NO MORE Crown Victorias double-parked outside Brox's apartment building. The search of detectives was done, but a change had been made since Iggy's last visit. He pulled down the brim of a ball cap as he walked past the doorman, a brand-new face.

Had to be a cop.

This was going to be dicey.

Turning a corner, he approached the side entrance for deliveries and moving men. There, the building handyman—

the same one, not a cop—was hauling a piece of broken furniture out to the curb for trash collection. Iggy slowed his steps for a glance at the propped-open door. Inside that storage area, a uniformed officer sat on a shipping carton, reading a newspaper.

If the police had two entries covered, he could count on at least one cop positioned inside the rooftop door. This could only mean that the police were planning to release Dwayne Brox from custody. That might be good news if they had no evidence to hold him. But police never got this fancy when they were only keeping an eye on a suspect. Had Brox become the NYPD's star witness—or was he just a cop's idea of bait?

THE WARMTH OF THE DEN was in the colored spines of books that lined the walls and also in the presence of the man seated at the desk. The rabbi's build was lean, his beard neatly trimmed, and his eyes were a bit too wide at the moment, but horror had that effect on this charter member of the Louis Markowitz Floating Poker Game. Obviously, he thought she was asking too much of him. However, by Mallory's lights, since David Kaplan had been her foster parents' rabbi and their oldest friend—she *owned* him.

Yet he said, "No. . . . These people are grieving for their little boy. They're sitting shiva. I'm not going to tell them his grave *may* have been violated . . . that *maybe* his heart was cut out. You can't know if this is the—"

"You're right," she said. "Call it a leap of faith. I'm all in on this one grave."

Not *exactly* the truth. While she pursued this lead, the

ME's investigators were still working through her list of dead and missing boys in the tri-state area, asking local police to call on distraught families and beg for personal effects that might yield DNA.

"Jonah Quill doesn't have much time left," she said. "Tell the parents about *that* kid. A hit man went to a lot of trouble to pass off a bogus heart. He hasn't killed Jonah, not yet, but that could change any minute. This is my chance to find him alive . . . if I can pin down this grave site. The hit man's getting sloppy. He might've left me some tracks, witnesses. I need that body dug up today. Talk to the mother. She'll understand."

No, it was clear that she could not even make the rabbi understand this need. The whole prospect mortified him. Such a tender soul. So . . . what else might she bludgeon him with?

"Rabbi, I don't want to waste time on a forced exhumation." And she could never make a legal case for one. "But if that's the only way to . . ." Mallory let the words trail off, as if she might be unwilling to even speak of this act of last resort. She left it to him to imagine the state brutalizing a grief-stricken mother and father, leaving them powerless, crying at the graveside. "It's better if this is the parents' decision. Tell them it could save the other boy."

Now she had him. His eyes turned sad, as if he already stood with the parents beside the open grave of their mutilated son. He nodded. "I'll speak to them."

"I'll drive you over there." She was not inclined to lose time waiting for this very gentle man to brace himself for the ordeal ahead. He could do that in the car.

* * *

SAD PEOPLE WALKED DOWN this quiet New Jersey street of shade trees, green lawns and single-family houses. They carried covered dishes of kosher food for the parents of the dead boy and those who came to call on them. By custom coupled with heartbreak, Mr. and Mrs. Phelps could not fend for themselves while sitting shiva for their only child.

Mallory waited outside in her personal car, adhering to Rabbi Kaplan's orders. Every word spoken in that house of grief must be softly said and kind. Apparently, he found her incapable of that.

The screen door flew open with such force its frame bounced off the wall of the front porch. A woman came flying out of the house, her feet only lighting on every other step before she hit the walkway on the run. Barefoot. Her hair in wild tangles. This could only be Mrs. Phelps—wearing a mother's raw anguish. Every cop knew it on sight.

The woman's mouth hung open. Her eyes had the dark circles of no sleep. Swiping tears away did her no good. Her face was awash in fresh rivers. And blinded this way, she stumbled, slamming one knee into the silver convertible's door. She gripped the edge of the ragtop roof, steadying herself, staring at the cop inside the car. Mrs. Phelps's lips worked in dumb show, only strangled sobs for words, her features contorted in pain. The rabbi came out of the house to walk up behind her and gently place one hand on her shoulder. She shook him off. Her mouth was still opening and closing, as she struggled so hard to find her voice. Fists tightening. Frustration mounting. Now she banged on the side of the car, once, twice, *three* times. And she said to Mallory, *screamed* at her, "You *find* that little boy! You find Jonah! You bring him home to his family!"

* * *

DAVID KAPLAN took his place in the passenger seat and handed over the consent form signed by the parents. He shook his head to warn Kathy, to tell that she should know better than to thank him for his part in this.

They drove to the cemetery in silence. He noticed that she was abiding by the speed limit, her only sign of contrition.

The ugly machine for unearthing a child was waiting for them at the grave. Kathy was first to leave the vehicle, and she gave a thumbs-up to the backhoe's operator. The engine was loud, and birds made their own fearful sounds, rising en masse from branches of every tree.

The rabbi was slow to approach. He had given certain assurances to the family, and now he had promises to keep. And so he must watch this horror unfold in its noisy mechanical way. At one end of the backhoe's long neck, an iron bucket with monstrous teeth was lowered to the earth for a first bite.

DWAYNE BROX had declined the option of going to the NYPD safe house, which was probably some low-rent hotel room with cops and bedbugs for roommates. *No, thank you.* He had opted for the comforts of his own apartment.

Detective Janos asked, "Did you hear me?"

Dwayne felt no need to respond. Could this fool not see that he was busy? He continued to work his remote control, surfing TV channels.

The detective walked up to the wall-mounted television set and turned it off the old-fashioned way. He ripped the plug from its socket, saying, "Listen up." The big man's voice was soft, but his patience was waning. He began again, explaining that the police officers posted in the building were there for Dwayne's protection. They were not jailing him here. They were *guarding* him. "You got that? The entrances are covered, and we'll have a cop sitting outside in the hall." Janos locked the balcony doors, and then he pulled the cord to close the draperies. "Stay away from *all* the windows, okay?"

THE UNEARTHED COFFIN was opened by a local medical examiner. The state of New Jersey required a pathologist to witness every desecration of a grave.

Mallory had everything she wanted. The dead child's small body had been cut open. Ribs broken. Heart stolen.

The small casket was loaded into a waiting van, and Rabbi Kaplan climbed in beside it. He had promised the mother that her son would never be alone, that he would remain with the dead boy until the body was returned to the earth. Before that could happen, the corpse must first undergo the formal gathering of evidence for the crime committed here.

Mallory raised the hand that held her car keys. "I'll pick you up at the—"

"I'll find my own way back," said the rabbi.

Understood. No offense taken.

This day had cost each of them something. And David Kaplan was still paying for it. He was to be the unwilling observer of an autopsy on Mrs. Phelps's little boy.

She knew that scene was going to destroy the rabbi.

And he was going to forgive her—in time.

* * *

INSIDE THE WORKROOM behind the garage's false wall, Iggy Conroy stood before an open locker jammed with useful clothes. Most of these outfits had patches with logos to fit the jobs of menials, invisible people. Witnesses would only recall the designations of delivery guys and movers, repairmen and utility workers. He pulled out a hanger holding a gray coverall and packed it in his duffel bag. It would fit with the magnetic sign he had slapped on the side of his van. He planned to drive back to the city as a cable repairman.

What else? He would also need a police uniform. He searched the hangers on the rack. Where was it? He ripped out every article of clothing and flung it, hanger by hanger, at the wall. What had he done with the damn thing?

Ah, wait. Months ago, he had wrecked the only one he owned. Yeah. That was why he had taken down a cop on the night he dumped those bodies at Gracie Mansion. And that cop's stolen uniform had gone into the river.

How the hell could he have forgotten a thing like that?

Iggy heard the distant howl of the dog in the basement. This was no warning bark, but a wail trailing off in a moan. The mutt was hungry. He had forgotten to feed the damn dog. And the boy—he had forgotten about him altogether. And what else? WHAT ELSE?

He sank down to the floor, hands covering his eyes and then tightening into fists. Everything was falling apart. He had screwed up so bad. He was down to playing a brainless game of whack-a-mole with the loose ends. His fists hit the floor, drumming, banging.

Done.

No more anger now. No feeling at all.

* * *

ACRES OF GREEN HILLS sloped down to valleys cut by pathways of white gravel. Some of the dead resided in small but grand stone houses, and others had graves adorned with marble statues.

"People come from all over the state," said the wiry gray-haired man. "We're famous. We got two rock stars buried here. But me, I never heard of 'em. Anyway, the place is huge." The cemetery groundskeeper looked down at the drawing in his gnarly hands. "Well, this could be anybody." He looked up at the detective. "Between the visitors and the funeral crowds, you know how many people I seen come through here?"

He opened the door to a small outlying building. Mallory followed him inside to see the promised array of surveillance monitors.

"This ain't the first case of vandalism, but nobody ever robbed a casket before. We had the cameras installed a few years back after somebody ripped off the stained-glass window in a mausoleum. You know what those things cost? The cops caught the guy—a building contractor two towns over. You're flat outta luck if *your* guy dug up that kid's body in the dark. Every rotten thing happens at night, but we got no infrared cameras."

"And no digital storage." Mallory was picking through shelves of cassette tapes that belonged to another era, all labeled by date and cemetery section.

"Well, this stuff's old. That's why they got it so cheap. I been here through three generations of Elroys, all penny-pinching bastards." He watched her hand graze the labels of last night's tapes. "You won't see much. No pictures of the grave robber, not even the grave. Cameras don't cover everything. In the daylight shots, we only got pictures for a few of the mourners."

She already knew the hit man would not be there. The locations of the security cameras were too easy to spot.

"Sorry, Miss. I thought Bobby was in here. Must be slackin' off somewhere. The kid's my assistant. He's the one who works all this crap."

"I know how it works." She pulled out cassettes that had been switched out in the early daylight hours before the funeral. Maybe the killer had been here checking markers, looking for dates of a fresh corpse, and he might have seen the backhoe digging a child-size grave before the funeral.

The groundskeeper was taking a second hard look at the suspect drawing, holding it to the light of a window as he squinted and rubbed his chin. "Most of it don't match, but there's somethin' about the eyes. We got a regular visitor here. When I see him, I never look him in the eye no more. Makes my skin crawl. You know what I mean?" The old man walked to the shelves and pulled down a tape. Handing it to her, he said, "Try this one. It's his regular day, and he always passes this building. No way around it if you park in the lot. Always goes by with a big bouquet of roses."

"Red roses?"

"Yeah."

She flipped a power switch, then fed the tape into the mouth of the machine and pressed the play button for the center monitor. The camera range was narrow. In the mistaken assumption that the electronic equipment might have some value, only this small building was covered. And now she saw the back of a man with a blue baseball cap and a bouquet of roses.

"That's my guy," said the groundskeeper. "The cap, the walk—that's him. You won't never see his face. Sorry 'bout that. No camera ever caught him on the way back to the parking lot."

"I don't suppose you ever followed him."

"Never, not *that* guy."

And she took this last remark as a positive ID for a stone killer.

THE VISITOR with the blue baseball cap had appeared in two other tapes, but only the back of him. One that captured him without his roses gave Mallory a rough idea of where he had been. The grave of the Phelps boy provided a direction, and beyond that, an absence of security cameras gave her a path through an old section, closed now for lack of room to fit one more headstone. Visitors were not so common here. In company with the groundskeeper, she had found six plots with red roses among the floral offerings. Half were ruled out for flowers too fresh or too wilted to fit the timing of the hit man's last bouquet.

She phoned her shortlist in to Riker. "Check the state tax roles for these three." She fed him names and dates of birth and death. "Whatever you can find on them."

"Okay, let's go," she said to the groundskeeper. He walked alongside her on the path to the main building of the Elroy Cemetery, where all the records were kept.

"Don't get your hopes up, Miss. The boss's computer is secondhand crap—almost as old as the cameras. No Internet. Penny-pinching bastard."

PENNY-PINCHING did not fit with the décor. Even Charles Butler, her walking, talking reference book for all things antique, would have approved the appointments of this private office. The furniture dated back to the mid 1800s, when the first grave was dug. The detective and the groundskeeper sat in matching high-back leather armchairs from the same period.

The young man behind the mahogany desk was the descendant of a long line of Elroys. He stared at another antique, his outmoded desktop computer, as he searched it for names of the dead and buried. He had found all but one from her shortlist. "This last one? You must've made an error when you—"

"I was *there,*" said the groundskeeper, taking offense on Mallory's behalf. "I *know* she wrote down the right names. Section and plot numbers, too."

"Impossible," said Elroy. "That last one's in a section that was closed over fifty years ago." Done with the old man, he flashed a toothy smile for Mallory. "But we *do* cross-index." He scrolled down a list of numbers and names. "Ah, plot 947. Like I said, we've got no Moira Conroy buried anywhere in this cemetery. That plot belongs to Moira *Kenna*. That's the name that would've appeared on her temporary marker, the one we always put down for the funeral. So . . . I can see what happened here. When the monument company finished carving her permanent headstone, obviously they delivered the wrong one, a stone for an entirely different Moira. We can't be expected to keep track of things like that. And, apparently, the Kenna family never made a complaint."

A corpse with an alias carved in stone?

Mallory reached out to swivel his monitor sideways for a look at the screen of names and numbers. She pointed to the end of one line. "Check out the dates for birth and death. Explain *that.*"

He leaned in to peer at the glowing numerals that followed Moira Kenna's name. "She died in 1931 . . . at the age of five." And now he consulted the notebook page with Mallory's neatly printed date of death for Moira Conroy, a woman who had lived much longer and died only nine years ago. "Oh, yes, I see." It was highly unlikely that it had taken the stone carver more than eighty years to deliver the wrong monument.

"That's why the family never complained," said Mallory. "They were all dead when you illegally sold that grave the *second* time." Did she believe this? No, she had a better theory. But menace inspired cooperation.

Mr. Elroy got off to a sputtering start. "N-n-no! We would *never*—"

"*Prove* it! You still have paperwork on that plot? Forms with next of kin? A funeral home?"

"Our paperwork dates back more than a hundred and fifty years, and it's all intact. Most of it's on *real* paper." He said this as if it might be a good thing to run a business in the wrong century. "The older sections haven't been scanned into the computer yet. So the Kenna child is downstairs with the rest of the backlog."

OR NOT.

In the basement storage area, Mallory stood before an old wooden filing cabinet, one of many, and she waited for the flustered Mr. Elroy to go through the contents of one drawer—for the third time. The file for plot 947 was not to be found.

"Oh, dear," he said. "If she's been misfiled, we'll never find her until *all* the paperwork gets scanned. That might be *years* from now."

Mallory's scenario for that was *never.* But a theory was proving out by the evidence that could not be found.

The file might have disappeared nine years ago, shortly after the second interment, the burial of Moira Conroy's trespassing corpse. Or it might have been stolen earlier, maybe on a day when the hit man was trolling cemeteries, hunting for an identity to steal for a living woman with roughly the same date of birth, *another* Moira. An elderly woman might find it hard to give up her entire identity—easier to keep her own first name.

Only a dead child would do. Children left no paper trails in the system, and a little girl with the same first name would have been a greater stroke of luck in a smaller cemetery than this one. The buried girl's birth certificate was all that was needed to apply for a Social Security number and a fresh start with bogus credentials. This was theory, but it fit so well with a single fact: Mallory knew she could count on two bodies in that grave.

The man who brought flowers to the deceased poseur had ordered the replacement gravestone with the extra corpse's true name, an act of sentiment that had served a second purpose. It obliterated the last visible trace of the grave's first tenant.

But the stolen identity would have had a life span of its own, one that left tracks. Mallory phoned her partner to add another name to her list of searches. "Run a tri-state trace for a paper ghost, another Moira, last name *Kenna.*"

FOR THE LENGTH of a commercial break, all of Iggy Conroy's possibilities remained intact.

He waited for the news story promised by the teasing

mention of a suspicious death and the exhumation of a New Jersey grave—after a word from the sponsors. With the tap of the mute button on his remote control, he killed the TV volume and watched a silent parade of film clips to sell him this thing and that. How many ads could be smashed into a single minute?

Another minute.

An eternity of ads.

C'mon, c'mon.

The news anchor reappeared. Iggy turned on the volume as the picture changed to a field reporter on location in a parking lot. He recognized the old man standing alongside the young woman with the microphone. She introduced him as an employee of the Elroy Cemetery, the only one willing to speak to the media, though he did not *seem* all that willing. The reporter had boxed him in between two cars and the shrubs that lined the parking spaces.

Following her first question, the surly groundskeeper said, "No, lady, I ain't seen a cop car all day." Asked why the small casket had been exhumed and taken away in a van, he replied, "Ah, who knows? It's not like that never happens. Let's say you're dead, and you think you're all set in your final resting place. But then your family decides to take you with 'em when they move down to Florida. Better weather, right? And maybe your new grave's got an ocean view. . . . People are stupid. . . . But that kills your rumor on a grave robber, don't it? The relatives never haul off empty coffins." And now, on to the traffic report.

A *small* casket. A lying old man.

The cops had that kid's heart!

Had Dwayne Brox just handed it over to them? Was that why they let him go?

Iggy walked through all the rooms of his house, saying goodbye to every wall. It was time to torch his meat locker.

26

The tumbledown house, a shelter to vermin and squatters, sat on the ragged edge of a slum that used to be a town. Even the rats here were down to skin and bone. The only thriving life forms were weeds that came up through cracks in the pavement. Harvey Madden, the wasting man on the front stoop, smiled wide as Iggy Conroy cruised past him to park the van at the end of the block.

Years ago, before Harvey had started sampling what he sold, he had been a pharmacist who owned his own drugstore and drove a nice car. Today the addict was a marginal man, such a puny man that he crouched below the notice of narcs, and no one would miss him if he never went back to that house for his bedroll. There was no muscle on him, but the height and age were roughly right. The skeletal junkie was coming down the sidewalk as Iggy opened the rear door of the van.

Harvey obligingly climbed inside, and with him came the smell of underwear never washed. Every dime made on deals went to feed his habit. Nothing left for soap. Between a bony finger and thumb, he held up the promised sugar cube. "Not your usual buy," nothing like the drugs he supplied for Iggy's murder kit. "This is primo, my friend. Packed with hallucinogens for the trip of a lifetime. Forget *Paris.*" He dropped the cube into the hand of his best customer. "Made to order for a quick dissolve with no aftertaste. And it kicks in fast. You'll love it."

"It's goin' in a pint of water."

"No problem. I promise you, it's *packed.*" And Harvey had been about to say more, but he felt the jab of the dart in his neck, whispered the words, *Oh . . . rats,* and then he lay sprawled on the floor of the van.

Only paralyzed.

There needed to be smoke in Harvey's lungs when he died.

Iggy's exit plan was simple. Torch everything. Kill everybody.

DETECTIVE GONZALES sang out, "Road trip!"

All around the squad room, men were opening and slamming drawers. Some clipped sidearms to their belts. Others favored shoulder holsters.

"Hey, Mallory. You still at the cemetery?" Riker cradled the desk phone's receiver between his shoulder and chin, freeing his hands to hide his eyeglasses and find his gun. "Your paper ghost, Moira Kenna—she's still pretty lively. Pays utility bills, property taxes. . . . Naw, no driver's license, but she's the registered owner of a vintage Jag. . . . Yeah, I thought you'd like that. But get this. Twelve years ago, she bought a house for cash. . . . Right, that was the year she applied for a Social Security number."

Janos called out to him from three desks away, "Tell her Moira Kenna's still writing checks on her bank account!"

"Hear that? Mallory, you're gonna *love* this. The date

of birth you gave me for the other woman—that fits a Moira Conroy in New York. She dropped off the tax rolls the year Moira Kenna bought the house in Jersey. . . . Yeah, twenty-two Birch Drive in Lowell. Everybody's on the move. The whole squad. We'll meet you there."

When he ended the call, the other detectives were filing out the stairwell door. He shouted to them, "Sirens all the way! We need speed! Mallory doesn't want any backup from the locals!"

"Smart move," said Gonzales. "They'd just fuck it up."

So true. If one patrol car pulled in the driveway, it would get the boy killed. Cops, too. The alternate game plan for the Jersey police would be dicking around for hours, waiting for a hostage negotiator to show up on the scene. Either way, the kid was dead, and their hit man was out the back door.

This was a job for shock and awe and a battering ram.

Washington pumped the address into his smartphone and squinted at the map on the little screen. "Right across the bridge and down the road we go. We're a helluva lot closer than Mallory. That cemetery's seventy miles from this address."

Obviously, Washington, smart man, had never ridden in a car with Mallory behind the wheel. And so Riker said, "I got twenty that says she beats us to the house."

Every man on the squad had a sporting nature, and this guaranteed him more speed on the road. He would cover every single bet and hope to lose—rather than have her go in alone.

IGGY CONROY stood at the kitchen counter with ingredients culled from his drug stash. After mashing pills with mortar and pestle, he emptied powder from the bowl and cut it into two parts with a razor blade, but the doses were not equal. He had become proficient in estimating the weight of the meat—the measure of a drug.

And now for something different. He dropped Harvey Madden's sugar cube into one of the water bottles, a promise of pretty pictures for a boy who could not see, not with his eyes.

Iggy thought he finally had the hang of blindness, and maybe it should not be called that. There was seeing—and there was *seeing*.

AS MALLORY TORE up the access road that led to the freeway, she had a name for the hit man: Ignatius Conroy, only child of the late Moira Conroy. He was also the beneficiary of his mother's life insurance—which he had never collected. No death certificate had ever been issued for the woman buried in that plot nine years ago.

Mrs. Conroy, alias Kenna, could never be allowed to die, not on paper, not while her son was alive with all his assets in her name. Very creative, using a woman for his paper persona—but why steal the heart of a little boy from that cemetery? It was a place he knew well, a comfort zone for grave robbing, but why the risk?

Why not just cut out Jonah's heart?

IGGY OPENED THE DOOR that led down to the basement. The dog was yapping, so happy to hear him coming. By the time he cleared the stairs and crossed the cement floor to unbolt the laundry-room door, the mutt had barked himself into a coughing fit. Iggy leaned down to pour the contents of one bottle into the dog's dry water bowl.

Beyond the doorway, Jonah sat cross-legged on the mattress. No fresh blood had seeped through the gauze wrapped round his head to cover the damage done by a stone troll, but, despite the antibiotics, pus oozed from the bandage on his leg. Dog bites were a bitch to heal.

Iggy wished the boy would close those broken eyes.

BURNING DOWN THE ON-RAMP and into four lanes of traffic, Mallory had no portable siren for her silver convertible. That kind of warning was futile. Few motorists would take this *cute* Volkswagen for a police vehicle, even *with* a screaming siren, and time would be lost to their confusion. This was the rationale she had given to her partner for silent running, and she half believed it.

The detective drove up on the tail of the pickup truck ahead, quickly turning a frail old man into a road-rage crazy. He *did* get out of her way, but then he tried to chase her down with the mistaken idea that his junker could beat the Porsche engine hidden under her hood.

Some things in life were just more fun than guns.

Next she bore down on a sports car that could give her at least *some* competition—should the driver fall into a vehicular-homicide state of mind. Nothing could make this motorist crazier than a VW in his rearview mirror, keeping pace with his *real* car, coming up to kiss his very expensive paint and maybe take a bite out of his fiberglass shell.

* * *

THE CONVOY OF DETECTIVES, stuck in city traffic, created a deafening scream of sirens and horns trained on motorists up ahead. Civilian drivers were jangled enough to brave the red light, and some pulled into a one-way side street to face oncoming traffic—anything to get out of the way, to escape the noise that played with their nerve endings. Other vehicles were crawling up on sidewalks to startle pedestrians, who turned en masse to face the string of wailing, honking cop cars, and they waved to the detectives, middle fingers extended in that New York salutation of *Hi, how are ya—and go fuck yourselves.*

BEYOND THE OPEN LAUNDRY-ROOM DOOR, the dog lapped at his bowl with thirsty gusto.

"Here." The man pressed a small bottle into Jonah's hands. "No tricks. The water's drugged. Pretty soon, this house is gonna be one big ball of fire. You don't want that, kid. . . . Burnin' alive? . . . Naw."

"You could let me go."

The cigarette lighter clicked. "There won't be any pain. I slipped in somethin' extra, a little somethin' for the road. You'll like it. . . . Up to you. I'm not gonna pour the stuff down your throat. But you really don't wanna wait for the smoke to come downstairs."

Jonah rocked himself as he strained to listen. No bells. No sirens. No one was coming to carry him away.

"Arson is where I really shine. It'll start in the back of the house. Then it's gonna rip along the hall and into the front room. . . . I wish you could see what I'm lookin' at, kid. The support beams for the floor—they're right over your head. No termites now, but they had a go at that wood for years before I bought this place. Brittle, dried out, fulla holes. It won't take much to bring the floor down . . . and down comes the fire. . . . But maybe the smoke gets you first. It's like breathin' in acid. You cough your insides out. Then you choke. You can't breathe. You go *nuts.* Total panic. I don't know what's worse. The flames or the smoke. So . . . drink the water. Don't drink it. Up to you, kid. But I know your Aunt Angie would want it this way. No fear, no pain."

Outside the laundry room, the lapping at the pit bull's water bowl had stopped. There was thump to the floor, but this was not a lie-down-to-sleep sound. More like a dropped sandbag. "You killed the dog?"

"He's not dead. Not yet. Wanna see?" Footsteps crossed the threshold and, seconds later, returned to the room.

Fur grazed Jonah's toes as the dog was laid on the floor, not with another thump, but gently. The man took the boy's hand and lowered it to the animal's pelt. Jonah could hear the pit bull's breathing, and he could feel it by the rise and fall of the ribs. And then came the familiar whistle the dog always made while asleep, a lullaby of old lungs.

"Oh, *hey,*" said Cigarette Man. "You gotta see this."

He moved Jonah's hand down the dog's fur to rest it on a lively haunch, and the boy's blind fingers walked up the animal's kicking leg.

"That's how you know he's dreamin'," said the man. "He's runnin' around in his dreams, chasin' down squirrels. . . . If that ain't Dog Heaven."

The kicking subsided.

The leg dropped.

The dog's song, the whistle of lungs, that stopped, too.

"You'll last longer," said Cigarette Man. "Not such a bad way to go. Up to you, kid."

RIKER RODE IN THE BACKSEAT. Despite the racket, the freeway traffic ahead was slow to divide and yield them a free lane.

Janos, behind the wheel, shouted reassurances to be heard over the sirens of their six-car convoy. "She can't beat us there! Not with a seventy-mile handicap!"

But Mallory would be driving most of that distance on open road—no red lights or city gridlock. They had already lost so much time along their escape route out of Manhattan.

Washington, who rode shotgun, turned around in his seat, offering Riker more comfort in a louder scream. "I saw Mallory when she left for Jersey! She's driving her VW! A damn *bug!*"

A bug. Yeah, *right.* No worries there—a Porsche disguised as a Volkswagen Beetle.

She liked her little jokes.

If Mallory had only taken a Crown Victoria to Jersey, the rest of the squad would stand a fair chance in this race. But her incognito engine was revved up way beyond factory settings. She was melting away her handicap.

IGGY STRUNG SHEER WHITE CURTAINS on one of the bedroom windows. These had come from his arson kit. With no flame-retardant qualities, they were better than tinder. He wondered that sunlight did not set them on fire.

The second window was left bare. He opened it by a crack. Fire loved oxygen.

The second set of curtains were wadded up, and he tossed them on the mattress with their metal rod—as if this chore had been left undone, work forsaken to take a nap. He set an ashtray next to the pile of flimsy material.

A lit cigarette was dropped. The flash was quick. The meat locker was as good as torched.

The door closed—like someone had come in behind him. A trick of drafts? This house had lots of pranks to play: a bang of pipes, a creak of beams and mouse crumbles inside the walls. But he had to spin around. He *had* to look.

No one there. And no one on the other side of the door. Flames crackling behind him, he walked down the hall—and stopped—dead still now.

What the hell was *that*?

He stared at the square door in the ceiling, the attic access. A footstep? Up there? Oh, Christ, were the police already here?

No. *Idiot!* Cops in the attic? *Gimme a break!*

But rodents lacked the weight to account for that sound. Iggy took the revolver from his waistband. Then he pulled a hooked pole from the linen closet and held it high to snag the latch for the overhead door. Before the ladder could slide out of that square hole in the ceiling and into his outstretched hand, his mouth opened wide, but he did not scream.

He shut the attic door.

Dropped the pole.

And ran.

CIGARETTE MAN had left him the music of a boxy plug-in radio. Jonah rested one hand on top of it, and his palm tingled with the vibrations of golden oldies. He hugged himself and rocked his body, but the motion could not calm him anymore. His fear had a drumbeat and the wicked-fast riff of a guitar. He rocked fast now.

Faster.

Smoke!

The smell was the distant size of a whiff, but it was coming for him. Soon it would be seeping, creeping under the bolted door—to *get* him.

Jonah found the radio's volume dial and turned up the music because he had lost his faith. He was done waiting for jingle bells on the stairs out there. His rocking stopped. It was time to choose between the fire and the water. He lifted the bottle to his nose. Death had no smell, but a tentative sip told him it was sugary. He drank one big gulp. And another. How long would it take? The dog had lasted for minutes.

His eyelids were heavy. Closing. The bottle dropped from his hand to slosh and roll away. Jonah knew he was going into the blink of Cigarette Man's eye, the one closed eye where the nothingness was—no air, no life. Not even ghosts could live there.

27

Jonah curled into a ball. Shrinking. Soon he would disappear into—

He was *flying! Zooming!* Air rushed past him. An object flew alongside him, brushing against his hand. Cold. Metallic. He wrapped his fingers round it, the better to see it, and he made out the shape. The hood ornament! The car! And then it was gone, diving down out of his grasp. And he was falling, too, air whooshing all around him as he dropped through empty space—and fell into the front seat and, beneath his bare feet, was the sensation of rolling down smooth pavement.

Aunt Angie was driving. He saw her in the scent of perfume, a hand caressing his face. The car radio came alive in a stream of quick musical notes, a piano riff. It must be late. She always said that jazz belonged to night, and she liked a boogie rhythm to work with the blinking taillights of after-dark traffic. Now they shifted into daytime, and the sun was warm on his skin. Their new road song was a blast of rock 'n' roll. The car picked up speed.

"I love you," he said. "I *love—*"

Aunt Angie roughly pulled the hair at the back of his head, and she jammed her fingers into his mouth, all the way to the back of his tongue, and pressed down till he gagged. Vomit poured out of him in a thick smelly river. Far off, he heard a soft rush of words in a silken thread. "Sick it up," she said. And he puked more slime in waves of nausea. Oh, *so* sick. He gulped stinking air as his limp body rose off the mattress, lifted in her arms.

She carried him up the stairs. Through the thick acid smog of the house. The terrible heat of an oven. *Crackle* and *roar.* Into the cool wind of the out-of-doors, a war of stink and perfume, smoke and roses.

Her footsteps slowed.

Stopped.

He was falling, slowly sliding out of her arms, down and down, to feel the grass with his spread hands. He had no more breath, not a sip of air. And he could not fight for it. And he did not want to. It was irresistible, this sinking sensation. Letting go. Spent, he lay quiet and still. Soft hair curled across his neck as her head pressed to his chest. Then she pounded his ribs. Again. *Again.* Louder now, silk threads snapped, she commanded him to *"Breathe!"* Patience lost, she breathed for him, velvet lips covering his mouth.

First kiss—and then the stench of bile exploded through his teeth.

Burning his throat.

He coughed and spewed vomit as his body was dragged across the grass. The air smelled sweeter here. She laid him down.

Before she fell.

Sirens! So loud! So many! Tires spit pebbles and rocks to knock on the underbelly of a car in its rush up the driveway. More were coming. They were *here!* The high-pitched wailing shut down. Shut off. And now the sounds of many car doors opening—and *left* open. Feet on the run.

Jonah reached out for the one who lay beside him. But he could not rouse her. She had carried him out of the fire on last legs, and now—

Nearby, a man's anguished voice screamed, *"Mallory!"*

THE NEW JERSEY HOSPITAL was small, more the size of a clinic, and the walls were thin. The detectives of Special Crimes could hear a baby being born down the corridor from this exam room, where they waited for Mallory to be discharged.

She sat tailor-fashion on a gurney and sucked air from an oxygen mask. The stink of vomit had been thrown away with her cast-off linen blazer, but the smell of smoke hung all around her. How much of it had she taken into her lungs during her search of the house? Riker reached out to touch a strand of her hair singed by flames and frizzed like blond steel wool. *"Nice."*

"Just one more question, okay?" Janos had offered to write up her report, and he wanted to meet her insane standard for detail. "The ER doc says the tox screen backed you up, but how'd you know the kid was poisoned?"

Mallory lowered the clear plastic mask. "The water in the dog's bowl was colored—doctored. Hardly any smoke in the basement, but the dog was dead. And the kid was out cold."

Colored water in a dog's bowl? Of all the detectives in this room, only Mallory would stop to look at that one odd thing—*in a burning house.* Before the report hit Jack Coffey's desk, Riker planned to edit out those lines.

"Good enough." Janos closed his notebook and said to her, "What you did—that was awesome."

"Yet stupid," said Riker. *"The house was on fire!"*

Testy, prickly, she said, "The fire was in a back room. The way to the basement was *clear!"*

"Oh, sure. *That* makes sense. The basement would've been the *last* place you checked."

"I followed the music."

That got everybody's attention. There had been only sirens and shouts, the roar of fire and the breaking of glass from a blown-out window—hardly music. Riker fingered the oxygen mask that hung loose around her neck. "Does this stuff get you high?"

In the next moment, he wished that he could take back every caustic word, though the hero halo was not a good fit for his partner. Jonah Quill owed his life to a defect in her, the lack of a healthy sense of fear. That was Mallory's weakness, even back in her puppy days, and one day it would get her killed. From the time she had entered the Police Academy, Lou Markowitz had known that his kid would surely die young. While sitting side by side on bar stools late one night, the old man had said to Riker, "When it happens, don't hold it against her. It won't be her fault."

Detective Gonzales crossed the room to join the rest of the squad. "I talked to the fire marshal. He doesn't see it as arson. His guys found a corpse in the back bedroom. Adult male. *Totally* cooked. He figures the guy was smoking in bed and—"

"I don't think we could be that lucky," said Mallory.

"Me, either," said Gonzales. "There was only one car in the garage—a Jag smashed to shit. The Jersey cops found the oil slick from a second vehicle, but they still like the fire marshal's theory. They don't plan to waste any time looking for Conroy. And I'm guessing whoever died in that bed, he's not gonna be missed."

Mallory nodded. "Any idea when they plan to release the other body?"

"It's a done deal," said Riker. "The Phelps kid—"

"He's been returned to his grave." Rabbi Kaplan stepped inside the circle of detectives. "And the stolen heart was buried with him." When Mallory showed surprise to see him standing there, he shrugged. "I was in the neighborhood," a neighborhood that extended for seventy miles.

Now Riker learned that the rabbi had ridden here with Dr. Slope and not the detectives sent to fetch him.

"Edward brought the heart from the city so the boy could be made whole before—"

"That heart was *evidence!*" Mallory punctuated this with a raised fist. "Where does Slope get *off*—"

Undaunted by her anger, the rabbi said, "I told Edward he could kiss his poker nights goodbye if that little boy was reburied without his heart." David Kaplan wore a winner's smile. Like every player in the Louis Markowitz Floating Poker Game, this man gambled for penny-ante stakes that were still tailored to a child's allowance money. And that child, a twelve-year-old Kathy Mallory, had described it as an old-ladies-night-out kind of game. So the rabbi had to grab his big wins elsewhere.

Riker was certainly impressed. Dr. Slope had never caved in so fast for—

"Kathy," said Rabbi Kaplan, one of the few to use her given name with no fear of reprisal. "I told Mrs. Phelps her boy's heart was restored. She was grateful. . . . When I told her you found Jonah alive, she was overjoyed."

Son of a bitch! All these detectives and not one of them had thought to take the rabbi's cell phone away from him?

Gonzales gave Riker a nod to say that he had received the unspoken *son of a bitch* loud and clear. He held up his own phone as he backed through the door, pulling the rabbi along with him to plug that leak with a call to Mrs. Phelps.

Heads turned when Dr. Slope walked in to announce that Jonah had just been dispatched by helicopter to a facility across the river. "This hospital isn't up to the standards of a New York trauma center. If he isn't properly treated for the wound on his leg, he could lose—" And now the doctor must have seen something that *might* be concern in Mallory's eyes. Or maybe not. It was a crapshoot. And he said, "The boy's wound is septic, but the prognosis is excellent."

And *she* said, "That heart was *evidence!*" But that was not her only complaint.

OUTSIDE THE HOSPITAL, the medical examiner sat on a stone bench, answering questions for the detective whose chore of damage control was nearly done.

Riker's cigarette had gone dark and smokeless. He crushed it in his hand, neatly palming this only sign of anger. The first mistake of the day had been to invite Rabbi Kaplan here so he would not be stranded on this side of the bridge—with too much dangerous information. And now the grieving Mrs. Phelps knew that Jonah was alive. But it was Dr. Slope who had blown security all to hell.

Thanks for that, you bastard!

Less than an hour ago, the squad had nailed down containment. The Jersey firefighters never knew that a child had been taken from the burning house. And here at the hospital, the emergency-room staff had not recognized the unconscious boy with the sooty, swollen face. A gang of men with badges aplenty had supplied them with the story of just another ordinary kid doing party drugs and poison while playing with matches and a mad dog.

"So, Doc, what name did you give the—"

"*John Doe!* Did you really think I'd tell the pilot he was transporting Jonah Quill?"

Oh, no. Perish the thought. The chief medical examiner could be trusted to keep case details to himself—even if he could *not* be trusted to keep a goddamn heart under lock and key, even though Slope had taken it upon himself to whisk a little boy away from a squad of police protection—*hanging the kid out in the line of fire!*

However, mopping up damage took precedence over revenge, and so Riker had robbed his partner of the chance to debrief this man. Though he wished it was Mallory sitting here with a loaded gun.

Dr. Slope had yet to finish ragging on her, and this did not sit well with Riker.

The detective stood up, an invitation for the doctor to join him in a stroll to the far side of the parking lot. At the end of an aisle of cars, David Kaplan sat in the passenger seat of Slope's black sedan, waiting for his ride home. This had been a long brutal day for that very gentle man, though the rabbi did seem at peace with the outcome.

Not so for Dr. Slope, who railed against Mallory as he walked. "I'll tell you the real crime here. David's already forgiven her. Do you have any idea what she put him through today? And the damage she did to the Phelps boy's parents, those poor people. *No* remorse. A total lack of empathy—a complete disconnect from their grief, their *pain*. It's . . . cold."

"Yeah, I hear you, Doc. You're absolutely right. Grieving family—that's somethin' Mallory can't handle worth shit. . . . I guess we all remember the comical look on her face when her old man died."

The doctor broke stride with a stumble.

Riker gallantly opened the car door, and a more subdued Edward Slope got in behind the wheel.

Small satisfaction.

The detective moseyed back across the parking lot, his mind on damages to come. How long would the kid's John Doe alias hold up? Minutes? Hours? How much time did they have before a hit man went roaming the corridors of New York City hospitals, hunting down a little boy?

Two more questions occurred to him before he reached the other side of the lot: How many cops would it take to protect one kid from a professional killer? And how many presidents had the Secret Service lost to amateurs?

ALL THE PREP work was done. In the back of the van, Iggy buttoned up the coverall that he had packed in the duffel bag. Around the corner of this block, an NYPD cop was still wearing the uniform that Iggy coveted for his next change of clothing.

Using the duffel as a pillow, he laid himself down to catch a nap before dark, but he could not shut down his brain. What had he done to himself? For the first time in his life, he was homeless, and he grieved for his house, though he would not miss that *thing* in the attic.

* * *

THE DOOR to the Connecticut home was opened by Gail Rawly's widow, a high-maintenance type with four different shades of salon highlights in her light brown hair. If this woman had not loved her husband, she would have filed down the jagged edge of that one broken fingernail in an otherwise perfect manicure. And she appeared not to notice that one of the detectives on her doorstep smelled of smoke.

Mallory held up her cell phone so Mary Rawly could see the small-screen image from a high-school yearbook. This was the only existing photograph of Ignatius Conroy, son of Moira Conroy. "He's nineteen years older now."

"I'm sorry. I've never seen him before." After inviting them in, she sent her child out to play in the backyard. The widow raised her hands, and then let them fall limp at her sides. This gesture conceded that, yes, her little girl should be in pajamas by now, but her husband was dead, and all the mom rules were suspended today.

The sun was still shining in a low orbit, but inside the house it was dark. The air was stale. The detectives followed her into the kitchen, the only room with an unshuttered window and natural light. Mrs. Rawly sat down at the table with Riker, who said, "I'm sorry for your loss, ma'am."

The window had a view of the backyard. Close by was another house, a little one built to the scale of Mrs. Rawly's daughter. There were expensive toys scattered here and there, but Mallory liked the swing best. It was an old rubber tire suspended from a tree limb by a rope. Finest kind. And there was Patty Rawly, riding high on the tire, toes pointing up to the sun—*happy* in this moment. "She doesn't know?"

Mrs. Rawly covered her face with both hands. "Patty saw an ambulance in the driveway. I pulled her inside before it left . . . before the others came for his body. She thinks Gail's in the hospital—and he's only sick. *I* didn't tell her that. I didn't know *what* to tell her."

Mallory sat down beside the woman. "I'd like to show Patty the photo. Maybe she saw the man around the house when you weren't home. . . . I won't say anything about the murder."

With the mother's nod of permission, Mallory left by the kitchen door and walked into the sweet smell of fresh air. Casting a long shadow, she crossed the grass to stand near the swinging tire's wide arc. She held out the cell phone to show the child Conroy's photograph. "Do you know this man?"

The girl swung up close, touching distance, to stare at the small screen, and then she swung down and away. "He doesn't have hair anymore," said Patty on the back-swing. "He shaved it off." On the upswing, she added, "He's got a five o'clock shadow like Daddy's." The swinging slowed. "But it's all over his head." The tire dangled. The child turned pensive. "Iggy's one of those things we don't tell Mommy about."

"You can tell *me.*" Mallory smiled. "I won't rat on you. Promise."

"He never comes to the front door. He goes in that way." Patty pointed to the French doors at the back of the house. "I don't *like* him. I *don't* like his eyes. . . . That's all I know."

"Are there other things you're not supposed to tell Mommy?"

Patty drummed her fingers on the tire's rim, giving this grave consideration. "Well, there's the clown in my bedroom. His head comes off, but Mommy doesn't know that. And Daddy's the only one who knows how to take it off. He does it after lights out . . . when he thinks I'm asleep. I tried to pull the head off myself—but I just can't do it."

"I could help you with that. . . . No one else has to know."

Patty liked this idea. She liked it a lot. Her smile was adorably evil.

Hand in hand, they walked back to the house, entering by the French doors of Gail Rawly's low-tech office. A standard landline sat on the desk beside a laptop that was six years out of date. Even the fax machine was a dinosaur. At Patty's insistence, they crept down the hallway on their toes.

The stuffed clown had a chair of its own in the corner of the pink bedroom, where it lay facedown because the child *hated* clowns. "And I think Daddy knows that, but *he* gave it to me. So we both pretend I like it."

Very smart. Mallory picked up the large doll with the red bulbous nose. This would be the toy that Patty was least likely to play with, cuddle with, and maybe notice the faint rattle in its belly. If only Daddy had known how much the trick feature intrigued the little clown hater, who longed to rip off its head.

Mallory unfastened the buttons that held a ruffled collar in place. When the ceramic neck was bare, she could see the hinge at the front and a tiny keyhole on the other side.

Would the mother mind this search, this act of breaking into the head of a clown? In a worst-case scenario for evidence not in plain sight, the need for a warrant would lead to a war with the local cops who owned Gail Rawly's murder. In any case, time would be lost. She reached into her back pocket and pulled out a velvet pouch of lock picks. "Patty, this is another one of those things we don't tell Mommy about. So . . . whatever we find inside the clown . . . ?"

The little girl gave her a thumbs-up agreement that the less Mommy knew, the better.

When the small lock was undone, the clown's head swung forward like a lid, and inside the body was a stash of tiny cassettes, the ones used in early-model answering machines for landlines. At the bottom of the belly, she found an old palm-size recorder with the jury-rigged look of something customized. Its bay was just large enough to hold the cassettes, and its add-on connection port held a cell-phone jack for the illegal covert taping of calls. Gail Rawly, a man who favored outmoded technology, could have used a speakerphone feature to record conversations the old-fashioned way, but not with a child running through the house. Patty might overhear details of murder for hire—one more thing that Mommy should not be told about.

GAIL RAWLY's recorder sat on Mallory's desk. She played a small cassette with the voice of Dwayne Brox ordering the death of a twelve-year-old boy.

"Not good enough," said ADA Joseph Walton.

Assistant district attorneys were prime obstacles of law and order. They were not the brightest, not top of the class, and Walton had the further disadvantage of a smarmy attitude, but it was the silly pencil-line mustache that really offended Riker.

"No, this won't do at all," said the lawyer. "It may *sound* like Mr. Brox, but let's nail it down, shall we? Send the cassette to One Police Plaza for voice-print analysis. *Then* you'll get an arrest warrant."

Mallory turned to Jack Coffey, who said, "It's the ADA's call."

"We don't want a lawsuit for false arrest, now *do* we?" Walton said this to Mallory in the tone of talking down to imbeciles.

Fifteen detectives and their boss waited for her to shoot him, but they were disappointed.

Unbloodied and smug, the ADA sidled past Charles Butler at the stairwell door. The tall psychologist crossed the room with a broad smile, a good sign that he had been allowed to visit Jonah in the hospital. When the man was two steps away, Riker asked, "How's the kid?"

"Jonah won't lose his leg. He'll be out of intensive care in a few more hours, but he can't be moved to another hospital."

Riker guessed that Charles was anticipating a problem with his report. The big man picked up a chair, as if it weighed no more than a paper clip, and he set it down in Switzerland, that borderland on the line between the detectives' joined desks, and he said, "I finished my assessment. The boy's a credible witness."

"Yeah, *right,*" said Mallory. "Is he still talking to the dead nun?"

"Yes, and his aunt talks back, but Jonah's only intuiting what she might say, and he knows that. He's not insane, not actually hearing voices."

"Just acting like it," said Riker. "Please tell me he doesn't do that in front of the doctors and nurses."

"Jonah doesn't do it in front of anyone. It's not a performance. It's a private conversation."

"With a dead woman," said Mallory. "That has to stop. When we catch the hit man, Jonah has to make a voice ID. That won't hold up in court if Conroy's lawyer finds out our witness talks to a ghost—and the ghost talks back. You have to fix this."

"Oh, right," said Charles.

Riker smiled. This shrink was more accommodating than most.

"Just flip a switch? Wave a magic wand? *That* sort of thing?"

Maybe not so accommodating.

"After what Jonah's been through," said Charles, "he belongs in therapy. I've found him a good child psychiatrist."

"No more shrinks till he makes that ID," said Mallory. "Just fix him."

"Jonah doesn't *need* fixing. It's a coping mechanism. Over time, he'll slough off his ghost like a coat he doesn't need anymore. The boy's not insane. He's *grieving*. Therapy and time is what he needs."

"I don't *have* that kind of time," said Mallory. "And I don't want a defense lawyer asking Jonah about his psychiatrist."

Riker leaned in to translate. "If you put Jonah and a shrink in the same sentence—goodbye witness ID. The jury's gonna stop listening right there. Out in Jersey, there's a burnt-up corpse to take the fall for kidnapping the boy. Reasonable doubt for a jury. And our hit man's a pro at staging fires. We'll never get a finding of arson."

"Oh, I can help you with that," said Charles. "He told Jonah he was going to burn down the house."

"Great," said Mallory with no enthusiasm, "assuming anyone can believe a kid who talks to a dead nun."

"Heads up," said Jack Coffey, and all eyes turned his way. "We caught a break on containment. The Jersey ME can't ID the corpse in Conroy's bed. No dental records, no DNA reference. If he can't notify next of kin, no press release goes out on the fire. And nobody in that Jersey hospital's gonna make a connection to the kid with the sooty face and smoke in his lungs. Gonzales says they didn't even know Jonah was blind."

"But now Jonah's awake—in another hospital," said Mallory. "The staff sure as hell knows who he is."

Riker chimed in with "And their husbands, wives, drinking buddies—"

"Okay," said Coffey, "we're screwed. But right now, the media's got nothing, and our perp thinks the kid's dead. We bought some time."

THE SLOW-ROLLING white van passed the driveway for the mayor's residence. There were no more reporters on the avenue. The story must be winding down. So far, the NYPD had not made a connection between a crispy-critter drug dealer in the torched bed—and a dead boy in the basement.

He had time.

Iggy Conroy drove on.

THE FURNITURE of Gracie Mansion's spacious foyer was carted into the adjoining dining room, giving technicians more space to set up their pole lights and cameras. A lectern was decked out in microphones bearing logos for TV stations. Reporters milled about, keeping their distance from the door to the library, where Mayor Polk was swaddled with a bib as a makeup artist powdered the shine from his skin.

Samuel Tucker handed his boss the final list of talking points—with a surprise ending. Andrew Polk looked up from his reading of the final item. With a flick of his fingers, the makeup artist was shooed away, and the mayor lowered his voice to ask, "Tuck, you're sure about this?"

"My source at the DA's Office guarantees it." Tuck grinned wide, awaiting praise—the reward of a smile at the very least, but there was only suspicion in the mayor's face. "Sir, this is solid information." He watched his boss heft the sheet of paper, as if weighing it, questioning its worth.

Not worthy enough, said the mayor's shiny little eyes.

And though they were alone, Tuck whispered, "My guy's the ADA assigned to the Special Crimes Unit."

"That would be Joe Walton, right? Affected little asshole. I know his family. Not a brain in the pack." The mayor shook his head. "The cops would *never* give him—"

"They didn't. And Joe's not a *complete* idiot. He asked me if there was a survivor or a witness. On his way into the SoHo station house, Joe overheard a desk sergeant's call to another precinct. The sergeant was sending his own cop to the Upper West Side—a cop to guard a hospital room. That change was authorized by the commander of the Special Crimes Unit. *I* worked out the rest of it. I *went* to that hospital. I know a kid was transported to the roof by helicopter, a boy. He's the right age. And Special Crimes is only working *one* case. So why—"

"Witness protection."

Yes! Samuel Tucker expelled a happy sigh. If he only had a tail, he would wag it. Intently, he watched for every nuance of his master's expression. To his amazement, this corroboration did not make the man happy.

"Okay, Tuck." The mayor ripped off his makeup bib. "Did you win any friends at that hospital?"

Did he bribe anyone? Of course. "Yes, sir, an orderly."

"Good. The orderlies go everywhere. Now you go back there. Give your guy some flowers for the room with a cop posted at the door. That's all you tell him. Then *follow those flowers.* If there's no cop on that door any-more, the boy's dead."

Tuck was out the door and into the thick of reporters in the foyer. They were gathering before the lectern like parishioners. They had a hungry look about them, but no communion wafers for this crew; they were praying for more blood and guts and, God willing, a dead child as a broadcast tease for news at eleven.

28

The man dressed in orderly's whites held a bouquet of carnations, and this should have been his ticket off the elevator, but "No," said the guard in the gray uniform of hospital security. "Nobody gets off on this floor."

"What's going on?" The orderly leaned into the corridor. "I was up here an hour ago."

"Then you must've come up on the north side." The security guard put one hand on the smaller man's chest and pushed him back into the elevator. "This area's off-limits. We got a contagious case here."

When the metal door slid shut, the irritated orderly turned to the passenger at the back of the elevator. "That was bullshit. The guard would've been wearing a mask if there was anything that catchy. And they wouldn't just seal off one section, either. They'd quarantine the whole damn floor."

"Did you notice any policemen in the hall? *Real* cops?"

"Yeah, there's one sitting in a chair outside the kid's room. He's not wearing a mask, either."

Samuel Tucker texted his boss to say, "Still here. Still alive."

AS THE METAL DOORS slid open, Iggy Conroy pulled down the brim of a tri-cornered cap. He could count on a security camera in this elevator, and now its lens would be looking down on the uniform of an NYPD cop. The man who owned these clothes would sleep the night away in his underwear.

Iggy listened to the chatter of a police-band radio clipped to the cop's utility belt. Apart from the codes for domestic violence and a car wreck, this neighborhood was quiet. With the press of a button, Iggy was on the rise to a high floor. A fast ride. No stops.

When he left the elevator, he saw a wooden chair in the hall, but no officer on duty. Probably gone for a piss or a smoke. Well, finally, a piece of luck on a bad day.

He stood in plain view of the fish-eye lens on Dwayne Brox's door when he knocked, and said, "Police! Open up!"

THE MAYOR read Tucker's text on his cell phone as he listened to the grousing rabble on the other side of the door. Perhaps the ladies and gentlemen of the press had been kept waiting too long.

Or maybe not long enough.

Andrew Polk glanced at his watch. With only a slightly longer stall, the news stations would go to a live feed for the eleven o'clock news, and nothing could be edited out.

* * *

THE BRANDY SNIFTER was held at a tilt, and spilt booze puddled on the carpet. Dwayne Brox wore a shitfaced grin. Totally trashed? Yeah, this fool was way too happy to have a stone killer for company tonight, and Iggy took offense. There should be fear—a little respect.

Brox turned his back, another insult, and leaned down to the coffee table to lift a bottle with a fancy gold label. "Could I interest you in Napoléon brandy?"

"Naw. You got beer?"

Brox stared at the low table littered with bottles of hard liquor and wine, an ice bucket with the shine of real silver, and three different kinds of dirty glasses with stems. He leaned down for a closer inspection, as if it might be hard to recognize beer in that mix. "I'll check the fridge." He walked away, though not in a straight line, and disappeared around the corner of a far wall, pressing one hand against it for support as he made this turn too fast.

Six-year-old girls could hold their liquor better.

Iggy found the remote control among the clutter on the coffee table. He aimed it at the wide screen on the wall and tuned the TV to a channel favored by news junkies. Soon enough, the cop on guard duty would return to his post outside in the hall, and so the volume was jacked up to mask conversation.

Dwayne Brox came weaving back into the room to hand a cold beer bottle to his dangerous guest, and now he turned his back on Iggy—*again*—to fill the cart's silver bucket with a tray of ice cubes and the remainder of a six-pack.

This guy must believe that he was going to live for five more beers.

"This can't be no kidnap for ransom." Iggy popped the bottle cap with his thumb and took a long swig. " 'Cause that's just nuts. Every time there's a ransom—and I mean a hundred percent of the time, the NYPD brings 'em back alive. So I know you never asked for no money." Not true. He knew damn well there was money in play here, but he was fishing for something more solid. He wanted this to *make sense!*

"Here's all you need to know." Brox spread out his arms and fell backward to land his butt deep in the cushions of the couch. Goofy smile. "My plan is foolproof."

"Ain't no such thing." Not in any scheme of amateurs. "The city's never gonna give you a dime for—"

"Not the city—the *mayor.*"

"No way. Nobody like him pays ransom for strangers."

"Polk will. And nothing comes back on me . . . or you."

"Hey, the police hauled your ass in *three times* . . . but you don't think they're onto you?" Any day now, the cops would realize that all they had to do was take this guy out for a few drinks.

"You can be certain I told them nothing." Dwayne Brox had a swagger about him, even when he was sitting down. He even *talked* swagger. And that stupid smirk was just begging for a fist to break every tooth in his head.

Yet Iggy flopped down beside him and spoke as if they were equals. "I'll tell you why ransom's a chump's game. You got no way to get paid without gettin' caught. There's cops on the mayor twenty-four-seven. So he can't make a cash drop, right? And you better believe they got a bug ridin' his computer. Even if Polk's got offshore accounts like yours—"

"That's not necessary. A personal check will do."

"How crazy *are* you?"

"My plan is brilliant," said Brox, slurring every word

out of his mouth. "And me getting caught? That's the last thing the mayor wants."

Make sense, you fucking idiot!

ANDREW POLK's press secretary had run out of stalls for the crowd of reporters outside in the foyer. She pressed her back against the door, as if expecting them to charge in with flaming torches. "Please, sir?"

Poor old girl. She was begging now. "Mr. Mayor, it's almost airtime!"

Almost was not quite good enough. He wanted a guarantee of live airtime. He opened door to the foyer by a crack, just wide enough for him to be seen with a dead cell phone pressed to his ear. Oh, the ripple of excitement from the media was palpable. Only reporters and hyenas had ears that could stand at attention. "Go out there, Nancy. Tell them I'm talking to cops, getting breaking news on the case. Tell them it's worth waiting for."

"YOU DIDN'T KNOW any of those people," said Iggy. "You didn't care who got killed."

"It didn't matter." Brox was having difficulty opening a fresh bottle of brandy. "The mayor was out of town for the first four murders. Out to sea. Even the police didn't know that till—"

"But *you* knew."

"Yes, and I took advantage of it. It's all about pressure. You see, the fun didn't really begin till you dumped those four bodies on the mayor's lawn. That was like a billboard sign to bring out the cops, the reporters . . . all those cameras. All that *lovely* pressure on Polk."

"Did you give him the kid's heart?"

"All the hearts." Brox continued to fiddle with the seal on the brandy bottle. "That last one? I popped it into a mailman's bag. It sailed right past the cops on the avenue. And the mayor's police bodyguards?" Brox snorted. "Everything sails past *them*."

No, the police *had* that heart. How else could they have found the grave of the boy who used to own it? Iggy drained his beer and reached for another. "Let's say the mayor gave the hearts and the ransom notes to the cops on day one—the day those bodies landed on the grass."

"Well, then it would've been game over. But obviously he didn't do that."

Polk had probably done just that. "The cops gotta know you ordered those hits. Why ain't you in jail? Tell me just one thing that makes sense."

"The mayor knows who I am now, but he doesn't want me caught." Brox handed the brandy bottle to Iggy. "Do you mind?"

Iggy sighed, pulled out his knife, and—*click*—a six-inch blade shot up from the handle. After slashing the seal and opening the bottle, he sloshed liquor into the idiot's glass, priming the drunken pump. "So you got somethin' on that bastard."

"The mayor? Yes . . . and no. My father didn't give up any sordid details before his . . . *accident* with dear old Mom. I was expecting a huge inheritance. You know what I got? A nondisclosure agreement and a long string of numbers for a bank account in the Cook Islands. You know what was left of the family fortune after losses in the market? A little over *five percent!*"

"Yeah, yeah. So you wanted money." Iggy nodded, hardly paying attention anymore. He was stuck on the word *accident* and the little note of joy that Brox had attached to the death of his parents. "This ain't your first time out with a hit man, is it, kid?" Oh, there was that smirk again. He was onto something. "When your folks had their accident, I bet you were a thousand miles away."

"On a ski trip in Vail. And you'll love this. . . . My bookie paid for it."

Iggy could fill in the rest. Hiring a pro to murder rich parents—that would have been the bookmaker's solution to a large debt left owing, one with damn little hope of payment by other means. And now Brox had implicated that bookie in a double murder for hire. So easily, too. And this moron was not done *yet.*

"It was a car crash in Vermont. My parents had a getaway cabin up there. It *appeared* that my father fell asleep at the wheel. That bit of speculation was in the police report. His chest was crushed when his car went off the road to hit a tree. Clearly dead on impact. That tended to knock his other heirs out of the running for the estate. You see, the old man had four children from a previous marriage. But Mom only had me. There was no doubt that she outlived him. Her body was found ten feet from the wreck. Thrown clear. That's what the police said. Legs broken. No chance of being heard from the road. She lasted nearly three days with no food or water. . . . Sound familiar?"

"That's where you got the idea to keep those people alive for—"

"Yes, professional methods. *Your* profession. I'd thought you'd appreciate that touch. When you dumped those bodies, it had to be clear that those people were kidnapped one by one. Held for days—well, obviously held for ransom. Even the idiot cops could see that much."

Iggy had a better opinion of the NYPD. And this sick little bastard sitting beside him was just too stupid to live.

Brox drained his glass. "Satisfied?"

No! But Iggy's voice was amiable, casual when he asked, "So who was your partner—your inside man?"

"My *what?*"

"You knew the mayor was out of town for the first four kills. Even the cops didn't know that. And that little back gate in the brick wall—you called it the mayor's hooker entrance. I *read* the gossip columns, kid. The mayor's pretty damn discreet about his whores. Not one line about 'em in print or on the Net. Then there's the cop at the front gate on the avenue. You said he'd be nappin' that night, and he was. Nobody watchin' the cameras go dark. What for? The mayor's outta town—like you said. So you got a partner on the inside."

"Oh, I see. That *flake* . . . he's not my partner. The dweeb only lives to impress people. Give him a drink and a pat on the head, he'll talk you to death. There's bartenders all over town who probably have the same inside information. He loves to bang on about the mayor's inner circle."

"I need a name for that guy." Iggy wanted *all* the details of this game that had cost him a house and a Jaguar.

"Your job is done. You got paid. Now it's been fun, but I'm off to bed. So finish your beer and—"

"First I gotta take a piss." And then the fun would begin. He was owed an EXPLANATION!

ASSISTANT DISTRICT ATTORNEY Joseph Walton was in a bad temper. Riker would describe it as a hissy fit. When this lawyer had failed to return every phone call, uniformed officers had escorted him out of bed and into the station house, and now he sat in the interrogation room.

"This is going to cost you," said Walton in a squawk of menace.

"Check this out." Mallory pushed the Tech Support file across the table. "The voice-print analysis was solid. Dwayne Brox hired the murders of *five* people."

"Fine. The arrest can wait till morning." Walton made a show of yawning. "It's a bit late to wake up a judge." His eyes turned sly. "It's a pity you can't drag Mr. Brox in here one more time, not without an arrest warrant. I trust that your boss received a copy of the harassment charges *and* the injunction? There's a photo of the ham sandwich attached to the paperwork. That little screwup of yours went over *so* well with the judge. . . . What're the odds he'll put any faith in your voice analysis?" The lawyer lightly slapped the tabletop. "So we're done here. For now, the guard on Brox's door is all that's allowed. You two can't get within a hundred yards of that man." His chair pushed back. "Well, then . . . till tomorrow." Walton stood up, all too ready to leave them.

"Sit!" Riker rose from the table, the smaller man sank down—surprised. "A hit man's going off the rails. He's cleanin' up his tracks, and he racked up more victims today. So either we arrest Brox right now or he dies, too."

"You're being melodramatic. The guards on Brox's—"

"If a pro wants to get you," said Mallory, "he gets you."

"I don't care. And don't try going behind my back one more time. I know how you got your search warrants. Did you think I wouldn't find out?"

"You weasel." Riker banged a fist on the table. "*That's* why you don't take our calls? 'Cause we left you out of the loop on a few warrants?" And now he understood why no one else in the DA's Office would return messages tonight. This little bastard was on a get-even mission to poison every other avenue for a—

"Let's call it a lesson," said Walton. "You two have to learn not to fuck with me. And the DA won't help you, either. I can promise you that old fool won't give a shit if Dwayne Brox lives or dies tonight. Now if Brox does die . . . well, that's all on you."

"Payback?" Mallory turned around to face the one-way glass. "Play that last bit for me?"

And the ADA's last lines came back to him over the intercom. "You can't record me in a—"

"Sure we can," said Mallory. "If we charge you with collusion and obstruction. You're Samuel Tucker's mole in the DA's Office."

Riker slapped a sheet of paper on the table. "Phone records. Yours. Tucker's. You were the inside man. But now you're just a complication. And that might land you on a hit man's list."

"I know you made ours," said Mallory, "after we talked to Tucker."

And now it was Riker's turn to lie. "He's resting up in a holding cell." The detective opened his laptop. "I guess we were too hard on him." The computer was turned around so the ADA could view a soundless film of Janos's days-old interview with the mayor's aide, replete with a shine of sweat on Samuel Tucker's face. This video should have been destroyed along with everything else connected to the aide's bogus arrest and the purloined SEC document, but Mallory was not inclined to waste anything. Without a sound track, this old conversation did look more interesting—and incriminating. Bug-eyed Joe

Walton apparently thought so. His chair inched back to the wall.

"We can't get you arraigned tonight," said Mallory, "but we have a nice little cot downstairs in the lockup . . . if we decide to charge you. So you get one phone call. What'll it be?"

ADA Walton decided, to no one's surprise, on using his call to wake up a judge for an arrest warrant on Dwayne Brox.

WHEN THIS WAS OVER, Iggy Conroy planned to sleep for days and days. He watched the water rising in the tub as he set a half-empty bottle of brandy on the floor of Dwayne Brox's bathroom.

Clothes or no clothes? Naked worked better. The necessary knock to the head would leave a bruise that worked with the finding of a bathtub fall. Amateurs who held their victims down while drowning them always left telltale marks on the flesh, bruising that would show up hours after death. But medical examiners rarely questioned the bop-and-drops that left only scalp wounds.

A cell phone beeped in his shirt pocket. The cop who owned it was about to miss this check-in call, and soon, a patrol car would be sent to find him. But before that happened, the cop on the roof would get a call—and so would the one parked outside Brox's door. No sweat with those two. Right now they were probably telling their sergeant that everything was *A*-okay.

He could count on ten minutes before patrolmen came looking for the downstairs cop, the half-naked guy asleep in a refrigerator carton. Iggy could allow a few minutes more for the search of the storage area—the ride up here in the elevator. And a bathtub drowning? That could take three or four minutes.

Yeah, he was good for the timing.

From the living room, he heard Dwayne Brox yell, "You *screwed* me!" Iggy left the bathroom on the run, and he found Brox standing in front of the TV set, weaving and red-faced.

"Shut your mouth!" Iggy glanced at the wide-screen image, a close-up of the mayor, who was answering questions shouted by reporters.

"Yes, the boy's going to be in the hospital for a few days." In response to another reporter, Polk said, "No, Jonah's had a rough time of it. He's under sedation, so he won't be making a statement to the police until tomorrow morning."

No, no, no! Iggy wanted to rip the TV off the wall.

Brox shouted, "That kid's still alive! You fucking screwed me!"

With one tap, not even all that hard, Iggy laid him out on the floor. Glass-jawed little shit. "I *told* you to shut up."

Another loose end. Every time he tied one off, *another* one—

Brox was rising from the floor. This idiot did not know *when* to be afraid. And before he could open his mouth one more time, Iggy stomped on his gut, and that shut him up. *Hard to breathe, Dwayne?* Oh, yeah.

Iggy gripped Brox's ankles and dragged him down the hall. "Take little breaths, nice and easy, okay? You'll be fine."

Just keep breathing.

There had to be water sucked into the lungs.

* * *

THERE WAS A KNOCK at the door and a voice in the hall. "Everything okay in there?"

"Yeah, yeah." With minutes to spare and water marks blending into his dark uniform, Iggy opened the front door, never breaking stride as he walked past the surprised police officer, saying, "I covered your ass. Don't leave your post one more time. Hear me?" He continued down the hall, assured that the cop was buying him as a brother in NYPD blue. Iggy stopped before the elevator. In sidelong vision, he saw the cop unfolding a sheet of paper. The man reached for his weapon, but before it cleared the holster, his other hand went to the shoulder where the medi-dart was lodged.

The dart gun was back in Iggy's pocket before the cop's legs failed him, and now the man hit the floor. Paralyzed. The sheet of paper lay beside him. Iggy hunkered down for a closer look. It was a bad drawing of himself in leaner, hairier days, but he thought the sketchy portrait had gotten the eyes right.

THE MAYOR'S PRESS CONFERENCE had been played and replayed on every channel. The lieutenant muted his office television. "That was cold."

"I'd call it murder," said Mallory. "It's like Polk took out a contract to kill that boy."

"At least he didn't mention the name of the hospital. That gives Jonah a sporting chance to make it through the night." Jack Coffey had been left on hold, his landline receiver pressed against one ear, and now he resumed his conversation with the commander of the Upper East Side precinct. Mallory was moving toward the door when he yelled, "Goddammit!" and she stopped, as if this might be her other name.

He said to the man on the line, "Greg, I know you guys *got* the damn picture! Why didn't you circulate it?"

The irritated uptown commander transferred Coffey's call to the man in charge of the hospital detail. Sergeant Murray picked up on the first ring with a surly, *"Speak!"* That word was packed with warning. The caller had better state his business *real* fast because the sergeant was one damn busy man tonight.

Coffey identified himself and said, "You don't have an updated picture of the perp. So tell your guys to be on the lookout for a cop they don't know. He might be wearing an NYPD uniform, and—"

"Count on it," said Murray. "*I* did 'cause . . . like I told *your* guys, he was wearin' one when he dumped those bodies on the mayor's lawn." The sergeant waited a beat, maybe daring the lieutenant to say one more word. "So . . . I got this *covered,* okay?" And the slammed-down phone said, *Call me back—and I'll put you on hold for twenty years.*

Oh, crap and miscommunication. With computerized scissors, Mallory had removed the long haircut from Ignatius Conroy's high-school yearbook picture, and the face had been aged to give every cop in the city a decent likeness. All that time and effort wasted. The killer might have strolled past dozens of uniforms tonight.

The lieutenant checked his watch. Janos and Washington should be at Dwayne Brox's place by now. He swiveled his chair to face Mallory. "You and Riker get over to Gracie Mansion. I'll deal with the hospital."

When she was out the door and gone, he phoned the guard on the boy's hospital room, a young cop from his own station house, and he said to Officer Devon, "Check on him. Do it now."

"I just did, sir. He's fine. And there's local uniforms on the street outside, maybe five guys out front. More in the back."

Outside? Not inside where they belonged? Only one hospital in the city would have a visible police presence on the street tonight. "You mean they like . . . hung out a sign?" Oh, yes indeed. A public show of uniformed cops, well, that was as good as a light left burning in the window to welcome a hit man.

IGGY CONROY drove the streets with a powered-up laptop on the passenger seat of his van. He had downloaded locations of more than twenty hospitals, and that was just freaking Manhattan. If the kid had been taken to another borough, this drive could last past sunup and land him in rush-hour traffic.

The list had been chopped by dropping small clinics and specialty shops for eye, ear, nose and throat, but that did not pare this night down to anything manageable. He was hemorrhaging time, though all he needed was a slow drive-by for every medical center. He would know the place when he saw it. The media had snitches everywhere, hospitals, too. Reporters always knew where the story was.

And there they were.

Double-parked news-show vehicles shared the street with patrol cars. Iggy rolled past them to park on the next block. He walked back to the hospital with no hurry to his steps, ambling along like any other cop reporting for duty. Getting past the five men guarding the entrance was no trouble. They were undermanned, fending off the media and checking IDs for staff and visitors. Iggy's stolen uniform blended in well with the chaos of cops in shouting matches with civilians, trading obscenities shot for shot. None of them gave Iggy a glance as he backed through a glass door, and no one in the lobby thought to question his right to enter a stairwell door that was marked do not enter.

He climbed to the second floor, where all was quiet at the nurses' station. No police in sight. He walked every corridor seeking a cop on guard duty to mark the boy's room for him. Iggy planned an easy suffocation. Jonah would freak out, but not for long. Three minutes tops. Respiratory failure would fit nice with smoke inhalation. But there were no cops on this floor.

All those uniforms outside—it was like they expected a hit on the kid, but why? The police should have closed out all the murders when they found the drug dealer's body in the burning bed back at the house. In Iggy's experience of staging fatal accidents, they should have gone for the easy close. He should be dead to police on both sides of the bridge. He pushed through the stairwell door and climbed to the third floor, when he stopped to sag against the wall.

The cops knew that fire was arson.

His body folded to a hard sit-down on a concrete step. He had *told* the boy he was going to torch the house.

Loose ends. How many now? He had a picture of them wriggling like spider legs. Cut off one, and two grew back. Oh, and the mistakes. No one would buy Dwayne Brox as an accidental death, not with those marks on the body, not when they found the cop in the hall and the one downstairs stuffed in that carton.

Instead of a bathtub drowning, he might as well have slit the creep's throat. All too clearly now, Iggy recalled the pounding he had given to Brox. Why? For two seconds of satisfaction? Did his mind have an off button? His memory had holes in it for sure. His eyes were trained on the steps leading down, as if searching them for a crucial piece of his brain that he was missing tonight.

Blame it on lost sleep. He had gotten none in the van. He emptied a vial of pills into his hand. Down to five tablets, he dry-mouthed them all. The rush kicked in. His heart jackhammered a million beats a minute. And he was on his feet. Jangled. Angry. His chest tightened up, and one fist broke through the plaster of the stairwell wall. This had to STOP! STOP! STOP!

He climbed the stairs.

29

The bathroom was enormous by New York standards and not the least bit crowded by a party of four, all of them wearing latex gloves. The on-call pathologist stood by the door waiting for a go-ahead from the woman with the camera. The crime-scene photographer took a picture of the brandy bottle on the floor. "I've seen this before," she said. "I'd say it started out as a staged accident, and then it all went haywire. You're sure a *pro* did this?"

"Yeah," said Detective Janos. "Our guy's just getting sloppy."

"Angry, too." Washington stared at the fully-dressed corpse in the bloody water of the bathtub. The nose of the late Dwayne Brox was broken, smashed to one side, and there were front teeth missing. But their hit man could be pardoned for this lapse in professionalism. When their soaking-wet victim was alive, every aspect of him had screamed, *Smack me!* He turned toward the door. "There's blood drops out there by the TV. So that's where Conroy snapped."

Janos followed his partner back to the front room and

the litter of empty bottles for beer and brandy. "I say the perp's just barely holding it together."

"That won't last." Washington held a green bottle up to the light. "I figure him for the beer drinker, and this wasn't wiped down." His glance passed over an ashtray with half-smoked girly cigarillos to fix on the one full of unfiltered stubbed-out cigarettes. "He didn't clean up his butts this time."

Janos looked down at the blood drops on the carpet, and then he faced the television. It was still tuned to the city's twenty-four-hour news station. "So Conroy's watching TV, knocking back booze—"

"And there's Andrew Fucking Polk on the screen, telling him the kid's still alive. . . . I'm gonna check on Jonah." Washington phoned the uptown sergeant in charge of the hospital security detail. It was a short conversation. "Bastard hung up on me. Says he's getting calls from Special Crimes dicks every six minutes, and that's gotta stop."

THE BAREFOOT MAYOR in robe and pajamas stood on the staircase, barring the way to his personal quarters on the floor above. "I'm not worried."

Mallory believed him. "Our perp's on a killing spree."

"He's jacking up his body count," said Riker. "But not for the money this time. You get it now? He's killing loose ends. You think he won't come after you?"

"Why should he? I'm the *victim* in all this."

Yeah, sure you are. "The hit man's little chat with Dwayne Brox was three beers long," said Mallory. "And Brox took a beating before he died. Whatever he had on you—his killer knows it now."

"Knows *what,* Detective?" The mayor's tone made this a challenge.

Mallory smiled. "Did you know your aide and Dwayne Brox were classmates at Fayton Prep? They still meet for drinks."

Only Riker registered surprise. She had shared Samuel Tucker's cell-phone history to net them a mole in the DA's Office—but not *all* the minutia of her background check and surveillance.

Polk lifted one shoulder in a shrug to say that this was of no consequence—but the timing was off. This was bad news to him. He looked down at the bodyguard standing by the banister. "Brogan, could you make me a sandwich?" Addressing the man's partner, he said, "Courtney, give him a hand with that." And the two detectives assigned to protect him walked away to do the job of kitchen maids with guns.

Riker was not liking this, watching cops being shamed, though Mallory knew he had no use for those two screwups. She looked up at the mayor. "How much do you trust your security detail? A lot got past them."

"All those ransom notes and body parts," said Riker. "What if they miss something tonight? Oh, I don't know—say a hit man walks in the door?"

"Not likely, Detective." The mayor flicked his fingers to send them on their way.

"We saw your help-wanted ad on TV tonight—the press conference," said Mallory. "It's like you begged a stone killer to murder a little boy. Is that why you think he won't come after you? Because you're his new client?"

This test of the waters should have brought on outrage and threats on her badge. But Polk only wore a smarmy expression, an unspoken suggestion to prove it or *shove it.* Apparently, he had tired of making an effort to hide what he was. Playing nicely with cops had become tedious.

She marched up the stairs, advancing on Polk, as if she planned to walk right over him on her way to the upper floor. The mayor stepped aside. They *all* did that.

"Mallory, that's enough," said Riker, playing peacemaker tonight—and philosopher, too. "If the mayor dies, he dies. . . . It's all good." Facing startled Andrew Polk, he said, "We'll just do a walk-through—check windows and doors, make sure the alarm system's working. Now *that's* gonna happen. . . . So you might wanna clean up any dope or body parts you got lyin' around . . . *sir.*"

OH, SWEET JESUS. The kid's uncle?

Iggy pulled the door shut to kill the crack of bright light from the hospital corridor.

He had spent the load of his dart gun on the cop who lay at his feet. And now a second dart, pulled from his pocket, was jammed into the other man before he could rise from his chair. Harold Quill had not cried out. He had missed that chance in the confusion of taking Iggy for another cop, and now, wide awake, terrified, paralyzed, he slumped back down in his chair by the hospital bed.

The small war for the room was over in five seconds, and so quietly that it did not wake the boy. All the light that remained was the little bulb mounted on the headboard of the bed, dim as a nightlight, and it only lit Jonah's face. The uncle sat slumped over in shadow.

Iggy stared at this man, this brand-new complication in his life. And what had the kid said to Uncle Harry?

Screw it! He would do them both. First Jonah.

The room stank of flowers. It smelled like home. Iggy saw no vases in the surrounding darkness, but somebody must have cleaned out every rose in the hospital gift shop. He leaned into the patch of light over the bed. Gently, he lifted the sleeping boy's head to steal a pillow.

Jonah's eyes snapped open.

Iggy backstepped to the foot of the bed. Why would the kid *do* that? What use were eyes to him?

The boy sat up. Nose high. Deep breath. "Aunt Angie?" He knuckled grains of sleep from his eyes and grinned wide as he threw off his bed sheets. "I know you're here."

No, kid. They don't come back. Blame it on the stinking roses.

Or maybe Jonah had not yet shaken off his dreams.

Iggy gripped the pillow, and he sank down on the mattress. The boy turned toward him—*so over-the-moon happy*—his hands reaching out to touch, to *see.*

"Lie down," said Iggy. "It's not gonna hurt."

Jonah's body stiffened, and his smile was a frozen mistake. Then he sagged, as if he had no bones, and collapsed, falling back to lie flat on the bed. His lower lip curled under his front teeth, and he bit down hard. He was *not* going to cry. This was the boy's last get-even act. No tears.

Stubborn kid. *Good for you.*

Jonah's face was in shadow now.

The pillow blocked the light.

WHEN THE OFFICER'S cell phone beeped, Harold Quill's eyes jumped in their sockets. A nurse leaned into the room for a moment, and then she withdrew, closing the door, shutting out the quick crack of light from the hospital corridor. Plunged back into shadows, he could no longer see the body on the floor, sticking out from the hem of the sheet by one black shoe. Like that paralyzed policeman, Harry could not speak, nor could he move one finger, but his wide-open terrified eyes madly darted like ricochet marbles.

30

Rookies never partnered with rookies, but Sergeant Murray had made an exception. Not one to waste manpower, he had counted these two as half a man each and posted them on the least likely access point for Gracie Mansion. Parked in the driveway with their taillights hanging out on East End Avenue, the youngsters had a view of the Wagner Wing beyond the gate, but the patrol car all by itself would guarantee that the hit man would not come this way, and so it was the safest place for kiddie cops tonight.

The sergeant leaned down to the open window on the passenger side, and he pointed to the computer on Officer Rowinski's lap. "Keep your eyes on that video feed." This was busywork, but it should keep them alert or at least awake. The screen was broken up into squares the size of postage stamps, one for each security camera in the park. Some were lit by spotlights, and others relied on the path lamps.

"Three of these got hardly any pictures," said this rookie riding shotgun. "They're not night-vision cameras, right?"

"You're a genius, Rowinski." At times like this, Murray saw himself as a babysitter with a sergeant's stripe. "But our perp ain't as smart as you." Well, *that* was a damn lie. "Before the guy dumped those four bodies, he took out half the park cameras with a paintball gun. So . . . if you see a camera go out, that's a clue he's in the park. Got it?" Now he glared at Officer Morris, the kid behind the wheel. "Just keep *your* eyes on the wing's front door."

"And if I see something? We got no contact numbers for the mayor's protection detail."

"No, Morris, you don't. . . . You have a *gun*. This is why we hand out so *many* guns." And now it seemed necessary to remind both of them, "No check-in calls, no calls to anybody." That had been Riker's idea, and it was a good one. A patrol cop on a phone or a radio might rattle a hit man turned spree killer. Conroy would just kill everybody in sight, and maybe take out the mayor, too.

Murray walked away from the car, assured that the kids would see no action tonight. He had other cops to check on, the grownups on foot patrol in the park. This operation was all eyeballs and guns. Farther down the block, his knock on the side of the surveillance van as he passed by was the announcement that all was well on the sergeant's watch.

INSIDE THE VAN, the monitors showed video feeds from security cameras—piss-poor security in the estimation of Carlstad, a civilian borrowed from Tech Support. He watched the uniformed police walking in and out of shots. The areas outside camera range were too large for this kind of surveillance to be effective. The only clear monitors were lit by spotlights on the mansion's roof. Others were dependent on path lamps through the surrounding parkland, and they were not all that bright. It was hard to tell if some of his monitors were even working. "Three of these feeds are useless," he said to no one who might care.

Behind him, two detectives were watching screens with live images of the streets and the promenade. The third cop, Mallory, sat at the audio station, wearing a headset to kill Carlstad's complaints, though she was from the planet of Pretty Chicks who did not actually need earphones to tune him out.

He covertly watched her reflection in the dark glass of one dead monitor. And now she creeped him out. As if she sensed his eyes on her, she turned her head to watch *him*.

A movement called his attention back to the live monitors. He followed a figure in the bright shots around the mansion perimeter, but it was only Murray doing his rounds, checking on his men again. With these overhead shots, Carlstad could not make out the sergeant's stripe, but now he was familiar with the man's build and gait.

In the civilian's geek opinion, this strategy of camera positions really sucked. They were all too high. He checked the monitor for the wing's rear entry to the basement level. Another cop was posted there. This one was seated on a chair. No movement at all, and everything was—

Carlstad sucked in his breath.

Mallory was right beside him, bending low, her head an inch away from his, and he was in hands-clammy panic mode even before she said, "Conroy's inside!"

No! Not possible!

"Where inside?" asked Riker. "What'd you hear?"

"Nothing. Look at this." She pointed to the camera shot of the cop in the chair.

And Riker said, "Goddamn!"

Behind him, Carlstad heard the van's door sliding open, detectives leaving, the door closing. He never took his eyes off the monitor. What had she seen? How did she know? The guard's face was obscured by the brimmed hat. A minute ticked by as Carlstad continued to stare at this cop, who never moved, never shifted his butt or kicked out a leg to keep a foot from going to sleep. The guard on the wing's basement door was as still as a photograph.

THE MASTER BEDROOM of Gracie Mansion was less than grand, but large enough to accommodate a couch and armchairs, and the formal mantelpiece was not overwhelming. Two windows overlooked the river, and the walls were painted a calming green, the color of money, and lit by the glow of a single lamp. One might call it a tranquil setting. The small man in the four-poster bed reached under the pillow, but his gun was not there.

The thug looming over him wore a police uniform, yet this offered the mayor no sense of security. The stranger's eyes were disturbing, and then there was the fist so close to— Oh, *there* was the missing gun. It was all but lost in the large clenched hand of the intruder. "I take it you're not a police officer."

"You got that right." The man sat down on the edge of the mattress. The tiny derringer now rested on his open palm. "*This* is a peashooter. It's only good for pissing off—"

"I'm not going to yell."

"Go on. Scream your head off."

"Did you kill the—"

"Naw, I don't do cops. But those guys won't be gettin' up again any time soon." The faux policeman removed his tri-cornered hat and dropped it on the bedcovers. Either his mother had taught him to remove his hat indoors, or he planned to stay awhile—just getting comfortable—and death was not imminent.

"Let's you and me talk about hearts and a few other loose ends."

"I assure you, I won't turn you in if—"

"I know. I had a little talk with Dwayne Brox. *I* get caught, *you* go to jail—just like you done all those murders yourself."

"I understand that you . . . *eliminated* Mr. Brox." The mayor sat up and reached for the pillow on the other side of the bed. He stacked it on the one behind him so that he could lean back in comfort. "So allow me to thank you for—"

"I know what Brox did with those hearts. He sent them to you."

"All marked proof of death. Yes, very dramatic."

"Where are they now?"

"Forgive a cliché, they sleep with the fishes . . . in the East River. Except for the last one. The *counterfeit* heart? The police took that one away."

"But first you got Jonah's picture—the one with him holding a newspaper."

"Proof of life. Yes, that's gone, too. No worries. I erased it from my cell phone."

"You *wanted* that kid to die."

"I've never met a child worth any part of my stock portfolio. I assume you've paid the boy a visit by now?"

"Yeah, thanks for the tipoff. I caught your act on TV."

"My pleasure. But we both know you're not going to kill *me*. The mayor of New York City? You'd never walk away from something like—"

"How did Brox figure to get away with it? He said the plan was foolproof."

"It was. It was brilliant. I could never turn on him. Or you. Incidentally, I have a yacht at your disposal. It can take you anywhere you like. But I want something in return. My aide, Tucker—he might be involved. Or maybe not. I can't be sure. He lives at—"

"What was the payoff plan for Brox? You got an offshore account?"

"No, not anymore. Foreign banks are falling like dominoes. Round heels, I call them. They spread their legs like whores, one new tax treaty after another. But the ransom wouldn't require an offshore transfer of funds."

"So how'd Brox expect to get paid?" The thug pounded the mattress, and there was frustration in his voice.

"You don't just *want* to know." Andrew Polk smiled. "You *need* to know. It's making you a little crazy, isn't it? Well, I think we can work this out. What shall I call you?"

"Damn amateurs, the two a you, playin' your little murder games." The man put the derringer on the nightstand. "No stupid toys." He reached into a back pocket. Now, what looked like a penknife protruded from his fist. "*This* is a weapon."

Click.

Not a penknife. A switchblade. Such a *long* blade, and rather wicked looking. And—*Oh, my*—the tip of it was hesitating in the air, a bare inch twixt sharp tip and a mayoral eyeball. Without so much as a tremor in his voice, Andrew said, "You can't do this, can you? You really *need* to know—"

"*Idiot.* You got *two* eyes. And me? I got the time."

So distracting was the blade, the mayor never saw the detective, only her hand—red fingernails—a big gun, its muzzle gently pressed to the knife wielder's temple.

Her voice was soft, one pure silk note. *"Don't."*

"Conroy!" Her partner was standing on the other side of the bed, aiming his weapon.

The knife never wavered. Andrew Polk resumed his cross-eyed stare at the blade's sharp point.

Detective Mallory said, "I've got all your answers, Conroy."

The knife dropped to the mattress.

Excellent. One might say the relief was an orgasmic release—all the fireworks splendor of sex.

RIKER'S EARPIECE DANGLED from one pocket by a wire, and now he could hear the feet of other men on the stairs beyond the door.

Detective Gonzales bent the hit man over the mattress. He had his prisoner handcuffed before the two young rookies entered the room to deliver the body count for the house and grounds.

"Four officers down," said Rowinski.

"Ambulances on the way," said his partner, Morris.

"So . . . about that stiff you left back in Jersey." Gonzales yanked Conroy to his feet. "The one who died in your bed? We figure him for a homeless guy. I don't suppose you got his name?"

"They have names?"

"Sorry, man. Stupid question." And Gonzales said this with all due sincerity.

Riker had to agree with the sentiment. A pro was unlikely to implicate himself in burning a man alive—but what the hell. Worth a try.

Mallory held up a Miranda card. "Ignatious Conroy, you have the right to—"

"*Iggy.* Call me Iggy."

"Iggy," said Riker, "your client, Dwayne Brox, died tonight. . . . We're sorry for your loss." He snapped on a latex glove and picked up the knife. "What've we got here? You and the mayor got some weird little sex fantasy going on? 'Cause I'd be willin' to buy that—my hand to God."

"Cut the sarcasm, Detective." The mayor smoothed out his bedding and fluffed his pillows. "Oh, no," he said, as if five more detectives were filing into his bedroom just to irritate him. "Get out, all of you. Just take your prisoner and go."

"Iggy stays for now." Riker never responded well to that tone for ordering servants around. He tipped back a lamp on the nightstand and removed a small metal pellet from its base. "Mr. Mayor, you're the one who's leaving."

"You *bugged* my—"

"Yeah, when we did that walk-through. We got 'em all over the mansion." Riker laid a folded sheet of paper on the mayor's lap. "That's the warrant for the bugs. I told a judge your security detail was doin' a shabby job. I'm not sure he really cared. That judge didn't vote for you, but he signed the warrant anyway . . . for your protection. And your confession to conspiracy? Hey, that was a bonus."

"A confession under duress is no good in court. I was only—"

"The mayor's got a point," said Riker. "I suppose we could just use the part where he admits to siccing Conroy on the kid in the hospital."

"No," said Mallory, as though this might be a serious negotiation. "I like the part where he tries to hire a hit on his aide. We should play that for Tucker. See if he wants to roll on his boss." She turned to their audience of grinning detectives and two rookie officers—one hit man. "Any volunteers to cuff Mayor Polk and read him his rights?"

Hands went up all around the room, and Mallory picked the winners.

Andrew Polk was so startled, he inadvertently invoked his right to remain silent before those words were read to him. He barefooted out of the room, cuffed and in the custody of the youngsters in uniform. Mallory's selection of these officers was taken for generosity that netted thumbs up from other detectives. A high-profile collar would make those two rookies shine tonight. But Riker put it down to his partner's sick sense of fun. When their sergeant saw them come down the staircase with the mayor in handcuffs, that poor bastard would faint dead away.

Iggy Conroy stood manacled between Lonahan and Gonzales. Mallory pointed to the armchair by the bed. "Sit him down."

Great idea. The lights were low. The furniture was comfortable. No lawyers in sight.

She finished reading his Miranda rights, with a small elaboration. "If you invoke your right of silence, I can't tell you about—"

"Okay, you got questions," said Conroy. "Me, too. Go for it. But first you gotta tell me the game those two clowns was playin'."

"I can do that," said Mallory. "When Polk was a Wall Street broker, he swindled ten of his own investors with bogus information on a stock offering. Then he bribed the victims with hush money—just a small percent of their losses. When they signed off on that deal and lied to the feds, every one of them was complicit in Polk's felony."

"*Screw* that part. What was the damn *game*? How was Brox gonna collect on it?"

Mallory sat down on the edge of the bed, facing Conroy, only inches between her knees and his. "When those four bodies turned up on the mayor's lawn, he took it for the work of an investor. One of them wanted restitution for the stock losses. The terms were all spelled out in the first ransom note."

Those ransom notes were long gone to ashes. Riker had to wonder why she would lie about that.

"If Polk had only known who was behind it, the game would've ended with those four kills. Brox never had any leverage. His parents got swindled, not him." Mallory leaned back on one arm, eyes half closed like a drowsing cat. "And I *know* they didn't tell their kid a damn thing about insider trading . . . or that would've been in the ransom notes."

The notes she had never read.

Taking his cue from Mallory's body language, Conroy relaxed every muscle, more at ease with this conversation—and with her. "So that little freak Brox, he was all hot air."

"No, he had a plan," said Mallory, "a good one."

And there they sat, as if they were alone in this room,

the cop and the hit man, just two people discussing their workday in the after hours. All that was missing was the beer.

"So," she said, "by the time Polk finds out it's Brox—an outsider who can't do him any harm with the feds—it's too late. The mayor's already trashed evidence on four murders, and he's gotten himself snagged into a kidnap-murder conspiracy for Jonah. *Now* Brox has leverage for a plea bargain . . . *if* he gets caught. And he's on the news, every damn channel, laughing it up for the cameras—*advertising* guilt. It's like Brox is begging to get caught. Very smart. *More* pressure on Polk. A first-rate squeeze play."

Oh, better than that. Riker saw it as a cop's idea of high art.

"Get to the payoff," said Iggy Conroy. "The mayor's got eyes on him every damn minute. No offshore accounts. How the hell could a ransom get paid?"

"Without Brox getting caught? That was the easy part," she said. "No risk at all. When I found out about the stock swindle, it only took me six seconds to figure that out."

Every cop's eyes were now trained on Riker. By a bare inch, he moved his head side to side to tell these men that she *had* to be lying. But what if she was telling it straight? If she had been holding back on the rest of the squad all this time—

The room full of detectives got very quiet.

"There's only one way it could work," said Mallory. "Brox wanted Polk to pay back *all* the losses to *everyone* he scammed on that stock deal. No need to collect any ransom. Brox would've gotten a check in the mail—like the rest of Polk's victims. By my count, that would amount to less than a third of the mayor's holdings . . . but he didn't plan to pay out a dime."

"A standoff," said Conroy.

Mallory nodded. "That was the flaw."

And that backed up Charles Butler's theory of Polk and Brox as two of a kind—twins in greed and sociopathy.

"It could only end in a draw." Mallory raised her eyebrows and exchanged you-gotta-love-it smiles with the hit man. "But it should've worked out fine on *your* end. Gail Rawly didn't leave us any ties to you. And Brox didn't lie about his plan being foolproof—for *you*. No chance you'd ever get caught. If you hadn't palmed off the heart of a graveyard corpse, we wouldn't even know your name. You could've just walked away with the money. So . . . here's *my* question. Why didn't you cut out—"

"Cut out *Jonah's* heart? . . . I couldn't do it."

Mallory was *up* on her feet—*so* fast—and there was a touch of outrage in her voice when she asked, "Why the hell *not?*" It was like this psycho in handcuffs had been somehow unreasonable—or worse, ripped her off. She was *owed* an explanation. A *deal* was a damn *deal*.

"It was the bells," said Iggy Conroy. "Jingle bells in the sky. . . . I want my lawyer now."

31

Another hospital visitor had left a newspaper behind in the waiting room. It was a tabloid, not his first choice for news of the day, but Charles Butler found the front-page story irresistible. And now he learned that Ignatius Conroy had become a media darling, granting press interviews with the blessings of the Manhattan District Attorney. Given a plethora of evidence against Andrew Polk, now painted in the blackest publicity, he could be prosecuted for any crime, real or imagined, and a jury could be counted upon to hang him from the handiest lamppost.

So ended the era of the *enfants terribles,* a mayoral string of tiny kings with Napoleon dreams. A deputy mayor had stepped into the vacated office, and the newspaper heralded him as a man of average means—but above-average height.

Charles looked up from his reading to glance at his watch, a Swiss timepiece that had never dropped the smallest increment of a second. There was only one minute to go before the appointed hour.

Not *soon* enough.

This area of the pediatrics wing was a cheerful place of

bright-colored walls. However, it reeked of fragrant diapers, spilt milk and five kinds of foods being imbibed by harried visiting parents and their noisy offspring. He folded the newspaper and turned to the elevator. The metal doors slid open, and Mallory stepped out, right on time.

When she was seated beside him, he said, "So, your hit man confessed, and I understand the mayor's aide turned state's witness."

Mallory took the newspaper away from him. "Why do you read this trash? I planted half the stuff in that article."

"But Conroy's confession—"

"No, that part's true, but Tucker's not locked in yet. Then there's Andrew Polk. He's got the best lawyers a rich man can buy, and a judge could toss his taped confession. . . . I need more. I need Jonah's testimony."

"If Conroy confessed, how could Jonah possibly matter to—"

"He figures in Polk's trial. I used to have one really great piece of evidence—a little boy's heart."

"The *wrong* boy's—"

"It was a *kid's heart,* Charles. It just doesn't get any better than that. The jury could've held it in their hands. But Dr. Slope just *gave* it away. Hell, he even sewed it back in."

Oh, yes, evil *bastard,* pissing her off that way, all for the sake of a child's grieving parents. "But Edward said you had photos and tissue samples."

The wave of her hand told him, *Sadly, it's just not the same.* "But I've got Jonah Quill. Polk colluded in a murder plot, and he all but drew the hit man a map to the hospital—to kill a twelve-year-old. So what do we *do* about that, Charles? . . . Bygones?"

"But Jonah isn't—"

"The jury needs to see a little boy on the witness stand . . . so they can hate Andrew Polk and *convict* him. If my tape gets thrown out, obstruction might be the only charge that sticks—if anything sticks. So . . . no more conversations with a dead nun. The kid's ghost has to go."

WHEN CHARLES entered the room, he saw Lucinda Wells standing by Jonah's bed. She was playing nurse today, dutifully plucking medicinal pieces of chocolate from a heart-shaped box and feeding them to her patient. Oh, but she looked so unhappy.

No—that was not quite *it*. This little girl was *worried*.

Jonah's uncle rose from his chair by the window. "Did you—"

"Yes," said Mallory. "I tracked down the roses."

Harold Quill smiled and thanked her for this strange errand. Late at night, a bouquet had appeared out of nowhere, and there had been no card to give away the sender. The boy's uncle had begged the police for a solution to this mystery that had had such an adverse effect on his nephew.

Mallory had been happy to oblige—entirely too happy to disabuse a child of his belief in a haunted hospital room. And, of course, she must still wonder why this boy's heart had not been cut out of him. But then there was the greater puzzle of how Jonah had survived the night of the hit man's killing spree.

A fanatically tidy detective, she hated the straggle of loose ends.

But first . . . the roses.

She began with the legend of Angie Quill among the nuns. Years ago, the monastery had raised only fruits and vegetables for sustenance and meager trade for goods. "Then your aunt joined up. She was good with all kinds of plants. Now they have a larger crop, a cash crop." The young acolyte had even coaxed rosebushes to grow in small patches, here and there, on land that had previously not even yielded weeds. "No ordinary flowers," said Mallory. Those were the words of the prioress, who had put all of this in a letter, and she had sent it with the bouquet, but it must have been lost along the way. "The Reverend Mother wouldn't tell me how she knew you were alive—or *where* to send the roses. I figure she badgered the cardinal, and he leaned on the police commissioner."

Mallory had even caught the culprit who had left the flowers in the boy's room. "You and Jonah were sleeping. The cop on guard duty didn't want to disturb you. There wasn't any space on the dresser, and that's why he put the vase in the corner on the floor."

Out of sight when a hit man came calling.

That vase had since been moved to a small table by the window. *Fabulous.* Dozens of roses were in full bloom, and their scent was potent. The prioress was right. These were no ordinary flowers, although they *were* a common breed, and thus he had to wonder how and why—

"So they're *Aunt Angie's* roses." By Jonah's tone of voice, this seemed to vindicate him in some way. "That's how she scared him off." The child must believe that his aunt had worked in God-like ways—via messenger service. Insistent now, the boy said, "Her roses scared him away. . . . You don't believe me, do you?" Apparently, like Mallory, the boy could read much into silences. Jonah turned toward his uncle's chair. "*Tell* her."

"There might be something to it," said Harold Quill, somewhat reluctantly. "I had no idea where that smell came from. The room was dark. I couldn't see any flowers, and neither could that man. He had a pillow in his hands. I know what he was planning to do with it. Well, the scent of roses *was* very strong. And Jonah was still half asleep. He thought it was Angie's perfume, Angie in the room with him."

"And so did that man," said Jonah. "He *knew* she was here. She *scared* him."

The uncle might have supported this claim, but here was another telling silence, a confession by omission, and thus Charles knew there had been no sign of fear in Conroy's face. So what had stayed a killer's hand that night? This was surely the theme of Mallory's wordless conversation with the uncle—her quizzical glance and his answering shrug of *Who knows?*

Charles had a theory of his own, a simple one based on an earlier visit with Mallory's young witness. No degrees in psychology had been necessary to arrive at it—and no one in this room would want to hear it.

This had nothing to do with the deceased nun.

It was all about the child.

The boy had eaten Cheerios and barbecued burgers with a stone killer, a man who lived in rural isolation. They had shared stories, watched TV, and, even further afield from a kidnap scenario, that man had taught Jonah how to drive a car. Perhaps when Conroy had come here to do murder, he had realized only then that—he had *missed* the boy.

"Before that," said Jonah, "Aunt Angie did it with the bells. That time she made him *cry.*" Both his hands balled into angry fists. "She brought him down on his *knees.*"

"Bells . . . jingle bells," said Mallory. "Where did the sound come from?"

The boy pointed to the ceiling.

"The upper floor?"

"No," he said, "we were outside that night. . . . The bells were in the sky."

And Mallory's expression said, *The hell they were.*

WHEN THE DETECTIVE quit the hospital room, Charles knew she was on a mission to reduce the boy's delusion to dead flesh and, ultimately, dust. Mallory was going over the bridge and up the wooded road to the hit man's house—to find that ghostly bell ringer and drag it back here so she could rip it to pieces it in front of a child.

Poor child.

At core, this was a matter of the heart. If there was truth to rumors that Mallory had no heart of her own, she could be forgiven for not knowing how it worked—and how it broke.

Charles never did find out how the day ended. She would not talk about it, and this would puzzle him for decades to come. Well into his nineties, he would still wonder what *did* happen when she revisited Iggy Conroy's house.

Ah, Mallory. She had a humorous side, though it was the dark side of her. She knew this never-answered question would drive him crazy as long as he lived, and *that* would be her final punch line. He would not resolve this day's mystery, but close upon the last hour of his life, he *would* get the joke—and laugh.

32

A thin odor of smoke mingled with a floral scent, though the only visible flowers were carved into the eaves, the shutters and the door to Iggy Conroy's house.

The front wall was unharmed, but the lawn was marred by ruts of tire tracks, puddles of water and bushes trampled by the feet of firemen. Mallory followed this trail of damage around a corner of the house to see half a wall charred but still standing. Close to the blackened foundation, there was a rosebush—alive and not even wilted from the smoke and the heat of the fire.

She reduced this miracle to Nature's parlor trick of windage.

The detective circled back to the front door, where she ignored a fire marshal's posted warning not to trespass. After stripping away a seal of tape, she picked the first lock. Now the second one. She opened the door.

And heard the bells.

Jingle bells.

But the sound had not come from within. It came from above. She stepped well back from the house to coolly survey the rooftop. Nothing there. Turning toward the undamaged side of the house, she stared at a nearby oak tree. Something about it was—*wrong*. Her eye for perfect symmetry detected the off-kilter effect on half the branches, but this could not be the work of firemen.

Compelled all her life to examine every odd thing, Mallory crossed the lawn and the dirt driveway to stand before the tree. Nothing in the grass or foliage here had been disturbed by the crew of firefighters. No, some other agent, maybe a local storm, had caused a crack in the trunk's first fork of a tree limb, and it was a recent injury judging by the run of sap. She looked up to see that a leafy branch had pierced a small eyelet window set just below the apex of the pitched roof. The sound of the bells must have come through that broken glass.

It *was* inside the house.

Mallory entered by the front door, gun in hand, for she had no faith in the spirit world; she only believed in what she could shoot. Once she was inside, the door shut itself, and she thought nothing of it. That was the way of old houses. Over time, they settled on an uneven keel, and the pull of gravity could swing a door on its hinge.

She stood in the wraparound smell of a wet ashtray. There were slicks of fire-hose water on the floor, and the walls were streaked with soot. Given only the poor light of smoke-grimed windowpanes, she made a cursory search and found no staircase to a second floor. The hallway leading to the burned-out bedroom was a blackened tunnel. She clicked on a penlight and found the entryway to the attic, a latched door in the scorched ceiling. Lying on the floor at her feet was a metal pole with a hook at one end. Dropped there in haste? Not by a fireman. Had Iggy Conroy also heard the sound of bells up there?

Raising the pole high, she fitted its hook into the overhead latch and pulled on it. The attic door opened downward, and down came a ladder, unfolding in the silence of well-greased joints. She climbed the wooden steps until she was head and shoulders above the attic floor, aiming her weapon at a heap of clothing in a tangle of hangers from a fallen wardrobe rack. Next the gun was turned on cardboard cartons and plastic ones, dusty suitcases—and one tree branch invading the house by several feet.

The air was thick with the scent of flowers carried on a breeze through the broken window glass. Was that why Iggy Conroy had dropped the latch pole? What had gotten to him first, the scent of roses where they did not grow or bells that could not ring themselves?

Stealthy, she climbed higher and caught a movement in the shadows. And then all was still as she stepped from the ladder to stand between the intruding tree branch—and the cat.

It stood over a mewling kitten nested in the heap of a moth-eaten coat. The mother cat's eyes were wide, its body frozen in a moment of consideration: Fight for the baby or flight?

Self-interest triumphed, and then, in a run for the window, its collar jingled with small silver balls. *Bells.* The cat was quick. Not quick enough. Mallory had the animal in her hands, and it scratched her. *Not* a house cat. Too frantic to have ever been tame. Wild to get away from her. *Definitely* raised wild. Mallory bled from the scratch, but she did *not* fling the crazed animal into a wall. One hand flashed out to grab the hem of the coat, and she wrapped the cat tight, all but its head. It struggled more now, all panic and frenzy and fear, but Mallory *needed* that collar, hard evidence that Jonah could hold in his hand, bells he could ring. The cat tried to bite her. Its teeth tore her sleeve.

"*Hey!* I'm doing you a damn *favor!*"

And that was true enough. She knew this animal's story with only a glance at the collar that had no wear, that still had a price tag tied to it.

An idiot in the neighborhood, maybe a lover of chipmunks or birds, must have captured this feral cat when its belly was swollen with kittens, when it could not run so fast. Then it had been hobbled with bells so that, unlike Mallory, it could not sneak up on its prey. By the skin and bones of this animal, she knew it had starved. For what crime? Had it hunted too close to some bastard's damn birdfeeder?

When the small catch was undone and the collar was in Mallory's hand, the feline was set free to leap for the tree limb, to dance along the branch, out the window and into the wide world, free at last to creep up on the little birdies—and eat them alive.

Mallory looked down at the left-behind kitten. So much for motherlove. It was tiny, only days old, and that would fit the time frame for the haunted jingle bells. There was only one, though the cat would have dropped a litter here. The mother must have been scared off by fire engines, and today it had returned to move the litter, kitten by kitten, to some new shelter.

Mallory pocketed the collar, her proof for the boy that the world was not magical, and his aunt was no longer a part of it. She turned around to descend the ladder and heard a noise behind her—so like a footfall. There were no hiding places up here, and nothing larger than the cat could pass through the glass shards of the small window.

But she was not alone. She knew this by the warning rise of fine hairs. The prickle of flesh.

The cat. It had come back for the last of its young, making a drop from the branch to the floor. Nothing else would fit. Yet she would not turn around to face it, nor would she even turn her head for a backward glance, and there was integrity in that resolve. No evidence was needed to preserve the iron rules of Mallory's planet, a bleak place and a cold one, where cats were the bell ringers, where the endgame of life was a corpse, then dust, then—nothing.

The detective returned to her car in the driveway. Out here, there was no longer any trace of smoke in the air, only the floral perfume—stronger now—though there was not one live flower in the front yard. She followed the scent along a flagstone walkway that led her around the garage and past the broken oak to the back of the house. There, she stood on a patio and looked out over a meadow ringed by woodland. Given the great beauty of it, Mallory could not help but do the dry math—averaging the number of blooms to a bush, even measuring time by old growth grading down, row by row, to small green shoots, and then factoring in the space allotted to each plant in this plot of at least a half acre—

Hundreds of thousands of red roses grew in the hit man's garden.

If she could believe in the story told to a child, every one of them had come from seeds planted after a girl had deserted the gardener—all this backbreaking work, *years* of it, all done on just the slender chance that, one day, the girl would return.

* * *

BRIGHT DAY graded into dusk on the Upper West Side, and Kathy Mallory never noticed the dimming of the light, never thought to turn on the lamp next to her chair. With only the mind's eye to see by, and with a vengeance, she worked on her ledger of debts and losses: what the world owed her for what had been torn away.

Unforgivable acts.

Till the end of her life, she so badly needed to get even.

She never did.

Rare visitors to her apartment found no sign of any such quest. They saw it as a stark place of too much empty space and no personality, as if uninhabited—as if her foster mother, Helen, did not live in all the spice jars. Lou Markowitz's best pipe and a pouch of makings dwelled in a drawer, and whenever Mallory opened it to find the aroma gone stale, she bought a fresh pouch of tobacco. Other residents of this crowded apartment emanated from objects hidden away in cupboards and closets.

And the cat's collar was in her hand.

She never saw the boy again.

Jonah was left to believe that his aunt had lived on in bells and roses. By Mallory's cold reckoning of a tally sheet for love and the sudden death of it, there were endings that could not and should not be borne.